THE SPIRIT
OF THE
BORDER

·

THE
LAST
TRAIL

ZANE GREY

A TOM DOHERTY ASSOCIATES BOOK | NEW YORK

THE SPIRIT OF THE BORDER AND THE LAST TRAIL

The Spirit of the Border was originally published in 1906. *The Last Trail* was originally published in 1909.

A Forge Book
Published by Tom Doherty Associates, LLC
175 Fifth Avenue
New York, NY 10010

www.tor-forge.com

Forge® is a registered trademark of Tom Doherty Associates, LLC.

ISBN 978-0-7653-7854-5

Forge books may be purchased for educational, business, or promotional use. For information on bulk purchases, please contact Macmillan Corporate and Premium Sales Department at 1-800-221-7945, extension 5442, or write specialmarkets@macmillan.com.

First Mass Market Edition: October 2014

Printed in the United States of America

0 9 8 7 6 5 4 3 2 1

CONTENTS

THE SPIRIT
OF THE
BORDER

INTRODUCTION

The author does not intend to apologize for what many readers may call the "brutality" of the story; but rather to explain that its wild spirit is true to the life of the Western border as it was known only a little more than one hundred years ago.

The writer is the fortunate possessor of historical material of undoubted truth and interest. It is the long-lost journal of Colonel Ebenezer Zane, one of the most prominent of the hunter-pioneers who labored in the settlement of the Western country.

The story of that tragic period deserves a higher place in historical literature than it has thus far been given, and this unquestionably because of a lack of authentic data regarding the conquering of the wilderness. Considering how many years the pioneers struggled on the border of this country, the history of their efforts is meager and obscure.

If the years at the close of the eighteenth and the beginning of the nineteenth century were full of stirring adventure on the part of the colonists along the Atlantic coast, how crowded must they have been for the almost forgotten pioneers who daringly invaded the trackless wilds! None there was to chronicle the fight of these sturdy travelers toward the setting sun. The story of their stormy lives, of their heroism, and of their sacrifice for the benefit of future generations is too little known.

It is to a better understanding of those days that the author has labored to draw from his ancestor's notes a new and striking portrayal of the frontier; one which shall paint the pioneer's fever of freedom, that powerful impulse which lured so many to unmarked graves; one which shall show his work, his love, the effect of the causes which rendered his life so hard, and surely one which does not forget the wronged Indian.

The frontier in 1777 produced white men so savage as to be men in name only. These outcasts and renegades lived among the savages, and during thirty years harassed the border, perpetrating all manner of fiendish cruelties upon the settlers. They were no less cruel to the redmen whom they ruled, and at the height of their bloody careers made futile the Moravian missionaries' long labors, and destroyed the beautiful hamlet of the Christian Indians, called Gnaddenhutten, or Village of Peace.

And while the border produced such outlaws so did it produce hunters like Boone, the Zanes, the McCollochs, and Wetzel, that strange, silent man whose deeds are still whispered in the country where he once roamed in his insatiate pursuit of savages and renegades, and who was purely a product of the times. Civilization could not have brought forth a man like Wetzel. Great revolutions, great crises, great moments come, and produce the men to deal with them.

The border needed Wetzel. The settlers would have needed many more years in which to make permanent homes had it not been for him. He was never a pioneer; but always a hunter after Indians. When not on the track of the savage foe, he was in the settlement, with his keen eye and ear ever alert for signs of the enemy. To the superstitious Indians he was a shadow, a spirit of the border, which breathed menace from the dark forests. To the settlers he was the right arm of defense, a fitting leader for those few implacable and unerring frontiersmen who made the settlement of the West a possibility.

And if this story of one of his relentless pursuits shows the man as he truly was, loved by pioneers, respected and feared by redmen, and hated by renegades; if it softens a little the ruthless name history accords him, the writer will have been well repaid.

Z.G.

CHAPTER I

"Nell, I'm growing powerful fond of you."

"So you must be, Master Joe, if often telling makes it true."

The girl spoke simply, and with an absence of that roguishness which was characteristic of her. Playful words, arch smiles, and a touch of coquetry had seemed natural to Nell; but now her grave tone and her almost wistful glance disconcerted Joe.

During all the long journey over the mountains she had been cheerful and bright, while now, when they were about to part, perhaps never to meet again, she showed him the deeper and more earnest side of her character. It checked his boldness as nothing else had done. Suddenly there came to him the real meaning of a woman's love when she bestows it without reservation. Silenced by the thought that he had not understood her at all, and the knowledge that he had been half in sport, he gazed out over the wild country before them.

The scene impressed its quietness upon the young couple and brought more forcibly to their minds the fact that they were at the gateway of the unknown West; that somewhere beyond this rude frontier settlement, out there in those unbroken forests stretching dark and silent before them, was to be their future home.

From the high bank where they stood the land sloped

and narrowed gradually until it ended in a sharp point which marked the last bit of land between the Allegheny and Monongahela rivers. Here these swift streams merged and formed the broad Ohio. The newborn river, even here at its beginning proud and swelling as if already certain of its faraway grandeur, swept majestically round a wide curve and apparently lost itself in the forest foliage.

On the narrow point of land commanding a view of the rivers stood a long, low structure enclosed by a stockade fence, on the four corners of which were little box-shaped houses that bulged out as if trying to see what was going on beneath. The massive timbers used in the construction of this fort, the square, compact form, and the small, dark holes cut into the walls, gave the structure a threatening, impregnable aspect.

Below Nell and Joe, on the bank, were many log cabins. The yellow clay which filled the chinks between the logs gave these a peculiar striped appearance. There was life and bustle in the vicinity of these dwellings, in sharp contrast with the still grandeur of the neighboring forests. There were canvas-covered wagons around which curly-headed youngsters were playing. Several horses were grazing on the short grass, and six red and white oxen munched at the hay that had been thrown to them. The smoke of many fires curled upward, and near the blaze hovered ruddy-faced women who stirred the contents of steaming kettles. One man swung an axe with a vigorous sweep and the clean, sharp strokes rang on the air; another hammered stakes into the ground on which to hang a kettle. Before a large cabin a fur trader was exhibiting his wares to three Indians. A second redskin was carrying a pack of pelts from a canoe drawn up on the riverbank. A small group of persons stood near; some were indifferent, and others gazed curiously at the savages. Two children peeped from behind their mother's skirts as if half-curious, half-frightened.

From this scene, the significance of which had just dawned on him, Joe turned his eyes again to his companion. It was a sweet face he saw; one that was sedate, but had a promise of innumerable smiles. The blue eyes could not long hide flashes of merriment. The girl turned, and the two young people looked at each other. Her eyes softened with a woman's gentleness as they rested upon him, for, broad of shoulder, and lithe and strong as a deer stalker, he was good to look at.

"Listen," she said. "We have known each other only three weeks. Since you joined our wagon train, and have been so kind to me and so helpful to make that long, rough ride endurable, you have won my regard. I—I cannot say more, even if I would. You told me you ran away from your Virginian home to seek adventure on the frontier, and that you knew no one in all this wild country. You even said you could not, or would not, work at farming. Perhaps my sister and I are as unfitted as you for this life; but we must cling to our uncle because he is the only relative we have. He has come out to join the Moravians, and to preach the gospel to these Indians. We shall share his life, and help him all we can. You have been telling me you—you cared for me, and now that we are about to part I—I don't know what to say to you—unless it is: Give up this intention of yours to seek adventure, and come with us. It seems to me you need not hunt for excitement here; it will come unsought."

"I wish I were Jim," said he, suddenly.

"Who is Jim?"

"My brother."

"Tell me of him."

"There's nothing much to tell. He and I are all that are

left of our people, as you and Kate of yours. Jim's a preacher, and the best fellow—oh! I cared a lot for Jim."

"Then why did you leave him?"

"I was tired of Williamsburg—I quarreled with a fellow, and hurt him. Besides, I wanted to see the West; I'd like to hunt deer and bear and fight Indians. Oh, I'm not much good."

"Was Jim the only one you cared for?" asked Nell, smiling. She was surprised to find him grave.

"Yes, except my horse and dog, and I had to leave them behind," answered Joe, bowing his head a little.

"You'd like to be Jim because he's a preacher, and could help Uncle convert the Indians?"

"Yes, partly that, but mostly because—somehow— something different you've said or done has made me care for you in a different way, and I'd like to be worthy of you."

"I don't think I can believe it, when you say you are 'no good,'" she replied.

"Nell," he cried, and suddenly grasped her hand.

She wrenched herself free, and leaped away from him. Her face was bright now, and the promise of smiles was made good.

"Behave yourself, sir." She tossed her head with a familiar backward motion to throw the chestnut hair from her face, and looked at him with eyes veiled slightly under their lashes. "You will go with Kate and me?"

Before he could answer, a cry from someone on the plain below attracted their attention. They turned and saw another wagon train pulling into the settlement. The children were shouting and running alongside the weary oxen; men and women went forward expectantly.

"That must be the train Uncle expected. Let us go down," said Nell.

Joe did not answer; but followed her down the path. When they gained a clump of willows near the cabins he bent forward and took her hand. She saw the reckless gleam in his eyes.

"Don't. They'll see," she whispered.

"If that's the only reason you have, I reckon I don't care," said Joe.

"What do you mean? I didn't say—I didn't tell—oh! let me go!" implored Nell.

She tried to release the hand Joe had grasped in his broad palm, but in vain; the more she struggled the firmer was his hold. A frown wrinkled her brow and her eyes sparkled with spirit. She saw the fur trader's wife looking out of the window, and remembered laughing and telling the good woman she did not like this young man; it was, perhaps, because she feared those sharp eyes that she resented his audacity. She opened her mouth to rebuke him; but no words came. Joe had bent his head and softly closed her lips with his own.

For a single instant during which Nell stood transfixed, as if with surprise, and looking up at Joe, she was dumb. Usually the girl was ready with sharp or saucy words and impulsive in her movements; but now the bewilderment of being kissed, particularly within view of the trader's wife, confused her. Then she heard voices, and as Joe turned away with a smile on his face, the unusual warmth in her heart was followed by an angry throbbing.

Joe's tall figure stood out distinctly as he leisurely strolled toward the incoming wagon train without looking backward. Flashing after him a glance that boded wordy trouble in the future, she ran into the cabin.

As she entered the door it seemed certain the grizzled frontiersman sitting on the bench outside had grinned knowingly at her, and winked as if to say he would keep her secret. Mrs. Wentz, the fur trader's wife, was seated by the open window which faced the fort; she was a large woman, strong of feature, and with that calm placidity of expression common to people who have lived long in sparsely populated districts. Nell glanced furtively at her and thought she detected the shadow of a smile in the gray eyes.

"I saw you and your sweetheart kissing behind the willow," Mrs. Wentz said in a matter-of-fact voice. "I don't see why you need hide to do it. We folks out here like to see the young people sparkin'. Your young man is a fine-appearin' chap. I felt certain you was sweethearts, for all you allowed you'd known him only a few days. Lize Davis said she saw he was sweet on you. I like his face. Jake, my man, says as how he'll make a good husband for you, and he'll take to the frontier like a duck does to water. I'm sorry you'll not tarry here awhile. We don't see many lasses, especially any as pretty as you, and you'll find it more quiet and lonesome the farther West you get. Jake knows all about Fort Henry, and Jeff Lynn, the hunter outside, he knows Eb and Jack Zane, and Wetzel, and all those Fort Henry men. You'll be gettin' married out there, won't you?"

"You are—quite wrong," said Nell, who all the while Mrs. Wentz was speaking grew rosier and rosier. "We're not anything—"

Then Nell hesitated and finally ceased speaking. She saw that denials or explanations were futile; the simple woman had seen the kiss, and formed her own conclusions. During the few days Nell had spent at Fort Pitt she had come to understand that the dwellers on the frontier took everything as a matter of course. She had seen them manifest a certain pleasure; but neither surprise, concern, nor any of the quick impulses so common among other people. And this was another lesson Nell took to heart. She realized that she was entering upon a life absolutely different from her former one, and the thought caused her to shrink from the ordeal. Yet all the suggestions regarding her future home; the stories told about Indians, renegades, and of the wild border life, fascinated her. These people who had settled in this wild region were simple, honest, and brave; they accepted what came as facts not to be questioned, and believed what looked true. Evidently the fur trader's wife and her female neighbors had settled in their minds the relation in which the girl stood to Joe.

This latter reflection heightened Nell's resentment toward her lover. She stood with her face turned away from Mrs. Wentz; the little frown deepened, and she nervously tapped her foot on the floor.

"Where is my sister?" she presently asked.

"She went to see the wagon train come in. Everybody's out there."

Nell deliberated a moment and then went into the open air. She saw a number of canvas-covered wagons drawn up in front of the cabins; the vehicles were dusty and the wheels encrusted with yellow mud. The grizzled frontiersman who had smiled at Nell stood leaning on his gun, talking to three men, whose travel-stained and worn homespun clothes suggested a long and toilsome journey. There was the bustle of excitement incident to the arrival of strangers; to the quick exchange of greetings, the unloading of wagons, and unharnessing of horses and oxen.

Nell looked here and there for her sister. Finally she saw her standing near her uncle while he conversed with one of the teamsters. The girl did not approach them; but glanced quickly around in search of someone else. At length she saw Joe unloading goods from one of the wagons; his back was turned toward her, but she at once recognized the challenge conveyed by the broad shoulders. She saw no other person; gave heed to nothing save what was to her, righteous indignation.

Hearing her footsteps, the young man turned, and, glancing at her admiringly, said:

"Good evening, miss."

Nell had not expected such a matter-of-fact greeting from Joe. There was not the slightest trace of repentance in his calm face, and he placidly continued his labor.

"Aren't you sorry you—you treated me so?" burst out Nell.

His coolness was exasperating. Instead of contrition and apology that she had expected, and which was her due, he evidently intended to tease her, as he had done so often.

The young man dropped a blanket and stared.

"I don't understand," he said gravely. "I never saw you before."

This was too much for quick-tempered Nell. She had had some vague idea of forgiving him, after he had sued sufficiently for pardon; but now, forgetting her good intentions in the belief that he was making sport of her when he should have pleaded for forgiveness, she swiftly raised her hand and slapped him smartly.

The red blood flamed to the young man's face; as he staggered backward with his hand to his cheek, she heard a smothered exclamation behind her, and then the quick joyous barking of a dog.

When Nell turned she was amazed to see Joe standing beside the wagon, while a big white dog was leaping upon him. Suddenly she felt faint. Bewildered, she looked from Joe to the man she had just struck; but could not say which was the man who professed to love her.

"Jim! So you followed me!" cried Joe, starting forward and flinging his arms around the other.

"Yes, Joe, and right glad I am to find you," answered the young man, while a peculiar expression of pleasure came over his face.

"It's good to see you again! And here's my old dog Mose! But how on earth did you know? Where did you strike my trail? What are you going to do out here on the frontier? Tell me all. What happened after I left—"

Then Joe saw Nell standing nearby, pale and distressed, and he felt something was amiss. He glanced quickly from her to his brother; she seemed to be dazed, and Jim looked grave.

"Nell, this is my brother Jim, the one I told you about. Jim, this is my friend, Miss Wells."

"I am happy to meet Miss Wells," said Jim, with a smile, "even though she did slap my face for nothing."

"Slapped you? What for?" Then the truth dawned on Joe, and he laughed until the tears came into his eyes. "She took you for me! Ha, ha, ha! Oh, this is great!"

Nell's face was now rosy red and moisture glistened in her eyes; but she tried bravely to stand her ground. Humiliation had taken the place of anger.

"I—I am sorry, Mr. Downs. I did take you for him. He—he has insulted me." Then she turned and ran into the cabin.

CHAPTER II

J oe and Jim were singularly alike. They were nearly the same size, very tall, but so heavily built as to appear of medium height, while their gray eyes and, indeed, every feature of their clean-cut faces corresponded so exactly as to proclaim them brothers.

"Already up to your old tricks?" asked Jim, with his hand on Joe's shoulder, as they both watched Nell's flight.

"I'm really fond of her, Jim, and didn't mean to hurt her feelings. But tell me about yourself; what made you come West?"

"To teach the Indians, and I was, no doubt, strongly influenced by your being here."

"You're going to do as you ever have—make some sacrifice. You are always devoting yourself; if not to me, to some other. Now it's your life you're giving up. To try to convert the redskins and influence me for good is in both cases impossible. How often have I said there wasn't any good in me! My desire is to kill Indians, not preach to them, Jim. I'm glad to see you; but I wish you hadn't come. This wild frontier is no place for a preacher."

"I think it is," said Jim, quietly.

"What of Rose—the girl you were to marry?"

Joe glanced quickly at his brother. Jim's face paled slightly as he turned away.

"I'll speak once more of her, and then, never again," he

answered. "You knew Rose better than I did. Once you tried to tell me she was too fond of admiration, and I rebuked you; but now I see that your wider experience of women had taught you things I could not then understand. She was untrue. When you left Williamsburg, apparently because you had gambled with Jewett and afterward fought him, I was not misled. You made the game of cards a pretense; you sought it simply as an opportunity to wreak your vengeance on him for his villainy toward me. Well, it's all over now. Though you cruelly beat and left him disfigured for life, he will live, and you are saved from murder, thank God! When I learned of your departure I yearned to follow. Then I met a preacher who spoke of having intended to go West with a Mr. Wells, of the Moravian Mission. I immediately said I would go in his place, and here I am. I'm fortunate in that I have found both him and you."

"I'm sorry I didn't kill Jewett; I certainly meant to. Anyway, there's some comfort in knowing I left my mark on him. He was a sneaking, cold-blooded fellow, with his white hair and pale face, and always fawning round the girls. I hated him, and gave it to him good." Joe spoke musingly and complacently as though it was a trivial thing to compass the killing of a man.

"Well, Jim, you're here now, and there's no help for it. We'll go along with this Moravian preacher and his nieces. If you haven't any great regrets for the past, why, all may be well yet. I can see that the border is the place for me. But now, Jim, for once in your life take a word of advice from me. We're out in the frontier, where every man looks after himself. Your being a minister won't protect you here where every man wears a knife and a tomahawk, and where most of them are desperadoes. Cut out that soft voice and most of your gentle ways, and be a little more like your brother. Be as kind as you like, and preach all you want to; but when some of these buckskin-legged frontiersmen try to walk all over you, as they will, take your own part in a way you have never taken it before. I had my lesson the first few days out with that wagon train. It was a case of four fights; but I'm all right now."

"Joe, I won't run, if that's what you mean," answered Jim, with a laugh. "Yes, I understand that a new life begins here, and I am content. If I can find my work in it, and remain with you, I shall be happy."

"Ah! old Mose! I'm glad to see you," Joe cried to the big dog who came nosing round him. "You've brought this old fellow; did you bring the horses?"

"Look behind the wagon."

With the dog bounding before him, Joe did as he was directed, and there found two horses tethered side by side. Little wonder that his eyes gleamed with delight. One was jet-black; the other iron-gray; and in every line the clean-limbed animals showed the thoroughbred. The black threw up his slim head and whinnied, with affection clearly shining in his soft, dark eyes as he recognized his master.

"Lance, old fellow, how did I ever leave you?" murmured Joe, as he threw his arm over the arched neck. Mose stood by looking up, and wagging his tail in token of happiness at the reunion of the three old friends. There were tears in Joe's eyes when, with a last affectionate caress, he turned away from his pet.

"Come, Jim, I'll take you to Mr. Wells."

They started across the little square, while Mose went back under the wagon; but at a word from Joe he bounded after them, trotting contentedly at their heels. Halfway to the cabins a big, raw-boned teamster, singing in a drunken voice, came staggering toward them. Evidently he had just left the group of people who had gathered near the Indians.

"I didn't expect to see drunkenness out here," said Jim, in a low tone.

"There's lots of it. I saw that fellow yesterday when he couldn't walk. Wentz told me he was a bad customer."

The teamster, his red face bathed in perspiration, and his sleeves rolled up, showing brown, knotty arms, lurched toward them. As they met he aimed a kick at the dog; but Mose leaped nimbly aside, avoiding the heavy boot. He did not growl, nor show his teeth; but the great white head sank forward a little, and the lithe body crouched for a spring.

"Don't touch that dog; he'll tear your leg off!" Joe cried sharply.

"Say, pard, cum an' hev a drink," replied the teamster, with a friendly leer.

"I don't drink," answered Joe, curtly, and moved on.

The teamster growled something of which only the word "parson" was intelligible to the brothers. Joe stopped and looked back. His gray eyes seemed to contract; they did not flash, but shaded and lost their warmth. Jim saw the change, and knowing what it signified, took Joe's arm as he gently urged him away. The teamster's shrill voice could be heard until they entered the fur trader's cabin.

An old man with long, white hair flowing from beneath his wide-brimmed hat, sat near the door holding one of Mrs. Wentz's children on his knee. His face was deep-lined and serious; but kindness shone from his mild blue eyes.

"Mr. Wells, this is my brother James. He is a preacher, and has come in place of the man you expected from Williamsburg."

The old minister arose, and extended his hand, gazing

earnestly at the newcomer meanwhile. Evidently he approved of what he saw in his quick scrutiny of the other's face, for his lips were wreathed with a smile of welcome.

"Mr. Downs, I am glad to meet you, and to know you will go with me. I thank God I shall take into the wilderness one who is young enough to carry on the work when my days are done."

"I will make it my duty to help you in whatsoever way lies in my power," answered Jim, earnestly.

"We have a great work before us. I have heard many scoffers who claim that it is worse than folly to try to teach these fierce savages Christianity; but I know it can be done, and my heart is in the work. I have no fear; yet I would not conceal from you, young man, that the danger of going among these hostile Indians must be great."

"I will not hesitate because of that. My sympathy is with the redman. I have had an opportunity of studying Indian nature and believe the race inherently noble. He has been driven to make war, and I want to help him into other paths."

Joe left the two ministers talking earnestly and turned toward Mrs. Wentz. The fur trader's wife was glowing with pleasure. She held in her hand several rude trinkets, and was explaining to her listener, a young woman, that the toys were for the children, having been brought all the way from Williamsburg.

"Kate, where's Nell?" Joe asked of the girl.

"She went on an errand for Mrs. Wentz."

Kate Wells was the opposite of her sister. Her motions were slow, easy, and consistent with her large, full form. Her brown eyes and hair contrasted sharply with Nell's. The greatest difference in the sisters lay in that Nell's face was sparkling and full of the fire of her eager young life, while Kate's was calm, like the unruffled surface of a deep lake.

"That's Jim, my brother. We're going with you," said Joe.

"Are you? I'm glad," answered the girl, looking at the handsome, earnest face of the young minister.

"Your brother's like you for all the world," whispered Mrs. Wentz.

"He does look like you," said Kate, with her slow smile.

"Which means you think, or hope, that that is all," retorted Joe, laughingly. "Well, Kate, there the resemblance ends, thank God for Jim!"

He spoke in a sad, bitter tone which caused both women to look at him wonderingly. Joe had to them ever been full of surprises; never until then had they seen evidences of sadness in his face. A moment's silence ensued. Mrs. Wentz gazed lovingly at the children who were playing with the trinkets; while Kate mused over the young man's remark, and began studying his half-averted face. She felt warmly drawn to him by the strange expression in the glance he had given his brother. The tenderness in his eyes did not harmonize with much of this wild and reckless boy's behavior. To Kate he had always seemed so bold, so cold, so different from other men, and yet here was proof that Master Joe loved his brother.

The murmured conversation of the two ministers was interrupted by a low cry from outside the cabin. A loud, coarse laugh followed, and then a husky voice:

"Hol' on, my purty lass."

Joe took two long strides, and was on the doorstep. He saw Nell struggling violently in the grasp of the half-drunken teamster.

"I'll jes' hev to kiss this lassie fer luck," he said in a tone of good humor.

At the same instant Joe saw three loungers laughing, and a fourth, the grizzled frontiersman, starting forward with a yell.

"Let me go!" cried Nell.

Just when the teamster had pulled her close to him, and was bending his red, moist face to hers, two brown, sinewy hands grasped his neck with an angry clutch. Deprived thus of breath, his mouth opened, his tongue protruded; his eyes seemed starting from their sockets, and his arms beat the air. Then he was lifted and flung with a crash against the cabin wall. Falling, he lay in a heap on the grass, while the blood flowed from a cut on his temple.

"What's this?" cried a man, authoritatively. He had come swiftly up, and arrived at the scene where stood the grizzled frontiersman.

"It was purty handy, Wentz. I couldn't hev did better myself, and I was comin' for that purpose," said the frontiersman. "Leffler was tryin' to kiss the lass. He's been drunk fer two days. That little girl's sweetheart kin handle himself some, now you take my word on it."

"I'll agree Leff's bad when he's drinkin'," answered the fur trader, and to Joe he added, "he's liable to look you up when he comes around."

"Tell him if I am here when he gets sober, I'll kill him," Joe cried in a sharp voice. His gaze rested once more on the fallen teamster, and again an odd contraction of his eyes was noticeable. The glance was cutting, as if with the flash of cold gray steel. "Nell, I'm sorry I wasn't round sooner," he said, apologetically, as if it was owing to his neglect the affair had happened.

As they entered the cabin Nell stole a glance at him. This was the third time he had injured a man because of her. She had on several occasions seen that cold, steely glare in his eyes, and it had always frightened her. It was gone, however, before they were inside the building. He said something which she did not hear distinctly, and his calm voice allayed her excitement. She had been angry with him; but now she realized that her resentment had disappeared. He had spoken so kindly after the outburst. Had he not shown that he considered himself her protector and lover? A strange emotion, sweet and subtle as the taste of wine, thrilled her, while a sense of fear because of his strength was mingled with her pride in it. Any other girl would have been glad to have such a champion; she would, too, hereafter, for he was a man of whom to be proud.

"Look here, Nell, you haven't spoken to me," Joe cried suddenly, seeming to understand that she had not even heard what he said, so engrossed had she been with her reflections. "Are you mad with me yet?" he continued. "Why, Nell, I'm in—I love you!"

Evidently Joe thought such a fact a sufficient reason for any act on his part. His tender tone conquered Nell, and she turned to him with flushed cheeks and glad eyes.

"I wasn't angry at all," she whispered, and then, eluding the arm he extended, she ran into the other room.

CHAPTER III

Joe lounged in the doorway of the cabin, thoughtfully contemplating two quiet figures that were lying in the shade of a maple tree. One he recognized as the Indian with whom Jim had spent an earnest hour that morning; the red son of the woods was wrapped in slumber. He had placed under his head a many-hued homespun shirt which the young preacher had given him; but while asleep his head had rolled off this improvised pillow, and the bright garment lay free, attracting the eye. Certainly it had led to the train of thought which had found lodgment in Joe's fertile brain.

The other sleeper was a short, stout man whom Joe had seen several times before. This last fellow did not appear to be well-balanced in his mind, and was the butt of the settlers' jokes, while the children called him "Loorey." He, like the Indian, was sleeping off the effects of the previous night's dissipation.

During a few moments Joe regarded the recumbent figures with an expression on his face which told that he thought in them were great possibilities for sport. With one quick glance around he disappeared within the cabin, and when he showed himself at the door, surveying the village square with mirthful eyes, he held in his hand a small basket of Indian design. It was made of twisted grass, and simply contained several bits of soft, chalky stone such as the Indians used for painting, which collection Joe had discovered among the fur trader's wares.

He glanced around once more, and saw that all those in sight were busy with their work. He gave the short man a push, and chuckled when there was no response other than a lazy grunt. Joe took the Indian's gaudy shirt, and, lifting Loorey, slipped it around him, shoved the latter's arm through the sleeves, and buttoned it in front. He streaked the round face with red and white paint, and then, dexterously extracting the eagle plume from the Indian's headdress, stuck it in Loorey's thick shock of hair. It was all done in a moment, after which Joe replaced the basket, and went down to the river.

Several times that morning he had visited the rude wharf where Jeff Lynn, the grizzled old frontiersman, busied himself with preparations for the raft journey down the Ohio.

Lynn had been employed to guide the missionary's party to Fort Henry, and as the brothers had acquainted him with their intention of accompanying the travelers, he had constructed a raft for them and their horses.

Joe laughed when he saw the dozen two-foot logs fastened together, upon which a rude shack had been erected for shelter. This slight protection from the sun and storm was all the brothers would have on their long journey.

Joe noted, however, that the larger raft had been prepared with some thought for the comfort of the girls. The floor of the little hut was raised so that the waves which broke over the logs could not reach it. Taking a peep into the structure, Joe was pleased to see that Nell and Kate would be comfortable, even during a storm. A buffalo robe and two red blankets gave to the interior a cosy, warm look. He observed that some of the girls' luggage was already on board.

"When'll we be off?" he inquired.

"Sun-up," answered Lynn, briefly.

"I'm glad of that. I like to be on the go in the early morning," said Joe, cheerfully.

"Most folks from over Eastways ain't in a hurry to tackle the river," replied Lynn, eyeing Joe sharply.

"It's a beautiful river, and I'd like to sail on it from here to where it ends, and then come back to go again," Joe replied, warmly.

"In a hurry to be a-goin'? I'll allow you'll see some slim red devils, with feathers in their hair, slippin' among the trees along the bank, and mebbe you'll hear the ping which's made when whistlin' lead hits. Perhaps you'll want to be back here by termorrer sundown."

"Not I," said Joe, with his short, cool laugh.

The old frontiersman slowly finished his task of coiling up a rope of wet cowhide, and then, producing a dirty pipe, he took a live ember from the fire and placed it on the bowl. He sucked slowly at the pipe-stem, and soon puffed out a great cloud of smoke. Sitting on a log, he deliberately surveyed the robust shoulders and long, heavy limbs of the young man, with a keen appreciation of their symmetry and strength. Agility, endurance, and courage were more to a borderman than all else; a newcomer on the frontier was always "sized-up" with reference to these "points," and respected in proportion to the measure in which he possessed them.

Old Jeff Lynn, riverman, hunter, frontiersman, puffed slowly at his pipe while he mused thus to himself: "Mebbe I'm wrong in takin' a likin' to this youngster so sudden. Mebbe it's because I'm fond of his sunny-haired lass, an' ag'in mebbe it's because I'm gettin' old an' likes young folks better'n I onct did. Anyway, I'm kinder thinkin', if this young feller gits worked out, say fer about twenty pounds less, he'll lick a whole raft-load of wildcats."

Joe walked to and fro on the logs, ascertained how the raft was put together, and took a pull on the long, clumsy steering oar. At length he seated himself beside Lynn. He was eager to ask questions; to know about the rafts, the river, the forest, the Indians—everything in connection with this wild life; but already he had learned that questioning these frontiersmen is a sure means of closing their lips.

"Ever handle the long rifle?" asked Lynn, after a silence.

"Yes," answered Joe, simply.

"Ever shoot anythin'?" the frontiersman questioned, when he had taken four or five puffs at his pipe.

"Squirrels."

"Good practice, shootin' squirrels," observed Jeff, after another silence, long enough to allow Joe to talk if he was so inclined. "Kin ye hit one—say, a hundred yards?"

"Yes, but not every time in the head," returned Joe. There was an apologetic tone in his answer.

Another interval followed in which neither spoke. Jeff was slowly pursuing his line of thought. After Joe's last remark he returned his pipe to his pocket and brought out a tobacco pouch. He tore off a large portion of the weed and thrust it into his mouth. Then he held out the little buckskin sack to Joe.

"Hev a chaw," he said.

To offer tobacco to anyone was absolutely a borderman's guarantee of friendliness toward that person.

Jeff expectorated half a dozen times, each time coming a little nearer the stone he was aiming at, some five yards distant. Possibly this was the borderman's way of oiling up his conversational machinery. At all events, he commenced to talk.

"Yer brother's goin' to preach out here, ain't he? Preachin' is all right, I'll allow; but I'm kinder doubtful about preachin' to redskins. Howsumever, I've knowed Injuns who are good fellows, and there's no tellin'. What are ye goin' in fer—farmin'?"

"No, I wouldn't make a good farmer."

"Jest cum out kinder wild like, eh?" rejoined Jeff, knowingly.

"I wanted to come West because I was tired of tame life. I love the forest; I want to fish and hunt; and I think I'd like to—to see Indians."

"I kinder thought so," said the old frontiersman, nodding his head as though he perfectly understood Joe's case. "Well, lad, where you're goin' seein' Injuns ain't a matter of choice. You has to see 'em, and fight 'em, too. We've had bad times for years out here on the border, and I'm thinkin' wuss is comin'. Did ye ever hear the name Girty?"

"Yes; he's a renegade."

"He's a traitor, and Jim and George Girty, his brother, are p'isin rattlesnake Injuns. Simon Girty's bad enough; but Jim's the wust. He's now wusser'n a full-blooded Delaware. He's all the time on the lookout to capture white wimen to take to his Injun teepee. Simon Girty and his pals, McKee and Elliott, deserted from that thar fort right afore yer eyes. They're now livin' among the redskins down Fort Henry way, raisin' as much hell fer the settlers as they kin."

"Is Fort Henry near the Indian towns?" asked Joe.

"There's Delawares, Shawnees, and Hurons all along the Ohio below Fort Henry."

"Where is the Moravian Mission located?"

"Why, lad, the Village of Peace, as the Injuns call it, is right in the midst of that Injun country. I s'pect it's a matter of a hundred miles below and cross-country a little from Fort Henry."

"The fort must be an important point, is it not?"

"Wal, I guess so. It's the last place on the river," answered Lynn, with a grim smile. "There's only a stockade there, an' a handful of men. The Injuns hev swarmed down on it time and ag'in, but they hev never burned it. Only such men as Colonel Zane, his brother Jack, and Wetzel could hev kept that fort standin' all these bloody years. Eb Zane's got but a few men, yet he kin handle 'em some, an' with such scouts as Jack Zane and Wetzel, he allus knows what's goin' on among the Injuns."

"I've heard of Colonel Zane. He was an officer under Lord Dunmore. The hunters here speak often of Jack Zane and Wetzel. What are they?"

"Jack Zane is a hunter an' guide. I knowed him well a few years back. He's a quiet, mild chap; but a streak of chain-lightnin' when he's riled. Wetzel is an Injunkiller. Some people say as how he's crazy over scalp-huntin'; but I reckon that's not so. I've seen him a few times. He don't hang round the settlement 'cept when the Injuns are up, an' nobody sees him much. At home he sets round silent-like, an' then mebbe next mornin' he'll be gone, an' won't show up fer days or weeks. But all the frontier knows of his deeds. Fer instance, I've hearn of settlers gettin' up in the mornin' an' findin' a couple of dead and scalped Injuns right in front of their cabins. No one knowed who killed 'em, but everybody says 'Wetzel.' He's allus warnin' the settlers when they need to flee to the fort, and sure he's right every time, because when these men go back to their cabins they find nothin' but ashes. There couldn't be any farmin' done out there but fer Wetzel."

"What does he look like?" questioned Joe, much interested.

"Wetzel stands straight as the oak over thar. He'd hev to go sideways to git his shoulders in that door, but he's as light of foot an' fast as a deer. An' his eyes—why, lad, ye kin hardly look into 'em. If you ever see Wetzel you'll know him to onct."

"I want to see him," Joe spoke quickly, his eyes lighting with an eager flash. "He must be a great fighter."

"Is he? Lew Wetzel is the heftiest of 'em all, an' we hev some as kin fight out here. I was down the river a few years ago and joined a party to go out an' hunt up some redskins as had been reported. Wetzel was with us. We soon struck Injun sign, and then come on to a lot of the pesky varmints. We was all fer goin' home, because we had a small force. When we started to go we finds Wetzel sittin' calmlike on a log. We said: 'Ain't ye goin' home?' and he replied, 'I cum out to find redskins, an' now as we've found 'em, I'm not goin' to run away.' An' we left him settin' thar. Oh, Wetzel is a fighter!"

"I hope I shall see him," said Joe once more, the warm light, which made him look so boyish, still glowing in his face.

"Mebbe ye'll git to; and sure ye'll see redskins, an' not tame ones, nuther."

At this moment the sound of excited voices near the cabins broke in upon the conversation. Joe saw several persons run toward the large cabin and disappear behind it. He smiled as he thought perhaps the commotion had been caused by the awakening of the Indian brave.

Rising to his feet, Joe went toward the cabin, and soon saw the cause of the excitement. A small crowd of men and women, all laughing and talking, surrounded the Indian brave and the little stout fellow. Joe heard someone groan, and then a deep, guttural voice:

"Paleface—big steal—ugh! Injun mad—heap mad—kill paleface."

After elbowing his way into the group, Joe saw the Indian holding Loorey with one hand, while he poked him in the ribs with the other. The captive's face was the picture of dismay: even the streaks of paint did not hide his look of fear and bewilderment. The poor, half-witted fellow was so badly frightened that he could only groan.

"Silvertip scalp paleface. Ugh!" growled the savage, giving Loorey another blow. This time he bent over in pain. The bystanders were divided in feeling; the men laughed, while the women murmured sympathetically.

"This's not a bit funny," muttered Joe, as he pushed his way nearly to the middle of the crowd. Then he stretched out a long arm that, bare and brawny, looked as though it might have been blacksmith's, and grasped the Indian's sinewy wrist with a force that made him loosen his hold on Loorey instantly.

"I stole the shirt—fun—joke," said Joe. "Scalp me if you want to scalp anyone."

The Indian looked quickly at the powerful form before him. With a twist he slipped his arm from Joe's grasp.

"Big paleface heap fun—all squaw play," he said, scornfully. There was a menace in his somber eyes as he turned abruptly and left the group.

"I'm afraid you've made an enemy," said Jake Wentz to Joe. "An Indian never forgets an insult, and that's how he regarded your joke. Silvertip has been friendly here because he sells us his pelts. He's a Shawnee chief. There he goes through the willows!"

By this time Jim and Mr. Wells, Mrs. Wentz and the

girls had joined in the group. They all watched Silvertip get into his canoe and paddle away.

"A bad sign," said Wentz, and then, turning to Jeff Lynn, who joined the party at that moment, he briefly explained the circumstances.

"Never did like Silver. He's a crafty redskin, an' not to be trusted," replied Jeff.

"He has turned round and is looking back," Nell said quickly.

"So he has," observed the fur trader.

The Indian was now several hundred yards down the swift river, and for an instant had ceased paddling. The sun shone brightly on his eagle plumes. He remained motionless for a moment, and even at such a distance the dark, changeless face could be discerned. He lifted his hand and shook it menacingly.

"If ye don't hear from that redskin ag'in, Jeff Lynn don't know nothin'," calmly said the old frontiersman.

CHAPTER IV

As the rafts drifted with the current the voyagers saw the settlers on the landing place diminish until they had faded from indistinct figures to mere black specks against the green background. Then came the last wave of a white scarf, faintly in the distance, and at length the dark outline of the fort was all that remained to their regretful gaze. Quickly that, too, disappeared behind the green hill, which, with its bold front, forces the river to take a wide turn.

The Ohio, winding in its course between high, wooded bluffs, rolled on and on into the wilderness.

Beautiful as was the ever-changing scenery, rugged, gray-faced cliffs on one side contrasting with green-clad hills on the other, there hovered over land and water something more striking than beauty. Above all hung a still atmosphere of calmness—of loneliness.

And this penetrating solitude marred somewhat the pleasure which might have been found in the picturesque scenery, and caused the voyagers, to whom this country was new, to take less interest in the gaily feathered birds and stealthy animals that were to be seen on the way. By the forms of wild life along the banks of the river, this strange intruder on their peace was regarded with attention. The birds and beasts evinced little fear of the floating rafts. The sandhill crane, stalking along the shore, lifted his long neck as the unfamiliar thing came floating by, and then stood still and silent as a statue until the rafts disappeared from view. Blue herons feeding along the bars, saw the unusual spectacle, and, uttering surprised "booms," they spread wide wings and lumbered away along the shore. The crows circled above the voyagers, cawing in not unfriendly excitement. Smaller birds alighted on the raised poles, and several—a robin, a catbird, and a little brown wren—ventured with hesitating boldness to peck at the crumbs the girls threw to them. Deer waded knee-deep in the shallow water, and, lifting their heads, instantly became motionless and absorbed. Occasionally a buffalo appeared on a level stretch of bank, and, tossing his huge head, seemed inclined to resent the coming of this stranger into his domain.

All day the rafts drifted steadily and swiftly down the river, presenting to the little party ever-varying pictures of densely wooded hills, of jutting, broken cliffs with scant evergreen growth; of long reaches of sandy bar that glistened golden in the sunlight, and over the all flight and call of wildfowl, the flitting of woodland songsters, and now and then the whistle and bellow of the horned watchers in the forest.

The intense blue of the vault above began to pale, and low down in the west a few fleecy clouds, gorgeously golden for a fleeting instant, then crimson-crowned for another, shaded and darkened as the setting sun sank behind the hills. Presently the red rays disappeared, a pink glow suffused the heavens, and at last, as gray twilight stole down over the hilltops, the crescent moon peeped above the wooded fringe of the western bluffs.

"Hard an' fast she is," sang out Jeff Lynn, as he fastened the rope to a tree at the head of a small island. "All off now, an' we'll hev supper. Thar's a fine spring under yon curly birch, an' I fetched along a leg of deer meat. Hungry, little 'un?"

He had worked hard all day steering the rafts, yet Nell had seen him smiling at her many times during the journey, and he had found time before the early start to arrange for her a comfortable seat. There was now a solicitude in the frontiersman's voice that touched her.

"I am famished," she replied, with her bright smile. "I am afraid I could eat a whole deer."

They all climbed the sandy slope, and found themselves on the summit of an oval island, with a pretty glade in the middle surrounded by birches. Bill, the second raftsman, a stolid, silent man, at once swung his axe upon a log of driftwood. Mr. Wells and Jim walked to and fro under the birches, and Kate and Nell sat on the grass watching with great interest the old helmsman as he came up from the river, his brown hands and face shining from the scrubbing he had given them. Soon he had a fire cheerfully blazing, and after laying out the few utensils, he addressed himself to Joe:

"I'll tell ye right here, lad, good venison kin be spoiled by bad cuttin' and cookin'. You're slicin' it too thick. See— thar! Now salt good, an' keep outen the flame; on the red coals is best."

With a sharpened stick Jeff held the thin slices over the fire for a few moments. Then he laid them aside on some clean white oak chips Bill's axe had provided. The simple meal of meat, bread, and afterward a drink of the cold spring water, was keenly relished by the hungry voyagers. When it had been eaten, Jeff threw a log on his fire and remarked:

"Seein' as how we won't be in redskin territory fer awhile yit, we kin hev a fire. I'll allow ye'll all be chilly and damp from river mist afore long, so toast yerselves good."

"How far have we come today?" inquired Mr. Wells, his mind always intent on reaching the scene of his cherished undertaking.

"'Bout thirty-odd miles, I reckon. Not much on a trip, thet's sartin, but we'll pick up termorrer. We've some quicker water, an' the rafts hev to go separate."

"How quiet!" exclaimed Kate, suddenly breaking the silence that followed the frontiersman's answer.

"Beautiful!" impetuously said Nell, looking up at Joe. A quick flash from his gray eyes answered her; he did not speak; indeed he had said little to her since the start, but his glance showed her how glad he was that she felt the sweetness and content of this wild land.

"I was never in a wilderness before," broke in the earnest voice of the young minister. "I feel an almost overpowering sense of loneliness. I want to get near you all, I feel lost. Yet it is grand, sublime!"

"Here is the promised land—the fruitful life—Nature as it was created by God," replied the old minister, impressively.

"Tell us a story," said Nell to the old frontiersman, as he once more joined the circle round the fire.

"So, little 'un, ye want a story?" queried Jeff, taking up a live coal and placing it in the bowl of his pipe. He took off his coonskin cap and carefully laid it aside. His weatherbeaten face beamed in answer to the girl's request. He drew a long and audible pull at his black pipe, and sent forth slowly a cloud of white smoke. Deliberately poking the fire with a stick, as if stirring into life dead embers of the past, he sucked again at his pipe, and emitted a great puff of smoke that completely enveloped the grizzled head. From out that white cloud came his drawling voice.

"Ye've seen thet big curly birch over thar—thet 'un as bends kind of sorrowful like. Wal, it used to stand straight

an' proud. I've knowed thet tree all the years I've navi-
gated this river, an' it seems natural like to me thet it now
droops dyin', fer it shades the grave of as young, an' sweet,
an' purty a lass as yerself, Miss Nell. Rivermen called this
island George's Island, 'cause Washington onct camped
here; but of late years the name's got changed, an' the men
say suthin' like this: 'We'll try an' make Milly's birch
afore sundown,' jest as Bill and me hev done today. Some
years agone I was comin' up from Fort Henry an' had on
board my slow old scow a lass named Milly—we never
learned her other name. She come to me at the fort, an'
tells as how her folks had been killed by Injuns, an' she
wanted to git back to Pitt to meet her sweetheart. I was
ag'in her comin' all along, an' fust off I said 'No.' But
when I seen tears in her blue eyes, an' she puts her little
hand on mine, I jest wilted, an' says to Jim Blair, 'She
goes.' Wal, jest as might hev been expected—an' fact is I
looked fer it—we wus tackled by redskins. Somehow, Jim
Girty got wind of us hevin' a lass aboard, an' he ketched
up with us jest below here. It's a bad place, called Shawnee
Rock, an' I'll show it to ye termorrer. The renegade, with
his red devils, attacked us thar, an' we had a fierce fight.
Jim Blair, he was killed, an' we had a time gittin' away.
Milly wus shot. She lived fer awhile, a couple of days, an'
all the time was so patient, an' sweet, an' brave with thet
renegade's bullet in her—fer he shot her, when he seen he
couldn't capture her—thet thar wusn't a blame man of us
who wouldn't hev died to grant her prayer, which wus that
she could live to onct more see her lover."

There was a long silence, during which the old frontiersman sat gazing into the fire with sad eyes.

"We couldn't do nuthin', an' we buried her thar under
thet birch, where she smiled her last sad, sweet smile, an'
died. Ever since then the river has been eatin' away at this

island. It's only half as big as it was onct, an' another flood will take away this sandbar, these few birches—an' Milly's grave."

The old frontiersman's story affected all his listeners. The elder minister bowed his head and prayed that no such fate might overtake his nieces. The young minister looked again, as he had many times that day, at Nell's winsome face. The girls cast grave glances at the drooping birch, and their bright tears glistened in the fire glow. Once more Joe's eyes glinted with that steely flash, and as he gazed out over the wide, darkening expanse of water his face grew cold and rigid.

"I'll allow I might hev told a more cheerful story, an' I'll do so next time; but I wanted ye all, particular the lasses, to know somethin' of the kind of country ye're goin' into. The frontier needs women; but jist yit it deals hard with them. An' Jim Girty, with more of his kind, ain't dead yit."

"Why don't someone kill him?" was Joe's sharp question.

"Easier said than done, lad. Jim Girty is a white traitor, but he's a cunnin' an' fierce redskin in his ways an' life. He knows the woods as a crow does, an' keeps outer sight 'cept when he's least expected. Then ag'in, he's got Simon Girty, his brother, an' almost the whole redskin tribe behind him. Injuns stick close to a white man that has turned ag'inst his own people, an' Jim Girty hain't ever been ketched. Howsumever, I heard last trip thet he'd been tryin' some of his tricks round Fort Henry, an' thet Wetzel is on his trail. Wal, if it's so thet Lew Wetzel is arter him, I wouldn't give a pinch o' powder fer the white redskin's chances of a long life."

No one spoke, and Jeff, after knocking the ashes from his pipe, went down to the raft, returning shortly afterward with his blanket. This he laid down and rolled himself in. Presently from under his coonskin cap came the words:

"Wal, I've turned in, an' I advise ye all to do the same."

All save Joe and Nell acted on Jeff's suggestion. For a long time the young couple sat close together on the bank, gazing at the moonlight on the river.

The night was perfect. A cool wind fanned the dying embers of the fire and softly stirred the leaves. Earlier in the evening a single frog had voiced his protest against the loneliness; but now his dismal croak was no longer heard. A snipe, belated in his feeding, ran along the sandy shore uttering his *tweet-tweet*, and his little cry, breaking in so softly on the silence, seemed only to make more deeply felt the great, vast stillness of the night.

Joe's arm was around Nell. She had demurred at first, but he gave no heed to her slight resistance, and finally her head rested against his shoulder. There was no need of words.

Joe had a pleasurable sense of her nearness, and there was a delight in the fragrance of her hair as it waved against his cheek; but just then love was not uppermost in his mind. All day he had been silent under the force of an emotion which he could not analyze. Some power, some feeling in which the thought of Nell had no share, was drawing him with irresistible strength. Nell had just begun to surrender to him in the sweetness of her passion; and yet even with that knowledge knocking reproachfully at his heart, he could not help being absorbed in the shimmering water, in the dark reflection of the trees, the gloom, and shadow of the forest.

Presently he felt her form relax in his arms; then her soft, regular breathing told him she had fallen asleep, and he laughed low to himself. How she would pout on the morrow when he teased her about it! Then, realizing that she was tired with her long day's journey, he reproached himself for keeping her from the needed rest, and instantly decided to carry her to the raft. Yet such was the novelty of the situation that he yielded to its charm and did not go at once. The moonlight found bright threads in her wavy hair; it shone caressingly on her quiet face, and tried to steal under the downcast lashes.

Joe made a movement to rise with her, when she muttered indistinctly as if speaking to someone. He remembered then she had once told him that she talked in her sleep, and how greatly it annoyed her. He might hear something more with which to tease her; so he listened.

"Yes—Uncle—I will go—Kate, we must—go . . ."

Another interval of silence, then more murmurings. He distinguished his own name, and presently she called clearly, as if answering some inward questioner.

"I—love him—yes—I love Joe—he has mastered me. Yet I wish he were—like Jim—Jim who looked at me—so—with his deep eyes—and I . . ."

Joe lifted her as if she were a baby, and carrying her down to the raft, gently laid her by her sleeping sister.

The innocent words which he should not have heard were like a blow. What she would never have acknowledged in her waking hours had been revealed in her dreams. He recalled the glance of Jim's eyes as it had rested on Nell many times that day, and now these things were most significant.

He found at the end of the island a great, mossy stone. On this he climbed, and sat where the moonlight streamed, upon him. Gradually that cold bitterness died out from his face, as it passed from his heart, and once more he became engrossed in the silver sheen on the water, the lapping of the waves on the pebbly beach, and in that speaking, mysterious silence of the woods.

When the first faint rays of red streaked over the eastern hilltops, and the river mist arose from the water in a vapory cloud, Jeff Lynn rolled out his blanket, stretched his long limbs, and gave a hearty call to the morning. His cheerful welcome awakened all the voyagers except Joe, who had spent the night in watching and the early morning in fishing.

"Wal, I'll be darned," ejaculated Jeff as he saw Joe. "Up afore me, an' ketched a string of fish."

"What are they?" asked Joe, holding up several bronze-backed fish.

"Bass—black bass, an' thet big feller is a lammin' hefty 'un. How'd ye ketch 'em?"

"I fished for them."

"Wal, so it 'pears," growled Jeff, once more reluctantly yielding to his admiration for the lad. "How'd ye wake up so early?"

"I stayed up all night. I saw three deer swim from the mainland, but nothing else came around."

"Try yer hand at cleanin' 'em fer breakfast," continued Jeff, beginning to busy himself with preparations for that meal. "Wal, wal, if he ain't surprisin'! He'll do somethin' out here on the frontier, sure as I'm a born sinner," he muttered to himself, wagging his head in his quaint manner.

Breakfast over, Jeff transferred the horses to the smaller raft, which he had cut loose from his own, and giving a few directions to Bill, started downstream with Mr. Wells and the girls.

The rafts remained close enough together for a while but as the current quickened and was more skillfully taken advantage of by Jeff, the larger raft gained considerable headway, gradually widening the gap between the two.

All day they drifted. From time to time Joe and Jim waved their hands to the girls; but the greater portion of their attention was given to quieting the horses. Mose, Joe's big white dog, retired in disgust to the hut, where he watched and dozed by turns. He did not fancy this kind of voyaging. Bill strained his sturdy arms all day on the steering oar.

About the middle of the afternoon Joe observed that the hills grew more rugged and precipitous, and the river ran faster. He kept a constant lookout for the wall of rock which marked the point of danger. When the sun had disappeared behind the hills, he saw ahead a gray rock protruding from the green foliage. It was ponderous, overhanging, and seemed to frown down on the river. This was Shawnee Rock. Joe looked long at the cliff, and wondered if there was now an Indian scout hidden behind the pines that skirted the edge. Prominent on the top of the bluff a large, dead tree projected its hoary twisted branches.

Bill evidently saw the landmark, for he stopped in his monotonous walk to and fro across the raft, and pushing his oar amidships he looked ahead for the other raft. The figure of the tall frontiersman could be plainly seen as he labored at the helm.

The raft disappeared round a bend, and as it did so Joe saw a white scarf waved by Nell.

Bill worked the clumsy craft over toward the right shore where the current was more rapid. He pushed with all his strength, and when the oar reached its widest sweep, he lifted it and ran back across the raft for another push. Joe scanned the river ahead. He saw no rapids; only rougher water whirling over some rocks. They were where the channel narrowed and ran close to the right-hand bank. Under a willow-flanked lodge was a sandbar. To Joe there seemed nothing hazardous in drifting through this pass.

"Bad place ahead," said Bill, observing Joe's survey of the river.

"It doesn't look so," replied Joe.

"A raft ain't a boat. We could pole a boat. You has to hev water to float logs, an' the river's run out considerable. I'm only afeerd fer the hosses. If we hit or drag, they might plunge around a bit."

When the raft passed into the head of the bend it struck the rocks several times, but finally gained the channel safely, and everything seemed propitious for an easy passage.

But, greatly to Bill's surprise, the wide craft was caught directly in the channel, and swung round so that the steering oar pointed toward the opposite shore. The water roared a foot deep over the logs.

"Hold hard on the hosses!" yelled Bill. "Somethin's wrong. I never seen a snag here."

The straining mass of logs, insecurely fastened together, rolled and then pitched loose again, but the short delay had been fatal to the steering apparatus.

Joe would have found keen enjoyment in the situation, had it not been for his horse, Lance. The thoroughbred was difficult to hold. As Bill was making strenuous efforts to get in a lucky stroke of the oar, he failed to see a long length of grapevine floating like a brown snake on the water below. In the excitement they heeded not the barking of Mose. Nor did they see the grapevine straighten and become taut just as they drifted upon it; but they felt the raft strike and hold on some submerged object. It creaked and groaned and the foamy water surged, gurgling, between the logs.

Jim's mare snorted with terror, and rearing high, pulled her halter loose and plunged into the river. But Jim still held her, at risk of being drawn overboard.

"Let go! She'll drag you in!" yelled Joe, grasping him with his free hand. Lance trembled violently and strained at the rope, which his master held with a strong grip.

"*Crack!*"

The stinging report of a rifle rang out above the splashing of the water.

Without a cry, Bill's grasp on the oar loosened; he fell over it limply, his head striking the almost submerged log. A dark-red fluid colored the water; then his body slipped over the oar and into the river, where it sank.

"My God! Shot!" cried Jim, in horrified tones.

He saw a puff of white smoke rising above the willows. Then the branches parted, revealing the dark forms of several Indian warriors. From the rifle in the foremost savage's hand a slight veil of smoke rose. With the leap of a panther the redskin sprang from the strip of sand to the raft.

"Hold, Jim! Drop that ax! We're caught!" cried Joe.

"It's that Indian from the fort!" gasped Jim.

The stalwart warrior was indeed Silvertip. But how changed! Stripped of the blanket he had worn at the settlement, now standing naked but for his buckskin breechcloth, with his perfectly proportioned form disclosed in all its sinewy beauty, and on his swarthy, evil face an expression of savage scorn, he surely looked a warrior and a chief.

He drew his tomahawk and flashed a dark glance at Joe. For a moment he steadily regarded the young man;

but if he expected to see fear in the latter's face he was mistaken, for the look was returned coolly.

"Paleface steal shirt," he said in his deep voice. "Fool paleface play—Silvertip no forget."

CHAPTER V

Silvertip turned to his braves, and giving a brief command, sprang from the raft. The warriors closed in around the brothers; two grasping each by the arms, and the remaining Indian taking care of the horse. The captives were then led ashore, where Silvertip awaited them.

When the horse was clear of the raft, which task necessitated considerable labor on the part of the Indians, the chief seized the grapevine, that was now plainly in sight, and severed it with one blow of his tomahawk. The raft dashed forward with a lurch and drifted downstream.

In the clear water Joe could see the cunning trap which had caused the death of Bill, and insured the captivity of himself and his brother. The crafty savages had trimmed a six-inch sapling and anchored it under the water. They weighted the heavy end, leaving the other pointing upstream. To this last had been tied the grapevine. When the drifting raft reached the sapling, the Indians concealed in the willows pulled hard on the improvised rope; the end of the sapling stuck up like a hook, and the raft was caught and held. The killing of the helmsman showed the Indians' foresight; even had the raft drifted on downstream the brothers would have been helpless on a craft they could not manage. After all, Joe thought, he had not been so far wrong when he half fancied that an Indian lay behind Shawnee Rock, and he marveled at this clever trick which had so easily effected their capture.

But he had little time to look around at the scene of action. There was a moment only in which to survey the river to learn if the unfortunate raftsman's body had appeared. It was not to be seen. The river ran swiftly and hid all evidence of the tragedy under its smooth surface. When the brave who had gone back to the raft for the goods joined his companion the two hurried Joe up the bank after the others.

Once upon level ground Joe saw before him an open forest. On the border of this the Indians stopped long enough to bind the prisoners' wrists with thongs of deerhide. While two of the braves performed this office, Silvertip leaned against a tree and took no notice of the brothers. When they were thus securely tied one of their captors addressed the chief, who at once led the way westward through the forest. The savages followed in single file, with Joe and Jim in the middle of the line. The last Indian tried to mount Lance; but the thoroughbred would have none of him, and after several efforts the savage was compelled to desist. Mose trotted reluctantly along behind the horse.

Although the chief preserved a dignified mien, his braves were disposed to be cheerful. They were in high glee over their feat of capturing the palefaces, and kept up an incessant jabbering. One Indian, who walked directly behind Joe, continually prodded him with the stock of a rifle; and whenever Joe turned, the brawny redskin grinned as he grunted, "Ugh!" Joe observed that this huge savage had a broad face of rather a lighter shade of red than his companions. Perhaps he intended those rifle prods in friendliness, for although they certainly amused him, he would allow no one else to touch Joe; but it would have been more pleasing had he shown his friendship in a gentle manner. This Indian carried Joe's pack, much to his own delight, especially as his companions evinced an envious curiosity. The big fellow would not, however, allow them to touch it.

"He's a cheerful brute," remarked Joe to Jim.

"Ugh!" grunted the big Indian, jamming Joe with his rifle-stock.

Joe took heed to the warning and spoke no more. He gave all his attention to the course over which he was being taken. Here was his first opportunity to learn something of Indians and their woodcraft. It occurred to him that his captors would not have been so pleased and careless had they not believed themselves safe from pursuit, and he concluded they were leisurely conducting him toward one of the Indian towns. He watched the supple figure before him, wondering at the quick step, light as the fall of a leaf, and tried to walk as softly. He found, however, that where the Indian readily avoided the sticks and brush, he was unable to move without snapping twigs. Now and then he would look up and study the lay of the land ahead; and as he came nearer to certain rocks and trees he scrutinized them closely, in order to remember their shape and general appearance. He believed he was blazing out in his mind this woodland trail, so that should fortune favor him and he contrive to escape, he would be able to find his way back to the river. Also, he was enjoying the wild scenery.

This forest would have appeared beautiful, even to one indifferent to such charms, and Joe was far from that. Every movement he felt steal stronger over him a subtle influence which he could not define. Half unconsciously he tried to analyze it, but it baffled him. He could no more explain what fascinated him than he could understand what caused the melancholy quiet which hung over the glades and hollows. He had pictured a real forest so differently from this. Here was a long lane paved with springy moss and fenced by bright-green sassafras; there a secluded dale, dotted with pale-blue blossoms, over which the giant cottonwoods leaned their heads, jealously guarding the delicate flowers from the sun. Beech trees, growing close in clanny groups, spread their straight limbs gracefully; the white birches gleamed like silver wherever a stray sunbeam stole through the foliage, and the oaks, monarchs of the forest, rose over all, dark, rugged, and kingly.

Joe soon understood why the party traveled through such open forest. The chief, seeming hardly to deviate from his direct course, kept clear of broken ground, matted thickets, and tangled windfalls. Joe got a glimpse of dark ravines and heard the music of tumbling waters; he saw gray cliffs grown over with vines, and full of holes and crevices; steep ridges, covered with dense patches of briar and hazel, rising in the way. Yet the Shawnee always found an easy path.

The sun went down behind the foliage in the west, and shadows appeared low in the glens; then the trees faded into an indistinct mass; a purple shade settled down over the forest, and night brought the party to a halt.

The Indians selected a sheltered spot under the lee of a knoll, at the base of which ran a little brook. Here in this inclosed space were the remains of a campfire. Evidently the Indians had halted there that same day, for the logs still smoldered. While one brave fanned the embers, another took from a neighboring branch a haunch of deer meat. A blaze was soon coaxed from the dull coals, more fuel was added, and presently a cheerful fire shone on the circle of dusky forms.

It was a picture which Joe had seen in many a boyish

dream; now that he was a part of it he did not dwell on the hopelessness of the situation, nor of the hostile chief whose enmity he had incurred. Almost, it seemed, he was glad of this chance to watch the Indians and listen to them. He had been kept apart from Jim, and it appeared to Joe that their captors treated his brother with a contempt which they did not show him. Silvertip had, no doubt, informed them that Jim had been on his way to teach the Indians of the white man's God.

Jim sat with drooping head; his face was sad, and evidently he took the most disheartening view of his capture. When he had eaten the slice of venison given to him he lay down with his back to the fire.

Silvertip, in these surroundings, showed his real character. He had appeared friendly in the settlement; but now he was the relentless savage, a son of the wilds, free as an eagle. His dignity as a chief kept him aloof from his braves. He had taken no notice of the prisoners since the capture. He remained silent, steadily regarding the fire with his somber eyes. At length, glancing at the big Indian, he motioned toward the prisoners, and with a single word stretched himself on the leaves.

Joe noted the same changelessness of expression in the other dark faces as he had seen in Silvertip's. It struck him forcibly. When they spoke in their soft, guttural tones, or burst into a low, not unmusical laughter, or sat gazing stolidly into the fire, their faces seemed always the same, inscrutable, like the depths of the forest now hidden in the night. One thing Joe felt rather than saw—these savages were fierce and untamable. He was sorry for Jim, because, as he believed, it would be as easy to teach the panther gentleness toward his prey as to instil into one of these wild creatures a belief in Christ.

The braves manifested keen pleasure in anticipation as

to what they would get out of the pack, which the Indian now opened. Time and again the big brave placed his broad hand on the shoulder of a comrade Indian and pushed him backward.

Finally the pack was opened. It contained a few articles of wearing apparel, a pair of boots, and a pipe and pouch of tobacco. The big Indian kept the latter articles, grunting with satisfaction, and threw the boots and clothes to the others. Immediately there was a scramble. One brave, after a struggle with another, got possession of both boots. He at once slipped off his moccasins and drew on the white man's foot covering. He strutted around in them a few moments, but his proud manner soon changed to disgust.

Cowhide had none of the soft, yielding qualities of buckskin, and hurt the Indian's feet. Sitting down, he pulled one off, not without difficulty, for the boots were wet; but he could not remove the other. He hesitated a moment, being aware of the subdued merriment of his comrades, and then held up his foot to the nearest one. This chanced to be the big Indian, who evidently had a keen sense of humor. Taking hold of the boot with both hands, he dragged the luckless brave entirely around the campfire. The fun, however, was not to be all onesided. The big Indian gave a more strenuous pull, and the boot came off suddenly. Unprepared for this, he lost his balance and fell down the bank almost into the creek. He held on to the boot, nevertheless, and getting up, threw it into the fire.

The braves quieted down after that, and soon lapsed into slumber, leaving the big fellow, to whom the chief had addressed his brief command, acting as guard. Observing Joe watching him as he puffed on his new pipe, he grinned, and spoke in broken English that was intelligible, and much of a surprise to the young man.

"Paleface—tobac'—heap good."

Then, seeing that Joe made no effort to follow his brother's initiative, for Jim was fast asleep, he pointed to the recumbent figures and spoke again.

"Ugh! Paleface sleep—Injun wigwams—near setting sun."

On the following morning Joe was awakened by the pain in his legs, which had been bound all night. He was glad when the bonds were cut and the party took up its westward march.

The Indians, though somewhat quieter, displayed the same carelessness: they did not hurry, nor use particular caution, but selected the most open paths through the forest. They even halted while one of their number crept up on a herd of browsing deer. About noon the leader stopped to drink from a spring; his braves followed suit and permitted the white prisoners to quench their thirst.

When they were about to start again the single note of a bird far away in the woods sounded clearly on the quiet air. Joe would not have given heed to it had he been less attentive. He instantly associated this peculiar bird-note with the sudden stiffening of Silvertip's body and his attitude of intense listening. Low exclamations came from the braves as they bent to catch the lightest sound. Presently, above the murmur of the gentle fall of water over the stones, rose that musical note once more. It was made by a bird, Joe thought, and yet, judged by the actions of the Indians, how potent with meaning beyond that of the simple melody of the woodland songster! He turned, half expecting to see somewhere in the treetops the bird which had wrought so sudden a change in his captors. As he did so from close at hand came the same call, now louder, but identical with the one that had deceived him. It was an answering signal, and had been given by Silvertip.

It flashed into Joe's mind that other savages were in the forest; they had run across the Shawnees' trail, and were thus communicating with them. Soon dark figures could be discerned against the patches of green thicket; they came nearer and nearer, and now entered the open glade where Silvertip stood with his warriors.

Joe counted twelve, and noted that they differed from his captors. He had only time to see that this difference consisted in the headdress, and in the color and quantity of paint on their bodies, when his gaze was attracted and riveted to the foremost figures.

The first was that of a very tall and stately chief, toward whom Silvertip now advanced with every show of respect. In this Indian's commanding stature, in his reddish bronze face, stern and powerful, there were readable the characteristics of a king. In his deepset eyes, gleaming from under a ponderous brow, in his mastifflike jaw; in every feature of his haughty face were visible all the high intelligence, the consciousness of past valor, and the power and authority that denote a great chieftain.

The second figure was equally striking for the remarkable contrast it afforded to the chief's. Despite the gaudy ornaments, the paint, the fringed and beaded buckskin leggings—all the Indian accoutrements and garments which bedecked this person, he would have been known anywhere as a white man. His skin was burned to a dark bronze, but it had not the red tinge which characterizes the Indian. This white man had, indeed, a strange physiognomy. The forehead was narrow and sloped backward from the brow, denoting animal instincts. The eyes were close together, yellowish brown in color, and had a peculiar vibrating movement, as though they were hung on a pivot, like a compass needle. The nose was long and hooked, and the mouth set in a thin, cruel line. There was in the man's aspect an extraordinary combination of ignorance, vanity, cunning, and ferocity.

While the two chiefs held a short consultation, this savage-appearing white man addressed the brothers.

"Who're you, an' where you goin'?" he asked gruffly, confronting Jim.

"My name is Downs. I am a preacher, and was on my way to the Moravian Mission to preach to the Indians. You are a white man; will you help us?"

If Jim expected the information would please his interrogator, he was mistaken.

"So you're one of 'em? Yes, I'll do suthin' fer you when I git back from this hunt. I'll cut your heart out, chop it up, an' feed it to the buzzards," he said fiercely, concluding his threat by striking Jim a cruel blow on the head.

Joe paled deathly white at this cowardly action, and his eyes, as they met the gaze of the ruffian, contracted with their characteristic steely glow, as if some powerful force within the depths of his being were at white heat and only this pale flash came to the surface.

"You ain't a preacher?" questioned the man, meeting something in Joe's glance that had been absent from Jim's.

Joe made no answer, and regarded his questioner steadily.

"Ever see me afore? Ever hear of Jim Girty?" he asked boastfully.

"Before you spoke I knew you were Girty," answered Joe quietly.

"How d'you know? Ain't you afeared?"

"Of what?"

"Me—me?"

Joe laughed in the renegade's face.

"How'd you know me?" growled Girty. "I'll see thet you hev cause to remember me after this."

"I figured there was only one so-called white man in these woods who is coward enough to strike a man whose hands are tied."

"Boy, ye're too free with your tongue. I'll shet off your wind." Girty's hand was raised, but it never reached Joe's neck.

The big Indian had an hour or more previous cut Joe's bonds, but he still retained the thong which was left attached to Joe's left wrist. This allowed the young man free use of his right arm, which, badly swollen or not, he brought into quick action.

When the renegade reached toward him Joe knocked up the hand, and, instead of striking, he grasped the hooked nose with all the powerful grip of his fingers. Girty uttered a frightful curse; he writhed with pain, but could not free himself from the viselike clutch. He drew his tomahawk and with a scream aimed a vicious blow at Joe. He missed his aim, however, for Silvertip had intervened and turned the course of the keen hatchet. But the weapon struck Joe a glancing blow, inflicting a painful, though not dangerous wound.

The renegade's nose was skinned and bleeding profusely. He was frantic with fury, and tried to get at Joe; but Silvertip remained in front of his captive until some of the braves led Girty into the forest, where the tall chief had already disappeared.

The nose-pulling incident added to the gayety of the Shawnees, who evidently were pleased with Girty's discomfiture. They jabbered among themselves and nodded approvingly at Joe, until a few words spoken by Silvertip produced a sudden change.

What the words were Joe could not understand, but to him they sounded like French. He smiled at the absurdity of imagining he had heard a savage speak a foreign language. At any rate, whatever had been said was trenchant with meaning. The Indians changed from cheerful to grave; they picked up their weapons and looked keenly on every side; the big Indian at once retied Joe, and then all crowded round the chief.

"Did you hear what Silvertip said, and did you notice the effect it had?" whispered Jim, taking advantage of the moment.

"It sounded like French, but of course it wasn't," replied Joe.

"It was French. *'Le Vent de la Mort.'* "

"By Jove, that's it. What does it mean?" asked Joe, who was not a scholar.

"The Wind of Death."

"That's English, but I can't apply it here. Can you?"

"No doubt it is some Indian omen."

The hurried consultation over, Silvertip tied Joe's horse and dog to the trees, and once more led the way; this time he avoided the open forest and kept on low ground. For a long time he traveled in the bed of the brook, wading when the water was shallow, and always stepping where there was the least possibility of leaving a footprint. Not a word was spoken. If either of the brothers made the lightest splash in the water, or tumbled a stone into the brook, the Indian behind rapped him on the head with a tomahawk handle.

At certain places, indicated by the care which Silvertip exercised in walking, the Indian in front of the captives turned and pointed where they were to step. They were hiding the trail. Silvertip hurried them over the stony places; went more slowly through the water, and picked his way carefully over the soft ground it became necessary to cross. At times he stopped, remaining motionless many seconds.

This vigilance continued all the afternoon. The sun sank; twilight spread its gray mantle, and soon black night enveloped the forest. The Indians halted, but made no fire; they sat close together on a stony ridge, silent and watchful.

Joe pondered deeply over this behavior. Did the Shawnees fear pursuit? What had that Indian chief told Silvertip? To Joe it seemed that they acted as if believing foes were on all sides. Though they hid their tracks, it was, apparently, not the fear of pursuit alone which made them cautious.

Joe reviewed the afternoon's march and dwelt upon the possible meaning of the catlike steps, the careful brushing aside of branches, the roving eyes, suspicious and gloomy, the eager watchfulness of the advance as well as to the rear, and always the strained effort to listen, all of which gave him the impression of some grave, unseen danger.

And now as he lay on the hard ground, nearly exhausted by the long march and suffering from the throbbing wound, his courage lessened somewhat, and he shivered with dread. The quiet and gloom of the forest; these fierce, wild creatures, free in the heart of their own wilderness yet menaced by a foe, and that strange French phrase which kept recurring in his mind—all had the effect of conjuring up giant shadows in Joe's fanciful mind.

During all his life, until this moment, he had never feared anything; now he was afraid of the darkness. The spectral trees spread long arms overhead, and phantom forms stalked abroad; somewhere out in that dense gloom stirred this mysterious foe—the "Wind of Death."

Nevertheless, he finally slept. In the dull-gray light of early morning the Indians once more took up the line of march toward the west. They marched all that day, and at dusk halted to eat and rest. Silvertip and another Indian stood watch.

Some time before morning Joe suddenly awoke. The night was dark, yet it was lighter than when he had fallen asleep. A pale, crescent moon shone dimly through the murky clouds. There was neither movement of the air nor the chirp of an insect. Absolute silence prevailed.

Joe saw the Indian guard leaning against a tree, asleep. Silvertip was gone. The captive raised his head and looked around for the chief. There were only four Indians left, three on the ground and one against the tree.

He saw something shining near him. He looked more closely, and made out the object to be an eagle plume Silvertip had worn in his headdress. It lay on the ground near the tree. Joe made some slight noise which awakened the guard. The Indian never moved a muscle; but his eyes roved everywhere. He, too, noticed the absence of the chief.

At this moment from out of the depths of the woods came a swelling sigh, like the moan of the night wind. It rose and died away, leaving the silence apparently all the deeper.

A shudder ran over Joe's frame. Fascinated, he watched the guard. The Indian uttered a low gasp; his eyes started and glared wildly; he rose very slowly to his full height and stood waiting, listening. The dark hand which held the tomahawk trembled so that little glints of moonlight glanced from the bright steel.

From far back in the forest deeps came that same low moaning:

"Um-m-mm-woo-o-o-o!"

It rose from a faint murmur and swelled to a deep moan, soft but clear, and ended in a wail like that of a lost soul.

The break it made in that dead silence was awful. Joe's blood seemed to have curdled and frozen; a cold sweat oozed from his skin, and it was as if a clammy hand clutched at his heart. He tried to persuade himself that the fear displayed by the savage was only superstition, and that that moan was but the sigh of the night wind.

The Indian sentinel stood as if paralyzed an instant after that weird cry, and then, swift as a flash, and as noiseless, he was gone into the gloomy forest. He had fled without awakening his companions.

Once more the moaning cry arose and swelled mournfully on the still night air. It was close at hand!

"The Wind of Death," whispered Joe.

He was shaken and unnerved by the events of the past two days, and dazed from his wound. His strength deserted him, and he lost consciousness.

CHAPTER VI

One evening, several days previous to the capture of the brothers, a solitary hunter stopped before a deserted log cabin which stood on the bank of a stream fifty miles or more inland from the Ohio River. It was rapidly growing dark; a fine, drizzling rain had set in, and a rising wind gave promise of a stormy night.

Although the hunter seemed familiar with his surroundings, he moved cautiously, and hesitated as if debating whether he should seek the protection of this lonely hut, or remain all night under dripping trees. Feeling of his hunting frock, he found that it was damp and slippery. This fact evidently decided him in favor of the cabin, for he stooped his tall figure and went in. It was pitch-dark inside; but having been there before, the absence of a light did not trouble him. He readily found the ladder leading to the loft, ascended it, and lay down to sleep.

During the night a noise awakened him. For a moment he heard nothing except the fall of the rain. Then came the hum of voices, followed by the soft tread of moccasined feet. He knew there was an Indian town ten miles across the country, and believed some warriors, belated on a hunting trip, had sought the cabin for shelter.

The hunter lay perfectly quiet, awaiting developments. If the Indians had flint and steel, and struck a light, he was almost certain to be discovered. He listened to their low conversation, and understood from the language that they were Delawares.

A moment later he heard the rustling of leaves and twigs, accompanied by the metallic click of steel against some hard substance. The noise was repeated, and then followed by a hissing sound, which he knew to be the burning of powder on a piece of dry wood, after which rays of light filtered through cracks of the unstable floor of the loft.

The man placed his eye to one of these crevices, and counted eleven Indians, all young braves, with the exception of the chief. The Indians had been hunting; they had haunches of deer and buffalo tongues, together with several packs of hides. Some of them busied themselves drying their weapons; others sat down listlessly, plainly showing their weariness, and two worked over the smouldering fire. The damp leaves and twigs burned faintly, yet there was light enough to cause the hunter fear that he might be discovered. He believed he had not much to worry about from the young braves, but the hawk-eyed chief was dangerous.

And he was right. Presently the stalwart chief heard, or saw, a drop of water fall from the loft. It came from the hunter's wet coat. Almost anyone save an Indian scout would have fancied this came from the roof. As the chief's gaze roamed everywhere over the interior of the cabin his expression was plainly distrustful. His eye searched the wet clay floor, but hardly could have discovered anything there, because the hunter's moccasined tracks had been obliterated by the footprints of the Indians. The chief's suspicions seemed to be allayed.

But in truth this chief, with the wonderful sagacity natural to Indians, had observed matters which totally escaped the eyes of the young braves, and, like a wily old fox, he waited to see which cub would prove the keenest.

Not one of them, however, noted anything unusual. They sat around the fire, ate their meat and parched corn, and chatted volubly.

The chief arose and walking to the ladder, ran his hand along one of the rungs.

"Ugh!" he exclaimed.

Instantly he was surrounded by ten eager, bright-eyed braves. He extended his open palm; it was smeared with wet clay like that under his feet. Simultaneously with their muttered exclamations the braves grasped their weapons. They knew there was a foe above them. It was a paleface, for an Indian would have revealed himself.

The hunter, seeing he was discovered, acted with the unerring judgment and lightninglike rapidity of one long accustomed to perilous situations. Drawing his tomahawk and noiselessly stepping to the hole in the loft, he leaped into the midst of the astounded Indians.

Rising from the floor like the rebound of a rubber ball, his long arm with the glittering hatchet made a wide sweep, and the young braves scattered like frightened sheep.

He made a dash for the door and, incredible as it may seem, his movements were so quick he would have escaped from their very midst without a scratch but for one unforeseen circumstance. The clay floor was wet and slippery; his feet were hardly in motion before they slipped from under him and he fell headlong.

With loud yells of triumph the band jumped upon him. There was a convulsive, heaving motion of the struggling mass, one frightful cry of agony, and then hoarse commands. Three of the braves ran to their packs from which they took cords of buckskin. So exceedingly powerful was the hunter that six Indians were required to hold him while the others tied his hands and feet. Then, with grunts and chuckles of satisfaction, they threw him into a corner of the cabin.

Two of the braves had been hurt in the brief struggle, one having a badly wrenched shoulder and the other a broken arm. So much for the hunter's power in that single moment of action.

The loft was searched, and found to be empty. Then the excitement died away, and the braves settled themselves down for the night. The injured ones bore their hurts with characteristic stoicism; if they did not sleep, both remained quiet and not a sigh escaped them.

The wind changed during the night, the storm abated, and when daylight came the sky was cloudless. The first rays of the sun shone in the open door, lighting up the interior of the cabin.

A sleepy Indian who had acted as guard stretched his limbs and yawned. He looked for the prisoner, and saw him sitting up in the corner. One arm was free, and the other nearly so. He had almost untied the thongs which bound him; a few moments more and he would have been free.

"Ugh!" exclaimed the young brave, awakening his chief and pointing to the hunter.

The chief glanced at his prisoner; then looked more closely, and with one spring was on his feet, a drawn tomahawk in his hand. A short, shrill yell issued from his lips. Roused by that clarion call, the young braves jumped up, trembling in eager excitement. The chief's summons had been the sharp war cry of the Delawares.

He manifested as intense emotion as could possibly have been betrayed by a matured, experienced chieftain, and pointing to the hunter, he spoke a single word.

* * *

At noonday the Indians entered the fields of corn which marked the outskirts of the Delaware encampment.

"Kol-loo—kol-loo—kol-loo."

The long signal, heralding the return of the party with important news, pealed throughout the quiet valley; and scarcely had the echoes died away when from the village came answering shouts.

Once beyond the aisles of waving corn the hunter saw over the shoulders of his captors the home of the redmen. A grassy plain, sloping gradually from the woody hill to a winding stream, was brightly beautiful with chestnut trees and long, well-formed lines of lodges. Many-hued blankets hung fluttering in the sun, and rising lazily were curling columns of blue smoke. The scene was picturesque and reposeful; the vivid hues suggesting the Indian's love of color and ornament; the absence of life and stir, his languorous habit of sleeping away the hot noonday hours.

The loud whoops, however, changed the quiet encampment into a scene of animation. Children ran from the wigwams, maidens and braves dashed here and there, squaws awakened from their slumber, and many a doughty warrior rose from his rest in the shade. French fur traders stared curiously from their lodges, and renegades hurriedly left their blankets, roused to instant action by the well-known summons.

The hunter, led down the lane toward the approaching crowd, presented a calm and fearless demeanor. When the Indians surrounded him one prolonged, furious yell rent the air, and then followed an extraordinary demonstration of fierce delight. The young braves' staccato yell, the maidens' scream, the old squaws' screech, and the deep war cry of the warriors intermingled in a fearful discordance.

Often had this hunter heard the name which the Indians called him; he had been there before, a prisoner; he had run the gauntlet down the lane; he had been bound to a stake in front of the lodge where his captors were now leading him. He knew the chief, Wingenund, sachem of the Delawares. Since that time, now five years ago, when Wingenund had tortured him, they had been bitterest foes.

If the hunter heard the hoarse cries, or the words hissed into his ears; if he saw the fiery glances of hatred, and sudden giving way to ungovernable rage, unusual to the Indian nature; if he felt in their fierce exultation the hopelessness of succor or mercy, he gave not the slightest sign.

"Atelang! Atelang! Atelang!" rang out the strange Indian name.

The French savages, like real savages, ran along with the procession, their feathers waving, their paint shining, their faces expressive of as much excitement as the Indians' as they cried aloud in their native tongue:

"Le Vent de la Mort! Le Vent de la Mort! Le Vent de la Mort!"

The hunter, while yet some paces distance, saw the lofty figure of the chieftain standing in front of his principal men. Well he knew them all. There were the crafty Pipe, and his savage comrade, the Half King; there was Shingiss, who wore on his forehead a scar—the mark of the hunter's bullet; there were Kotoxen, the Lynx, and Misseppa, the Source, and Winstonah, the War-cloud, chiefs of sagacity and renown. Three renegades completed the circle; and these three traitors represented a power which had for ten years left an awful, bloody trail over the country. Simon Girty, the so-called White Indian, with his keen, authoritative face turned expectantly; Elliott, the Tory deserter, from Fort Pitt, a wiry, spiderlike little man; and last, the gaunt and gaudily arrayed form of the demon of the frontier—Jim Girty.

The procession halted before this group, and two brawny braves pushed the hunter forward. Simon Girty's face betrayed satisfaction; Elliott's shifty eyes snapped, and the dark, repulsive face of the other Girty exhibited an exultant joy. These desperadoes had feared this hunter.

Wingenund, with a majestic wave of his arms, silenced the yelling horde of frenzied savages and stepped before the captive.

The deadly foes were once again face to face. The chieftain's lofty figure and dark, sleek head, now bare of plumes, towered over the other Indians, but he was not obliged to lower his gaze in order to look straight into the hunter's eyes.

Verily this hunter merited the respect which shone in the great chieftain's glance. Like a mountain-ash he stood, straight and strong, his magnificent frame tapering wedge-like from his broad shoulders. The bulging line of his thick neck, the deep chest, the knotty contour of his bared forearm, and the full curves of his legs—all denoted a wonderful muscular development.

The power expressed in this man's body seemed intensified in his features. His face was white and cold, his jaw squared and set; his coal-black eyes glittered with almost a superhuman fire. And his hair, darker than the wing of a crow, fell far below his shoulders; matted and tangled as it was, still it hung to his waist, and had it been combed out, must have reached his knees.

One long moment Wingenund stood facing his foe, and then over the multitude and through the valley rolled his sonorous voice:

"Deathwind dies at dawn!"

The hunter was tied to a tree and left in view of the

Indian populace. The children ran fearfully by; the braves gazed long at the great foe of their race; the warriors passed in gloomy silence. The savages' tricks of torture, all their diabolical ingenuity of inflicting pain were suppressed, awaiting the hour of sunrise when this hated Long Knife was to die.

Only one person offered an insult to the prisoner; he was a man of his own color. Jim Girty stopped before him, his yellowish eyes lighted by a tigerish glare, his lips curled in a snarl, and from between them issuing the odor of the fur traders' vile rum.

"You'll soon be feed fer the buzzards," he croaked, in his hoarse voice. He had so often strewed the plains with human flesh for the carrion birds that the thought had a deep fascination for him. "D'ye hear, scalp-hunter? Feed for buzzards!" He deliberately spat in the hunter's face. "D'ye hear?" he repeated.

There was no answer save that which glittered in the hunter's eye. But the renegade could not read it because he did not meet that flaming glance. Wild horses could not have dragged him to face this man had he been free. Even now a chill crept over Girty. For a moment he was enthralled by a mysterious fear, half paralyzed by a fore-shadowing of what would be this hunter's vengeance. Then he shook off his craven fear. He was free; the hunter's doom was sure. His sharp face was again wreathed in a savage leer, and he spat once more on the prisoner.

His fierce impetuosity took him a step too far. The hunter's arms and waist were fastened, but his feet were free. His powerful leg was raised suddenly; his foot struck Girty in the pit of the stomach. The renegade dropped limp and gasping. The braves carried him away, his gaudy feathers trailing, his long arms hanging inertly, and his face distorted with agony.

The maidens of the tribe, however, showed for the prisoner an interest that had in it something of veiled sympathy. Indian girls were always fascinated by white men. Many records of Indian maidens' kindness, of love, of heroism for white prisoners brighten the dark pages of frontier history. These girls walked past the hunter, averting their eyes when within his range of vision, but stealing many a sidelong glance at his impressive face and noble proportions. One of them, particularly, attracted the hunter's eye.

This was because, as she came by with her companions, while they all turned away, she looked at him with her soft, dark eyes. She was a young girl, whose delicate beauty bloomed fresh and sweet as that of a wild rose. Her costume, fringed, beaded, and exquisitely wrought with fanciful designs, betrayed her rank—she was Wingenund's daughter. The hunter had seen her when she was a child, and he recognized her now. He knew that the beauty of Aola, of Whispering Winds Among the Leaves, had been sung from the Ohio to the Great Lakes.

Often she passed him that afternoon. At sunset, as the braves untied him and led him away, he once more caught the full, intense gaze of her lovely eyes.

That night as he lay securely bound in the corner of a lodge, and the long hours wore slowly away, he strained at his stout bonds, and in his mind revolved different plans of escape. It was not in this man's nature to despair; while he had life he would fight. From time to time he expanded his muscles, striving to loosen the wet buckskin thongs.

The dark hours slowly passed, no sound coming to him save the distant bark of a dog and the monotonous tread of his guard; a dim grayness pervaded the lodge. Dawn was close at hand—his hour was nearly come.

Suddenly his hearing, trained to a most acute sensibility, caught a faint sound, almost inaudible. It came from without, on the other side of the lodge. There it was again, a slight tearing sound, such as is caused by a knife when it cuts through soft material.

Someone was slitting the wall of the lodge.

The hunter rolled noiselessly over and over until he lay against the skins. In the dim grayness he saw a bright blade moving carefully upward through the deerhide. Then a long knife was pushed into the opening; a small, brown hand grasped the hilt. Another little hand followed and felt the wall and floor, reaching out with groping fingers.

The hunter rolled again so that his back was against the wall and his wrists in front of the opening. He felt the little hand on his arm; then it slipped down to his wrists. The contact of cold steel sent a tremor of joy through his heart. The pressure of his bonds relaxed, ceased; his arms were free. He turned to find the long-bladed knife on the ground. The little hands were gone.

In a twinkling he rose unbound, armed, desperate. In another second an Indian warrior lay upon the ground in his death throes, while a fleeing form vanished in the gray morning mist.

CHAPTER VII

J oe felt the heavy lethargy rise from him like the removal of a blanket; his eyes became clear, and he saw the trees and the forest gloom; slowly he realized his actual position.

He was a prisoner, lying helpless among his sleeping captors. Silvertip and the guard had fled into the woods, frightened by the appalling moan which they believed sounded their death knell. And Joe believed he might have fled himself had he been free. What could have caused that sound? He fought off the numbing chill that once again began to creep over him. He was wide awake now; his head was clear, and he resolved to retain his senses. He told himself there could be nothing supernatural in that wind, or wail, or whatever it was, which had risen murmuring from out the forest depths.

Yet, despite his reasoning, Joe could not allay his fears. That thrilling cry haunted him. The frantic flight of an Indian brave—nay, of a cunning, experienced chief—was not to be lightly considered. The savages were at home in these untracked wilds. Trained from infancy to scent danger and to fight when they had an equal chance, they surely would not run without good cause.

Joe knew that something moved under those dark trees. He had no idea what. It might be the fretting night wind, or a stealthy, prowling, soft-footed beast, or a savage alien to these wild Indians, and wilder than they by far. The chirp of a bird awoke the stillness. Night had given way to morning. Welcoming the light that was chasing away the gloom, Joe raised his head with a deep sigh of relief. As he did so he saw a bush move; then a shadow seemed to sink into the ground. He had seen an object lighter than the trees, darker than the gray background. Again that strange sense of the nearness of *something* thrilled him.

Moments passed—to him long as hours. He saw a tall fern waver and tremble. A rabbit, or perhaps a snake, had brushed it. Other ferns moved, their tops agitated, perhaps, by a faint breeze. No; that wavering line came straight toward him; it could not be the wind; it marked the course of a creeping, noiseless thing. It must be a panther crawling nearer and nearer.

Joe opened his lips to awaken his captors, but could not speak; it was as if his heart had stopped beating. Twenty feet away the ferns were parted to disclose a white, gleaming face, with eyes that seemingly glittered. Brawny shoulders were upraised, and then a tall, powerful man stood revealed. Lightly he stepped over the leaves into the little glade. He bent over the sleeping Indians. Once, twice, three times a long blade swung high. One brave shuddered, another gave a sobbing gasp, and the third moved two fingers—thus they passed from life to death.

"Wetzel!" cried Joe.

"I reckon so," said the deliverer, his deep, calm voice contrasting strangely with what might have been expected from his aspect. Then, seeing Joe's head covered with blood, he continued: "Able to get up?"

"I'm not hurt," answered Joe, rising when his bonds had been cut.

"Brothers, I reckon?" Wetzel said, bending over Jim.

"Yes, we're brothers. Wake up, Jim, wake up! We're saved!"

"What? Who's that?" cried Jim, sitting up and staring at Wetzel.

"This man has saved our lives! See, Jim, the Indians are dead! And, Jim, it's Wetzel, the hunter. You remember, Jeff Lynn said I'd know him if I ever saw him, and——"

"What happened to Jeff?" inquired Wetzel, interrupting. He had turned from Jim's grateful face.

"Jeff was on the first raft, and for all we know he is now safe at Fort Henry. Our steersman was shot, and we were captured."

"Has the Shawnee anythin' ag'inst you boys?"

"Why, yes, I guess so. I played a joke on him—took his shirt and put it on another fellow."

"Might jes' as well kick an' Injun. What has he ag'in you?"

"I don't know. Perhaps he did not like my talk to him," answered Jim. "I am a preacher, and have come west to teach the gospel to the Indians."

"They're good Injuns now," said Wetzel, pointing to the prostrate figures.

"How did you find us?" eagerly asked Joe.

"Run acrost yer trail two days back."

"And you've been following us?"

The hunter nodded.

"Did you see anything of another band of Indians? A tall chief and Jim Girty were among them."

"They've been arter me fer two days. I was followin' you when Silvertip got wind of Girty an' his Delawares. The big chief was Wingenund. I seen you pull Girty's nose. Arter the Delawares went I turned loose yer dog an' horse an' lit out on yer trail."

"Where are the Delawares now?"

"I reckon they're nosin' my back trail. We must be gittin'. Silvertip'll soon hev a lot of Injuns here."

Joe intended to ask the hunter about what had frightened the Indians, but despite his eager desire for information, he refrained from doing so.

"Girty nigh did fer you," remarked Wetzel, examining Joe's wound. "He's in a bad humor. He got kicked a few days back, and then hed the skin pulled offen his nose. Somebody'll hev to suffer. Wal, you fellers grab yer rifles, an' we'll be startin' fer the fort."

Joe shuddered as he leaned over one of the dusky forms to detach powder and bullet horn. He had never seen a dead Indian, and the tense face, the sightless, vacant eyes made him shrink. He shuddered again when he saw the hunter scalp his victims. He shuddered a third time when he saw Wetzel pick up Silvertip's beautiful white eagle plume, dabble it in a pool of blood, and stick it in the bark of a tree. Bereft of its graceful beauty, drooping with its gory burden, the long feather was a deadly message. It had been Silvertip's pride; it was now a challenge, a menace to the Shawnee chief.

"Come," said Wetzel, leading the way into the forest.

Shortly after daylight on the second day following the release of the Downs brothers the hunter brushed through a thicket of alder and said:

"That's Fort Henry."

The boys were on the summit of a mountain from which the land sloped in a long incline of rolling ridges and gentle valleys like a green, billowy sea, until it rose again abruptly into a peak higher still than the one upon which they stood. The broad Ohio, glistening in the sun, lay at the base of the mountain.

Upon the bluff overlooking the river, and under the brow of the mountain, lay the frontier fort. In the clear atmosphere it stood out in bold relief. A small, low structure surrounded by a high stockade fence was all, and yet it did not seem unworthy of its fame. Those watchful, forbidding loopholes, the blackened walls and timbers, told the history of ten long, bloody years. The whole effect was one of menace, as if the fort sent out a defiance to the wilderness, and meant to protect the few dozen log cabins clustered on the hillside.

"How will we ever get across that big river?" asked Jim, practically.

"Wade—swim," answered the hunter, laconically, and began the descent of the ridge. An hour's rapid walking brought the three to the river. Depositing his rifle in a clump of willows, and directing the boys to do the same with their guns, the hunter splashed into the water. His companions followed him into the shallow water, and waded a hundred yards, which brought them near the island that they now perceived hid the fort. The hunter swam the remaining distance, and, climbing the bank, looked back for the boys. They were close behind him. Then he strode across the island, perhaps a quarter of a mile wide.

"We've a long swim here," said Wetzel, waving his hand toward the main channel of the river. "Good fer it?" he inquired of Joe, since Jim had not received any injuries during the short captivity and consequently showed more endurance.

"Good for anything," answered Joe, with that coolness Wetzel had been quick to observe in him.

The hunter cast a sharp glance at the lad's haggard face, his bruised temple, and his hair matted with blood. In that look he read Joe thoroughly. Had the young man known the result of that scrutiny, he would have been pleased as well as puzzled, for the hunter had said to himself: "A brave lad an' the border fever's on him."

"Swim close to me," said Wetzel, and he plunged into the river. The task was accomplished without accident.

"See the big cabin, thar, on the hillside? Thar's Colonel Zane in the door," said Wetzel.

As they neared the building several men joined the one who had been pointed out as the colonel. It was evident the boys were the subject of their conversation. Presently Colonel Zane left the group and came toward them. The brothers saw a handsome, stalwart man, in the prime of life.

"Well, Lew, what luck?" he said to Wetzel.

"Not much. I treed five Injuns, an' two got away," answered the hunter as he walked toward the fort.

"Lads, welcome to Fort Henry," said Colonel Zane, a smile lighting his dark face. "The others of your party arrived safely. They certainly will be overjoyed to see you."

"Colonel Zane, I had a letter from my uncle to you," replied Jim; "but the Indians took that and everything else we had with us."

"Never mind the letter. I knew your uncle, and your father, too. Come into the house and change those wet clothes. And you, my lad, have got an ugly knock on the head. Who gave you that?"

"Jim Girty."

"What?" exclaimed the colonel.

"Jim Girty did that. He was with a party of Delawares who ran across us. They were searching for Wetzel."

"Girty and the Delawares! The devil's to pay now. And you say hunting Wetzel? I must learn more about it. It looks bad. But tell me, how did Girty come to strike you?"

"I pulled his nose."

"You did? Good! Good!" cried Colonel Zane, heartily. "By George, that's great! Tell me—but wait until you are more comfortable. Your packs came safely on Jeff's raft, and you will find them inside."

As Joe followed the colonel he heard one of the other men say:

"Like as two peas in a pod."

Farther on he saw an Indian standing a little apart from the others. Hearing Joe's slight exclamation of surprise, he turned, disclosing a fine, manly countenance, characterized by calm dignity. The Indian read the boy's thought.

"Ugh! Me friend," he said in English.

"That's my Shawnee guide, Tomepomehala. He's a good fellow, although Jonathan and Wetzel declare the only good Indian is a dead one. Come right in here. There are your packs, and you'll find water outside the door."

Thus saying, Colonel Zane led the brothers into a small room, brought out their packs, and left them. He came back presently with a couple of soft towels.

"Now you lads fix up a bit; then come out and meet my family and tell us all about your adventure. By that time dinner will be ready."

"Geminy! Don't that towel remind you of home?" said Joe, when the colonel had gone. "From the looks of things, Colonel Zane means to have comfort here in the wilderness. He struck me as being a fine man."

The boys were indeed glad to change the few articles of clothing the Indians had left them, and when they were shaved and dressed they presented an entirely different appearance. Once more they were twin brothers, in costume and feature. Joe contrived, by brushing his hair down on his forehead, to conceal the discolored bump.

"I think I saw a charming girl," observed Joe.

"Suppose you did—what then?" asked Jim, severely.

"Why—nothing—see here, mayn't I admire a pretty girl if I want?"

"No, you may not. Joe, will nothing ever cure you? I should think the thought of Miss Well's——"

"Look here, Jim; she don't care—at least, it's very little she cares. And I'm—I'm not worthy of her."

"Turn around here and face me," said the young minister sharply.

Joe turned and looked in his brother's eyes.

"Have you trifled with her, as you have with so many others? Tell me. I know you don't lie."

"No."

"Then what do you mean?"

"Nothing much, Jim, except I'm really not worthy of her. I'm no good, you know, and she ought to get a fellow like—like you."

"Absurd! You ought to be ashamed of yourself."

"Never mind me. See here; don't you admire her?"

"Why—why, yes," stammered Jim, flushing a dark guilty red at the direct question. "Who could help admiring her?"

"That's what I thought. And I know she admires you for qualities which I lack. Nell's like a tender vine just beginning to creep around and cling to something strong. She cares for me; but her love is like the vine. It may hurt her a little to tear that love away, but it won't kill her; and in the end it will be best for her. You need a good wife. What could I do with a woman? Go in and win her, Jim."

"Joe, you're sacrificing yourself again for me," cried Jim, white to the lips. "It's wrong to yourself and wrong to her. I tell you——"

"Enough!" Joe's voice cut in cold and sharp. "Usually you influence me; but sometimes you can't. I say this: Nell will drift into your arms as surely as the leaf falls. It will not hurt her—will be best for her. Remember, she is yours for the winning."

"You do not say whether that will hurt you," whispered Jim.

"Come—we'll find Colonel Zane," said Joe, opening the door.

They went out in the hallway which opened into the yard as well as the larger room through which the colonel had first conducted them. As Jim, who was in advance, passed into this apartment a trim figure entered from the yard. It was Nell, and she ran directly against him. Her face was flushed, her eyes were beaming with gladness, and she seemed the incarnation of girlish joy.

"Oh, Joe," was all she whispered. But the happiness and welcome in that whisper could never have been better expressed in longer speech. Then slightly, ever so slightly, she tilted her sweet face up to his.

It all happened with the quickness of thought. In a single instant Jim saw the radiant face, the outstretched hands, and heard the glad whisper. He knew that she had again mistaken him for Joe; but for his life he could not draw back his head. He had kissed her, and even as his lips thrilled with her tremulous caress he flushed with the shame of his deceit.

"You're mistaken again—I'm Jim," he whispered.

For a moment they stood staring into each other's eyes, slowly awakening to what had really happened, slowly conscious of a sweet, alluring power. Then Colonel Zane's cheery voice rang in their ears.

"Ah, here's Nellie and your brother! Now, lads, tell me which is which!"

"That's Jim, and I'm Joe," answered the latter. He appeared not to notice his brother, and his greeting to Nell was natural and hearty. For the moment she drew the attention of the others from them.

Joe found himself listening to the congratulations of a number of people. Among the many names he remembered were those of Mrs. Zane, Silas Zane, and Major McColloch. Then he found himself gazing at the most beautiful girl he had ever seen in his life.

"My only sister, Mrs. Alfred Clarke—once Betty Zane, and the heroine of Fort Henry," said Colonel Zane proudly, with his arm around the slender, dark-eyed girl.

"I would brave the Indians and the wilderness again for this pleasure," replied Joe gallantly, as he bowed low over the little hand she cordially extended.

"Bess, is dinner ready?" inquired Colonel Zane of his comely wife. She nodded her head, and the colonel led the way into the adjoining room. "I know you boys must be hungry as bears."

During the meal Colonel Zane questioned his guests about their journey, and as to the treatment they had received at the hands of the Indians. He smiled at the young minister's earnestness in regard to the conversion of the redmen, and he laughed outright when Joe said he guessed he came to the frontier because it was too slow at home.

"I am sure your desire for excitement will soon be satisfied, if indeed it is not so already," remarked the colonel. "But as to the realization of your brother's hopes I am not so sanguine. Undoubtedly the Moravian missionaries have accomplished wonders with the Indians. Not long ago I visited the Village of Peace—the Indian name for the mission—and was struck by the friendliness and industry which prevailed there. Truly it *was* a village of peace. Yet it is almost too early to be certain of permanent success of this work. The Indian's nature is one hard to understand. He is naturally roving and restless, which, however, may be owing to his habit of moving from place to place in search of good hunting grounds. I believe—though I must confess I haven't seen any pioneers who share my belief—that the savage has a beautiful side to his character. I know of many noble deeds done by them, and I believe, if they are honestly dealt with, they will return good for good. There are bad ones, of course; but the French traders, and men like the Girtys, have caused most of this long war. Jonathan and Wetzel tell me the Shawnees and Chippewas have taken the warpath again. Then the fact that the Girtys are with the Delawares is reason for alarm. We have been comparatively quiet here of late. Did you boys learn to what tribe your captors belong? Did Wetzel say?"

"He did not; he spoke little, but I will say he was exceedingly active," answered Joe, with a smile.

"To have seen Wetzel fight Indians is something you are not likely to forget," said Colonel Zane grimly. "Now, tell me, how did those Indians wear their scalplock?"

"Their heads were shaved closely, with the exception of a little place on top. The remaining hair was twisted into a tuft, tied tightly, and into this had been thrust a couple of painted pins. When Wetzel scalped the Indians the pins fell out. I picked one up, and found it to be bone."

"You will make a woodsman, that's certain," replied Colonel Zane. "The Indians were Shawnees on the warpath. Well, we will not borrow trouble, for when it comes in the shape of redskins it usually comes quickly. Mr. Wells seemed anxious to resume the journey down the river; but I shall try to persuade him to remain with us awhile. Indeed, I am sorry I cannot keep you all here at Fort Henry, and more especially the girls. On the border we need young people, and while I do not want to frighten the women, I fear there will be more than Indians fighting for them."

"I hope not; but we have come prepared for anything," said Kate, with a quiet smile. "Our home was with Uncle, and when he announced his intention of going west we decided our duty was to go with him."

"You were right, and I hope you will find a happy home," rejoined Colonel Zane. "If life among the Indians proves to be too hard, we shall welcome you here. Betty, show the girls your pets and Indian trinkets. I am going to take the boys to Silas' cabin to see Mr. Wells, and then show them over the fort."

As they went out Joe saw the Indian guide standing in exactly the same position as when they entered the building.

"Can't that Indian move?" he asked curiously.

"He can cover one hundred miles in a day, when he wants to," replied Colonel Zane. "He is resting now. An Indian will often stand or sit in one position for many hours."

"He's a fine-looking chap," remarked Joe, and then to himself: "but I don't like him. I guess I'm prejudiced."

"You'll learn to like Tome, as we call him."

"Colonel Zane, I want a light for my pipe. I haven't had a smoke since the day we were captured. That blamed redskin took my tobacco. It's lucky I had some in my other pack. I'd like to meet him again; also Silvertip and that brute Girty."

"My lad, don't make such wishes," said Colonel Zane, earnestly. "You were indeed fortunate to escape, and I can well understand your feelings. There is nothing I should like better than to see Girty over the sights of my rifle; but I never hunt after danger, and to look for Girty is to court death."

"But Wetzel——"

"Ah, my lad, I know Wetzel goes alone in the woods; but then, he is different from other men. Before you leave I will tell you all about him."

Colonel Zane went around the corner of the cabin and returned with a live coal on a chip of wood, which Joe placed in the bowl of his pipe, and because of the strong breeze stepped close to the cabin wall. Being a keen observer, he noticed many small, round holes in the logs. They were so near together that the timbers had an odd, speckled appearance, and there was hardly a place where he could have put his thumb without covering a hole. At first he thought they were made by a worm or bird peculiar to that region; but finally he concluded that they were bullet holes. He thrust his knife blade into one, and out rolled a leaden ball.

"I'd like to have been here when these were made," he said.

"Well, at the time I wished I was back on the Potomac," replied Colonel Zane.

They found the old missionary on the doorstep of the adjacent cabin. He appeared discouraged when Colonel Zane interrogated him, and said that he was impatient because of the delay.

"Mr. Wells, is it not possible that you underrate the danger of your enterprise?"

"I fear naught but the Lord," answered the old man.

"Do you not fear for those with you?" went on the colonel earnestly. "I am heart and soul with you in your work, but want to impress upon you that the time is not propitious. It is a long journey to the village, and the way is beset with dangers of which you have no idea. Will you not remain here with me for a few weeks, or, at least, until my scouts report?"

"I thank you; but go I will."

"Then let me entreat you to remain here for a few days, so that I may send my brother Jonathan and Wetzel with you. If any can guide you safely to the Village of Peace it will be they."

At this moment Joe saw two men approaching from the fort, and recognized one of them as Wetzel. He doubted not that the other was Lord Dunmore's famous guide and hunter, Jonathan Zane. In features he resembled the colonel, and was as tall as Wetzel, although not so muscular or wide of chest.

Joe felt the same thrill he had experienced while watching the frontiersmen at Fort Pitt. Wetzel and Jonathan spoke a word to Colonel Zane and then stepped aside. The hunters stood lithe and erect, with the easy, graceful poise of Indians.

"We'll take two canoes, day after tomorrow," said Jonathan, decisively, to Colonel Zane. "Have you a rifle for Wetzel? The Delawares got his."

Colonel Zane pondered over the question; rifles were not scarce at the fort, but a weapon that Wetzel would use was hard to find.

"The hunter may have my rifle," said the old missionary. "I have no use for a weapon with which to destroy God's creatures. My brother was a frontiersman; he left this rifle to me. I remember hearing him say once that if a man knew exactly the weight of lead and powder needed, it would shoot absolutely true."

He went into the cabin, and presently came out with a long object wrapped in linsey cloths. Unwinding the coverings, he brought to view a rifle, the proportions of which caused Jonathan's eyes to glisten, and brought an exclamation from Colonel Zane. Wetzel balanced the gun in his hands. It was fully six feet long; the barrel was large, and the dark steel finely polished; the stock was black walnut, ornamented with silver trimmings. Using Jonathan's powder flask and bullet pouch, Wetzel proceeded to load the weapon. He poured out a quantity of powder in the palm of his hand, performing the action quickly and dexterously, but was so slow while measuring it that Joe wondered if he were counting the grains. Next he selected a bullet out of a dozen which Jonathan held toward him. He examined it carefully and tried it in the muzzle of the rifle. Evidently it did not please him, for he took another. Finally he scraped a bullet with his knife, and placing it in the center of a small linsey rag, deftly forced it down. He adjusted the flint, dropped a few grains of powder in the pan, and then looked around for a mark at which to shoot.

Joe observed that the hunters and Colonel Zane were as serious regarding the work as if at that moment some important issue depended upon the accuracy of the rifle.

"There, Lew; there's a good shot. It's pretty far, even for you, when you don't know the gun," said Colonel Zane, pointing toward the river.

Joe saw the end of a log, about the size of a man's head, sticking out of the water, perhaps a hundred and fifty yards distant. He thought to hit it would be a fine shot; but was amazed when he heard Colonel Zane say to several men who had joined the group that Wetzel intended to shoot at a turtle on the log. By straining his eyes Joe succeeded in distinguishing a small lump, which he concluded was the turtle.

Wetzel took a step forward; the long, black rifle was raised with a stately sweep. The instant it reached a level a thread of flame burst forth, followed by a peculiarly clear, ringing report.

"Did he hit?" asked Colonel Zane, eagerly as a boy.

"I allow he did," answered Jonathan.

"I'll go and see," said Joe. He ran down the bank, along the beach, and stepped on the log. He saw a turtle about the size of an ordinary saucer. Picking it up, he saw a bullet hole in the shell near the middle. The bullet had gone through the turtle, and it was quite dead. Joe carried it to the waiting group.

"I allowed so," declared Jonathan.

Wetzel examined the turtle, and turning to the old missionary, said:

"Your brother spoke the truth, an' I thank you fer the rifle."

CHAPTER VIII

S o you want to know all about Wetzel?" inquired
Colonel Zane of Joe, when, having left Jim and Mr.
Wells, they returned to the cabin.

"I am immensely interested in him," replied Joe.

"Well, I don't think there's anything singular in that. I
know Wetzel better, perhaps, than any man living; but
have seldom talked about him. He doesn't like it. He is by
birth a Virginian; I should say, forty years old. We were
boys together, and I am a little beyond that age. He was like
any of the lads, except that he excelled us all in strength
and agility. When he was nearly eighteen years old a band
of Indians—Delawares, I think—crossed the border on a
marauding expedition far into Virginia. They burned the
old Wetzel homestead and murdered the father, mother,
two sisters, and a baby brother. The terrible shock nearly
killed Lewis, who for a time was very ill. When he recovered he went in search of his brothers, Martin and John
Wetzel, who were hunting, and brought them back to
their desolated home. Over the ashes of the home and the
graves of the loved ones the brothers swore sleepless and
eternal vengeance. The elder brothers have been devoted
all these twenty years and more to the killing of Indians;
but Lewis has been the great foe of the redman. You have
already seen an example of his deeds, and will hear of
more. His name is a household word on the border. Scores

of times he has saved, actually saved, this fort and settlement. His knowledge of savage ways surpasses by far
Boone's, Major McColloch's, Jonathan's, or any of the
hunters'."

"Then hunting Indians is his sole occupation?"

"He lives for that purpose alone. He is very seldom in
the settlement. Sometimes he stays here a few days, especially if he is needed; but usually he roams the forests."

"What did Jeff Lynn mean when he said that some
people think Wetzel is crazy?"

"There are many who think the man mad; but I do not.
When the passion for Indian hunting comes upon him he
is fierce, almost frenzied, yet perfectly sane. While here
he is quiet, seldom speaks except when spoken to, and is
taciturn with strangers. He often comes to my cabin and
sits beside the fire for hours. I think he finds pleasure in
the conversation and laughter of friends. He is fond of the
children, and would do anything for my sister Betty."

"His life must be lonely and sad," remarked Joe.

"The life of any borderman is that; but Wetzel's is particularly so."

"What is he called by the Indians?"

"They call him *Atelang*, or, in English, Deathwind."

"By George! That's what Silvertip said in French—'*Le
Vent de la Mort.*'"

"Yes; you have it right. A French fur trader gave Wetzel
that name years ago, and it has clung to him. The Indians
say the Deathwind blows through the forest whenever Wetzel stalks on their trail."

"Colonel Zane, don't you think me superstitious,"
whispered Joe, leaning toward the colonel, "but I heard
the wind blow through the forest."

"What!" exclaimed Colonel Zane. He saw that Joe was
in earnest, for the remembrance of the moan had more

than once paled his cheek and caused beads of perspiration to collect on his brow.

Joe related the circumstances of that night, and at the end of his narrative Colonel Zane sat silent and thoughtful.

"You don't really think it was Wetzel who moaned?" he asked, at length.

"No, I don't," replied Joe quickly; "but, Colonel Zane, I heard the moan as plainly as I can hear your voice. I heard it twice. Now, what was it?"

"Jonathan said the same thing to me once. He had been out hunting with Wetzel; they separated, and during the night Jonathan heard the wind. The next day he ran across a dead Indian. He believes Wetzel makes the noise, and so do the hunters; but I think it is simply the moan of the night wind through the trees. I have heard it at times, when my very blood ran cold."

"I tried to think it was the wind soughing through the pines, but am afraid I didn't succeed very well. Anyhow, I knew Wetzel instantly, just as Jeff Lynn said I would. He killed those Indians in an instant, and he must have an iron arm."

"Wetzel excels in strength and speed any man, red or white, on the frontier. He can run away from Jonathan, who is as swift as an Indian. He's stronger than any of the other men. I remember one day old Hugh Bennet's wagon wheels stuck in a bog down by the creek. Hugh tried, as several others did, to move the wheels; but they couldn't be made to bulge. Along came Wetzel, pushed away the men, and lifted the wagon unaided. It would take hours to tell you about him. In brief, among all the border scouts and hunters Wetzel stands alone. No wonder the Indians fear him. He is as swift as an eagle, strong as mountain ash, keen as a fox, and absolutely tireless and implacable."

"How long have you been here, Colonel Zane?"

"More than twelve years, and it has been one long fight."

"I'm afraid I'm too late for the fun," said Joe, with his quiet laugh.

"Not by about twelve more years," answered Colonel Zane, studying the expression on Joe's face. "When I came out here years ago I had the same adventurous spirit which I see in you. It has been considerably quelled, however. I have seen many a daring young fellow get the border fever, and with it his death. Let me advise you to learn the ways of the hunters; to watch someone skilled in woodcraft. Perhaps Wetzel himself will take you in hand. I don't mind saying that he spoke of you to me in a tone I never heard Lew use before."

"He did?" questioned Joe, eagerly, flushing with pleasure. "Do you think he'd take me out? Dare I ask him?"

"Don't be impatient. Perhaps I can arrange it. Come over here now to Metzar's place. I want to make you acquainted with him. These boys have all been cutting timber; they've just come in for dinner. Be easy and quiet with them; then you'll get on."

Colonel Zane introduced Joe to five sturdy boys and left him in their company. Joe sat down on a log outside a cabin and leisurely surveyed the young men. They all looked about the same: strong without being heavy, light-haired and bronzed-faced. In their turn they carefully judged Joe. A newcomer from the East was always regarded with some doubt. If they expected to hear Joe talk much they were mistaken. He appeared good-natured, but not too friendly.

"Fine weather we're havin'," said Dick Metzar.

"Fine," agreed Joe, laconically.

"Like frontier life?"

"Sure."

A silence ensued after this breaking of the ice. The boys were awaiting their turn at a little wooden bench upon which stood a bucket of water and a basin.

"Hear ye got ketched by some Shawnees?" remarked another youth, as he rolled up his shirt sleeves. They all looked at Joe now. It was not improbable their estimate of him would be greatly influenced by the way he answered this question.

"Yes; was captive for three days."

"Did ye knock any redskins over?" The question was artfully put to draw Joe out. Above all things, the border-men detested boastfulness; tried on Joe the ruse failed signally.

"I was scared speechless most of the time," answered Joe, with his pleasant smile.

"By gosh, I don't blame ye!" burst out Will Metzar. "I hed that experience onct, an' onct's enough."

The boys laughed and looked in a more friendly manner at Joe. Though he said he had been frightened, his cool and careless manner belied his words. In Joe's low voice and clear, gray eye there was something potent and magnetic, which subtly influenced those with whom he came in contact.

While his new friends were at dinner Joe strolled over to where Colonel Zane sat on the doorstep of his home.

"How did you get on with the boys?" inquired the colonel.

"All right, I hope. Say, Colonel Zane, I'd like to talk to your Indian guide."

Colonel Zane spoke a few words in the Indian language to the guide, who left his post and came over to them. The colonel then had a short conversation with him, at the conclusion of which he pointed toward Joe.

"How do—shake," said Tome, extending his hand.

Joe smiled, and returned the friendly hand pressure.

"Shawnee—ketch'um?" asked the Indian, in his fairly intelligible English.

Joe nodded his head, while Colonel Zane spoke once more in Shawnee, explaining the cause of Silvertip's enmity.

"Shawnee—chief—one—bad—Injun," replied Tome, seriously. "Silver—mad—thunder-mad. Ketch'um paleface—scalp'um sure."

After giving this warning the chief returned to his former position near the corner of the cabin.

"He can talk in English fairly well, much better than the Shawnee brave who talked with me the other day," observed Joe.

"Some of the Indians speak the language almost fluently," said Colonel Zane. "You could hardly have distinguished Logan's speech from a white man's. Cornplanter uses good English, as also does my brother's wife, a Wyandot girl."

"Did your brother marry an Indian?" And Joe plainly showed his surprise.

"Indeed he did, and a most beautiful girl she is. I'll tell you Isaac's story some time. He was a captive among the Wyandots for ten years. The chief's daughter, Myeerah, loved him, kept him from being tortured, and finally saved him from the stake."

"Well, that floors me," said Joe; "yet I don't see why it should. I'm just surprised. Where is your brother now?"

"He lives with the tribe. He and Myeerah are working hard for peace. We are now on more friendly terms with the great Wyandots, or Hurons, as we call them, than ever before."

"Who is the big man coming from the fort?" asked Joe, suddenly observing a stalwart frontiersman approaching.

"Major Sam McColloch. You have met him. He's the man who jumped his horse from yonder bluff."

"Jonathan and he have the same look, the same swing," observed Joe, as he ran his eye over the major. His faded buckskin costume, beaded, fringed, and laced, was similar to that of the colonel's brother. Powder flask and bullet pouch were made from cow horns and slung around his neck on deerhide strings. The hunting coat was unlaced, exposing, under the long, fringed borders, a tunic of the same well-tanned, but finer and softer, material. As he walked, the flaps of his coat fell back, showing a belt containing two knives, sheathed in heavy buckskin, and a bright tomahawk. He carried a long rifle in the hollow of his arm.

"These hunters have the same kind of buckskin suits," continued Joe; "still, it doesn't seem to me the clothes make the resemblance to each other. The way these men stand, walk, and act is what strikes me particularly, as in the case of Wetzel."

"I know what you mean. The flashing eye, the erect poise of expectation, and the springy step—those, my lad, come from a life spent in the woods. Well, it's a grand way to live."

"Colonel, my horse is laid up," said Major McColloch, coming to the steps. He bowed pleasantly to Joe.

"So you are going to Short Creek? You can have one of my horses; but first come inside and we'll talk over your expedition."

The afternoon passed uneventfully for Joe. His brother

and Mr. Wells were absorbed in plans for their future work, and Nell and Kate were resting; therefore he was forced to find such amusement or occupation as was possible in or near the stockade.

CHAPTER IX

J oe went to bed that night with a promise to himself to rise early next morning, for he had been invited to take part in a "raising," which term meant that a new cabin was to be erected, and such task was ever an event in the lives of the settlers.

The following morning Joe rose early, dressing himself in a complete buckskin suit, for which he had exchanged his good garments of cloth. Never before had he felt so comfortable. He wanted to hop, skip, and jump. The soft, undressed buckskin was as warm and smooth as silk plush; the weight so light, the moccasins so well-fitting and springy, that he had to put himself under considerable restraint to keep from capering about like a frolicsome colt.

The possession of this buckskin outfit, and the rifle and accoutrements which went with the bargain, marked the last stage in Joe's surrender to the border fever. The silent, shaded glens, the mystery of the woods, the breath of this wild, free life claimed him from this moment entirely and forever.

He met the others, however, with a serene face, showing no trace of the emotion which welled up strongly from his heart. Nell glanced shyly at him; Kate playfully voiced her admiration; Jim met him with a brotherly ridicule which bespoke his affection as well as his amusement; but Colonel Zane, having once yielded to the same burning, riotous craving for freedom which now stirred in the boy's heart, understood, and felt warmly drawn toward the lad. He said nothing, though as he watched Joe his eyes were grave and kind. In his long frontier life, where many a day measured the life and fire of ordinary years, he had seen lad after lad go down before this forest fever. It was well, he thought, because the freedom of the soil depended on these wild, light-footed boys; yet it always made him sad. How many youths, his brother among them, lay under the fragrant pine needle carpet of the forest, in their last earthly sleep!

The "raising" brought out all the settlement—the women to look on and gossip, while the children played; the men to bend their backs in the moving of the heavy timbers. They celebrated the erection of a new cabin as a noteworthy event. As a social function it had a prominent place in the settlers' short list of pleasures.

Joe watched the proceeding with the same pleasure and surprise he had felt in everything pertaining to border life.

To him this log-raising appeared the hardest kind of labor. Yet it was plain these hardy men, these low-voiced women, and merry children regarded the work as something far more significant than the mere building of a cabin. After a while he understood the meaning of the scene. A kindred spirit, the spirit of the pioneer, drew them all into one large family. This was another cabin; another home; another advance toward the conquering of the wilderness, for which these brave men and women were giving their lives. In the bright-eyed children's glee, when they clapped their little hands at the mounting logs, Joe saw the progress, the march of civilization.

"Well, I'm sorry you're to leave us tonight," remarked Colonel Zane to Joe, as the young man came over to where he, his wife, and sister watched the work. "Jonathan said all was ready for your departure at sundown."

"Do we travel by night?"

"Indeed, yes, my lad. There are Indians everywhere on the river. I think, however, with Jack and Lew handling the paddles, you will slip by safely. The plan is to keep along the south shore all night; then cross over at a place called Girty's Point, where you are to remain in hiding during daylight. From there you paddle up Yellow Creek; then portage across country to the head of the Tuscarawas. Another night's journey will then bring you to the Village of Peace."

Jim and Mr. Wells, with his nieces, joined the party now, and all stood watching as the last logs were put in place.

"Colonel Zane, my first log-raising is an education to me," said the young minister, in his earnest manner.

"This scene is so full of life. I never saw such good will among laboring men. Look at that brawny-armed giant standing on the topmost log. How he whistles as he swings his ax! Mr. Wells, does it not impress you?"

"The pioneers must be brothers because of their isolation and peril; to be brothers means to love one another; to love one another is to love God. What you see in this fraternity is God. And I want to see this same beautiful feeling among the Indians."

"I have seen it," said Colonel Zane, to the old missionary. "When I came out here alone twelve years ago the Indians were peaceable. If the pioneers had paid for land, as I paid Cornplanter, there would never have been a border war. But no; the settlers must grasp every acre they could. Then the Indians rebelled; then the Girtys and their allies spread discontent, and now the border is a bloody warpath."

"Have the Jesuit missionaries accomplished anything with these war tribes?" inquired Jim.

"No; their work has been chiefly among the Indians near Detroit and northward. The Hurons, Delawares, Shawnees, and other western tribes have been demoralized by the French traders' rum, and incited to fierce hatred by Girty and his renegades. Your work at Gnaddenhutten must be among these hostile tribes, and it is surely a hazardous undertaking."

"My life is God's," murmured the old minister. No fear could assail his steadfast faith.

"Jim, it strikes me you'd be more likely to impress these Indians Colonel Zane spoke of if you'd get a suit like mine and wear a knife and tomahawk," interposed Joe, cheerfully. "Then, if you couldn't convert, you could scalp them."

"Well, well, let us hope for the best," said Colonel Zane, when the laughter had subsided. "We'll go over to dinner now. Come, all of you. Jonathan, bring Wetzel. Betty, make him come, if you can."

As the party slowly wended its way toward the colonel's cabin Jim and Nell found themselves side by side. They had not exchanged a word since the evening previous, when Jim had kissed her. Unable to look at each other now, and finding speech difficult, they walked in embarrassed silence.

"Doesn't Joe look splendid in his hunting suit?" asked Jim, presently.

"I hadn't noticed. Yes; he looks well," replied Nell, carelessly. She was too indifferent to be natural.

"Are you angry with him?"

"Certainly not."

Jim was always simple and frank in his relations with women. He had none of his brother's fluency of speech, with neither confidence, boldness, nor understanding of the intricate mazes of a woman's moods.

"But—you are angry with—me?" he whispered.

Nell flushed to her temples, yet she did not raise her eyes nor reply.

"It was a terrible thing for me to do," went on Jim, hesitatingly. "I don't know why I took advantage—of—of your mistaking me for Joe. If you only hadn't held up your mouth. No—I don't mean that—of course you didn't. But—well, I couldn't help it. I'm guilty. I have thought of little else. Some wonderful feeling has possessed me ever since—since——"

"What has Joe been saying about me?" demanded Nell, her eyes burning like opals.

"Why, hardly anything," answered Jim, haltingly. "I took him to task about—about what I considered might be wrong to you. Joe has never been very careful of young ladies' feelings, and I thought—well, it was none of my business. He said he honestly cared for you, that you had taught him how unworthy he was of a good woman. But he's wrong there. Joe is wild and reckless, yet his heart is a well of gold. He is a diamond in the rough. Just now he is possessed by wild notions of hunting Indians and roaming through these forests; but he'll come round all right. I wish I could tell you how much he has done for me, how much I love him, how I know him! He can be made worthy of any woman. He will outgrow this fiery, daring spirit, and then—won't you help him?"

"I will, if he will let me," softly whispered Nell, irresistibly drawn by the strong, earnest love thrilling in his voice.

CHAPTER X

O nce more out under the blue-black vault of heaven, with its myriads of twinkling stars, the voyagers resumed their westward journey. Whispered farewells of new but sincere friends lingered in their ears. Now the great looming bulk of the fort above them faded into the obscure darkness, leaving a feeling as if a protector had gone—perhaps forever. Admonished to absolute silence by the stern guides, who seemed indeed to have embarked upon a dark and deadly mission, the voyagers lay back in the canoes and thought and listened. The water eddied with soft gurgles in the wake of the racing canoes; but that musical sound was all they heard. The paddles might have been shadows, for all the splash they made; they cut the water swiftly and noiselessly. Onward the frail barks glided into black space, side by side, close under the overhanging willows. Long moments passed into long hours, as the guides paddled tirelessly as if their sinews were cords of steel.

With gray dawn came the careful landing of the canoes, a cold breakfast eaten under cover of a willow thicket, and the beginning of a long day while they were lying hidden from the keen eyes of Indian scouts, waiting for the friendly mantle of night.

The hours dragged until once more the canoes were launched, this time not on the broad Ohio, but on a stream that mirrored no shining stars as it flowed still and somber under the dense foliage.

The voyagers spoke not, nor whispered, nor scarcely moved, so menacing had become the slow, listening caution of Wetzel and Zane. Snapping of twigs somewhere in the inscrutable darkness delayed them for long moments. Any moment the air might resound with the horrible Indian war whoop. Every second was heavy with fear. How marvelous that these scouts, penetrating the wilderness of gloom, glided on surely, silently, safely! Instinct, or the eyes of the lynx, guided their course. But another dark night wore on to the tardy dawn, and each of its fearful hours numbered miles past and gone.

The sun was rising in ruddy glory when Wetzel ran his canoe into the bank just ahead of a sharp bend in the stream.

"Do we get out here?" asked Jim, seeing Jonathan turn his canoe toward Wetzel's.

"The village lies yonder, around the bend," answered the guide. "Wetzel cannot go there, so I'll take you all in my canoe."

"There's no room; I'll wait," replied Joe, quietly. Jim noted his look—a strange, steady glance it was—and then saw him fix his eyes upon Nell, watching her until the canoe passed around the green-bordered bend in the stream.

Unmistakable signs of an Indian town were now evident. Dozens of graceful birchen canoes lay upon the well-cleared banks; a log bridge spanned the stream; above the slight ridge of rising ground could be seen the poles of Indian teepees.

As the canoe grated upon the sandy beach a little Indian boy, who was playing in the shallow water, raised his head and smiled.

"That's an Indian boy," whispered Kate.

"The dear little fellow!" exclaimed Nell.

The boy came running up to them, when they were landed, with pleasure and confidence shining in his dusky eyes. Save for tiny buckskin breeches, he was naked, and his shiny skin gleamed gold-bronze in the sunlight. He was a singularly handsome child.

"Me—Benny," he lisped in English, holding up his little hand to Nell.

The action was as loving and trusting as any that could have been manifested by a white child. Jonathan Zane stared with a curious light in his dark eyes; Mr. Wells and Jim looked as though they doubted the evidence of their own sight. Here, even in an Indian boy, was incontestable proof that the savage nature could be tamed and civilized.

With a tender exclamation Nell bent over the child and kissed him.

Jonathan Zane swung his canoe upstream for the purpose of bringing Joe. The trim little bark slipped out of sight round the bend. Presently its gray curved nose peeped from behind the willows; then the canoe swept into view again. There was only one person in it, and that was the guide.

"Where is my brother?" asked Jim, in amazement.

"Gone," answered Zane, quietly.

"Gone! What do you mean? Gone? Perhaps you have missed the spot where you left him."

"They're both gone."

Nell and Jim gazed at each other with slowly whitening faces.

"Come, I'll take you up to the village," said Zane, getting out of his canoe. All noticed that he was careful to take his weapons with him.

"Can't you tell us what it means—this disappearance?" asked Jim, his voice low and anxious.

"They're gone, canoe and all. I knew Wetzel was going, but I didn't calkilate on the lad. Mebbe he followed Wetzel, mebbe he didn't," answered the taciturn guide, and he spoke no more.

In his keen expectation and wonder as to what the village would be like, Jim momentarily forgot his brother's disappearance, and when he arrived at the top of the bank he surveyed the scene with eagerness. What he saw was more imposing than the Village of Peace which he had conjured up in his imagination. Confronting him was a level plain, in the center of which stood a wide, low structure surrounded by log cabins, and these in turn encircled by Indian teepees. A number of large trees, mostly full-foliaged maples, shaded the clearing. The settlement swarmed with Indians. A few shrill halloes uttered by the first observers of the newcomers brought braves, maidens, and children trooping toward the party with friendly curiosity.

Jonathan Zane stepped before a cabin adjoining the large structure, and called in at the open door. A short, stoop-shouldered white man, clad in faded linsey, appeared on the threshold. His serious, lined face had the unmistakable benevolent aspect peculiar to most teachers of the gospel.

"Mr. Zeisberger, I've fetched a party from Fort Henry," said Zane, indicating those he had guided. Then, without another word, never turning his dark face to the right or left, he hurried down the lane through the throng of Indians.

Jim remembered, as he saw the guide vanish over the bank of the creek, that he had heard Colonel Zane say that Jonathan, as well as Wetzel, hated the sight of an Indian. No doubt long years of war and bloodshed had rendered these two great hunters callous. To them there could be no discrimination—an Indian was an Indian.

"Mr. Wells, welcome to the Village of Peace!" exclaimed Mr. Zeisberger, wringing the old missionary's hand. "The years have not been so long but that I remember you."

"Happy, indeed, am I to get here, after all these dark, dangerous journeys," returned Mr. Wells. "I have brought my nieces, Nell and Kate, who were children when you left Williamsburg, and this young man, James Downs, a minister of God, and earnest in his hope for our work."

"A glorious work it is! Welcome, young ladies, to our peaceful village. And, young man, I greet you with heartfelt thankfulness. We need young men. Come in, all of you, and share my cabin. I'll have your luggage brought up. I have lived in this hut alone. With some little labor, and the magic touch women bring to the making of a home, we can be most comfortable here."

Mr. Zeisberger gave his own room to the girls, assuring them with a smile that it was the most luxurious in the village. The apartment contained a chair, a table, and a bed of Indian blankets and buffalo robes. A few pegs driven in the chinks between the logs completed the furnishings. Sparse as were the comforts, they appealed warmly to the girls, who, weary from their voyage, lay down to rest.

"I am not fatigued," said Mr. Wells, to his old friend. "I want to hear all about your work, what you have done, and what you hope to do."

"We have met with wonderful success, far beyond our wildest dreams," responded Mr. Zeisberger. "Certainly we have been blessed of God."

Then the missionary began a long, detailed account of the Moravian Mission's efforts among the western tribes.

The work lay chiefly among the Delawares, a noble nation of redmen, intelligent, and wonderfully susceptible to the teaching of the gospel. Among the eastern Delawares, living on the other side of the Allegheny Mountains, the missionaries had succeeded in converting many; and it was chiefly through the western exploration of Frederick Post that his Church decided the Indians of the west could as well be taught to lead Christian lives. The first attempt to convert the western redmen took place upon the upper Allegheny, where many Indians, including Allemewi, a blind Delaware chief, accepted the faith. The mission decided, however, it would be best to move farther west, where the Delawares had migrated and were more numerous.

In April 1770, more than ten years before, sixteen canoes, filled with converted Indians and missionaries, drifted down the Allegheny to Fort Pitt; thence down the Ohio to the Big Beaver; up that stream, and far into the Ohio wilderness.

Upon a tributary of the Muskingong, called the Tuscarawas, a settlement was founded. Near and far the news was circulated. Redmen from all tribes came flocking to the new colony. Chiefs and warriors, squaws and maidens, were attracted by the new doctrine of the converted Indians. They were astonished at the missionaries' teachings. Many doubted, some were converted, all listened. Great excitement prevailed when old Glickhican, one of the wisest chiefs of the Turtle tribe of the Delawares, became a convert to the palefaces' religion.

The interest widened, and in a few years a beautiful, prosperous town arose, which was called Village of Peace. The Indians of the warlike tribes bestowed the appropriate name. The vast forests were rich in every variety of game; the deep, swift streams were teeming with fish.

Meat and grain in abundance, buckskin for clothing, and soft furs for winter garments were to be had for little labor. At first only a few wigwams were erected. Soon a large log structure was thrown up and used as a church. Then followed a school, a mill, and a workshop. The verdant fields were cultivated and surrounded by rail fences. Horses and cattle grazed with the timid deer on the grassy plains.

The Village of Peace blossomed as a rose. The reports of the love and happiness existing in this converted community spread from mouth to mouth, from town to town, with the result that inquisitive savages journeyed from all points to see this haven. Peaceful and hostile Indians were alike amazed at the change in their brethren. The good fellowship and industry of the converts had a widespread and wonderful influence. More, perhaps, than any other thing, the great fields of waving corn, the hills covered with horses and cattle, those evidences of abundance, impressed the visitors with the well-being of the Christians. Bands of traveling Indians, whether friendly or otherwise, were treated with hospitality, and never sent away empty-handed. They were asked to partake of the abundance and solicited to come again.

A feature by no means insignificant in the popularity of the village was the church bell. The Indians loved music, and this bell charmed them. On still nights the savages in distant towns could hear at dusk the deep-toned, mellow notes of the bell summoning the worshippers to the evening service. Its ringing clang, so strange, so sweet, so solemn, breaking the vast dead wilderness quiet, haunted the savage ear as though it were a call from a woodland god.

"You have arrived most opportunely," continued Mr. Zeisberger. "Mr. Edwards and Mr. Young are working to establish other missionary posts. Heckewelder is here now in the interest of this branching out."

"How long will it take me to learn the Delaware language?" inquired Jim.

"Not long. You do not, however, need to speak the Indian tongue, for we have excellent interpreters."

"We heard much at Fort Pitt and Fort Henry about the danger, as well as uselessness, of our venture," Jim continued. "The frontiersmen declared that every rod of the way was beset with savage foes, and that, even in the unlikely event of our arriving safely at the Village of Peace, we would then be hemmed in by fierce, vengeful tribes."

"Hostile savages abound here, of course; but we do not fear them. We invite them. Our work is to convert the wicked, to teach them to lead good, useful lives. We will succeed."

Jim could not help warming to the minister for his unswervable faith, his earnest belief that the work of God could not fail; nevertheless, while he felt no fear and intended to put all his heart in the work, he remembered with disquietude Colonel Zane's warnings. He thought of the wonderful precaution and eternal vigilance of Jonathan and Wetzel—men of all men who most understood Indian craft and cunning. It might well be possible that these good missionaries, wrapped up in saving the souls of these children of the forest, so full of God's teachings as to have little mind for aught else, had no knowledge of the Indian nature beyond what the narrow scope of their work invited. If what these frontiersmen asserted was true, then the ministers' zeal had struck them blind.

Jim had a growing idea of the way in which the savages could be best taught. He resolved to go slowly; to study the redmen's natures; not to preach one word of the gospel to them until he had mastered their language and could convey to their simple minds the real truth. He would make Christianity as clear to them as were the deer trails on the moss and leaves of the forest.

"Ah, here you are. I hope you have rested well," said Mr. Zeisberger, when at the conclusion of this long recital Nell and Kate came into the room.

"Thank you, we feel much better," answered Kate. The girls certainly looked refreshed. The substitution of clean gowns for their former travel-stained garments made a change that called forth the minister's surprise and admiration.

"My! My! Won't Edwards and Young beg me to keep them here now!" he exclaimed, his pleased eyes resting on Nell's piquant beauty and Kate's noble proportions and rich coloring. "Come; I will show you over the Village of Peace."

"Are all these Indians Christians?" asked Jim.

"No, indeed. These Indians you see here, and out yonder under the shade, though they are friendly, are not Christians. Our converts employ themselves in the fields or shops. Come; take a peep in here. This is where we preach in the evenings and during inclement weather. On pleasant days we use the maple grove yonder."

Jim and the others looked in at the door of the large log structure. They saw an immense room, the floor covered with benches, and a raised platform at one end. A few windows let in the light. Spacious and barnlike was this apartment; but, undoubtedly, seen through the beaming eyes of the missionary, it was a grand amphitheater for worship. The hard-packed clay floor was velvet carpet; the crude seats soft as eiderdown; the platform with its white oak cross, an altar of marble and gold.

"This is one of our shops," said Mr. Zeisberger, leading them to a cabin. "Here we make brooms, harnesses for the horses, farming implements—everything useful that we can. We have a forge here. Behold an Indian blacksmith!"

The interior of the large cabin presented a scene of bustling activity. Twenty or more Indians bent their backs in earnest employment. In one corner a savage stood holding a piece of red-hot iron on an anvil, while a brawny brave wielded a sledgehammer. The sparks flew; the anvil rang. In another corner a circle of braves sat around a pile of dried grass and flags. They were twisting and fashioning these materials into baskets. At a bench three Indian carpenters were pounding and swaying. Young braves ran back and forth, carrying pails, rough-hewn boards, and blocks of wood.

Instantly struck by two things, Jim voiced his curiosity:

"Why do these Indians all wear long hair, smooth and shiny, without adornment?"

"They are Christians. They wear neither headdress, warbonnet, nor scalplock," replied Mr. Zeisberger, with unconscious pride.

"I did not expect to see a blacksmith's anvil out here in the wilderness. Where did you procure these tools?"

"We have been years getting them here. Some came by way of the Ohio River; others overland from Detroit. That anvil has a history. It was lost once, and lay for years in the woods, until some Indians found it again. It is called the Ringing Stone, and Indians come from miles around to see and hear it."

The missionary pointed out wide fields of corn, now growing yellow, and hillsides dotted with browsing cattle, droves of sturdy-limbed horses, and pens of fat, grunting pigs—all of which attested to the growing prosperity of the Village of Peace.

On the way back to the cabin, while the others listened to and questioned Mr. Zeisberger, Jim was silent and thoughtful, for his thoughts reverted to his brother.

Later, as he walked with Nell by the golden-fringed stream, he spoke of Joe.

"Joe wanted so much to hunt with Wetzel. He will come back; surely he will return to us when he has satisfied his wild craving for adventure. Do you not think so?"

There was an eagerness that was almost pleading in Jim's voice. What he so much hoped for—that no harm had befallen Joe, and that he would return—he doubted. He needed the encouragement of his hope.

"Never," answered Nell, solemnly.

"Oh, why—why do you say that?"

"I saw him look at you—a strange, intent glance. He gazed long at me as we separated. Oh! I can feel his eyes. No; he will never come back."

"Nell, Nell, you do not mean he went away deliberately—because, oh! I cannot say it."

"For no reason, except that the wilderness called him more than love for you or—me."

"No, no," returned Jim, his face white. "You do not understand. He really loved you—I know it. He loved me, too. Ah, how well! He has gone because—I can't tell you."

"Oh, Jim, I hope—he loved—me," sobbed Nell, bursting into tears. "His coldness—his neglect—those last few days—hurt me—so. If he cared—as you say—I won't be—so—miserable."

"We are both right—you when you say he will never return, and I when I say he loved us both," said Jim sadly, as the bitter certainty forced itself into his mind.

As she sobbed softly, and he gazed with set, stern face into the darkening forest, the deep, mellow notes of the church bell pealed out. So thrilled, so startled were they by this melody wondrously breaking the twilight stillness, that they gazed mutely at each other. Then they remembered. It was the missionary's bell summoning the Christian Indians to the evening service.

CHAPTER XI

The sultry, drowsy, summer days passed with no untoward event to mar their slumbering tranquility. Life for the newcomers to the Village of Peace brought a content, the like of which they had never dreamed of. Mr. Wells at once began active work among the Indians, preaching every day to them through an interpreter; Nell and Kate, in hours apart from household duties, busied themselves brightening their new abode, and Jim entered upon the task of acquainting himself with the modes and habits of the redmen. Truly, the young people might have found perfect happiness in this new and novel life, if only Joe had returned. His disappearance and subsequent absence furnished a theme for many talks and many a quiet hour of dreamy sadness. The fascination of his personality had been so impelling that long after it was withdrawn a charm lingered around everything which reminded them of him; a subtle and sweet memory, with perverse and half bitter persistence, returned hauntingly. No trace of Joe had been seen by any of the friendly Indian runners. He was gone into the mazes of deep-shadowed forests, where to hunt for him would be like striving to trail the flight of a swallow. Two of those he had left behind always remembered him, and in their thoughts followed him in his wanderings.

Jim settled down to his study of Indians with single-heartedness of purpose. He spent part of every morning with the interpreters, with whose assistance he rapidly acquired the Delaware language. He went freely among the Indians, endeavoring to win their goodwill. There were always fifty to a hundred visiting Indians at the village; sometimes, when the missionaries had advertised a special meeting, there were assembled in the shady maple grove as many as five hundred savages. Jim had, therefore, golden opportunities to practice his offices of friendliness.

Fortunately for him, he at once succeeded in establishing himself in the good graces of Glickhican, the converted Delaware chief. The wise old Indian was of inestimable value to Jim. Early in their acquaintance he evinced an earnest regard for the young minister, and talked with him for hours.

From Glickhican Jim learned the real nature of the redmen. The Indian's love of freedom and honor, his hatred of subjection and deceit, as explained by the good old man, recalled to Jim Colonel Zane's estimate of the savage character. Surely, as the colonel had said, the Indians had reason for their hatred of the pioneers. Truly, they were a blighted race.

Seldom had the rights of the redmen been thought of. The settler pushed onward, plodding, as it were, behind his plow with a rifle. He regarded the Indian as little better than a beast; he was easier to kill than to tame. How little the settler knew the proud independence, the wisdom, the stainless chastity of honor, which belonged so truly to many Indian chiefs!

The redmen were driven like hounded deer into the untrodden wilds. From freemen of the forest, from owners of the great boundless plains, they passed to stern, enduring fugitives on their own lands. Small wonder that they became cruel where once they had been gentle! Stratagem and cunning, the night assault, the daylight ambush took the place of their one-time open warfare. Their chivalrous courage, that sublime inheritance from ancestors who had never known the paleface foe, degenerated into a savage ferocity.

Interesting as was this history to Jim, he cared more for Glickhican's rich portrayal of the redmen's domestic life, for the beautiful poetry of his tradition and legends. He heard with delight the exquisite fanciful Indian lore. From these romantic legends, beautiful poems, and marvelous myths he hoped to get ideas of the Indian's religion. Sweet and simple as children's dreams were these quaint tales— tales of how the woodland fairies dwelt in fern-carpeted dells; how at sunrise they came out to kiss open the flowers; how the forest walks were spirit-haunted paths; how the leaves whispered poetry to the winds; how the rocks harbored Indian gods and masters who watched over their chosen ones.

Glickhican wound up his long discourse by declaring he had never lied in the whole course of his seventy years, he had never stolen, never betrayed, never murdered, never killed, save in self-defense. Gazing at the chief's fine features, now calm, yet showing traces of past storms, Jim believed he spoke the truth.

When the young minister came, however, to study the hostile Indians that flocked to the village, any conclusive delineation of character, or any satisfactory analysis of their mental state in regard to the paleface religion, eluded him. Their passive, silent, sphinx-like secretiveness was baffling. Glickhican had taught him how to propitiate the friendly braves, and with these he was successful. Little he learned, however, from the unfriendly ones. When making gifts to these redmen he could never be certain that his offerings were appreciated. The jewels and gold he had brought west with him went to the French traders, who in exchange gave him trinkets, baubles, bracelets, and weapons. Jim made hundreds of presents. Boldly going up to befeathered and befringed chieftains, he offered them knives, hatchets, or strings of silvery beads. Sometimes his kindly offerings were repelled with a haughty stare; at other times they would be accepted coldly, suspiciously, as if the gifts brought some unknown obligation.

For a white man it was a never-to-be-forgotten experience to see eight or ten of these grim, slowly stepping forest kings, arrayed in all the rich splendor of their costume, stalking among the teepees of the Village of Peace. Somehow, such a procession always made Jim shiver. The singing, praying, and preaching they heard unmoved. No emotion was visible on their bronzed faces; nothing changed their unalterable mien. Had they not moved, or gazed with burning eyes, they would have been statues. When these chieftains looked at the converted Indians, some of whom were braves of their nations, the contempt in their glances betrayed that they now regarded these Christian Indians as belonging to an alien race.

Among the chiefs Glickhican pointed out to Jim were Wingenund, the Delaware; Tellane, the Half King; Shingiss and Kotoxen—all of the Wolf tribe of the Delawares.

Glickhican was careful to explain that the Delaware nation had been divided into the Wolf and Turtle tribes; the former warlike people, and the latter peaceable. Few of the Wolf tribe had gone over to the new faith, and those who had were scorned. Wingenund, the great power of the Delawares—indeed, the greatest of all the western tribes—maintained a neutral attitude toward the Village of Peace. But it was well known that his right-hand war chiefs, Pipe and Wishtonah, remained coldly opposed.

Jim turned all he had learned over and over in his mind, trying to construct part of it to fit into a sermon that would be different from any the Indians had ever heard. He did not want to preach far over their heads. If possible, he desired to keep to their ideals—for he deemed them more beautiful than his own—and to conduct his teaching along the simple lines of their belief, so that when he stimulated and developed their minds he could pass from what they knew to the unknown Christianity of the white man.

His first address to the Indians was made one day during the indisposition of Mr. Wells—who had been overworking himself—and the absence of the other missionaries. He did not consider himself at all ready for preaching, and confined his efforts to a simple, earnest talk, a recital of the thoughts he had assimilated while living here among the Indians.

Amazement would not have described the state of his feelings when he learned that he had made a powerful impression. The converts were loud in his praise; the unbelievers silent and thoughtful. In spite of himself, long before he had been prepared, he was launched on his teaching. Every day he was called upon to speak; every day one savage, at least, was convinced; every day the throng of interested Indians was augmented. The elder missionaries were quite overcome with joy; they pressed him day after day to speak, until at length he alone preached during the afternoon service.

The news flew apace; the Village of Peace entertained more redmen than ever before. Day after day the faith gained a stronger foothold. A kind of religious trance affected some of the converted Indians, and this greatly influenced the doubting ones. Many of them half believed the Great Manitou had come.

Heckewelder, the acknowledged leader of the western Moravian Mission, visited the village at this time, and, struck by the young missionary's success, arranged a three days' religious festival. Indian runners were employed to carry invitations to all the tribes. The Wyandots in the west, the Shawnees in the south, and the Delawares in the north were especially requested to come. No deception was practiced to lure the distant savages to the Village of Peace. They were asked to come, partake of the feasts, and listen to the white man's teaching.

CHAPTER XII

From dawn until noon on Sunday bands of Indians arrived at the Village of Peace. Hundreds of canoes glided down the swift stream and bumped their prows into the pebbly beach. Groups of mounted warriors rode out of the forests into the clearing; squaws with pappooses, maidens carrying wicker baskets, and children playing with rude toys, came trooping along the bridle paths.

Gifts were presented during the morning, after which the visitors were feasted. In the afternoon all assembled in the grove to hear the preaching.

The maple grove wherein the service was to be conducted might have been intended by Nature for just such a purpose as it now fulfilled. These trees were large, spreading, and situated far apart. Mossy stones and the thick carpet of grass afforded seats for the congregation.

Heckewelder—a tall, spare, and kindly appearing man—directed the arranging of the congregation. He placed the converted Indians just behind the knoll upon which the presiding minister was to stand. In a half circle facing the knoll he seated the chieftains and important personages of the various tribes. He then made a short address in the Indian language, speaking of the work of the mission, what wonders it had accomplished, what more good work it hoped to do, and concluded by introducing the young missionary.

While Heckewelder spoke, Jim, who stood just behind, employed the few moments in running his eyes over the multitude. The sight which met his gaze was one he thought he would never forget. An involuntary word escaped him.

"Magnificent!" he exclaimed.

The shady glade had been transformed into a theater, from which gazed a thousand dark, still faces. A thousand eagle plumes waved, and ten thousand bright-hued feathers quivered in the soft breeze. The fantastically dressed scalps presented a contrast to the smooth, unadorned heads of the converted redmen. These proud plumes and defiant feathers told the difference between savage and Christian.

In front of the knoll sat fifty chiefs, attentive and dignified. Representatives of every tribe as far west as the Scioto River were numbered in that circle. There were chiefs renowned for war, for cunning, for valor, for wisdom. Their stately presence gave the meeting tenfold importance. Could these chiefs be interested, moved, the whole western world of Indians might be civilized.

Hepote, a Maumee chief, of whom it was said he had never listened to words of the paleface, had the central position in this circle. On his right and left, respectively, sat Shaushoto and Pipe, implacable foes of all white men. The latter's aspect did not belie his reputation. His copper-colored, repulsive visage compelled fear; it breathed vindictiveness and malignity. A singular action of his was that he always, in what must have been his arrogant vanity, turned his profile to those who watched him, and it was a remarkable one; it sloped in an oblique line from the top of his forehead to his protruding chin, resembling somewhat the carved bowl of his pipe, which was of flint and a famed inheritance from his ancestors. From it he took his name. One solitary eagle plume, its tip stained vermilion, stuck from his scalplock. It slanted backward on a line with his profile.

Among all these chiefs, striking as they were, the figure of Wingenund, the Delaware, stood out alone.

His position was at the extreme left of the circle, where he leaned against a maple. A long, black mantle, trimmed with spotless white, enveloped him. One bronzed arm, circled by a heavy bracelet of gold, held the mantle close about his lofty form. His headdress, which trailed to the ground, was exceedingly beautiful. The eagle plumes were of uniform length and pure white, except the black-pointed tips.

At his feet sat his daughter, Whispering Winds. Her maidens were gathered round her. She raised her soft, black eyes, shining with a wondrous light of surprise and expectation, to the young missionary's face.

Beyond the circle the Indians were massed together, even beyond the limits of the glade. Under the trees on every side sat warriors astride their steeds; some lounged on the green turf; many reclined in the branches of low-spreading maples.

As Jim looked out over the sea of faces he started in surprise. The sudden glance of fiery eyes had impelled his gaze. He recognized Silvertip, the Shawnee chief. The Indian sat motionless on a powerful black horse. Jim started again, for the horse was Joe's thoroughbred, Lance. But Jim had no further time to think of Joe's enemy, for Heckewelder stepped back.

Jim took the vacated seat, and, with a far-reaching, resonant voice, began his discourse to the Indians.

"Chieftains, warriors, maidens, children of the forest, listen, and your ears shall hear no lie. I am come from where the sun rises to tell you of the Great Spirit of the white man.

"Many, many moons ago, as many as blades of grass grow on yonder plain, the Great Spirit of whom I shall speak created the world. He made the sparkling lakes and swift rivers, the boundless plains and tangled forests, over which He caused the sun to shine and the rain to fall. He gave life to the kingly elk, the graceful deer, the rolling bison, the bear, the fox—all the beasts and birds and fishes. But He was not content; for nothing He made was perfect in His sight. He created the white man in His own image, and from this first man's rib He created his mate—a woman. He turned them free in a beautiful forest.

"Life was fair in the beautiful forest. The sun shone always, the birds sang, the waters flowed with music, the flowers cast sweet fragrance on the air. In this forest, where fruit bloomed always, was one tree, the Tree of Life, the apple of which they must not eat. In all this beautiful forest of abundance this apple alone was forbidden them.

"Now evil was born with woman. A serpent tempted her to eat of the apple of Life, and she tempted the man to eat. For their sin the Great Spirit commanded the serpent to crawl forever on his belly, and He drove them from the beautiful forest. The punishment for their sin was to be visited on their children, always, until the end of time. The two went afar into the dark forests to learn to live as best they might. From them all tribes descended. The world is wide. A warrior might run all his days and not reach the setting sun, where tribes of yellowskins live. He might travel half his days toward the southwind, where tribes of blackskins abound. People of all colors inhabited the world. They lived in hatred toward one another. They shed each other's blood; they stole each other's lands, gold, and women. They sinned.

"Many moons ago the Great Spirit sorrowed to see His chosen tribe, the palefaces, living in ignorance and sin. He sent His only Son to redeem them, and said if they would listen and believe, and teach the other tribes, He would forgive their sin and welcome them to the beautiful forest.

"That was moons and moons ago, when the paleface killed his brother for gold and lands, and beat his women slaves to make them plant his corn. The Son of the Great Spirit lifted the cloud from the palefaces' eyes, and they saw and learned. So pleased was the Great Spirit that He made the palefaces wiser and wiser, and masters of the world. He bid them go afar to teach the ignorant tribes.

"To teach you is why the young paleface journeyed from the rising sun. He wants no lands or power. He has given all that he had. He walks among you without gun or knife. He can gain nothing but the happiness of opening the redmen's eyes.

"The Great Spirit of whom I teach and the Great Manitou, your idol, are the same; the happy hunting ground of the Indian and the beautiful forest of the paleface are the same; the paleface and the redman are the same. There is but one Great Spirit, that is God; but one eternal home, that is heaven; but one human being, that is man.

"The Indian knows the habits of the beaver; he can follow the paths of the forests; he can guide his canoe through the foaming rapids; he is honest, he is brave, he is great; but he is not wise. His wisdom is clouded with the original sin. He lives in idleness; he paints his face; he makes his squaw labor for him, instead of laboring for her; he kills his brothers. He worships the trees and rocks. If he were wise he would not make gods of the swift arrow and bounding canoe; of the flowering ash and the flaming flint. For these things have not life. In his dreams he sees his arrow speed to the running deer. In his dreams he sees his canoes shoot over the crest of shining waves; and in his mind he gives them life, when his eyes are opened he will see they have no spirit. The spirit is in his own heart. It guides the arrow to the running deer, and steers the canoe over the swirling current. The spirit makes him find the untrodden paths, and do brave deeds, and love his children and his honor. It makes him meet his foe face to face, and if he is to die it gives him strength to die—a man. The spirit is what makes him different from the arrow, the canoe, the mountain, and all the birds and beasts. For it is born of the Great Spirit, the creator of all. Him you must worship.

"Redmen, this worship is understanding your spirit and teaching it to do good deeds. It is called Christianity. Christianity is love. If you will love the Great Spirit you will love your wives, your children, your brothers, your friends, your foes—you will love the palefaces. No more will you idle in winter and wage wars in summer. You will wear your knife and tomahawk only when you hunt for meat. You will be kind, gentle, loving, virtuous—you will have grown wise. When your days are done you will meet all your loved ones in the beautiful forest. There, where the flowers bloom, the fruits ripen always, where the pleasant water glides, and the summer winds whisper sweetly, there peace will dwell forever.

"Comrades, be wise, think earnestly. Forget the wicked paleface; for there are many wicked palefaces. They sell the serpent firewater; they lie and steal and kill. These palefaces' eyes are still clouded. If they do not open they will never see the beautiful forest. You have much to forgive, but those who forgive please the Great Spirit; you must give yourselves to love, but those who love are loved; you must work, but those who work are happy.

"Behold the Village of Peace! Once it contained few; now there are many. Where once the dark forest shaded the land, see the cabins, the farms, the horses, the cattle!

Field on field of waving, golden grain shine there under your eyes. The earth has blossomed abundance. Idling and fighting made not these rich harvests. Belief made love; love made wise eyes; wise eyes saw, and lo! there came plenty.

"The proof of love is happiness. These Christian Indians are happy. They are at peace with the redman and the paleface. They till the fields and work in the shops. In days to come cabins and farms and fields of corn will be theirs. They will bring up their children, not to hide in the forest to slay, but to walk hand in hand with the palefaces as equals.

"Oh, open your ears! God speaks to you; peace awaits you! Cast the bitterness from your hearts; it is the serpent poison. While you hate, God shuts His eyes. You are great on the trail, in the council, in war; now be great in forgiveness. Forgive the palefaces who have robbed you of your lands. Then will come peace. If you do not forgive, the war will go on; you will lose lands and homes, to find unmarked graves under the forest leaves. Revenge is sweet; but it is not wise. The price of revenge is blood and life. Root it out of your hearts. Love these Christian Indians; love the missionaries as they love you; love all living creatures. Your days are but few; therefore, cease the strife. Let us say, 'Brothers, that is God's word, His law; that is love; that is Christianity!' If you will say from your heart, brother, you are a Christian.

"Brothers, the paleface teacher beseeches you. Think not of this long, bloody war, of your dishonored dead, of your silenced wigwams, of your nameless graves, of your homeless children. Think of the future. One word from you will make peace over all this broad land. The paleface must honor a Christian. He can steal no Christian's land. All the palefaces, as many as the stars of the great white path, dare not invade the Village of Peace. For God smiles here. Listen to His words: 'Come unto me all ye that are weary and heavy laden, and I will give you rest.'"

Over the multitude brooded an impressive, solemn silence. Then an aged Delaware chief rose, with a mien of profound thought, and slowly paced before the circle of chiefs. Presently he stopped, turned to the awaiting Indians, and spoke:

"Netawatwees is almost persuaded to be a Christian." He resumed his seat.

Another interval of penetrating quiet ensued. At length a venerable-looking chieftain got up:

"White Eyes hears the rumbling thunder in his ears. The smoke blows from his eyes. White Eyes is the oldest chief of the Lenni-Lenape. His days are many; they are full; they draw near the evening of his life; he rejoices that wisdom is come before his sun is set.

"White Eyes believes the young White Father. The ways of the Great Spirit are many as the fluttering leaves; they are strange and secret as the flight of a loon; White Eyes believes the redman's happy hunting grounds need not be forgotten to love the palefaces' God. As a young brave pants and puzzles over his first trail, so the grown warrior feels in his understanding of his God. He gropes blindly through dark ravines.

"White Eyes speaks few words today, for he is learning wisdom; he bids his people hearken to the voice of the White Father. War is wrong; peace is best. Love is the way to peace. The paleface advances one step nearer his God. He labors for his home; he keeps the peace; he asks but little; he frees his women. That is well. White Eyes has spoken."

The old chief slowly advanced toward the Christian Indians. He laid aside his knife and tomahawk, and then his eagle plumes and warbonnet. Bare-headed, he seated himself among the converted redmen. They began chanting in low, murmuring tones.

Amid the breathless silence that followed this act of such great significance, Wingenund advanced toward the knoll with slow, stately step. His dark eye swept the glade with lightning scorn; his glance alone revealed the passion that swayed him.

"Wingenund's ears are keen; they have heard a feather fall in the storm; now they hear a soft-voiced thrush. Wingenund thunders to his people, to his friends, to the chiefs of other tribes: *'Do not bury the hatchet!'* The young White Father's tongue runs smooth like the gliding brook; it sings as the thrush calls its mate. Listen; but wait, wait! Let time prove his beautiful tale; let the moons go by over the Village of Peace.

"Wingenund does not flaunt his wisdom. He has grown old among his warriors; he loves them; he fears for them. The dream of the palefaces' beautiful forest glimmers as the rainbow glows over the laughing falls of the river. The dream of the paleface is too beautiful to come true. In the days of long ago, when Wingenund's forefathers heard not the paleface's ax, they lived in love and happiness such as the young White Father dreams may come again. They waged no wars. A white dove sat in every wigwam. The lands were theirs and they were rich. The paleface came with his leaden death, his burning firewater, his ringing ax, and the glory of the redmen faded forever.

"Wingenund seeks not to inflame his braves to anger. He is sick of blood-spilling—not from fear; for Wingenund cannot feel fear. But he asks his people to wait. Remember, the gifts of the paleface ever contained a poisoned arrow.

Wingenund's heart is sore. The day of the redman is gone. His sun is setting. Wingenund feels already the gray shades of evening."

He stopped for one long moment as if to gather breath for his final charge to his listeners. Then with a magnificent gesture he thundered:

"Is the Delaware a fool? When Wingenund can cross unarmed to the Big Water he shall change his mind. When Deathwind ceases to blow his bloody trail over the fallen leaves Wingenund will believe."

CHAPTER XIII

As the summer waned, each succeeding day, with its melancholy calm, its changing lights and shades, its cool, damp evening winds, growing more and more suggestive of autumn, the little colony of white people in the Village of Peace led busy, eventful lives.

Upwards of fifty Indians, several of them important chiefs, had become converted since the young missionary began preaching. Heckewelder declared that this was a wonderful showing, and if it could be kept up would result in gaining a hold on the Indian tribes which might not be shaken. Heckewelder had succeeded in interesting the savages west of the Village of Peace to the extent of permitting him to establish missionary posts in two other localities—one near Goshhocking, a Delaware town; and one on the Muskingong, the principal river running through central Ohio. He had, with his helpers, Young and Edwards, journeyed from time to time to these points, preaching, making gifts, and soliciting help from chiefs.

The most interesting feature, perhaps, of the varied life of the missionary party was a rivalry between Young and Edwards for the elder Miss Wells. Usually Nell's attractiveness appealed more to men than Kate's; however, in this instance, although the sober teachers of the gospel admired Nell's winsome beauty, they fell in love with Kate. The missionaries were both under forty, and good, honest men, devoted to the work which had engrossed them for years. Although they were ardent lovers, certainly they were not picturesque. Two homelier men could hardly have been found. Moreover, the sacrifice of their lives to missionary work had taken them far from the companionship of women of their own race, so that they lacked the ease of manner which women would like to see in men. Young and Edwards were awkward, almost uncouth. Embarrassment would not have done justice to their state of feeling while basking in the sunshine of Kate's quiet smile. They were happy, foolish, and speechless.

If Kate shared in the merriment of the others—Heckewelder could not conceal his, and Nell did not try very hard to hide hers—she never allowed a suspicion of it to escape. She kept the easy, even tenor of her life, always kind and gracious in her quaint way, and precisely the same to both her lovers. No doubt she well knew that each possessed, under all his rough exterior, a heart of gold.

One day the genial Heckewelder lost, or pretended to lose, his patience.

"Say, you worthy gentlemen are becoming ornamental instead of useful. All this changing of coals, trimming of mustaches, and eloquent sighing doesn't seem to have affected the young lady. I've a notion to send you both to Maumee town, one hundred miles away. This young lady is charming, I admit, but if she is to keep on seriously hindering the work of the Moravian Mission I must object. As for that matter, I might try conclusions myself. I'm as young as either of you, and, I flatter myself, much handsomer. You'll have a dangerous rival presently. Settle it! You can't both have her; settle it!"

This outburst from their usually kind leader placed the earnest but awkward gentlemen in a terrible plight.

On the afternoon following the crisis Heckewelder took Mr. Wells to one of the Indian shops, and Jim and Nell went canoeing. Young and Edwards, after conferring for one long, trying hour, determined on settling the question.

Young was a pale, slight man, very homely except when he smiled. His smile not only broke up the plainness of his face, but seemed to chase away a serious shadow, allowing his kindly, gentle spirit to shine through. He was nervous, and had a timid manner. Edwards was his opposite, being a man of robust frame, with a heavy face, and a manner that would have suggested self-confidence in another man.

They were true and tried friends.

"Dave, I couldn't ask her," said Young, trembling at the very thought. "Besides, there's no hope for me, I know it. That's why I'm afraid, why I don't want to ask her. What'd such a glorious creature see in a poor, puny little thing like me?"

"George, you're not over-handsome," admitted Dave, shaking his head. "But you can never tell about women. Sometimes they like even little, insignificant fellows. Don't be too scared about asking her. Besides, it will make it easier for me. You might tell her—about me—you know, sort of feel her out, so I'd——"

Dave's voice failed him here; but he had said enough, and that was most discouraging to poor George. Dave was so busy screwing up his courage that he forgot all about his friend.

"No; I couldn't," gasped George, falling into a chair. He was ghastly pale. "I couldn't ask her to accept me, let alone do another man's wooing. She thinks more of you. She'll accept you."

"You really think so?" whispered Dave, nervously.

"I know she will. You're such a fine, big figure of a

man. She'll take you, and I'll be glad. This fever and fretting has about finished me. When she's yours I'll not be
so bad. I'll be happy in your happiness. But, Dave, you'll
let me see her occasionally, won't you? Go! Hurry—get it
over!"

"Yes; we must have it over," replied Dave, getting up
with a brave effort. Truly, if he carried that determined
front to his lady love he would look like a masterful lover.
But when he got to the door he did not at all resemble a
conqueror.

"You're sure she—cares for me?" asked Dave, for the
hundredth time. This time, as always, his friend was faithful and convincing.

"I know she does. Go—hurry. I tell you I can't stand this
any longer," cried George, pushing Dave out of the door.

"You won't go—first?" whispered Dave, clinging to
the door.

"I won't go at all. I couldn't ask her—I don't want
her—go! Get out!"

Dave started reluctantly toward the adjoining cabin,
from the open window of which came the song of the
young woman who was responsible for all this trouble.
George flung himself on his bed. What a relief to feel it
was all over! He lay there with eyes shut for hours, as it
seemed. After a time Dave came in. George leaped to his
feet and saw his friend stumbling over a chair. Somehow,
Dave did not look as usual. He seemed changed, or
shrunken, and his face wore a discomfited, miserable expression.

"Well?" cried George, sharply. Even to his highly excited imagination this did not seem the proper condition
for a victorious lover.

"She refused—refused me," faltered Dave. "She was
very sweet and kind; said something about being my

sister—I don't remember just what—but she wouldn't have me."

"What did you say to her?" whispered George, a paralyzing hope almost rendering him speechless.

"I—I told her everything I could think of," replied Dave, despondently; "even what you said."

"What I said? Dave, what did you tell her I said?"

"Why, you know—about she cared for me—that you were sure of it, and that you didn't want her——"

"Jackass!" roared George, rising out of his meekness like a lion from slumber.

"Didn't you—say so?" inquired Dave, weakly.

"No! No! No! Idiot!"

As one possessed, George rushed out of the cabin, and a moment later stood disheveled and frantic before Kate.

"Did that fool say I didn't love you!" he demanded.

Kate looked up, startled; but as an understanding of George's wild aspect and wilder words dawned upon her, she resumed her usual calm demeanor. Looking again to see if this passionate young man was indeed George, she turned her face as she said:

"If you mean Mr. Edwards, yes; I believe he did say as much. Indeed, from his manner he seemed to have monopolized all the love near the Village of Peace."

"But it's not true. I *do* love you. I love you to distraction. I have loved you ever since I first saw you. I told Dave that. Heckewelder knows it; even the Indians know it," cried George, protesting vehemently against the disparaging allusion to his affections. He did not realize he was making a most impassioned declaration of love. When he was quite out of breath he sat down and wiped his moist brow.

A pink bloom tinged Kate's cheeks, and her eyes glowed with a happy light; but George never saw these womanly evidences of pleasure.

"Of course I know you don't care for me——"

"Did Mr. Edwards tell you so?" asked Kate, glancing up quickly.

"Why, yes, he has often said he thought that. Indeed, he always seemed to regard himself as the fortunate object of your affections. I always believed he was."

"But it wasn't true."

"What?"

"It's not true."

"What's not true?"

"Oh—about my—not caring."

"Kate!" cried George, quite overcome with rapture. He fell over two chairs getting to her; but he succeeded, and fell on his knees to kiss her hand.

"Foolish boy! It has been you all the time," whispered Kate, with her quiet smile.

L ook here, Downs; come to the door. See there," said Heckewelder to Jim.

Somewhat surprised at Heckewelder's grave tone, Jim got up from the supper table and looked out of the door. He saw two tall Indians pacing to and fro under the maples. It was still early twilight, and light enough to see clearly. One Indian was almost naked; the lithe, graceful symmetry of his dark figure standing out in sharp contrast to the gaunt, gaudily costumed form of the other.

"Silvertip! Girty!" exclaimed Jim, in a low voice.

"Girty I knew, of course; but I was not sure the other was the Shawnee who captured you and your brother," replied Heckewelder, drawing Jim into another room.

"What do they mean by loitering around the village?" inquired Jim, apprehensively. Whenever he heard Girty's name mentioned, or even thought of him, he remembered with a shudder the renegade's allusion to the buzzards.

Jim never saw one of these carrion birds soaring overhead but his thoughts instantly reverted to the frontier
ruffian and his horrible craving.

"I don't know," answered Heckewelder. "Girty has
been here several times of late. I saw him conferring with
Pipe at Goshhocking. I hope there's no deviltry afoot.
Pipe is a relentless enemy of all Christians, and Girty is a
fiend, a hyena. I think, perhaps, it will be well for you and
the girls to stay indoors while Girty and Silvertip are in
the village."

That evening the entire missionary party were gathered in Mr. Wells' room. Heckewelder told stories of Indian life, Nell sang several songs, and Kate told of many
amusing things said and done by the little Indian boys in
her class at the school. Thus the evening passed pleasantly
for all.

"So next Wednesday I am to perform the great cere-
mony," remarked Heckewelder, laying his hand kindly on
Young's knee. "We'll celebrate the first white wedding in
the Village of Peace."

Young looked shyly down at his boots; Edwards crossed
one leg over the other, and coughed loudly to hide his embarrassment. Kate wore, as usual, her pensive smile; Nell's
eyes twinkled, and she was about to speak, when Heck-
welder's quizzical glance in her direction made her lips
mute.

"I hope I'll have another wedding on my hands soon,"
he said, placidly.

This ordinary remark had an extraordinary effect. Nell
turned with burning cheeks and looked out of the window. Jim frowned fiercely and bit his lips. Edwards began
to laugh, and even Mr. Wells' serious face lapsed into a
smile.

"I mean I've picked out a nice little Delaware squaw

for Dave," said Heckewelder, seeing his badinage had somehow gone amiss.

"Oh-h!" suddenly cried Nell, in shuddering tones.

They all gazed at her in amazement. Every vestige of color had receded from her face, leaving it marblelike. Her eyes were fixed in startled horror. Suddenly she relaxed her grasp on the windowsill and fell back limp and senseless.

Heckewelder ran to the door to look out, while the others bent over the unconscious girl, endeavoring to revive her. Presently a fluttering breath and a quivering of her dark lashes noted a return of suspended life. Then her beautiful eyes opened wide to gaze with wonder and fear into the grave faces bent so anxiously over her.

"Nell, dearest, you are safe. What was it? What frightened you so?" said Kate, tenderly.

"Oh, it was fearful!" gasped Nell, sitting up. She clung to her sister with one hand, while the other grasped Jim's sleeve.

"I was looking out into the dark, when suddenly I beheld a face, a terrible face!" cried Nell. Those who watched her marveled at the shrinking, awful fear in her eyes. "It was right by the window. I could have touched it. Such a greedy, wolfish face, with a long, hooked nose! The eyes, oh! the eyes! I'll never forget them. They made me sick; they paralyzed me. It wasn't an Indian's face. It belonged to that white man, that awful white man! I never saw him before; but I knew him."

"Girty!" said Heckewelder, who had come in with his quiet step. "He looked in at the window. Calm yourself, Nellie. The renegade has gone."

The incident worried them all at the time, and made Nell nervous for several days; but as Girty had disappeared, and nothing more was heard of him, gradually they forgot. Kate's wedding day dawned with all the little party well and happy. Early in the afternoon Jim and Nell, accompanied by Kate and her lover, started out into the woods just beyond the clearing for the purpose of gathering wildflowers to decorate the cabin.

"We are both thinking of—him," Jim said, after he and Nell had walked some little way in silence.

"Yes," answered Nell, simply.

"I hope—I pray Joe comes back, but if he doesn't—Nell—won't you care a little for me?"

He received no answer. But Nell turned her face away.

"We both loved him. If he's gone forever our very love for him should bring us together. I know—I know he would have wished that."

"Jim, don't speak of love to me now," she whispered. Then she turned to the others. "Come quickly; here are great clusters of wild clematis and goldenrod. How lovely! Let us gather a quantity."

The young men had almost buried the girls under huge masses of the beautiful flowers, when the soft tread of moccasined feet caused them all to turn in surprise. Six savages stood waist-deep in the bushes, where they had lain concealed. Fierce, painted visages scowled from behind leveled rifles.

"Don't yell!" cried a hoarse voice in English. Following the voice came a snapping of twigs, and then two other figures came into view. They were Girty and Silvertip.

"Don't yell, er I'll leave you layin' here fer the buzzards," said the renegade. He stepped forward and grasped Young, at the same time speaking in the Indian language and pointing to a nearby tree. Strange to relate, the renegade apparently wanted no bloodshed. While one of the savages began to tie Young to the tree, Girty turned his gaze on the girls. His little, yellow eyes glinted; he stroked his chin with a bony hand, and his dark, repulsive face was wreathed in a terrible, meaning smile.

"I've been layin' fer you," he croaked, eyeing Nell. "Ye're the purtiest lass, 'ceptin' mebbe Bet Zane, I ever seed on the border. I got cheated outen her, but I've got you; arter I feed yer Injun preacher to ther buzzards mebbe ye'll larn to love me."

Nell gazed one instant into the monster's face. Her terror-stricken eyes were piteous to behold. She tried to speak; but her voice failed. Then, like a stricken bird, she fell on the grass.

CHAPTER XIV

Not many miles from the Village of Peace rose an irregular chain of hills, the first faint indication of the Appalachian mountain system; these ridges were thickly wooded with white oak, poplar, and hickory, among which a sentinel pine reared here and there its evergreen head. There were clefts in the hills, passes lined by gray-stoned cliffs, below which ran clear brooks, tumbling over rocks in a hurry to meet their majestic father, the Ohio.

One of these valleys, so narrow that the sun seldom brightened the merry brook, made a deep cut in the rocks. The head of this valley tapered until the walls nearly met; it seemed to lose itself in the shade of fern-faced cliffs, shadowed as they were by fir trees leaning over the brink as though to search for secrets of the ravine. So deep and dark and cool was this sequestered nook that here late summer had not dislodged early spring. Everywhere was a soft, fresh, bright green. The old gray cliffs were festooned with ferns, lichens, and moss. Under a great, shelving rock, damp and stained by the copper-colored water dripping down its side, was a dewy dell into which the sunshine had never peeped. Here the swift book tarried lovingly, making a wide turn under the cliff, as though loath to leave this quiet nook, and then leaped once more to enthusiasm in its murmuring flight.

Life abounded in this wild, beautiful, almost inaccessible spot. Little brown and yellow birds flitted among the trees; thrushes ran along the leaf-strewn ground; orioles sang their melancholy notes; robins and flickers darted beneath the spreading branches. Squirrels scurried over the leaves like little whirlwinds, and leaped daringly from the swinging branches or barked noisily from woody perches. Rabbits hopped inquisitively here and there while nibbling at the tender shoots of sassafras and laurel.

Along this flower-skirted stream a tall young man, carrying a rifle, cautiously stepped, peering into the branches overhead. A gray flash shot along a limb of a white oak; then the bushy tail of a squirrel flitted into a well-protected notch, from whence, no doubt, a keen little eye watched the hunter's every movement.

The rifle was raised; then lowered. The hunter walked around the tree. Presently up in the treetop, snug under a knotty limb, he espied a little ball of gray fur. Grasping a branch of underbrush, he shook it vigorously. The thrashing sound worried the gray squirrel, for he slipped from his retreat and stuck his nose over the limb. *Crack!* With a scratching and tearing of bark the squirrel loosened his hold and then fell, alighting with a thump. As the hunter picked up his quarry a streak of sunshine glinting through the treetop brightened his face.

The hunter was Joe.

He was satisfied now, for after stowing the squirrel in the pocket of his hunting coat he shouldered his rifle and went back up the ravine. Presently a dull roar sounded above the babble of the brook. It grew louder as he threaded his way carefully over the stones. Spots of white foam flecked the brook. Passing under the gray, stained cliff, Joe turned around a rocky corner, and came to an abrupt end of the ravine. A waterfall marked the spot where the brook entered. The water was brown as it took the leap, light green when it thinned out; and below, as it dashed on the stones, it became a beautiful, sheeny white.

Upon a flat rock, so near the cascade that spray flew over him, sat another hunter. The roaring falls drowned all other sounds, yet the man roused from his dreamy contemplation of the waterfall when Joe rounded the corner.

"I heerd four shots," he said, as Joe came up.

"Yes; I got a squirrel for every shot."

Wetzel led the way along a narrow foot trail which gradually wound toward the top of the ravine. This path emerged presently, some distance above the falls, on the brink of the bluff. It ran along the edge of the precipice a few yards, then took a course back into densely wooded thicket. Just before stepping out on the open cliff Wetzel paused and peered keenly on all sides. There was no living thing to be seen; the silence was the deep, unbroken calm of the wilderness.

Wetzel stepped to the bluff and looked over. The stony wall opposite was only thirty feet away, and somewhat lower. From Wetzel's action it appeared as if he intended to leap the fissure. In truth, many a band of Indians pursuing the hunter into this rocky fastness had come out on the bluff, and, marveling at what they thought Wetzel's prowess, believed he had made a wonderful leap, thus eluding them. But he had never attempted that leap, first, because he knew it was well nigh impossible, and, secondly, there had never been any necessity for such risk.

Anyone leaning over this cliff would have observed, perhaps ten feet below, a narrow ledge projecting from the face of the rock. He would have imagined if he were to drop on that ledge there would be no way to get off and he would be in a worse predicament.

Without a moment's hesitation Wetzel swung himself

over the ledge. Joe followed suit. At one end of this lower ledge grew a hardy shrub of the ironwood species, and above it a scrub pine leaned horizontally out over the ravine. Laying his rifle down, Wetzel grasped a strong root and cautiously slid over the side. When all of his body had disappeared, with the exception of his sinewy fingers, they loosened their hold on the root, grasped the rifle, and dragged it down out of sight. Quietly, with similar caution, Joe took hold of the same root, let himself down, and when at full length swung himself in under the ledge. His feet found a pocket in the cliff. Letting go of the root, he took his rifle, and in another second was safe.

Of all Wetzel's retreats—for he had many—he considered this one the safest. The cavern under the ledge he had discovered by accident. One day, being hotly pursued by Shawnees, he had been headed off on this cliff, and had let himself down on the ledge, intending to drop from it to the tops of the trees below. Taking advantage of every little aid, he swung over by means of the shrub, and was in the act of leaping when he saw that the cliff shelved under the ledge, while within reach of his feet was the entrance to a cavern. He found the cave to be small, with an opening at the back into a split in the rock. Evidently the place had been entered from the rear by bears, who used the hole for winter sleeping quarters. By crawling on his hands and knees, Wetzel found the rear opening. Thus he had established a hiding place where it was almost impossible to locate him. He provisioned his retreat, which he always entered by the cliff and left by the rear.

An evidence of Wetzel's strange nature, and of his love for this wild home, manifested itself when he bound Joe to secrecy. It was unlikely, even if the young man ever did get safely out of the wilderness, that any stories he might relate would reveal the hunter's favorite rendezvous. But

Wetzel seriously demanded this secrecy, as earnestly as if the forest were full of Indians and white men, all prowling in search of his burrow.

Joe was in the seventh heaven of his delight, and took to the free life as a wild gosling takes to the water. No place had ever appealed to him as did this dark, silent hole far up on the side of a steep cliff. His interest in Wetzel soon passed into a great admiration, and from that deepened to love.

This afternoon, when they were satisfied that all was well within their refuge, Joe laid aside his rifle, and, whistling softly, began to prepare supper. The back part of the cave permitted him to stand erect, and was large enough for comparative comfort. There was a neat, little stone fireplace, and several cooking utensils and gourds. From time to time Wetzel had brought these things. A pile of wood and a bundle of pinecones lay in the corner. Haunches of dried beef, bear, and buffalo meat hung from pegs; a bag of parched corn, another of dried apples lay on a rocky shelf. Nearby hung a powder-horn filled with salt and pepper. In the cleft back of the cave was a spring of clear, cold water.

The wants of woodsmen are few and simple. Joe and Wetzel, with appetites whetted by their stirring outdoor life, relished the frugal fare as they could never have enjoyed a feast. As the shadows of evening entered the cave, they lighted their pipes to partake of the hunger's sweetest solace, a quiet smoke.

Strange as it may appear this lonely, stern Indian hunter and the reckless, impulsive boy were admirably suited for companionship. Wetzel had taken a liking to the young man when he led the brothers to Fort Henry. Subsequent events strengthened his liking, and now, many days after, Joe having followed him into the forest, a strong attachment had been insensibly forged between them.

Wetzel understood Joe's burning desire to roam the forests; but he half expected the lad would soon grow tired of this roving life, but exactly the opposite symptoms were displayed. The hunter had intended to take his comrade on a hunting trip, and to return with him, after that was over, to Fort Henry. They had now been in the woods for weeks, and every day in some way had Joe showed his mettle. Wetzel finally admitted him into the secrets of his most cherished hiding place. He did not want to hurt the lad's feelings by taking him back to the settlement; he could not send him back. So the days wore on swiftly; full of heart-satisfying incident and life, with man and boy growing closer in an intimacy that was as warm as it was unusual.

Two reasons might account for this: First, there is no sane human being who is not better off for companionship. An exile would find something of happiness in one who shared his misery. And, secondly, Joe was a most acceptable comrade, even for a slayer of Indians. Wedded as Wetzel was to the forest trails, to his lonely life, to the Nemesis pursuit he had followed for eighteen long years, he was still a white man, kind and gentle in his quiet hours, and because of this, though he knew it not, still capable of affection. He had never known youth; his manhood had been one pitiless warfare against his sworn foes; but once in all those years had his sore, cold heart warmed; and that was toward a woman who was not for him. His life had held only one purpose—a bloody one. Yet the man had a heart, and he could not prevent it from responding to another. In his simple ignorance he rebelled against this affection for anything other than his forest homes. Man is weak against hate; what can he avail against love? The dark caverns of Wetzel's great heart opened, admitting to their gloomy depths this stranger.

So now a new love was born in that cheerless heart, where for so long a lonely inmate, the ghost of old love, had dwelt in chill seclusion.

The feeling of comradeship which Wetzel had for Joe was something altogether new in the hunter's life. True he had hunted with Jonathan Zane, and accompanied expeditions where he was forced to sleep with another scout; but a companion, not to say friend, he had never known. Joe was a boy, wilder than an eagle, yet he was a man. He was happy and enthusiastic, still his good spirits never jarred on the hunter; they were restrained. He never asked questions, as would seem the case in any eager lad; he waited until he was spoken to. He was apt; he never forgot anything; he had the eye of a born woodsman, and lastly, perhaps what went far with Wetzel, he was as strong and supple as a young lynx, and absolutely fearless.

On this evening Wetzel and Joe followed their usual custom; they smoked a while before lying down to sleep. Tonight the hunter was even more silent than usual, and the lad, tired out with his day's tramp, lay down on a bed of fragrant boughs.

Wetzel sat there in the gathering gloom while he puffed slowly on his pipe. The evening was very quiet; the birds had ceased their twittering; the wind had died away; it was too early for the bay of a wolf, the wail of a panther, or hoot of an owl; there was simply perfect silence.

The lad's deep, even breathing caught Wetzel's ear, and he found himself meditating, as he had often of late, on this new something that had crept into his life. For Joe loved him; he could not fail to see that. The lad had preferred to roam with the lonely Indian hunter through the forests, to encounter the perils and hardships of a wild life, rather than accept the smile of fortune and of love. Wetzel knew that Colonel Zane had taken a liking to the boy, and had offered him work and a home; and, also, the hunter remembered the warm light he had seen in Nell's hazel eyes. Musing thus, the man felt stir in his heart an emotion so long absent that it was unfamiliar. The Avenger forgot, for a moment, his brooding plans. He felt strangely softened. When he laid his head on the rude pillow it was with some sense of gladness that, although he had always desired a lonely life, and wanted to pass it in the fulfillment of his vow, his loneliness was now shared by a lad who loved him.

Joe was awakened by the merry chirp of a chipmunk that every morning ran along the seamy side of the opposite wall of the gorge. Getting up, he went to the back of the cave, where he found Wetzel combing out his long hair. The lad thrust his hands into the cold pool, and bathed his face. The water was icy cold, and sent an invigorating thrill through him. Then he laughed as he took a rude comb Wetzel handed to him.

"My scalp is nothing to make an Indian very covetous, is it?" said he, eyeing in admiration the magnificent black hair that fell over the hunter's shoulders.

"It'll grow," answered Wetzel.

Joe did not wonder at the care Wetzel took of his hair, nor did he misunderstand the hunter's simple pride. Wetzel was very careful of his rifle, he was neat and clean about his person, he brushed his buckskin costume, he polished his knife and tomahawk; but his hair received more attention than all else. It required much care. When combed out it reached fully to his knees. Joe had seen him, after he returned from a long hunt, work patiently for an hour with his wooden comb, and not stop until every little burr was gone, or tangle smoothed out. Then he would comb it again in the morning—this of course, when time permitted—and twist and tie it up so as to offer small resistance to his slipping through the underbrush. Joe knew the hunter's simplicity was such, that if he cut off his hair it would seem he feared the Indians—for that streaming black hair the Indians had long coveted and sworn to take. It would make any brave a famous chief, and was the theme of many a savage war tale.

After breakfast Wetzel said to Joe:

"You stay here, an' I'll look round some; mebbe I'll come back soon, and we'll go out an' kill a buffalo. Injuns sometimes foller up a buffalo trail, and I want to be sure none of the varlets are chasin' that herd we saw today."

Wetzel left the cave by the rear. It took him fifteen minutes to crawl to the end of the tortuous, stony passage. Lifting the stone which closed up the aperture, he looked out and listened. Then, rising, he replaced the stone, and passed down the wooded hillside.

It was a beautiful morning; the dew glistened on the green leaves, the sun shone bright and warm, the birds warbled in the trees. The hunter's moccasins pressed so gently on the moss and leaves that they made no more sound than the soft foot of a panther. His trained ear was alert to catch any unfamiliar noise; his keen eyes sought first the remoter open glades and glens, then bent their gaze on the mossy bluff beneath his feet. Fox squirrels dashed from before him into bushy retreats; grouse whirred away into the thickets; startled deer whistled, and loped off with their white flags upraised. Wetzel knew from the action of these denizens of the woods that he was the only creature, not native to these haunts, who had disturbed them this morning. Otherwise the deer would not have been grazing, but lying low in some close thicket; fox squirrels seldom or never were disturbed by a hunter twice in one day, for after being frightened these little animals, wilder and shyer than gray squirrels, remained hidden for hours, and grouse that have been flushed a little while before, always get up unusually quick, and fly very far before alighting.

Wetzel circled back over the hill, took a long survey from a rock eminence, and then reconnoitered the lowland for several miles. He located the herd of buffalo, and satisfying himself there were no Indians near—for the bison were grazing quietly—he returned to the cave. A soft whistle into the back door of the rocky home told Joe that the hunter was waiting.

"Coast clear?" whispered the lad, thrusting his head out of the entrance. His gray eyes gleamed brightly, showing his eager spirit.

The hunter nodded, and, throwing his rifle in the hollow of his arm, proceeded down the hill. Joe followed closely, endeavoring, as Wetzel had trained him, to make each step precisely in the hunter's footprint. The lad had soon learned to step nimbly and softly as a cat. When halfway down the hill Wetzel paused.

"See anythin'?" he whispered.

Joe glanced on all sides. Many mistakes had taught him to be cautious. He had learned from experience that for every woodland creature he saw, there were ten watching his every move. Just now he could not see even a little red squirrel. Everywhere were sturdy hickory and oak trees, thickets and hazelnuts, slender ash saplings, and, in the open glades, patches of sumach. Rotting trees lay on the ground, while ferns nodded long, slender heads over the fallen monarchs. Joe could make out nothing but the colors of the woods, the gray of the tree trunks, and, in the openings through the forest green, the dead purple haze of forests farther on. He smiled, and, shaking his head at the hunter, by his action admitted failure.

"Try again. Dead ahead," whispered Wetzel.

Joe bent a direct gaze on the clump of sassafras one hundred feet ahead. He searched the open places, the shadows—even the branches. Then he turned his eyes slowly to the right. Whatever was discernible to human vision he studied intently. Suddenly his eye became fixed on a small object protruding from behind a beech tree. It was pointed, and in color darker than the gray bark of the beech. It had been a very easy matter to pass over this little thing; but now that the lad saw it, he knew to what it belonged.

"That's a buck's ear," he replied.

Hardly had he finished speaking when Wetzel intentionally snapped a twig. There was a crash and commotion in the thicket; branches moved and small saplings waved; then out into the open glade bounded a large buck with a whistle of alarm. Throwing his rifle to a level, Joe was trying to cover the bounding deer, when the hunter struck up his piece.

"Lad, don't kill fer the sake of killin'," he said, quietly. "We have plenty of venison. We'll go arter a buffalo. I hev a hankerin' fer a good rump steak."

Half an hour later, the hunters emerged from the forest into a wide plain of waving grass. It was a kind of oval valley, encircled by hills, and had been at one time, perhaps, covered with water. Joe saw a herd of large animals browsing, like cattle, in a meadow. His heart beat high, for until that moment the only buffalo he had seen were the few which stood on the riverbanks as the raft passed down the Ohio. He would surely get a shot at one of these huge fellows.

Wetzel bade Joe do exactly as he did, whereupon he dropped on his hands and knees and began to crawl through the long grass. This was easy for the hunter, but very hard for the lad to accomplish. Still, he managed to keep his comrade in sight, which was a matter for congratulation, because the man crawled as fast as he walked. At length, after what to Joe seemed a very long time, the hunter paused.

"Are we near enough?" whispered Joe, breathlessly.

"Nope. We're just circlin' on 'em. The wind's not right, an' I'm afeered they'll get our scent."

Wetzel rose carefully and peeped over the top of the grass; then, dropping on all fours, he resumed the advance.

He paused again, presently and waited for Joe to come up.

"See here, young fellar, remember, never hurry unless the bizness calls fer speed, an' then act like lightnin'."

Thus admonishing the eager lad, Wetzel continued to crawl. It was easy for him. Joe wondered how those wide shoulders got between the weeds and grasses without breaking, or, at least, shaking them. But so it was.

"Flat now," whispered Wetzel, putting his broad hand on Joe's back and pressing him down. "Now's yer time fer good practice. Trail yer rifle over yer back—if yer careful it won't slide off—an' reach out far with one arm an' dig yer fingers in deep. Then pull yerself forrard."

Wetzel slipped through the grass like a huge buckskin snake. His long, lithe body wormed its way among the reeds. But for Joe, even with the advantage of having the hunter's trail to follow, it was difficult work. The dry reeds broke under him, and the stalks of saw grass shook. He worked persistently at it, learning all the while, and improving with every rod. He was surprised to hear a swish, followed by a dull blow on the ground. Raising his head, he looked forward. He saw the hunter wipe his tomahawk on the grass.

"Snake," whispered Wetzel.

Joe saw a huge blacksnake squirming in the grass. Its head had been severed. He caught glimpses of other snakes gliding away, and glossy round moles darting into their holes. A gray rabbit started off with a leap.

"We're near enough," whispered Wetzel, stopping behind a bush. He rose and surveyed the plain; then motioned Joe to look.

Joe raised himself on his knees. As his gaze reached the level of the grassy plain his heart leaped. Not fifty yards away was a great, shaggy, black buffalo. He was the king of the herd; but ill at ease, for he pawed the grass and shook his huge head. Near him were several cows and a half-grown calf. Beyond was the main herd, extending as far as Joe could see—a great sea of black humps! The lad breathed hard as he took in the grand sight.

"Pick out the little fellar—the reddish brown one—an' plug him behind the shoulder. Shoot close now, fer if ye miss, mebbe I can't hit one, because I'm not used to shootin' at sich small marks."

Wetzel's rare smile lighted up his dark face. Probably he could have shot a fly off the horn of the bull, if one of the big flies or bees, plainly visible as they swirled around the huge head, had alighted there.

Joe slowly raised his rifle. He had covered the calf, and was about to pull the trigger, when, with a sagacity far beyond his experience as hunter, he whispered to Wetzel:

"If I fire, they may run toward us."

"Nope; they'll run away," answered Wetzel, thinking the lad was as keen as an Indian.

Joe quickly covered the calf again, and pulled the trigger. Bellowing loud the big bull dashed off. The herd swung around toward the west, and soon were galloping off with a lumbering roar. The shaggy humps bobbed up and down like short, angry waves on a storm-blackened sea.

Upon going forward, Wetzel and Joe found the calf lying dead in the grass.

"You might hev did better'n that," remarked the hunter, as he saw where the bullet had struck. "You went a little too fer back, but mebbe that was 'cause the calf stepped as you shot."

CHAPTER XV

So the days passed swiftly, dreamily, each one bringing Joe a keener delight. In a single month he was as good a woodsman as many pioneers who had passed years on the border, for he had the advantage of a teacher whose woodcraft was incomparable. Besides, he was naturally quick in learning, and with all his interest centered upon forest lore, it was no wonder he assimilated much of Wetzel's knowledge. He was ever willing to undertake anything whereby he might learn. Often when they were miles away in the dense forest, far from their cave, he asked Wetzel to let him try to lead the way back to camp. And he never failed once, though many times he got off a straight course, thereby missing the easy traveling.

Joe did wonderfully well, but he lacked, as nearly all white men do, the subtler, intuitive forest instinct, which makes the Indian as much at home in the woods as in his teepee. Wetzel had this developed to a high degree. It was born in him. Years of training, years of passionate, unrelenting search for Indians, had given him a knowledge of the wilds that was incomprehensible to white men, and appalling to his red foes.

Joe saw how Wetzel used this ability, but what it really was baffled him. He realized that words were not adequate to explain fully this great art. Its possession required a marvelously keen vision, an eye perfectly familiar with every creature, tree, rock, shrub, and thing belonging in the forest; an eye so quick in sight as to detect instantly the slightest change in nature, or anything unnatural to that environment. The hearing must be delicate, like that of a deer, and the finer it is, the keener will be the woodsman. Lastly, there is the feeling that prompts the old hunter to say: "No game today." It is something in him that speaks when, as he sees a nighthawk circling low near the ground, he says: "A storm tomorrow." It is what makes an Indian at home in any wilderness. The clouds may hide the guiding star; the northing may be lost; there may be no moss on the trees, or difference in their bark; the ridges may be flat or lost altogether, and there may be no watercourses; yet the Indian brave always goes for his teepee, straight as a crow flies. It was this voice which rightly bade Wetzel, when he was baffled by an Indian's trail fading among the rocks, to cross, or circle, or advance in the direction taken by his wily foe.

Joe had practiced trailing deer and other hoofed game, until he was true as a hound. Then he began to perfect himself in the art of following a human being through the forest. Except a few old Indian trails, which the rain had half obliterated, he had no tracks to discover save Wetzel's, and these were as hard to find as the airy course of a grosbeak. On soft ground or marshy grass, which Wetzel avoided where he could, he left a faint trail, but on a hard surface, for all the traces he left, he might as well not have gone over the ground at all.

Joe's persistence stood him in good stead; he hung on, and the more he failed, the harder he tried. Often he would slip out of the cave after Wetzel had gone, and try to find which way he had taken. In brief, the lad became a fine marksman, a good hunter, and a close, persevering student of the wilderness. He loved the woods, and all they contained. He learned the habits of the wild creatures. Each deer, each squirrel, each grouse that he killed, taught him some lesson.

He was always up with the lark to watch the sun rise red and grand over the eastern hills, and chase away the white mist from the valleys. Even if he was not hunting, or roaming the woods, if it was necessary for him to lie low in camp awaiting Wetzel's return, he was always content. Many hours he idled away lying on his back, with the west wind blowing softly over him, his eye on the distant hills, where the cloud shadows swept across with slow, majestic movement, like huge ships at sea.

If Wetzel and Joe were far distant from the cave, as was often the case, they made camp in the open woods, and it was here that Joe's contentment was fullest. Twilight shades stealing down over the campfire; the cheery glow of red embers; the crackling of dry stocks; the sweet smell of wood smoke, all had for the lad a subtle, potent charm.

The hunter would broil a venison steak, or a partridge, on the coals. Then they would light their pipes and smoke while twilight deepened. The oppressive stillness of the early evening hour always brought to the younger man a sensation of awe. At first he attributed this to the fact that he was new to this life; however, as the days passed and the emotion remained, nay, grew stronger, he concluded it was imparted by this close communion with nature. Deep, solemn, tranquil, the gloaming hour brought him no ordinary fullness of joy and clearness of perception.

"Do you ever feel this stillness?" he asked Wetzel one evening, as they sat near their flickering fire.

The hunter puffed his pipe and like an Indian seemed to let the question take deep root.

"I've scalped redskins every hour of the day, 'ceptin' twilight," he replied.

Joe wondered no longer whether the hunter was too hardened to feel this beautiful tranquility. That hour which wooed Wetzel from his implacable pursuit was indeed a bewitching one.

There was never a time, when Joe lay alone in camp waiting for Wetzel, that he did not hope the hunter would return with information of Indians. The man never talked about the savages, and if he spoke at all it was to tell of some incident of his day's travel. One evening he came back with a large, black fox that he had killed.

"What beautiful, glossy fur!" said Joe. "I never saw a black fox before."

"I've been layin' fer this fellar some time," replied Wetzel, as he began his first evening task, that of combing his hair. "Jest back here in a clump of cottonweeds there's a holler log full of leaves. Happen' to see a blacksnake sneakin' round, I thought mebbe he was up to somethin', so I investigated, an' found a nest full of young rabbits. I killed the snake, an' arter that took an interest in 'em. Every time I passed I'd look in at the bunnies, an' each time I seen signs that some tarnal varmint had been prowlin' round. One day I missed a bunny, an' next day another; so on until only one was left, a peart white and gray little scamp. Somethin' was stealin' of 'em, and it made me mad. So yistidday an' today I watched, an' finally I plugged this black thief. Yes, he's got a glossy coat; but he's a bad un for all his fine looks. These black foxes are bigger, stronger an' cunniner than red ones. In every litter you'll find a dark one, the black sheep of the family. Because he grows so much faster, an' steals all the food from the others, the mother jest takes him by the nape of the neck an' chucks him out in the world to shift fer hisself. An' it's a good thing."

The next day Wetzel told Joe that they would go across

country to seek new game fields. Accordingly the two set out and tramped industriously until evening. They came upon a country no less beautiful than the one they had left though the picturesque cliffs and rugged hills had given way to a rolling land, the luxuriance of which was explained by the abundant springs and streams. Forests and fields were thickly interspersed with bubbling springs, narrow and deep streams and here and there a small lake with a running outlet.

Wetzel had said little concerning this region, but that little was enough to rouse all Joe's eagerness, for it was to the effect that they were now in a country much traversed by Indians, especially runners and hunting parties traveling from north to south. The hunter explained that through the center of this tract ran a buffalo road; that the buffalo always picked out the straightest, lowest, and dryest path from one range to another, and the Indians followed these first pathfinders.

Joe and Wetzel made camp on the bank of a stream that night, and as the lad watched the hunter build a hidden campfire, he peered furtively around, half expecting to see dark forms scurrying through the forest. Wetzel was extremely cautious. He stripped pieces of bark from fallen trees and built a little hut over his firewood. He rubbed some powder on a piece of punk, and then with flint and steel dropped two or three sparks on the inflammable substance. Soon he had a blaze. He arranged the covering so that not a ray of light escaped. When the flames had subsided, and the wood had burned down to a glowing bed of red, he threw aside the bark, and broiled the strips of venison they had brought with them.

They rested on a bed of boughs which they had cut and arranged alongside a huge log. For hours Joe lay awake; he could not sleep. He listened to the breeze rustling the leaves, and shivered at the thought of the sighing wind he had once heard moan through the forest. Presently he turned over. The slight noise instantly awakened Wetzel, who lifted his dark face while he listened intently. He spoke one word: "Sleep," and lay back again on the leaves. Joe forced himself to be quiet, relaxed all his muscles, and soon slumbered.

On the morrow Wetzel went out to look over the hunting prospects. About noon he returned. Joe was surprised to find some slight change in the hunter. He could not tell what it was.

"I seen Injun sign," said Wetzel. "There's no tellin' how soon we may run agin the sneaks. We can't hunt here. Like as not there's Hurons and Delawares skulkin' round. I think I'd better take you back to the village."

"It's all on my account you say that," said Joe.

"Sure," Wetzel replied.

"If you were alone what would you do?"

"I calkilate I'd hunt fer some redskinned game."

The supreme moment had come. Joe's heart beat hard. He could not miss this opportunity; he must stay with the hunter. He looked closely at Wetzel.

"I won't go back to the village," he said.

The hunter stood in his favorite position, leaning on his long rifle, and made no response.

"I won't go," continued Joe, earnestly. "Let me stay with you. If at any time I hamper you, or cannot keep the pace, then leave me to shift for myself; but don't make me go until I weaken. Let me stay."

Fire and fearlessness spoke in Joe's every word, and his gray eyes contracted with their peculiar steely flash. Plain it was that, while he might fail to keep pace with Wetzel he did not fear this dangerous country, and, if it must be, would face it alone.

Wetzel extended his broad hand and gave his comrade's a viselike squeeze. To allow the lad to remain with him was more than he would have done for any other person in the world. Far better to keep the lad under his protection while it was possible, for Joe was taking that war trail which had for every hunter, somewhere along its bloody course, a bullet, a knife, or a tomahawk. Wetzel knew that Joe was conscious of this inevitable conclusion, for it showed in his white face, and in the resolve in his big, gray eyes.

So there, in the shade of a towering oak, the Indian killer admitted the boy into his friendship and into a life which would no longer be play, but eventful, stirring, hazardous.

"Wal, lad, stay," he said, with that rare smile which brightened his dark face like a ray of stray sunshine. "We'll hang round these diggin's a few days. First off, we'll take in the lay of the land. You go downstream a ways an' scout round some, while I go up, an' then circle down. Move slow, now, an' don't miss nothin'."

Joe followed the stream a mile or more. He kept close in the shade of willows, and never walked across an open glade without first waiting and watching. He listened to all sounds; but none were unfamiliar. He closely examined the sand along the stream, and the moss and leaves under the trees. When he had been separated from Wetzel several hours, and concluded he would slowly return to camp, he ran across a well-beaten path winding through the forest. This was, perhaps, one of the bridle trails Wetzel had referred to. He bent over the worn grass with keen scrutiny.

Crack!

The loud report of a heavily charged rifle rang out. Joe felt the zip of a bullet as it fanned his cheek. With an agile leap he gained the shelter of a tree, from behind which he peeped to see who had shot at him. He was just in time to detect the dark form of an Indian dart behind the foliage a hundred yards down the path. Joe expected to see other Indians, and to hear more shots, but he was mistaken. Evidently the savage was alone, for the tree Joe had taken refuge behind was scarcely large enough to screen his body, which disadvantage the other Indians would have been quick to note.

Joe closely watched the place where his assailant had disappeared, and presently saw a dark hand, then a naked elbow, and finally the ramrod of a rifle. The savage was reloading. Soon a rifle barrel protruded from behind the tree. With his heart beating like a triphammer, and the skin tightening on his face, Joe screened his body as best he might. The tree was small, but it served as a partial protection. Rapidly he revolved in his mind plans to outwit the enemy. The Indian was behind a large oak with a low limb over which he could fire without exposing his own person to danger.

"Bang!" The Indian's rifle bellowed; the bullet crumbled the bark close to Joe's face. The lad yelled loudly, staggered to his knees, and then fell into the path, where he lay quiet.

The redskin gave an exultant shout. Seeing that the fallen figure remained quite motionless he stepped forward, drawing his knife as he came. He was a young brave, quick and eager in his movements, and came nimbly up the path to gain his coveted trophy, the paleface's scalp.

Suddenly Joe sat up, raised his rifle quickly as thought, and fired point-blank at the Indian.

But he missed.

The redskin stopped aghast when he saw the lad thus seemingly come back to life. Then, realizing that Joe's aim had been futile, he bounded forward, brandishing his knife, and uttering infuriated yells.

Joe rose to his feet with rifle swung high above his head.

When the savage was within twenty feet, so near that his dark face, swollen with fierce passion, could be plainly discerned, a peculiar whistling noise sounded over Joe's shoulder. It was accompanied, rather than followed, by a clear, ringing rifle shot.

The Indian stopped as if he had encountered a heavy shock from a tree or stone barring his way. Clutching at his breast, he uttered a weird cry, and sank slowly on the grass.

Joe ran forward to bend over the prostrate figure. The Indian, a slender, handsome young brave, had been shot through the breast. He held his hand tightly over the wound, while bright red blood trickled between his fingers, flowed down his side and stained the grass.

The brave looked steadily up at Joe. Shot as he was, dying as he knew himself to be, there was no yielding in the dark eyes—only an unquenchable hatred. Then the eyes glazed; the fingers ceased twitching.

Joe was bending over a dead Indian.

It flashed into his mind, of course, that Wetzel had come up in time to save his life, but he did not dwell on the thought; he shrank from this violent death of a human being. But it was from the aspect of the dead, not from remorse for the deed. His heart beat fast, his fingers trembled, yet he felt only a strange coldness in all his being. The savage had tried to kill him, perhaps, even now, had it not been for the hunter's unerring aim, would have been gloating over a bloody scalp.

Joe felt, rather than heard, the approach of someone, and he turned to see Wetzel coming down the path.

"He's a lone Shawnee runner," said the hunter, gazing down at the dead Indian. "He was tryin' to win his eagle plumes. I seen you both from the hillside."

"You did!" exclaimed Joe. Then he laughed. "It was lucky for me. I tried the dodge you taught me, but in my eagerness I missed."

"Wal, you hadn't no call fer hurry. You worked the trick clever, but you missed him when there was plenty of time. I had to shoot over your shoulder, or I'd hev plugged him sooner."

"Where were you?" asked Joe.

"Up there by that bit of sumach!" and Wetzel pointed to an open ridge on a hillside not less than one hundred and fifty yards distant.

Joe wondered which of the two bullets, the death-seeking one fired by the savage, or the life-saving missile from Wetzel's fatal weapon, had passed nearest to him.

"Come," said the hunter, after he had scalped the Indian.

"What's to be done with this savage?" inquired Joe, as Wetzel started up the path.

"Let him lay."

They returned to camp without further incident. While the hunter busied himself reinforcing their temporary shelter—for the clouds looked threatening—Joe cut up some buffalo meat, and then went down to the brook for a gourd of water. He came hurriedly back to where Wetzel was working, and spoke in a voice which he vainly endeavored to hold steady:

"Come quickly. I have seen something which may mean a good deal."

He led the way down to the brookside.

"Look!" Joe said, pointing at the water.

Here the stream was about two feet deep, perhaps twenty wide, and had just a noticeable current. Shortly before, it had been as clear as a bright summer sky; it was now tinged with yellow clouds that slowly floated downstream, each one enlarging and becoming fainter as the clear water permeated and stained. Grains of sand glided along with the current, little pieces of bark floated on the surface, and minnows darted to and fro nibbling at these drifting particles.

"Deer wouldn't roil the water like that. What does it mean?" asked Joe.

"Injuns, an' not fer away."

Wetzel returned to the shelter and tore it down. Then he bent the branch of a beech tree low over the place. He pulled down another branch over the remains of the campfire. These precautions made the spot less striking. Wetzel knew that an Indian scout never glances casually; his roving eyes survey the forest, perhaps quickly, but thoroughly. An unnatural position of bush or log always leads to an examination.

This done, the hunter grasped Joe's hand and led him up the knoll. Making his way behind a well-screened tree, which had been uprooted, he selected a position where, hidden themselves, they could see the creek.

Hardly had Wetzel admonished Joe to lie perfectly still, when from a short distance up the stream came the sound of splashing water; but nothing could be seen above the open glade, as in that direction willows lined the creek in dense thickets. The noise grew more audible.

Suddenly Joe felt a muscular contraction pass over the powerful frame lying close beside him. It was a convulsive thrill such as passes through a tiger when he is about to spring upon his quarry. So subtle and strong was its meaning, so clearly did it convey to the lad what was coming, that he felt it himself; save that in his case it was a cold, chill shudder.

Breathless suspense followed. Then into the open space along the creek glided a tall Indian warrior. He was knee-deep in the water, where he waded with slow, cautious steps. His garish, befrilled costume seemed familiar to Joe. He carried a rifle at a low trail, and passed slowly ahead with evident distrust. The lad believed he recognized that head, with its tangled black hair, and when he saw the swarthy, villainous countenance turned full toward him, he exclaimed:

"Girty! By—"

Wetzel's powerful arm forced him so hard against the log that he could not complete the exclamation; but he could still see. Girty had not heard that stifled cry, for he continued his slow wading, and presently his tall, gaudily decorated form passed out of sight.

Another savage appeared in the open space, and then another. Close between them walked a white man, with hands bound behind him. The prisoner and guards disappeared downstream among the willows.

The splashing continued—grew even louder than before. A warrior came into view, then another, and another. They walked close together. Two more followed. They were wading by the side of a raft made of several logs, upon which were two prostrate figures that closely resembled human beings.

Joe was so intent upon the lithe forms of the Indians that he barely got a glimpse of their floating prize, whatever it might have been. Bringing up the rear was an athletic warrior, whose broad shoulders, sinewy arms, and shaved, polished head Joe remembered well. It was the Shawnee chief, Silvertip.

When he, too, passed out of sight in the curve of willows, Joe found himself trembling. He turned eagerly to Wetzel; but instantly recoiled.

Terrible, indeed, had been the hunter's transformation. All calmness of facial expression was gone; he was now stern, somber. An intense emotion was visible in his white face; his eyes seemed reduced to two dark shining points, and they emitted so fierce, so piercing a flash, so deadly a light, that Joe could not bear their glittering gaze.

"Three white captives, two of 'em women," muttered the hunter, as if weighing in his mind the importance of this fact.

"Were those women on the raft?" questioned Joe, and as Wetzel nodded, he continued. "A white man and two women, six warriors, Silvertip, and that renegade, Jim Girty!"

Wetzel deigned not to answer Joe's passionate outburst, but maintained silence and his rigid posture. Joe glanced once more at the stern face.

"Considering we'd go after Girty and his redskins if they were alone, we're pretty likely to go quicker now that they've got white women prisoners, eh?" And Joe laughed fiercely between his teeth.

The lad's heart expanded, while along every nerve tingled an exquisite thrill of excitement. He had yearned for wild, border life. Here he was in it, with the hunter whose name alone was to the savages a symbol for all that was terrible.

Wetzel evidently decided quickly on what was to be done, for in few words he directed Joe to cut up so much of the buffalo meat as they could stow in their pockets. Then bidding the lad to follow, he turned into the woods, walking rapidly, and stopping now and then for a brief instant. Soon they emerged from the forest into more open country. They faced a wide plain skirted on the right by a long, winding strip of bright green willows which marked the course of the stream. On the edge of this plain Wetzel broke into a run. He kept this pace for a distance of a hundred yards, then stopped to listen intently as he glanced sharply on all sides, after which he was off again.

Halfway across this plain Joe's wind began to fail, and his breathing became labored; but he kept close to the hunter's heels. Once he looked back to see a great wide expanse of waving grass. They had covered perhaps four miles at a rapid pace, and were nearing the other side of the plain. The lad felt as if his head was about to burst; a sharp pain seized upon his side; a blood-red film obscured his sight. He kept doggedly on, and when utterly exhausted fell to the ground.

When, a few minutes later, having recovered his breath, he got up, they had crossed the plain and were in a grove of beeches. Directly in front of him ran a swift stream, which was divided at the rocky head of what appeared to be a wooded island. There was only a slight ripple and fall of the water, and, after a second glance, it was evident that the point of land was not an island, but a portion of the mainland which divided the stream. The branches took almost opposite courses.

Joe wondered if they had headed off the Indians. Certainly they had run fast enough. He was wet with perspiration. He glanced at Wetzel, who was standing near. The man's broad breast rose and fell a little faster; that was the only evidence of exertion. The lad had a painful feeling that he could never keep pace with the hunter, if this five-mile run was a sample of the speed he would be forced to maintain.

"They've got ahead of us, but which crick did they take?" queried Wetzel, as though debating the question with himself.

"How do you know they've passed?"

"We circled," answered Wetzel, as he shook his head

and pointed into the bushes. Joe stepped over and looked into the thicket. He found a quantity of dead leaves, sticks, and litter thrown aside, exposing to light a long, hollowed place on the ground. It was what would be seen after rolling over a log that had lain for a long time. Little furrows in the ground, holes, mounds, and curious winding passages showed where grubs and crickets had made their homes. The frightened insects were now running round wildly.

"What was here? A log?"

"A twenty-foot canoe was hid under thet stuff. The Injuns has taken one of these streams."

"How can we tell which one?"

"Mebbe we can't; but we'll try. Grab up a few of them bugs, go below thet rocky point, an' crawl close to the bank so you can jest peep over. Be keerful not to show the tip of your head, an' don't knock nothin' off'n the bank into the water. Watch fer trout. Look everywhere, an' drop in a bug now and then. I'll do the same fer the other stream. Then we'll come back here an' talk over what the fish has to say about the Injuns."

Joe walked downstream a few paces, and, dropping on his knees, crawled carefully to the edge of the bank. He slightly parted the grass so he could peep through, and found himself directly over a pool with a narrow shoal running out from the opposite bank. The water was so clear he could see the pebbly bottom in all parts, except a dark hole near the bend in the shore close by. He did not see a living thing in the water, not a crawfish, turtle, nor even a frog. He peered round closely, then flipped in one of the bugs he had brought along. A shiny yellow fish flared up from the depths of the deep hole and disappeared with the cricket; but it was a bass or a pike, not a trout. Wetzel had said there were a few trout living near the cool springs of these streams. The lad tried again to coax one to the surface. This time the more fortunate cricket swam and hopped across the stream to safety.

When Joe's eyes were thoroughly accustomed to the clear water, with its deceiving lights and shades, he saw a fish lying snug under the side of a stone. The lad thought he recognized the snub-nose, the hooked, wolfish jaw, but he could not get sufficient of a view to classify him. He crawled to a more advantageous position farther downstream, and then he peered again through the weeds. Yes, sure enough, he had espied a trout. He well knew those spotted silver sides, that broad, square tail. Such a monster! In his admiration for the fellow, and his wish for a hook and line to try conclusions with him, Joe momentarily forgot his object. Remembering, he tossed out a big, fat cricket, which alighted on the water just above the fish. The trout never moved, nor even blinked. The lad tried again, with no better success. The fish would not rise. Thereupon Joe returned to the point where he had left Wetzel.

"I couldn't see nothin' over there," said the hunter, who was waiting. "Did you see any?"

"One, and a big fellow."

"Did he see you?"

"No."

"Did he rise to a bug?"

"No, he didn't; but then maybe he wasn't hungry," answered Joe, who could not understand what Wetzel was driving at.

"Tell me exactly what he did."

"That's just the trouble; he didn't do anything," replied Joe, thoughtfully. "He just lay, stifflike, under a stone. He never batted an eye. But his side fins quivered like an aspen leaf."

"Them side fins tell us the story. Girty an' his redskins

hev took this branch," said Wetzel, positively. "The other leads to the Huron towns. Girty's got a place near the Delaware camp somewheres. I've tried to find it a good many times. He's took more'n one white lass there, an' nobody ever seen her agin."

"Fiend! To think of a white woman, maybe a girl like Nell Wells, at the mercy of those red devils!"

"Young fellar, don't go wrong. I'll allow Injuns is bad enough; but I never hearn tell of one abusin' a white woman, as mayhap you mean. Injuns marry white women sometimes; kill an' scalp 'em often, but that's all. It's men of our own color, renegades like this Girty, as do worse'n murder."

Here was the amazing circumstance of Lewis Wetzel, the acknowledged unsatiable foe of all redmen, speaking a good word for his enemies. Joe was so astonished he did not attempt to answer.

"Here's where they got in the canoe. One more look, an' then we're off," said Wetzel. He strode up and down the sandy beach; examined the willows, and scrutinized the sand. Suddenly he bent over and picked up an object from the water. His sharp eyes had caught the glint of something white, which, upon being examined, proved to be a small ivory or bone buckle with a piece broken out. He showed it to Joe.

"By heavens! Wetzel, that's a buckle off Nell Wells' shoe. I've seen it too many times to mistake it."

"I was afraid Girty hed your friends, the sisters, an' mebbe your brother, too. Jack Zane said the renegade was hangin' round the village, an' that couldn't be fer no good."

"Come on. Let's kill the fiend!" cried Joe, white to the lips.

"I calkilate they're about a mile downstream, makin' camp fer the night. I know the place. There's a fine spring, an', look! D'ye see them crows flyin' round the big oak with the bleached top? Hear them cawin'? You might think they was chasin' a hawk, or king birds were arter 'em, but thet fuss the're makin' is because they see Injuns."

"Well?" asked Joe, impatiently.

"It'll be moonlight a while arter midnight. We'll lay low an' wait, an' then——"

The sharp click of his teeth, like the snap of a steel trap, completed the sentence. Joe said no more, but followed the hunter into the woods. Stopping near a fallen tree Wetzel raked up a bundle of leaves and spread them on the ground. Then he cut a few spreading branches from a beech, and leaned them against a log. Bidding the lad crawl in before him, he took one last look around and then made his way under the shelter.

It was yet daylight, which seemed a strange time to creep into this little nook; but, Joe thought, it was not to sleep, only to wait, wait, wait for the long hours to pass. He was amazed once more, because, by the time twilight had given place to darkness, Wetzel was asleep. The lad said then to himself that he would never again be surprised at the hunter. He assumed once and for all that Wetzel was capable of anything. Yet how could he lose himself in slumber? Feeling, as he must, over the capture of the girls; eager to draw a bead on the black-hearted renegade; hating Indians with all his soul and strength and lying there but a few hours before what he knew would be a bloody battle, Wetzel calmly went to sleep. Knowing the hunter to be as bloodthirsty as a tiger, Joe had expected he would rush to a combat with his foes, but, no, this man with his keen sagacity, knew when to creep upon his enemy; he bided that time, and, while he waited, slept.

Joe could not close his eyes in slumber. Through the interstices in the branches he saw the stars come out one by one, the darkness deepened, and the dim outline of tall trees over the dark hill came out sharply. The moments dragged. Each one an hour. He heard a whippoorwill call, lonely and dismal; then an owl hoot monotonously. A stealthy footed animal ran along the log, sniffed at the boughs, and then scurried away over the dry leaves. By and by the dead silence of night fell over all. Still Joe lay there wide awake, listening—his heart on fire. He was about to rescue Nell; to kill the hawk-nosed renegade; to fight Silvertip to the death.

The hours passed, but not Joe's passionate eagerness. When at last he saw the crescent moon gleam silver-white over the black hilltop he knew the time was nigh, and over him ran thrill on thrill.

CHAPTER XVI

When the waning moon rose high enough to shed a pale light over forest and field, two dark figures, moving silently from the shade of the trees, crossed the moonlit patches of ground, out to the open plain where low on the grass hung silver mists.

A timber wolf, gray and gaunt, came loping along with lowered nose. A new scent brought the animal to a standstill. His nose went up, his fiery eyes scanned the plain. Two men had invaded his domain, and with a short, dismal bark, he dashed away.

Like spectres, gliding swiftly with noiseless tread, the two vanished. The long grass had swallowed them.

Deserted once again seemed the plain. It became unutterably lonely. No stir, no sound, no life; nothing but a wide expanse bathed in sad, gray light.

The moon shone steadily; the silver radiance mellowed, the stars paled before this brighter glory.

Slowly the night hours wore away.

On the other side of the plain, near where the adjoining forest loomed darkling, the tall grass parted to disclose a black form. Was it only a deceiving shade cast by a leafy branch—only a shadow? Slowly it sank, and was lost. Once more the gray, unwavering line of silver-crested grass tufts was unbroken.

Only the night breeze, wandering caressingly over the

grass, might have told of two dark forms gliding, gliding, gliding so softly, so surely, so surely toward the forest. Only the moon and the pale stars had eyes to see these creeping figures.

Like avengers they moved, on a mission to slay and to save!

On over the dark line where plain merged into forest they crawled. No whispering, no hesitating; but a silent, slow, certain progress showed their purpose. In single file they slipped over the moss, the leader clearing the path. Inch by inch they advanced. Tedious was this slow movement, difficult and painful this journey which must end in lightninglike speed. They rustled no leaf, nor snapped a twig, nor shook a fern, but passed onward slowly, like the approach of Death. The seconds passed as minutes; minutes as hours; an entire hour was spent in advancing twenty feet!

At last the top of the knoll was reached. The Avenger placed his hand on his follower's shoulder. The strong pressure was meant to remind, to warn, to reassure. Then, like a huge snake, the first glided away.

He who was left behind raised his head to look into the open place, called the glade of the Beautiful Spring. An oval space lay before him, exceedingly lovely in the moonlight; a spring, as if a pearl, gemmed the center. An Indian guard stood statuelike against a stone. Other savages lay in a row, their polished heads shining. One slumbering form was bedecked with feathers and frills. Near him lay an Indian blanket, from the border of which peeped two faces, gleaming white and sad in the pitying moonlight.

The watcher quivered at the sight of those pale faces; but he must wait while long moments passed. He must wait for the Avenger to creep up, silently kill the guard, and release the prisoners without awakening the savages. If that plan failed, he was to rush into the glade, and in the excitement make off with one of the captives.

He lay there waiting, listening, wrought up to the intensest pitch of fierce passion. Every nerve was alert, every tendon strung, and every muscle strained ready for the leap.

Only the faint rustling of leaves, the low swish of swaying branches, the soft murmur of falling water, and over all the sigh of the night wind, proved to him that this picture was not an evil dream. His gaze sought the quiet figures, lingered hopefully on the captives, menacingly on the sleeping savages, and glowered over the gaudily arrayed form. His glance sought the upright guard, as he stood a dark blot against the gray stone. He saw the Indian's plume, a single feather waving silver-white. Then it became riveted on the bubbling, refulgent spring. The pool was round, perhaps five feet across, and shone like a burnished shield. It mirrored the moon, the twinkling stars, the spectre trees.

An unaccountable horror suddenly swept over the watching man. His hair stood straight up; a sensation as of cold stole chilling over him. Whether it was the climax of this long night's excitement, or anticipation of the bloody struggle soon to come, he knew not. Did this boiling spring, shimmering in the silver moon rays, hold in its murky depths a secret? Did these lonesome, shadowing trees, with their sad, drooping branches, harbor a mystery? If a future tragedy was to be enacted here in this quiet glade, could the murmuring water or leaves whisper its portent? No; they were only silent, only unintelligible with nature's mystery.

The waiting man cursed himself for a craven coward; he fought back the benumbing sense; he steeled his heart.

Was this his vaunted willingness to share the Avenger's danger? His strong spirit rose up in arms; once more he was brave and fierce.

He fastened a piercing gaze on the plumed guard. The Indian's lounging posture against the rock was the same as it had been before, yet now it seemed to have a kind of strained attention. The savage's head was poised, like that of a listening deer. The wary Indian scented danger.

A faint moan breathed low above the sound of gently splashing water somewhere beyond the glade.

"Woo-o-oo."

The guard's figure stiffened, and became rigidly erect; his blanket slowly slid to his feet.

"Ah-oo-o," sighed the soft breeze in the treetops.

Louder then, with a deep wail, a moan arose out of the dark gray shadows, swelled thrilling on the still air, and died away mournfully.

"Um-m-mmwoo-o-o-o!"

The sentinel's form melted into the shade. He was gone like a phantom.

Another Indian rose quietly, and glanced furtively around the glade. He bent over a comrade and shook him. Instantly the second Indian was on his feet. Scarcely had he gained a standing posture when an object, bounding like a dark ball, shot out of the thicket and hurled both warriors to the earth. A moonbeam glinted upon something bright. It flashed again on a swift, sweeping circle. A short, choking yell aroused the other savages. Up they sprang, alarmed, confused.

The shadow form darted among them. It moved with inconceivable rapidity; it became a monster. Terrible was the convulsive conflict. Dull blows, the click of steel, angry shouts, agonized yells, and thrashing, wrestling sounds mingled together and half drowned by an awful roar like that of a mad bull. The strife ceased as suddenly as it had begun. Warriors lay still on the grass; others writhed in agony. For an instant a fleeting shadow crossed the open lane leading out of the glade; then it vanished.

Three savages had sprung toward their rifles. A blinding flash, a loud report burst from the thicket overhead. The foremost savage sank lifelessly. The others were intercepted by a giant shadow with brandished rifle. The watcher on the knoll had entered the glade. He stood before the stacked rifles and swung his heavy gun. Crash! An Indian went down before that sweep, but rose again. The savages backed away from this threatening figure, and circled around it.

The noise of the other conflict ceased. More savages joined the three who glided to and fro before their desperate foe. They closed in upon him, only to be beaten back. One savage threw a glittering knife, another hurled a stone, a third flung his tomahawk, which struck fire from the swinging rifle.

He held them at bay. While they had no firearms he was master of the situation. With every sweep of his arms he brought the long rifle down and knocked a flint from the firelock of an enemy's weapon. Soon the Indians' guns were useless. Slowly then he began to edge away from the stone, toward the opening where he had seen the fleeing form vanish.

His intention was to make a dash for life, for he had heard a noise behind the rock, and remembered the guard.

He saw the savages glance behind him, and anticipated danger from that direction, but he must not turn. A second there might be fatal. He backed defiantly along the rock until he gained its outer edge. But too late! The Indians glided before him, now behind him; he was surrounded. He turned around and around, with the ever-circling rifle whirling in the faces of the baffled foe.

Once opposite the lane leading from the glade he changed his tactics, and plunged with fierce impetuosity into the midst of the painted throng. Then began a fearful conflict. The Indians fell before the sweep of his powerful arms; but grappled with him from the ground. He literally plowed his way through the struggling mass, warding off a hundred vicious blows. Savage after savage he flung off, until at last he had a clear path before him. Freedom lay beyond that shiny path. Into it he bounded.

As he left the glade the plumed guard stepped from behind a tree near the entrance of the path, and cast his tomahawk.

A white, glittering flash, it flew after the fleeing runner; its aim was true.

Suddenly the moonlight path darkened in the runner's sight; he saw a million flashing stars; a terrible pain assailed him; he sank slowly, slowly down; then all was darkness.

CHAPTER XVII

J oe awoke as from a fearsome nightmare. Returning consciousness brought a vague idea that he had been dreaming of clashing weapons, of yelling savages, of a conflict in which he had been clutched by sinewy fingers. An acute pain pulsed through his temples; a bloody mist glazed his eyes; a sore pressure cramped his arms and legs. Surely he dreamed this distress, as well as the fight. The red film cleared from his eyes. His wandering gaze showed the stern reality.

The bright sun, making the dewdrops glisten on the leaves, lighted up a tragedy. Near him lay an Indian whose vacant, sightless eyes were fixed in death. Beyond lay four more savages, the peculiar, inert position of whose limbs, the formlessness, as it were, as if they had been thrown from a great height and never moved again, attested that here, too, life had been extinguished. Joe took only one detail—the cloven skull of the nearest—when he turned away sickened. He remembered it all now. The advance, the rush, the fight—all returned. He saw again Wetzel's shadowy form darting like a demon into the whirl of conflict; he heard again that hoarse, booming roar with which the Avenger accompanied his blows. Joe's gaze swept the glade, but found no trace of the hunter.

He saw Silvertip and another Indian bathing a wound

on Girty's head. The renegade groaned and writhed in pain. Near him lay Kate, with white face and closed eyes. She was unconscious or dead. Jim sat crouched under a tree to which he was tied.

"Joe, are you badly hurt?" asked the latter, in deep solicitude.

"No, I guess not; I don't know," answered Joe." Is poor Kate dead?"

"No, she has fainted."

"Where is Nell?"

"Gone," replied Jim, lowering his voice, and glancing at the Indians. They were too busy trying to bandage Girty's head to pay any attention to their prisoners. "That whirlwind was Wetzel, wasn't it?"

"Yes; how'd you know?"

"I was awake last night. I had an oppressive feeling, perhaps a presentiment. Anyway, I couldn't sleep. I heard that wind blow through the forest, and thought my blood would freeze. The moan is the same as the night wind, the same soft sigh, only louder and somehow pregnant with superhuman power. To speak of it in broad daylight one seems superstitious, but to hear it in the darkness of this lonely forest, it is fearful! I hope I am not a coward; I certainly know I was deathly frightened. No wonder I was scared! Look at these dead Indians, all killed in a moment. I heard the moan; I saw Silvertip disappear, and the other two savages rise. Then something huge dropped from the rock; a bright object seemed to circle round the savages; they uttered one short yell, and sank to rise no more. Somehow at once I suspected that this shadowy form, with its lightninglike movements, its glittering hatchet, was Wetzel. When he plunged into the midst of the other savages I distinctly recognized him, and saw that he had a bundle, possibly his coat, wrapped round his left arm, and his right hand held the glittering tomahawk. I saw him strike that big Indian there, the one lying with split skull. His wonderful daring and quickness seemed to make the savages turn at random. He broke through the circle, swung Nell under his arm, slashed at my bonds as he passed by, and then was gone as he had come. Not until after you were struck, and Silvertip came up to me, was I aware my bonds were cut. Wetzel's hatchet had severed them; it even cut my side, which was bleeding. I was free to help, to fight, and I did not know it. Fool that I am!"

"I made an awful mess of my part of the rescue," groaned Joe. "I wonder if the savages know it was Wetzel."

"Do they? Well, I rather think so. Did you not hear them scream that French name? As far as I am able to judge, only two Indians were killed instantly. The others died during the night. I had to sit there, tied and helpless, listening as they groaned and called the name of their slayer, even in their death throes. Deathwind! They have named him well."

"I guess he nearly killed Girty."

"Evidently, but surely the evil one protects the renegade."

"Jim Girty's doomed," whispered Joe, earnestly. "He's as good as dead already. I've lived with Wetzel, and know him. He told me Girty had murdered a settler, a feeble old man, who lived near Fort Henry with his son. The hunter swore to kill the renegade; but mind you, he did not tell me that. I saw it in his eyes. It wouldn't surprise me to see him jump out of these bushes any moment. I'm looking for it. If he knows there are only three left, he'll be after them like a hound on a trail. Girty must hurry. Where's he taking you?"

"To the Delaware town."

"I don't suppose the chiefs will let any harm befall you; but Kate and I would be better off dead. If we can only delay the march, Wetzel will surely return."

"Hush! Girty's up."

The renegade staggered to an upright position, and leaned on the Shawnee's arm. Evidently he had not been seriously injured, only stunned. Covered with blood from a swollen, gashed lump on his temple, he certainly presented a savage appearance.

"Where's the yellow-haired lass?" he demanded, pushing away Silvertip's friendly arm. He glared around the glade. The Shawnee addressed him briefly, whereupon he raged to and fro under the tree, cursing with foam-flecked lips, and actually howling with baffled rage. His fury was so great that he became suddenly weak, and was compelled to sit down.

"She's safe, you villainous renegade!" cried Joe.

"Hush, Joe! Do not anger him. It can do no good," interposed Jim.

"Why not? We couldn't be worse off," answered Joe.

"I'll git her, I'll git her agin," panted Girty. "I'll keep her, an' she'll love me."

The spectacle of this perverted wretch speaking as if he had been cheated out of love was so remarkable, so pitiful, so monstrous, that for a moment Joe was dumfounded.

"Bah! You white-livered murderer!" Joe hissed. He well knew it was not wise to give way to his passion; but he could not help it. This beast in human guise, whining for love, maddened him. "Any white woman on earth would die a thousand deaths and burn for a million years afterward rather than love you!"

"I'll see you killed at the stake, beggin' for mercy, an' be feed fer buzzards," croaked the renegade.

"Then kill me now, or you may slip up in one of your cherished buzzard-feasts," cried Joe, with glinting eye and taunting voice. "Then go sneaking back to your hole like a hyena, and stay there. Wetzel is on your trail! He missed you last night; but it was because of the girl. He's after you, Girty; he'll get you one of these days, and when he does—My God!——"

Nothing could be more revolting than that swarthy, evil face turned pale with fear. Girty's visage was a ghastly, livid white. So earnest, so intense was Joe's voice, that it seemed to all as if Wetzel was about to dart into the glade, with his avenging tomahawk uplifted to wreak an awful vengeance on the abductor. The renegade's white, craven heart contained no such thing as courage. If he ever fought it was like a wolf, backed by numbers. The resemblance ceased here, for even a cornered wolf will show his teeth, and Girty, driven to bay, would have cringed and cowered. Even now at the mention of Wetzel's enmity he trembled.

"I'll shet yer wind," he cried, catching up his tomahawk and making for Joe.

Silvertip intervened, and prevented the assault. He led Girty back to his seat and spoke low, evidently trying to soothe the renegade's feelings.

"Silvertip, give me a tomahawk, and let me fight him," implored Joe.

"Paleface brave—like Injun chief. Paleface Shawnee's prisoner—no speak more," answered Silvertip, with respect in his voice.

"Oh, where's Nellie?"

A grief-stricken whisper caught Jim's ear. He turned to see Kate's wide, questioning eyes fixed upon him.

"Nell was rescued."

"Thank God!" murmured the girl.

"Come along," shouted Girty, in his harsh voice, as, grasping Kate's arm, he pulled the girl violently to her feet. Then, picking up his rifle, he led her into the forest. Silvertip followed with Joe, while the remaining Indian guarded Jim.

The great council lodge of the Delawares rang with savage and fiery eloquence. Wingenund paced slowly before the orators. Wise as he was, he wanted advice before deciding what was to be done with the missionary. The brothers had been taken to the chief, who immediately called council. The Indians sat in a half circle around the lodge. The prisoners, with hands bound, guarded by two brawny braves, stood in one corner gazing with curiosity and apprehension at this formidable array. Jim knew some of the braves, but the majority of those who spoke bitterly against the palefaces had never frequented the Village of Peace. Nearly all were of the Wolf tribe of Delawares. Jim whispered to Joe, interpreting that part of the speeches bearing upon the disposal to be made of them. Two white men, dressed in Indian garb, held prominent positions before Wingenund. The boys saw a resemblance between one of these men and Jim Girty, and accordingly concluded he was the famous renegade, or so-called White Indian, Simon Girty. The other man was probably Elliott, the Tory, with whom Girty had deserted from Fort Pitt. Jim Girty was not present. Upon nearing the encampment he had taken his captive and disappeared in a ravine.

Shingiss, seldom in favor of drastic measures with prisoners, eloquently urged initiating the brothers into the tribe. Several other chiefs were favorably inclined, though not so positive as Shingiss. Kotoxen was for the death penalty; the implacable Pipe for nothing less than burning at the stake. Not one was for returning the missionary to his Christian Indians. Girty and Elliott, though requested to speak, maintained an ominous silence.

Wingenund strode with thoughtful mien before his council. He had heard all his wise chiefs and his fiery warriors. Supreme was his power. Freedom or death for the captives awaited the wave of his hand. His impassive face gave not the slightest inkling of what to expect. Therefore the prisoners were forced to stand there with throbbing hearts while the chieftain waited the customary dignified interval before addressing the council.

"Wingenund has heard the Delaware wise men and warriors. The White Indian opens not his lips; his silence broods evil for the palefaces. Pipe wants the blood of the white men; the Shawnee chief demands the stake. Wingenund says free the white father who harms no Indian. Wingenund hears no evil in the music of his voice. The white father's brother should die. Kill the companion of Deathwind!"

A plaintive murmur, remarkable when coming from an assembly of stern-browed chiefs, ran round the circle at the mention of the dread appellation.

"The white father is free," continued Wingenund. "Let one of my runners conduct him to the Village of Peace."

A brave entered and touched Jim on the shoulder.

Jim shook his head and pointed to Joe. The runner touched Joe.

"No, no. I am not the missionary," cried Joe, staring aghast at his brother. "Jim, have you lost your senses?"

Jim sadly shook his head, and turning to Wingenund made known in a broken Indian dialect that his brother was the missionary, and would sacrifice himself, taking this opportunity to practice the Christianity he had taught.

"The white father is brave, but he is known," broke in Wingenund's deep voice, while he pointed to the door of the lodge. "Let him go back to his Christian Indians."

The Indian runner cut Joe's bonds, and once more attempted to lead him from the lodge. Rage and misery shone in the lad's face. He pushed the runner aside. He exhausted himself trying to explain, to think of Indian words enough to show he was not the missionary. He even implored Girty to speak for him. When the renegade sat there stolidly silent Joe's rage burst out.

"Curse you all for a lot of ignorant redskins. I am not a missionary. I am Deathwind's friend. I killed a Delaware. I was the companion of *La Vent de la Mort*!"

Joe's passionate vehemence, and the truth that spoke from his flashing eyes compelled the respect, if not the absolute belief of the Indians. The savages slowly shook their heads. They beheld the spectacle of two brothers, one a friend, the other an enemy of all Indians, each willing to go to the stake, to suffer an awful agony, for love of the other. Chivalrous deeds always stir an Indian's heart. It was like a redman to die for his brother. The indifference, the contempt for death, won their admiration.

"Let the white father stand forth," sternly called Wingenund.

A hundred somber eyes turned on the prisoners. Except that one wore a buckskin coat, the other a linsey one, there was no difference. The strong figures were the same, the white faces alike, the stern resolve in the gray eyes identical—they were twin brothers.

Wingenund once more paced before his silent chiefs. To deal rightly with this situation perplexed him. To kill both palefaces did not suit him. Suddenly he thought of a way to decide.

"Let Wingenund's daughter come," he ordered.

A slight, girlish figure entered. It was Whispering Winds. Her beautiful face glowed while she listened to her father.

"Wingenund's daughter has her mother's eyes, that were beautiful as a doe's, keen as a hawk's, far-seeing as an eagle's. Let the Delaware maiden show her blood. Let her point out the white father."

Shyly but unhesitatingly Whispering Winds laid her hand on Jim's arm.

"Missionary, begone!" came the chieftain's command. "Thank Wingenund's daughter for your life, not the God of your Christians!"

He waved his hand to the runner. The brave grasped Jim's arm.

"Good-bye, Joe," brokenly said Jim.

"Old fellow, good-bye," came the answer.

They took one last, long look into each other's eyes. Jim's glance betrayed his fear—he would never see his brother again. The light in Joe's eyes was the old steely flash, the indomitable spirit—while there was life there was hope.

"Let the Shawnee chief paint his prisoner black," commanded Wingenund.

When the missionary left the lodge with the runner, Whispering Winds had smiled, for she had saved him whom she loved to hear speak; but the dread command that followed paled her cheek. Black paint meant hideous death. She saw this man so like the white father. Her piteous gaze tried to turn from that white face; but the cold, steely eyes fascinated her.

She had saved one only to be the other's doom!

She had always been drawn toward white men. Many prisoners had she rescued. She had even befriended her nation's bitter foe, Deathwind. She had listened to the young missionary with rapture; she had been his savior. And now when she looked into the eyes of this young giant, whose fate had rested on her all unwitting words, she resolved to save him.

She had been a shy, shrinking creature, fearing to lift her eyes to a paleface's, but now they were raised clear and steadfast.

As she stepped toward the captive and took his hand, her whole person radiated with conscious pride in her power. It was the knowledge that still she could save. When she kissed his hand and knelt before him, she expressed a tender humility.

She had claimed the unquestionable right of an Indian maiden; she asked what no Indian dared refuse a chief's daughter; she took the paleface for her husband.

Her action was followed by an impressive silence. She remained kneeling. Wingenund resumed his slow march to and fro. Silvertip retired to his corner with gloomy face. The others bowed their heads as if the maiden's decree was irrevocable.

Once more the chieftain's sonorous command rang out. An old Indian, wrinkled and worn, weird of aspect, fanciful of attire, entered the lodge and waved his wampum wand. He mumbled strange words, and departed chanting a love song.

Whispering Winds arose, a soft, radiant smile playing over her face, and, still holding Joe's hand, she led him out of the lodge, through long rows of silent Indians, down a lane bordered by teepees, he following like one in a dream.

He expected to awaken at any minute to see the stars shining through the leaves. Yet he felt the warm, soft pressure of a little hand. Surely this slender, graceful figure was real.

She bade him enter a lodge of imposing proportions. Still silent, in amazement and gratitude, he obeyed.

The maiden turned to Joe. Though traces of pride still lingered, all her fire had vanished. Her bosom rose with each quick-panting breath; her lips quivered, she trembled like a trapped doe.

But at last the fluttering lashes rose. Joe saw two velvety eyes dark with timid fear, yet veiling in their lustrous depths an unuttered hope and love.

"Whispering Winds—save—paleface," she said, in a voice low and tremulous. "Fear—Father. Fear—tell—Wingenund—she—Christian."

Indian summer, that enchanted time, unfolded its golden, dreamy haze over the Delaware village. The forests blazed with autumn fire, the meadows bloomed in rich luxuriance. All day low down in the valleys hung a purple smoke which changed, as the cool evening shades crept out of the woodland, into a cloud of white mist. All day the asters along the brooks lifted golden-brown faces to the sun as if to catch the waning warmth of his smile. All day the plains and forests lay in melancholy repose. The sad swish of the west wind over the tall grass told that he was slowly dying away before the enemy, the north wind. The sound of dropping nuts was heard under the motionless trees.

For Joe the days were days of enchantment. His wild heart had found its mate. A willing captive he was now. All his fancy for other women, all his memories faded into love for his Indian bride.

Whispering Winds charmed the eye, mind, and heart. Every day her beauty seemed renewed. She was as apt to learn as she was quick to turn her black-crowned head, but her supreme beauty was her loving, innocent soul. Untainted as the clearest spring, it mirrored the purity and simplicity of her life. Indian she might be, one of a race whose morals and manners were alien to those of the man she loved, yet she would have added honor to the proudest name.

When Whispering Winds raised her dark eyes they showed radiant as a lone star; when she spoke low her voice made music.

"Beloved," she whispered one day to him, "teach the Indian maiden more love for you, and truth, and God. Whispering Winds yearns to go to the Christians, but she fears her stern father. Wingenund would burn the Village of Peace. The Indian tribes tremble before the thunder of his wrath. Be patient, my chief. Time changes the leaves, so it will the anger of the warriors. Whispering Winds will set you free, and be free herself to go far with you toward the rising sun, where dwell your people. Her love will be an eternal spring where blossoms bloom ever anew, and fresh, and sweet. She will love your people, and raise Christian children, and sit ever in the door of your home praying for the west wind to blow. Or, if my chief wills, we shall live the Indian life, free as two eagles on their lonely crag."

Although Joe gave himself up completely to his love for his bride, he did not forget that Kate was in the power of the renegade, and that he must rescue her. Knowing Girty had the unfortunate girl somewhere near the Delaware encampment, he resolved to find the place. Plans of all kinds he revolved in his mind. The best one he believed lay through Whispering Winds. First to find the whereabouts of Girty; kill him if possible, or at least free

Kate, and then get away with her and his Indian bride. Sanguine as he invariably was, he could not but realize the peril of this undertaking. If Whispering Winds betrayed her people, it meant death to her as well as to him. He would far rather spend the remaining days of his life in the Indian village, than doom the maiden whose love had saved him. Yet he thought he might succeed in getting away with her, and planned to that end. His natural spirit, daring, reckless, had gained while he was associated with Wetzel.

Meanwhile he mingled freely with the Indians, and here, as elsewhere, his winning personality, combined with his athletic prowess, soon made him well liked. He was even on friendly terms with Pipe. The swarthy war chief liked Joe because, despite the animosity he had aroused in some former lovers of Whispering Winds, he actually played jokes on them. In fact, Joe's pranks raised many a storm; but the young braves who had been suitors for Wingenund's lovely daughter, feared the muscular paleface, and the tribe's ridicule more; so he continued his trickery unmolested. Joe's idea was to lead the savages to believe he was thoroughly happy in his new life, and so he was, but it suited him better to be free. He succeeded in misleading the savages. At first he was closely watched, then the vigilance relaxed and finally ceased.

This last circumstance was owing, no doubt, to a ferment of excitement that had suddenly possessed the Delawares. Council after council was held in the big lodge. The encampment was visited by runner after runner. Some important crisis was pending.

Joe could not learn what it all meant, and the fact that Whispering Winds suddenly lost her gladsome spirit and became sad caused him further anxiety. When he asked her the reason for her unhappiness, she was silent. Moreover, he was surprised to learn, when he questioned her upon the subject of their fleeing together, that she was eager to go immediately. While all this mystery puzzled Joe, it did not make any difference to him or in his plans. It rather favored the latter. He understood that the presence of Simon Girty and Elliott, with several other renegades unknown to him, was significant of unrest among the Indians. These presagers of evil were accustomed to go from village to village, exciting the savages to acts of war. Peace meant the downfall and death of these men. They were busy all day and far into the night. Often Joe heard Girty's hoarse voice lifted in the council lodge. Pipe thundered incessantly for war. But Joe could not learn against whom. Elliott's suave, oily oratory exhorted the Indians to vengeance. But Joe could not guess upon whom. He was, however, destined to learn.

The third day of the councils a horseman stopped before Whispering Winds' lodge and called her. Stepping to the door, Joe saw a white man, whose dark, keen, handsome face seemed familiar. Yet Joe knew he had never seen this stalwart man.

"A word with you," said the stranger. His tone was curt, authoritative, as that of a man used to power.

"As many as you would like. Who are you?"

"I am Isaac Zane. Are you Wetzel's companion, or the renegade Deering?"

"I am not a renegade any more than you are. I was rescued by the Indian girl, who took me as her husband," said Joe coldly. He was surprised and did not know what to make of Zane's manner.

"Good! I'm glad to meet you," instantly replied Zane,

his tone and expression changing. He extended his hand to Joe. "I wanted to be sure. I never saw the renegade Deering. He is here now. I am on my way to the Wyandot town. I have been to Fort Henry, where my brother told me of you and the missionaries. When I arrived here I heard your story from Simon Girty. If you can, you must get away from here. If I dared I'd take you to the Huron village, but it's impossible. Go, while you have a chance."

"Zane, I thank you. I've suspected something was wrong. What is it?"

"Couldn't be worse," whispered Zane, glancing around to see if they were overheard. "Girty and Elliott, backed by this Deering, are growing jealous of the influence of Christianity on the Indians. They are plotting against the Village of Peace. Tarhe, the Huron chief, has been approached, and asked to join in a concerted movement against religion. Seemingly it is not so much the missionaries as the converted Indians, that the renegades are fuming over. They know if the Christian savages are killed, the strength of the missionaries' hold will be forever broken. Pipe is wild for blood. These renegades are slowly poisoning the minds of the few chiefs who are favorably disposed. The outlook is bad! bad!"

"What can I do?"

"Cut out for yourself. Get away, if you can, with a gun. Take the creek below, follow the current down to the Ohio, and then make east for Fort Henry.

"But I want to rescue the white girl Jim Girty has concealed here somewhere."

"Impossible! Don't attempt it unless you want to throw your life away. Buzzard Jim, as we call Girty, is a butcher; he has probably murdered the girl."

"I won't leave without trying. And there's my wife, the

Indian girl who saved me. Zane, she's a Christian. She wants to go with me. I can't leave her."

"I am warning you, that's all. If I were you I'd never leave without a try to find the white girl, and I'd never forsake my Indian bride. I've been through the same thing. You must be a good woodsman, or Wetzel wouldn't have let you stay with him. Pick out a favorable time and make the attempt. I suggest you make your Indian girl show you where Girty is. She knows, but is afraid to tell you, for she fears Girty. Get your dog and horse from the Shawnees. That's a fine horse. He can carry you both to safety. Take him away from Silvertip."

"How?"

"Go right up and demand your horse and dog. Most of these Delawares are honest, for all their blood-shedding and cruelty. With them might is right. The Delawares won't try to get your horse for you; but they'll stick to you when you assert your rights. They don't like the Shawnee, anyhow. If Silvertip refuses to give you the horse, grab him before he can draw a weapon, and beat him good. You're big enough to do it. The Delawares will be tickled to see you pound him. He's thick with Girty, that's why he lays round here. Take my word, it's the best way. Do it openly, and no one will interfere."

"By Heavens, Zane, I'll give him a drubbing. I owe him one, and am itching to get hold of him."

"I must go now. I shall send a Wyandot runner to your brother at the village. They shall be warned. Good-bye. Good luck. May we meet again."

Joe watched Zane ride swiftly down the lane and disappear in the shrubbery. Whispering Winds came to the door of the lodge. She looked anxiously at him. He went within, drawing her along with him, and quickly informed her that he had learned the cause of the councils, that he had resolved to get away, and she must find out Girty's hiding place. Whispering Winds threw herself into his arms declaring with an energy and passion unusual to her, that she would risk anything for him. She informed Joe that she knew the direction from which Girty always returned to the village. No doubt she could find his retreat. With a cunning that showed her Indian nature, she suggested a plan which Joe at once saw was excellent. After Joe got his horse, she would ride around the village, then off into the woods, where she could leave the horse and return to say he had run away from her. As was their custom during afternoons, they would walk leisurely along the brook, and, trusting to the excitement created by the councils, get away unobserved. Find the horse, if possible rescue the prisoner, and then travel east with all speed.

Joe left the lodge at once to begin the working out of the plan. Luck favored him at the outset, for he met Silvertip before the council lodge. The Shawnee was leading Lance and the dog followed at his heels. The spirit of Mose had been broken. Poor dog, Joe thought; he had been beaten until he was afraid to wag his tail at his old master. Joe's resentment blazed into fury, but he kept cool outwardly.

Right before a crowd of Indians waiting for the council to begin, Joe planted himself in front of the Shawnee, barring his way.

"Silvertip has the paleface's horse and dog," said Joe, in a loud voice.

The chief stared haughtily while the other Indians sauntered nearer. They all knew how the Shawnee had got the animals, and now awaited the outcome of the white man's challenge.

"Paleface—heap—liar," growled the Indian. His dark eyes glowed craftily, while his hand dropped, apparently in careless habit, to the haft of his tomahawk.

Joe swung his long arm; his big fist caught the Shawnee on the jaw, sending him to the ground. Uttering a frightful yell, Silvertip drew his weapon and attempted to rise, but the moment's delay in seizing the hatchet, was fatal to his design. Joe was upon him with tigerlike suddenness. One kick sent the tomahawk spinning, another landed the Shawnee again on the ground. Blind with rage, Silvertip leaped up, and without a weapon rushed at his antagonist; but the Indian was not a boxer, and he failed to get his hands on Joe. Shifty and elusive, the lad dodged around the struggling savage. One, two, three hard blows staggered Silvertip, and a fourth, delivered with the force of Joe's powerful arm, caught the Indian when he was off his balance, and felled him, battered and bloody, on the grass. The surrounding Indians looked down at the vanquished Shawnee, expressing their approval in characteristic grunts.

With Lance prancing proudly, and Mose leaping lovingly beside him, Joe walked back to his lodge. Whispering Winds sprang to meet him with joyful face. She had feared the outcome of trouble with the Shawnee, but no queen ever bestowed upon returning victorious lord a loftier look of pride, a sweeter glance of love, then the Indian maiden bent upon her lover.

Whispering Winds informed Joe that an important council was to be held that afternoon. It would be wise for them to make the attempt to get away immediately after the convening of the chiefs. Accordingly she got upon Lance and rode him up and down the village lane, much to the pleasure of the watching Indians. She scattered the idle crowds on the grass plots, she dashed through the side

streets, and let everyone in the encampment see her clinging to the black stallion. Then she rode him out along the
creek. Accustomed to her imperious will, the Indians
thought nothing unusual. When she returned an hour later,
with flying hair and dishevelled costume, no one paid particular attention to her.

That afternoon Joe and his bride were the favored of
fortune. With Mose running before them, they got clear
of the encampment and into the woods. Once in the forest
Whispering Winds rapidly led the way east. When they
climbed to the top of a rocky ridge she pointed down into
a thicket before her, saying that somewhere in this dense
hollow was Girty's hut. Joe hesitated about taking Mose.
He wanted the dog, but in case he had to run it was necessary Whispering Winds should find his trail, and for this
he left the dog with her.

He started down the ridge, and had not gone a hundred
paces when over some gray boulders he saw the thatched
roof of a hut. So wild and secluded was the spot, that he
would never have discovered the cabin from any other
point than this, which he had been so fortunate as to find.

His study and practice under Wetzel now stood him in
good stead. He picked out the best path over the rough
stones and through the brambles, always keeping under
cover. He stepped as carefully as if the hunter was behind
him. Soon he reached level ground. A dense laurel thicket
hid the cabin, but he knew the direction in which it lay.
Throwing himself flat on the ground, he wormed his way
through the thicket, carefully, yet swiftly, because he
knew there was no time to lose. Finally the rear of the
cabin stood in front of him.

It was made of logs, rudely hewn, and as rudely thrown
together. In several places clay had fallen from chunks
between the timbers, leaving small holes. Like a snake,

Joe slipped close to the hut. Raising his head he looked through one of the cracks.

Instantly he shrank back into the grass, shivering with horror. He almost choked in his attempt to prevent an outcry.

CHAPTER XVIII

The sight which Joe had seen horrified him, for several moments, into helpless inaction. He lay breathing heavily, impotent, in an awful rage. As he remained there stunned by the shock, he gazed up through the open space in the leaves, trying to still his fury, to realize the situation, to make no hasty move. The soft blue of the sky, the fleecy clouds drifting eastward, the fluttering leaves, and the twittering birds—all assured him he was wide awake. He had found Girty's den where so many white women had been hidden, to see friends and home no more. He had seen the renegade sleeping, calmly sleeping like any other man. How could the wretch sleep! He had seen Kate. It had been the sight of her that had paralyzed him. To make a certainty of his fears, he again raised himself to peep into the hole. As he did so a faint cry came from within.

Girty lay on a buffalo robe near a barred door. Beyond him sat Kate, huddled in one corner of the cabin. A long buckskin thong was knotted round her waist, and tied to a log. Her hair was matted and tangled, and on her face and arms were many discolored bruises. Worse still, in her plaintive moaning, in the meaningless movement of her head, in her vacant expression, was proof that her mind had gone. She was mad. Even as an agonizing pity came over Joe, to be followed by the surging fire of rage, blazing up in his breast, he could not but thank God that she was mad! It was merciful that Kate was no longer conscious of her suffering.

Like leaves in a storm wavered Joe's hands as he clenched them until the nails brought blood. "Be calm, be cool," whispered his monitor, Wetzel, ever with him in spirit. But God! Could he be cool? Bounding with lion spring he hurled his heavy frame against the door.

Crash! The door was burst from its fastenings.

Girty leaped up with startled yell, drawing his knife as he rose. It had not time to descend before Joe's second spring, more fierce even than the other, carried him directly on top of the renegade. As the two went down Joe caught the villain's wrist with a grip that literally cracked the bones. The knife fell and rolled away from the struggling men. For an instant they tumbled about on the floor, clasped in a crushing embrace. The renegade was strong, supple, slippery as an eel. Twice he wriggled from his foe. Gnashing his teeth, he fought like a hyena. He was fighting for life—life, which is never so dear as to a coward and a murderer. Doom glared from Joe's big eyes, and scream after scream issued from the renegade's white lips.

Terrible was this struggle, but brief. Joe seemingly had the strength of ten men. Twice he pulled Girty down as a wolf drags a deer. He dashed him against the wall, throwing him nearer and nearer the knife. Once within reach of the blade Joe struck the renegade a severe blow on the temple and the villain's wrestling became weaker. Planting his heavy knee on Girty's breast, Joe reached for the knife, and swung it high. Exultantly he cried, mad with lust for the brute's blood.

But the slight delay saved Girty's life.

The knife was knocked from Joe's hand and he leaped

erect to find himself confronted by Silvertip. The chief held a tomahawk with which he struck the weapon from the young man's grasp, and, to judge from his burning eyes and malignant smile, he meant to brain the now defenseless paleface.

In a single fleeting instant Joe saw that Girty was helpless for the moment, that Silvertip was confident of his revenge, and that the situation called for Wetzel's characteristic advice, "act like lightnin'."

Swifter than the thought was the leap he made past Silvertip. It carried him to a wooden bar which lay on the floor. Escape was easy, for the door was before him and the Shawnee behind, but Joe did not flee! He seized the bar and rushed at the Indian. Then began a duel in which the savage's quickness and cunning matched the white man's strength and fury. Silvertip dodged the vicious swings Joe aimed at him; he parried many blows, any one of which would have crushed his skull. Nimble as a cat, he avoided every rush, while his dark eyes watched for an opening. He fought wholly on the defensive, craftily reserving his strength until his opponent should tire.

At last, catching the bar on his hatchet, he broke the force of the blow, and then, with agile movement, dropped to the ground and grappled Joe's legs. Long before this he had drawn his knife, and now he used it, plunging the blade into the young man's side.

Cunning and successful as was the savage's ruse, it failed signally, for to get hold of the Shawnee was all Joe wanted. Feeling the sharp pain as they fell together, he reached his hand behind him and caught Silvertip's wrist. Exerting all his power, he wrenched the Indian's arm so that it was not only dislocated, but the bone cracked.

Silvertip saw his fatal mistake, but he uttered no sound. Crippled though he was, he yet made a supreme effort, struggling desperately, to whirl or writhe away from Joe; but it was as if he had been in the hands of a giant. The lad handled him with remorseless and resistless fury. Suddenly he grasped the knife, which Silvertip had been unable to hold with his crippled hand, and thrust it deeply into the Indian's side.

All Silvertip's muscles relaxed as if a strong tension had been removed. Slowly his legs straightened, his arms dropped, and from his side gushed a dark flow. A shadow crept over his face, not dark nor white, but just a shadow. His eyes lost their hate; they no longer saw the foe, they looked beyond with gloomy question, and then were fixed cold in death. Silvertip died as he had lived—a chief.

Joe glared round for Girty. He was gone, having slipped away during the fight. The lad turned to release the poor prisoner, when he started back with a cry of fear. Kate lay bathed in a pool of blood—dead. The renegade, fearing she might be rescued, had murdered her, and then fled from the cabin.

Almost blinded by horror, and staggering with weakness, Joe turned to leave the cabin. Realizing that he was seriously, perhaps dangerously, wounded he wisely thought he must not leave the place without weapons. He had marked the pegs where the renegade's rifle hung, and had been careful to keep between that and his enemies. He took down the gun and horns, which were attached to it, and, with one last shuddering glance at poor Kate, left the place.

He was conscious of a strange lightness in his head, but he suffered no pain. His garments were dripping with blood. He did not know how much of it was his, or the Indian's. Instinct rather than sight was his guide. He grew weaker and weaker, his head began to whirl, yet he kept on, knowing that life and freedom were his if he found

Whispering Winds. He gained the top of the ridge; his eyes were blurred, his strength gone. He called aloud, and then plunged forward on his face. He heard dimly, as though the sound were afar off, the whine of a dog. He felt something soft and wet on his face. Then consciousness left him.

When he regained his senses he was lying on a bed of ferns under a projecting rock. He heard the gurgle of running water mingling with the song of birds. Near him lay Mose, and beyond rose a wall of green thicket. Neither Whispering Winds nor his horse was visible.

He felt a dreamy lassitude. He was tired, but had no pain. Finding he could move without difficulty, he concluded his weakness was more from loss of blood than a dangerous wound. He put his hand on the place where he had been stabbed, and felt a soft, warm compress such as might have been made by a bunch of wet leaves. Someone had unlaced his hunting shirt—for he saw the strings were not as he usually tied them—and had dressed the wound. Joe decided, after some deliberation, that Whispering Winds had found him, made him as comfortable as possible, and, leaving Mose on guard, had gone out to hunt for food, or perhaps back to the Indian encampment. The rifle and horn he had taken from Girty's hut, together with Silvertip's knife, lay beside him.

As Joe lay there hoping for Whispering Winds' return, his reflections were not pleasant. Fortunate, indeed, he was to be alive; but he had no hope he could continue to be favored of fortune. Odds were now against his escape. Girty would have the Delawares on his trail like a pack of hungry wolves. He could not understand the absence of Whispering Winds. She would have died sooner than desert him. Girty had, perhaps, captured her, and was now scouring the woods for him.

"I'll get him next time, or he'll get me," muttered Joe, in bitter wrath. He could never forgive himself for his failure to kill the renegade.

The recollection of how nearly he had forever ended Girty's brutal career brought before Joe's mind the scene of the fight. He saw again Buzzard Jim's face, revolting, unlike anything human. There stretched Silvertip's dark figure, lying still and stark, and there was Kate's white form in its winding, crimson wreath of blood. Hauntingly her face returned, sad, stern in its cold rigidity.

"Poor girl, better for her to be dead," he murmured. "Not long will she be unavenged!"

His thoughts drifted to the future. He had no fear of starvation, for Mose could catch a rabbit or woodchuck at any time. When the strips of meat he had hidden in his coat were gone, he could start a fire and roast more. What concerned him most was pursuit. His trail from the cabin had been a bloody one, which would render it easily followed. He dared not risk exertion until he had given his wound time to heal. Then, if he did escape from Girty and the Delawares, his future was not bright. His experiences of the last few days had not only been sobered, but brought home to him this real border life. With all his fire and daring he knew he was no fool. He had eagerly embraced a career which, at the present stage of his training, was beyond his scope—not that he did not know how to act in sudden crisis, but because he had not had the necessary practice to quickly and surely use his knowledge.

Bitter, indeed, was his self-scorn when he recalled that of the several critical positions he had been in since his aquaintance with Wetzel, he had failed in all but one. The exception was the killing of Silvertip. Here his fury had made him fight as Wetzel fought with only his everyday incentive. He realized that the border was no place for any save the boldest and most experienced hunters—men who had become inured to hardship, callous as to death, keen as Indians. Fear was not in Joe nor lack of confidence; but he had good sense, and realized he would have done a wiser thing had he stayed at Fort Henry. Colonel Zane was right. The Indians were tigers, the renegades vultures, the vast untrammeled forests and plains their covert. Ten years of war had rendered this wilderness a place where those few white men who had survived were hardened to the spilling of blood, stern even in those few quiet hours which peril allowed them, strong in their sacrifice of all for future generations.

A low growl from Mose broke into Joe's reflections. The dog had raised his nose from his paws and sniffed suspiciously at the air. The lad heard a slight rustling outside, and in another moment was overjoyed at seeing Whispering Winds. She came swiftly, with a lithe, graceful motion, and, flying to him like a rush of wind, knelt beside him. She kissed him and murmured words of endearment.

"Winds, were have you been?" he asked her, in the mixed English and Indian dialect in which they conversed.

She told him the dog had led her to him two evenings before. He was insensible. She had bathed and bandaged his wound, and remained with him all that night. The next day, finding he was ill and delirious, she decided to risk returning to the village. If any questions arose, she could say he had left her. Then she would find a way to get back to him, bringing healing herbs for his wound and a soothing drink. As it turned out Girty had returned to the camp. He was battered and bruised, and in a white heat of passion. Going at once to Wingenund, the renegade openly accused Whispering Winds of aiding her paleface lover to escape. Wingenund called his daughter before him, and questioned her. She confessed all to her father.

"Why is the daughter of Wingenund a traitor to her race?" demanded the chief.

"Whispering Winds is a Christian."

Wingenund received this intelligence as a blow. He dismissed Girty and sent his braves from his lodge, facing his daughter alone. Gloomy and stern, he paced before her.

"Wingenund's blood might change, but would never betray. Wingenund is the Delaware chief," he said. "Go. Darken no more the door of Wingenund's wigwam. Let the flower of the Delawares fade in alien pastures. Go. Whispering Winds is free!"

Tears shone brightly in the Indian girl's eyes while she told Joe her story. She loved her father, and she would see him no more.

"Winds is free," she whispered. "When strength returns to her master she can follow him to the white villages. Winds will live her life for him."

"Then we have no one to fear?" asked Joe.

"No redman, now that the Shawnee chief is dead."

"Will Girty follow us? He is a coward; he will fear to come alone."

"The white savage is a snake in the grass."

Two long days followed, during which the lovers lay quietly in hiding. On the morning of the third day Joe felt that he might risk the start for the Village of Peace. Whispering Winds led the horse below the stone upon which the invalid stood, thus enabling him to mount. Then she got on behind him.

The sun was just gilding the horizon when they rode out of the woods into a wide plain. No living thing could be seen. Along the edge of the forest the ground was level, and the horse traveled easily. Several times during the morning Joe dismounted beside a pile of stones or a fallen tree. The miles were traversed without serious inconvenience to the invalid, except that he grew tired. Toward the middle of the afternoon, when they had ridden perhaps twenty-five or thirty miles, they crossed a swift, narrow brook. The water was a beautiful clear brown. Joe made a note of this, as it was an unusual circumstance. Nearly all the streams, when not flooded, were green in color. He remembered that during his wanderings with Wetzel they had found one stream of this brown, copper-colored water. The lad knew he must take a roundabout way to the village so that he might avoid Indian runners or scouts, and he hoped this stream would prove to be the one he had once camped upon.

As they were riding toward a gentle swell or knoll covered with trees and shrubbery, Whispering Winds felt something warm on her hand, and, looking, was horrified to find it covered with blood. Joe's wound had opened. She told him they must dismount here, and remain until he was stronger. The invalid himself thought this conclusion was wise. They would be practically safe now, since they must be out of the Indian path, and many miles from the encampment. Accordingly he got off the horse and sat down on a log, while Whispering Winds searched for a suitable place in which to erect a temporary shelter.

Joe's wandering gaze was arrested by a tree with a huge knotty formation near the ground. It was like many trees, but this peculiarity was not what struck Joe. He had seen it before. He never forgot anything in the woods that had once attracted his attention. He looked around on all sides. Just behind him was an opening in the clump of trees. Within this was a perpendicular stone covered with moss and lichens; above it a beech tree spread long, graceful branches. He thrilled with the remembrance these familiar marks brought. This was Beautiful Spring, the place where Wetzel rescued Nell, where he had killed the Indians in that night attack he would never forget.

CHAPTER XIX

One evening a week or more after the disappearance of Jim and the girls, George Young and David Edwards, the missionaries, sat on the cabin steps, gazing disconsolately upon the forest scenery. Hard as had been the ten years of their labor among the Indians, nothing had shaken them as the loss of their young friends.

"Dave, I tell you your theory about seeing them again is absurd," asserted George. "I'll never forget that wretch, Girty, as he spoke to Nell. Why, she just wilted like a flower blasted by fire. I can't understand why he let me go, and kept Jim, unless the Shawnee had something to do with it. I never wished until now that I was a hunter. I'd go after Girty. You've heard as well as I of his many atrocities. I'd rather have seen Kate and Nell dead than have them fall into his power. I'd rather have killed them myself!"

Young had aged perceptibly in these last few days. The blue veins showed at his temples; his face had become thinner and paler, his eyes had a look of pain. The former expression of patience, which had sat so well on him, was gone.

"George, I can't account for my fancies or feelings, else, perhaps, I'd be easier in mind," answered Dave. His face, too, showed the ravages of grief. "I've had strange thoughts lately, and dreams such as I never had before.

Perhaps it's this trouble which has made me so nervous. I don't seem able to pull myself together. I can neither preach nor work."

"Neither can I! This trouble has hit you as hard as it has me. But, Dave, we've still our duty. To endure, to endure— that is our life. Because a beam of sunshine brightened, for a brief time, the gray of our lives, and then faded away, we must not shirk nor grow sour and discontented."

"But how cruel is this border life!"

"Nature itself is brutal."

"Yes, I know, and we have elected to spend our lives here in the midst of this ceaseless strife, to fare poorly, to have no pleasure, never to feel the comfort of a woman's smiles, nor the joy of a child's caress, all because out in the woods are ten or twenty or a hundred savages we may convert."

"That is why, and it is enough. It is hard to give up the women you love to a black-souled renegade, but that is not my thought. What kills me is the horror for her—for her."

"I, too, suffer with that thought; more than that, I am morbid and depressed. I feel as if some calamity awaited us here. I have never been superstitious, nor have I had presentiments, but of late there are strange fears in my mind."

At this juncture Mr. Wells and Heckewelder came out of the adjoining cabin.

"I had word from a trustworthy runner today. Girty and his captives have not been seen in the Delaware towns," said Heckewelder.

"It is most unlikely that he will take them to the towns," replied Edwards. "What do you make of his capturing Jim?"

"For Pipe, perhaps. The Delaware Wolf is snapping his

teeth. Pipe is particularly opposed to Christianity, and—what's that?"

A low whistle from the bushes near the creek bank attracted the attention of all. The younger men got up to investigate, but Heckewelder detained them.

"Wait," he added. "There is no telling what that signal may mean."

They waited with breathless interest. Presently the whistle was repeated, and an instant later the tall figure of a man stepped from behind a thicket. He was a white man, but not recognizable at that distance, even if a friend. The stranger waved his hand as if asking them to be cautious, and come to him.

They went toward the thicket, and when within a few paces of the man Mr. Wells exclaimed:

"It's the man who guided my party to the village. It is Wetzel!"

The other missionaries had never seen the hunter, though, of course, they were familiar with his name, and looked at him with great curiosity. The hunter's buckskin garments were wet, torn, and covered with burrs. Dark spots, evidently bloodstains, showed on his hunting shirt.

"Wetzel?" interrogated Heckewelder.

The hunter nodded, and took a step behind the bush. Bending over he lifted something from the ground. It was a girl. It was Nell! She was very white—but alive. A faint, glad smile lighted up her features.

Not a word was spoken. With an expression of tender compassion Mr. Wells received her into his arms. The four missionaries turned fearful, questioning eyes upon the hunter, but they could not speak.

"She's well, an' unharmed," said Wetzel, reading their thoughts, "only worn out. I've carried her these ten miles."

"God bless you, Wetzel!" exclaimed the old missionary. "Nellie, Nellie, can you speak?"

"Uncle dear—I'm—all right," came the faint answer.

"Kate? What—of her?" whispered George Young with lips as dry as corn husks.

"I did my best," said the hunter with a simple dignity. Nothing but the agonized appeal in the young man's eyes could have made Wetzel speak of his achievement.

"Tell us," broke in Heckewelder, seeing that fear had stricken George dumb.

"We trailed 'em, an' got away with the golden-haired lass. The last I saw of Joe he was braced up agin a rock fightin' like a wildcat. I tried to cut Jim loose as I was goin' by. I s'pect the wust fer the brothers an' the other lass."

"Can we do nothing?" asked Mr. Wells.

"Nothin'!"

"Wetzel, has the capturing of James Downs any significance to you?" inquired Heckewelder.

"I reckon so."

"What?"

"Pipe an' his white-redskin allies are agin Christianity."

"Do you think we are in danger?"

"I reckon so."

"What do you advise?"

"Pack up a few of your traps, take the lass, an' come with me. I'll see you back in Fort Henry."

Heckewelder nervously walked up to the tree and back again. Young and Edwards looked blankly at one another. They both remembered Edwards' presentiment. Mr. Wells uttered an angry exclamation.

"You ask us to fail in our duty? No, never! To go back to the white settlements and acknowledge we were afraid to continue teaching the Gospel to the Indians! You can not understand Christianity if you advise that. You have no religion. You are a killer of Indians."

A shadow that might have been one of pain flitted over the hunter's face.

"No, I ain't a Christian, an' I am a killer of Injuns," said Wetzel, and his deep voice had a strange tremor. "I don't know nothin' much 'cept the woods an' fields, an' if there's a God fer me He's out thar under the trees an' grass. Mr. Wells, you're the first man as ever called me a coward, an' I overlook it because of your callin'. I advised you to go back to Fort Henry, because if you don't go now the chances are against your ever goin'. Christianity or no Christianity, such men as you hev no bisness in these woods."

"I thank you for your advice, and bless you for your rescue of this child; but I can not leave my work, nor can I understand why all this good work we have done should be called useless. We have converted Indians, saved their souls. Is that not being of some use, of some good here?"

"It's accordin' to how you look at it. Now I know the bark of an oak is different accordin' to the side we see it from. I'll allow, hatin' Injuns as I do, is no reason you oughtn't to try an' convert 'em. But you're bringin' on a war. These Injuns won't allow this Village of Peace here with its big fields of corn, an' shops an' workin' redskins. It's agin their nature. You're only sacrificin' your Christian Injuns."

"What do you mean?" asked Mr. Wells, startled by Wetzel's words.

"Enough. I'm ready to guide you to Fort Henry."

"I'll never go."

Wetzel looked at the other men. No one would have doubted him. No one could have failed to see he knew that some terrible danger hovered over the Village of Peace.

"I believe you, Wetzel, but I cannot go," said Heck-ewelder, with white face.

"I will stay," said George, steadily.

"And I," said Dave.

Wetzel nodded, and turned to depart when George grasped his arm. The young missionary's face was drawn and haggard; he fixed an intense gaze upon the hunter.

"Wetzel, listen;" his voice was low and shaken with deep feeling. "I am a teacher of God's word, and I am as earnest in that purpose as you are in your life work. I shall die here; I shall fill an unmarked grave; but I shall have done the best I could. This is the life destiny has marked out for me, and I will live it as best I may; but in this moment, preacher as I am, I would give all I have or hope to have, all the little good I may have done, all my life, to be such a man as you. For I would avenge the woman I loved. To torture, to kill Girty! I am only a poor, weak fellow who would be lost a mile from this village, and if not, would fall before the youngest brave. But you with your glorious strength, your incomparable woodcraft, you are the man to kill Girty. Rid the frontier of this fiend. Kill him! Wetzel, kill him. I beseech you for the sake of some sweet girl who even now may be on her way to this terrible country, and who may fall into Girty's power—for her sake, Wetzel, kill him. Trail him like a bloodhound, and when you find him remember my broken heart, re-member Nell, remember, oh, God! remember poor Kate!"

Young's voice broke into dry sobs. He had completely exhausted himself, so that he was forced to lean against the tree for support.

Wetzel spoke never a word. He stretched out his long, brawny arm and gripped the young missionary's shoul-der. His fingers clasped hard. Simple, without words as the action was, it could not have been more potent. And then, as he stood, the softer look faded slowly from his face. A ripple seemed to run over his features, which froze, as it subsided, into a cold, stone rigidity.

His arms dropped; he stepped past the tree, and, bounding lightly as a deer, cleared the creek, and disappeared in the bushes.

Mr. Wells carried Nell to his cabin where she lay for hours with wan face and listless languor. She swallowed the nourishing drink an old Indian nurse forced between her teeth; she even smiled weakly when the missionaries spoke to her; but she said nothing nor seemed to rally from her terrible shock. A dark shadow lay always before her eyes. At times she remained gazing straight before her, conscious of nothing present, living over again her frightful experience. Again she seemed sunk in dull apathy.

"Dave, we're going to lose Nell. She's fading slowly," said George, one evening, several days after the girl's return. "Wetzel said she was unharmed, yet she seems to have received a hurt more fatal than a physical one. It's her mind—her mind. If we cannot brighten her up to make her forget, she'll die."

"We've done all within our power. If she could only be brought out of this trance! She lies there all day long with those staring eyes. I can't look into them. They are the eyes of a child who has seen murder."

"We must try in some way to get her out of this stupor, and I have an idea. Have you noticed that Mr. Wells has failed very much in the last few weeks?"

"Indeed I have, and I'm afraid he's breaking down. He has grown so thin, eats very little, and doesn't sleep. He is old, you know, and, despite his zeal, this border life is telling on him."

"Dave, I believe he knows it. Poor, earnest old man! He

never says a word about himself, yet he must know he is going downhill. Well, we all begin, sooner or later, that descent which ends in the grave. I believe we might stir Nellie by telling her Mr. Wells' health is breaking."

"Let us try."

A hurried knock on the door interrupted their conversation.

"Come in," said Edwards.

The door opened to admit a man, who entered eagerly.

"Jim! Jim!" exclaimed both missionaries, throwing themselves upon the newcomer.

It was, indeed, Jim, but no answering smile lighted his worn, distressed face while he wrung his friends' hands.

"You're not hurt?" asked Dave.

"No, I'm uninjured."

"Tell us all. Did you escape? Did you see your brother? Did you know Wetzel rescued Nell?"

"Wingenund set me free in spite of many demands for my death. He kept Joe a prisoner, and intends to kill him, for the lad was Wetzel's companion. I saw the hunter come into the glade where we camped, break through the line of fighting Indians, and carry Nell off."

"Kate?" faltered Young, with ashen face.

"George, I wish to God I could tell you she is dead," answered Jim, nervously pacing the room. "But she was well when I last saw her. She endured the hard journey better than either Nell or I. Girty did not carry her into the encampment, as Silvertip did Joe and me, but the renegade left us on the outskirts of the Delaware town. There was a rocky ravine with dense undergrowth when he disappeared with his captive. I suppose he has his den somewhere in that ravine."

George sank down and buried his face in his arms; neither movement nor sound betokened consciousness.

"Has Wetzel come in with Nell? Joe said he had a cave where he might have taken her in case of illness or accident."

"Yes, he brought her back," answered Edwards, slowly.

"I want to see her," said Jim, his haggard face expressing a keen anxiety. "She's not wounded? hurt? ill?"

"No nothing like that. It's a shock which she can't get over, can't forget."

"I must see her," cried Jim, moving toward the door.

"Don't go," replied Dave, detaining him. "Wait. We must see what's best to be done. Wait till Heckewelder comes. He'll be here soon. Nell thinks you're dead, and the surprise might be bad for her."

Heckewelder came in at that moment, and shook hands warmly with Jim.

"The Delaware runner told me you were here. I am overjoyed that Wingenund freed you," said the missionary. "It is a most favorable sign. I have heard rumors from Goshocking and Sandusky that have worried me. This good news more than offsets the bad. I am sorry about your brother. Are you well?"

"Well, but miserable. I want to see Nell. Dave tells me she is not exactly ill, but something is wrong with her. Perhaps I ought not to see her just yet."

"It'll be exactly the tonic for her," replied Heckewelder. "She'll be surprised out of herself. She is morbid, apathetic, and, try as we may, we can't interest her. Come at once."

Heckewelder had taken Jim's arm and started for the door when he caught sight of Young, sitting bowed and motionless. Turning to Jim he whispered:

"Kate?"

"Girty did not take her into the encampment," answered Jim, in a low voice. "I hoped he would, because the Indians are kind, but he didn't. He took her to his den."

Just then Young raised his face. The despair in it would have melted a heart of stone. It had become the face of an old man.

"If only you'd told me she had died," he said to Jim, "I'd have been man enough to stand it, but—this—this kills me—I can't breathe!"

He staggered into the adjoining room, where he flung himself upon a bed.

"It's hard, and he won't be able to stand up under it, for he's not strong," whispered Jim.

Heckewelder was a mild, pious man, in whom no one would ever expect strong passion; but now depths were stirred within his heart that had ever been tranquil. He became livid, and his face was distorted with rage.

"It's bad enough to have these renegades plotting and working against our religion; to have them sow discontent, spread lies, make the Indians think we have axes to grind, to plant the only obstacle in our path—all this is bad; but to doom an innocent white woman to worse than death! What can I call it!"

"What can we do?" asked Jim.

"Do? That's the worst of it. We can do nothing, nothing. We dare not move."

"Is there no hope of getting Kate back?"

"Hope? None. That villain is surrounded by his savages. He'll lie low now for a while. I've heard of such deeds many a time, but it never before came so close home. Kate Wells was a pure, loving Christian woman. She'll live an hour, a day, a week, perhaps, in that snake's clutches, and then she'll die. Thank God!"

"Wetzel has gone on Girty's trail. I know that from his manner when he left us," said Edwards.

"Wetzel may avenge her, but he can never save her. It's too late. Hello——"

The exclamation was called forth by the appearance of Young, who entered with a rifle in his hands.

"George, where are you going with that gun?" asked Edwards, grasping his friend by the arm.

"I'm going after her," answered George, wildly. He tottered as he spoke, but wrenched himself free from Dave.

"Come, George, listen, listen to reason," interposed Heckewelder, laying hold of Young. "You are frantic with grief now. So are all of us. But calm yourself. Why, man, you're a preacher, not a hunter. You'd be lost, you'd starve in the woods before getting halfway to the Indian town. This is terrible enough; don't make it worse by throwing your life away. Think of us, your friends; think of your Indian pupils who rely so much on you. Think of the Village of Peace. We can pray, but we can't prevent these border crimes. With civilization, with the spread of Christianity, they will pass away. Bear up under this blow for the sake of your work. Remember we alone can check such barbarity. But we must not fight. We must sacrifice all that men hold dear, for the sake of the future."

He took the rifle away from George, and led him back into the little, dark room. Closing the door he turned to Jim and Dave.

"He's in a bad way, and we must carefully watch him for a few days."

"Think of George starting out to kill Girty!" exclaimed Dave. "I never fired a gun, but yet I'd go too."

"So would we all, if we did as our hearts dictate," retorted Heckewelder, turning fiercely upon Dave as if stung. "Man, we have a village full of Christians to look after. What would become of them? I tell you we've all we can do here to outwit these border ruffians. Simon Girty is plotting our ruin. I heard it today from the Delaware runner who is my friend. He is jealous of our influence, when all we desire is to save these poor Indians. And Jim, Girty has killed our happiness. Can we ever recover from the misery brought upon us by poor Kate's fate?"

The missionary raised his hand as if to exhort some power above.

"Curse the Girtys!" he exclaimed in a sudden burst of uncontrollable passion. "Having conquered all other obstacles, must we fail because of wicked men of our own race? Oh, curse them!"

"Come," he said, presently, in a voice which trembled with the effort he made to be calm. "We'll go in to Nellie."

The three men entered Mr. Wells' cabin. The old missionary, with bowed head and hands clasped behind his back, was pacing to and fro. He greeted Jim with glad surprise.

"We want Nellie to see him," whispered Heckewelder. "We think the surprise will do her good."

"I trust it may," said Mr. Wells.

"Leave it to me."

They followed Heckewelder into an adjoining room. A torch flickered over the rude mantel shelf, lighting up the room with fitful flare. It was a warm night, and the soft breeze coming in the window alternately paled and brightened the flame.

Jim saw Nell lying on the bed. Her eyes were closed, and her long, dark lashes seemed black against the marble paleness of her skin.

"Stand behind me," whispered Heckewelder to Jim.

"Nellie," he called softly, but only a faint flickering of her lashes answered him.

"Nellie, Nellie," repeated Heckewelder, his deep, strong voice thrilling.

Her eyes opened. They gazed at Mr. Wells on one side, at Edwards standing at the foot of her bed, at Heckewelder leaning over her, but there was no recognition or interest in her look.

"Nellie, can you understand me?" asked Heckewelder, putting into his voice all the power and intensity of feeling of which he was capable.

An almost imperceptible shadow of understanding shone in her eyes.

"Listen. You have had a terrible shock, and it has affected your mind. You are mistaken in what you think, what you dream of all the time. Do you understand? You are wrong!"

Nell's eyes quickened with a puzzled, questioning doubt. The minister's magnetic, penetrating voice had pierced her dulled brain.

"See, I have brought you Jim!"

Heckewelder stepped aside as Jim fell on his knees by the bed. He took her cold hands in his and bent over her. For the moment his voice failed.

The doubt in Nell's eyes changed to a wondrous gladness. It was like the rekindling of a smoldering fire.

"Jim?" she whispered.

"Yes, Nellie, it's Jim alive and well. It's Jim come back to you."

A soft flush stained her white face. She slipped her arm tenderly around his neck, and held her cheek close to his.

"Jim," she murmured.

"Nellie, don't you know me?" asked Mr. Wells, trembling, excited. This was the first word she had spoken in four days.

"Uncle!" she exclaimed, suddenly loosening her hold on Jim, and sitting up in bed, then she gazed wildly at the others.

"Was it all a horrible dream?"

Mr. Wells took her hand soothingly, but he did not attempt to answer her question. He looked helplessly at Heckewelder, but that missionary was intently studying the expression on Nell's face.

"A part of it was a dream," he answered, impressively.

"Then that horrible man did take us away?"

"Yes."

"Oh-h! but we're free now? This is my room. Oh, tell me?"

"Yes, Nellie, you're safe at home now."

"Tell—tell me," she cried, shudderingly, as she leaned to Jim and raised a white, imploring face to his. "Where is Kate?—Oh! Jim—say, say she wasn't left with Girty?"

"Kate is dead," answered Jim, quickly. He could not endure the horror in her eyes. He deliberately intended to lie, as had Heckewelder.

It was as if the tension of Nell's nerves was suddenly relaxed. The relief from her worst fear was so great that her mind took in only the one impression. Then, presently, a choking cry escaped her, to be followed by a paroxysm of sobs.

CHAPTER XX

Early on the following day Heckewelder, astride his horse, appeared at the door of Edwards' cabin.

"How is George?" he inquired of Dave, when the latter had opened the door.

"He had a bad night, but is sleeping now. I think he'll be all right after a time," answered Dave.

"That's well. Nevertheless keep a watch on him for a few days."

"I'll do so."

"Dave, I leave matters here to your good judgment. I'm off to Goshocking to join Zeisberger. Affairs there demand our immediate attention, and we must make haste."

"How long do you intend to be absent?"

"A few days; possibly a week. In case of any unusual disturbance among the Indians, the appearance of Pipe and his tribe, or any of the opposing factions, send a fleet runner at once to warn me. Most of my fears have been allayed by Wingenund's attitude toward us. His freeing Jim in the face of the opposition of his chiefs is a sure sign of friendliness. More than once I have suspected that he was interested in Christianity. His daughter, Whispering Winds, exhibited the same intense fervor in religion as has been manifested by all our converts. It may be that we have not appealed in vain to Wingenund and his daughter; but their high position in the Delaware tribe makes it impolitic for them to reveal a change of heart. If we could win over those two we'd have every chance to convert the whole tribe. Well, as it is we must be thankful for Wingenund's friendship. We have two powerful allies now. Tarhe, the Wyandot chieftain, remains neutral, to be sure, but that's almost as helpful as his friendship."

"I, too, take a hopeful view of the situation," replied Edwards.

"We'll trust in Providence, and do our best," said Heckewelder, as he turned his horse. "Good-bye."

"Godspeed!" called Edwards, as his chief rode away.

The missionary resumed his work of getting breakfast. He remained indoors all that day, except for the few moments when he ran over to Mr. Wells' cabin to inquire regarding Nell's condition. He was relieved to learn she was so much better that she had declared her intention of moving about the house. Dave kept a close watch on Young. He, himself, was suffering from the same blow which had prostrated his friend, but his physical strength and fortitude were such that he did not weaken. He was overjoyed to see that George rallied, and showed no further indication of breaking down.

True it was, perhaps, that Heckewelder's earnest prayer on behalf of the converted Indians had sunk deeply into George's heart and thus kept it from breaking. No stronger plea could have been made than the allusion to those gentle, dependent Christians. No one but a missionary could realize the sweetness, the simplicity, the faith, the eager hope for a good, true life which had been implanted in the hearts of these Indians. To bear it in mind, to think of what he, as a missionary and teacher, was to them, relieved him of half his burden, and for strength to bear the remainder he went to God. For all worry there is a sovereign cure, for all suffering there is a healing balm: it is religious faith. Happiness had suddenly flashed with a meteorlike radiance into Young's life only to be snuffed out like a candle in a windy gloom, but his work, his duty remained. So in his trial he learned the necessity of resignation. He chaffed no more at the mysterious, seemingly brutal methods of nature; he questioned no more. He wondered no more at the apparent indifference of Providence. He had one hope, which was to be true to his faith, and teach it to the end.

Nell mastered her grief by an astonishing reserve of strength. Undoubtedly it was that marvellously merciful power which enables a person, for the love of others, to bear up under a cross, or even to fight death himself. As Young had his bright-eyed Indian boys and girls, who had learned Christianity from him, and whose future depended on him, so Nell had her aged and weakening uncle to care for and cherish.

Jim's attentions to her before the deep affliction had not been slight, but now they were so marked as to be unmistakable. In some way Jim seemed changed since he had returned from the Delaware encampment. Although he went back to the work with his old aggressiveness, he was not nearly so successful as he had been before. Whether or not this was his fault, he took his failure deeply to heart. There was that in his tenderness which caused Nell to regard him, in one sense, as she did her uncle. Jim, too, leaned upon her, and she accepted his devotion where once she had repelled it. She had unconsciously betrayed a great deal when she had turned so tenderly to him in the first moments after her recognition, and he remembered. He did not speak of love to her; he let a thousand little acts of kindness, a constant thoughtfulness of her plead his cause.

The days succeeding Heckewelder's departure were

remarkable for several reasons. Although the weather was enticing, the number of visiting Indians gradually decreased. Not a runner from any tribe came into the village, and finally the day dawned when not a single Indian from the outlying towns was present to hear the preaching.

Jim spoke, as usual. After several days had passed and none but converted Indians made up the congregation, the young man began to be uneasy in mind.

Young and Edwards were unable to account for the unusual absence from worship, yet they did not see in it anything to cause especial concern. Often there had been days without visitation to the Village of Peace.

Finally Jim went to consult Glickhican. He found the Delaware at work in the potato patch. The old Indian dropped his hoe and bowed to the missionary. A reverential and stately courtesy always characterized the attitude of the Indians toward the young White Father.

"Glickhican, can you tell me why no Indians have come here lately?"

The old chief shook his head.

"Does their absence signify ill to the Village of Peace?"

"Glickhican saw a blackbird flitting in the shadow of the moon. The bird hovered above the Village of Peace, but sang no song."

The old Delaware vouchsafed no other than this strange reply.

Jim returned to his cabin decidedly worried. He did not at all like Glickhican's answer. The purport of it seemed to be that a cloud was rising on the bright horizon of the Christian village. He confided his fears to Young and Edwards. After discussing the situation, the three missionaries decided to send for Heckewelder. He was the leader of the Mission; he knew more of Indian craft than any of them, and how to meet it. If this calm in the heretofore busy life of the Mission was the lull before the storm, Heckewelder should be there with his experience and influence.

"For nearly ten years Heckewelder has anticipated trouble from hostile savages," said Edwards, "but so far he has always averted it. As you know, he has confined himself mostly to propitiating the Indians, and persuading them to be friendly, and listen to us. We'll send for him."

Accordingly they dispatched a runner to Goshocking. In due time the Indian returned with the startling news that Heckewelder had left the Indian village days before, as had, in fact, all the savages except the few converted ones. The same held true in the case of Sandusky, the adjoining town. Moreover, it had been impossible to obtain any news in regard to Zeisberger.

The missionaries were now thoroughly alarmed, and knew not what to do. They concealed the real state of affairs from Nell and her uncle, desiring to keep them from anxiety as long as possible. That night the three teachers went to bed with heavy hearts.

The following morning at daybreak, Jim was awakened from a sound sleep by someone calling at his window. He got up to learn who it was, and, in the gray light, saw Edwards standing outside.

"What's the matter?" questioned Jim, hurriedly.

"Matter enough. Hurry. Get into your clothes," replied Edwards. "As soon as you are dressed, quietly awaken Mr. Wells and Nellie, but do not frighten them."

"But what's the trouble?" queried Jim, as he began to dress.

"The Indians are pouring into the village as thickly as flying leaves in autumn."

Edwards' exaggerated assertion proved to be almost literally true. No sooner had the rising sun dispelled the mist than it shone on long lines of marching braves, mounted warriors, hundreds of packhorses approaching from the forest. The orderly procession was proof of a concerted plan on the part of the invaders.

From their windows the missionaries watched with bated breath; with wonder and fear they saw the long lines of dusky forms. When they were in the clearing the savages busied themselves with their packs. Long rows of teepees sprung up as if by magic. The savages had come to stay! The number of incoming visitors did not lessen until noon, when a few straggling groups marked the end of the invading host. Most significant of all was the fact that neither child, maiden, nor squaw accompanied this army.

Jim appraised the number at six or seven hundred, more than had ever before visited the village at one time. They were mostly Delawares, with many Shawnees, and a few Hurons among them. It was soon evident, however, that for the present, at least, the Indians did not intend any hostile demonstration. They were quiet in manner, and busy about their teepees and campfires, but there was an absence of the curiosity that had characterized the former sojourns of Indians at the peaceful village.

After a brief consultation with his brother missionaries, who all were opposed to his preaching that afternoon, Jim decided he would not deviate from his usual custom. He held the afternoon service, and spoke to the largest congregation that had ever sat before him. He was surprised to find that the sermon, which heretofore so strongly impressed the savages, did not now arouse the slightest enthusiasm. It was followed by a brooding silence of a boding, ominous import.

Four white men, dressed in Indian garb, had been

the most attentive listeners to Jim's sermon. He recognized three as Simon Girty, Elliott and Deering, the renegades, and he learned from Edwards that the other was the notorious McKee. These men went through the village stalking into the shops and cabins, and acting as do men who are on a tour of inspection.

So intrusive was their curiosity that Jim hurried back to Mr. Wells' cabin and remained there in seclusion. Of course, by this time Nell and her uncle knew of the presence of the hostile savages. They were frightened, and barely regained their composure when the young man assured them he was certain they had no real cause for fear.

Jim was sitting at the doorstep with Mr. Wells and Edwards when Girty, with his comrades, came toward them. The renegade leader was a tall, athletic man, with a dark, strong face. There was in it none of the brutality and ferocity which marked his brother's visage. Simon Girty appeared keen, forceful, authoritative, as, indeed, he must have been to have attained the power he held in the confederated tribes. His companions presented wide contrasts. Elliott was a small, spare man of cunning, vindictive aspect; McKee looked, as might have been supposed from his reputation, and Deering was a fit mate for the absent Girty. Simon appeared to be a man of some intelligence, who had been thrust into a degrading position, but who, once there, used all his power to make that position a great one. The other renegades were desperadoes.

"Where's Heckewelder?" asked Girty, curtly, as he stopped before the missionaries.

"He started out for the Indian towns on the Muskingong," answered Edwards. "But we have had no word from either him or Zeisberger."

"When d'ye expect him?"

"I can't say. Perhaps tomorrow, and then, again, maybe not for a week."

"His is in authority here, ain't he?"

"Yes; but he left me in charge of the Mission. Can I serve you in any way?"

"I reckon not," said the renegade, turning to his companions. They conversed in low tones for a moment. Presently McKee, Elliott, and Deering went toward the newly erected teepees.

"Girty, do you mean us any ill will?" earnestly asked Edwards. He had met the man on more than one occasion, and had no hesitation about questioning him.

"I can't say as I do," answered the renegade, and those who heard him believed him. "But I'm agin this redskin preachin', an' hev been all along. The Injuns are mad clear through, an' I ain't sayin' I've tried to quiet 'em any. This missionary work has got to be stopped, one way or another. Now what I waited here to say is this: I ain't quite forgot I was white once, an' believe you fellars are honest. I'm willin' to go outer my way to help you git away from here."

"Go away?" echoed Edwards.

"That's it," answered Girty, shouldering his rifle.

"But why? We are perfectly harmless; we are only doing good and hurt no one. Why should we go?"

"'Cause there's liable to be trouble," said the renegade, significantly.

Edwards turned slowly to Mr. Wells and Jim. The old missionary was trembling visibly. Jim was pale; but more with anger than fear.

"Thank you, Girty, but we'll stay," and Jim's voice rang clear.

CHAPTER XXI

Jim, come out here," called Edwards at the window of Mr. Wells' cabin.

The young man arose from the breakfast table, and when outside found Edwards standing by the door with an Indian brave. He was a Wyandot lightly built, lithe and wiry, easily recognizable as an Indian runner. When Jim appeared the man handed him a small packet. He unwound a few folds of some oily skin to find a square piece of birch bark, upon which were scratched the following words:

> "Rev. J. Downs. Greeting.
>
> "Your brother is alive and safe. Whispering Winds rescued him by taking him as her husband. Leave the Village of Peace. Pipe and Half King have been influenced by Girty.
>
> "ZANE."

"Now, what do you think of that?" exclaimed Jim, handing the message to Edwards. "Thank Heaven, Joe was saved!"

"Zane? That must be the Zane who married Tarhe's daughter," answered Edwards, when he had read the note. "I'm rejoiced to hear of your brother."

"Joe married to that beautiful Indian maiden! Well, of all wonderful things," mused Jim. "What will Nell say?"

"We're getting warnings enough. Do you appreciate that?" asked Edwards. "'Pipe and Half King have been influenced by Girty.' Evidently the writer deemed that brief sentence of sufficient meaning."

"Edwards, we're preachers. We can't understand such things. I am learning, at least something every day. Colonel Zane advised us not to come out here. Wetzel said 'Go back to Fort Henry.' Girty warned us, and now comes this peremptory order from Isaac Zane."

"Well?"

"It means that these border men see what we will not admit. We ministers have such hope and trust in God that we cannot realize the dangers of this life. I fear that our work has been in vain."

"Never. We have already saved many souls. Do not be discouraged."

All this time the runner had stood near at hand straight as an arrow. Presently Edwards suggested that the Wyandot was waiting to be questioned, and accordingly he asked the Indian if he had anything further to communicate.

"Huron—go by—paleface." Here he held up both hands and shut his fists several times, evidently enumerating how many white men he had seen. "Here—when—high—sun."

With that he bounded lightly past them and loped off with an even, swinging stride.

"What did he mean?" asked Jim, almost sure he had not heard the runner aright.

"He meant that a party of white men are approaching, and will be here by noon. I never knew an Indian runner to carry unreliable information. We have joyful news, both in regard to your brother, and the Village of Peace. Let us go in to tell the others."

The Huron runner's report proved to be correct. Shortly before noon signals from Indian scouts proclaimed the approach of a band of white men. Evidently Girty's forces had knowledge beforehand of the proximity of this band, for the signals created no excitement. The Indians expressed only a lazy curiosity. Soon several Delaware scouts appeared, escorting a large party of frontiersmen.

These men turned out to be Captain Williamson's force, which had been out on an expedition after a marauding tribe of Chippewas. This last-named tribe had recently harried the remote settlers and committed depredations on the outskirts of the white settlements eastward. The company was composed of men who had served in the garrison at Fort Pitt, and hunters and backwoodsmen from Yellow Creek and Fort Henry. The captain himself was a typical borderman, rough and bluff, hardened by long years of border life, and, like most pioneers, having no more use for an Indian than for a snake. He had led his party after the marauders, and surprised and slaughtered nearly all of them. Returning eastward he had passed through Goshocking, where he learned of the muttering storm rising over the Village of Peace, and had come more out of curiosity than hope to avert misfortune.

The advent of so many frontiersmen seemed a godsend to the perplexed and worried missionaries. They welcomed the newcomers most heartily. Beds were made in several of the newly erected cabins; the village was given over for the comfort of the frontiersmen. Edwards conducted Captain Williamson through the shops and schools, and the old borderman's weatherbeaten face expressed a comical surprise.

"Wal, I'll be durned If I ever expected to see a redskin work," was his only comment on the industries.

"We are greatly alarmed by the presence of Girty and

his followers," said Edwards. "We have been warned to leave, but have not been actually threatened. What do you infer from the appearance here of these hostile savages?"

"It hardly 'pears to me they'll bother you preachers. They're agin the Christian redskins, that's plain."

"Why have we been warned to go?"

"That's natural, seein' they're agin the preachin'."

"What will they do with the converted Indians?"

"Mighty onsartin. They might let them go back to the tribes, but 'pears to me these good Injuns won't go. Another thing, Girty is afeered of the spread of Christianity."

"'Pears likely."

"And you, also, think we'd do well to leave here."

"I do, sartin. We're startin' for Fort Henry soon. You'd better come along with us."

"Captain Williamson, we're going to stick it out, Girty or no Girty."

"You can't do no good stayin' here. Pipe and Half King won't stand for the singin', prayin' redskins, especially when they've got all these cattle and fields of grain."

"Wetzel said the same."

"Hev you seen Wetzel?"

"Yes; he rescued a girl from Jim Girty, and returned her to us."

"That so? I met Wetzel and Jack Zane back a few miles in the woods. They're layin' for somebody, because when I asked them to come along they refused, sayin' they had work as must be done. They looked like it, too. I never hearn tell of Wetzel advisin' anyone before; but I'll say if he told me to do a thing, by gosh! I'd do it."

"As men, we might very well take the advice given us; but as preachers we must stay here to do all we can for these Christian Indians. One thing more: Will you help us?"

"I reckon I'll stay here to see the thing out," answered Williamson. Edwards made a mental note of the frontiersman's evasive answer.

Jim had, meanwhile, made the acquaintance of a young minister, John Christy by name, who had lost his sweetheart in one of the Chippewa raids, and had accompanied the Williamson expedition in the hope he might rescue her.

"How long have you been out?" asked Jim.

"About four weeks now," answered Christy. "My betrothed was captured five weeks ago yesterday. I joined Williamson's band, which made up at Short Creek to take the trail of the flying Chippewas, in the hope I might find her. But not a trace! The expedition fell upon a band of redskins over on the Walhonding, and killed nearly all of them. I learned from a wounded Indian that a renegade had made off with a white girl about a week previous. Perhaps it was poor Lucy."

Jim related the circumstances of his own capture by Jim Girty, the rescue of Nell, and Kate's sad fate.

"Could Jim Girty have gotten your girl?" inquired Jim, in conclusion.

"It's hardly probable. The description doesn't tally with Girty's. This renegade was short and heavy, and noted especially for his strength. Of course, an Indian would first speak of some such distinguishing feature. There are, however, ten or twelve renegades on the border, and, excepting Jim Girty, one's bad as another."

"Then it's a common occurrence, this abducting girls from the settlements?"

"Yes, and the strange thing is that one never hears of such doings until he gets out on the frontier."

"For that matter, you don't hear much of anything, except of the wonderful richness and promise of the western country."

"You're right. Rumors of fat, fertile lands induce the colonist to become a pioneer. He comes west with his family; two out of every ten lose their scalps, and in some places the average is much greater. The wives, daughters, and children are carried off into captivity. I have been on the border two years, and know that the rescue of any captive, as Wetzel rescued your friend, is a remarkable exception."

"If you have so little hope of recovering your sweetheart what then is your motive for accompanying this band of hunters?"

"Revenge!"

"And you are a preacher?" Jim's voice did not disguise his astonishment.

"I was a preacher, and now I am thirsting for vengeance," answered Christy, his face clouding darkly. "Wait until you learn what frontier life means. You are young here yet; you are flushed with the success of your teaching; you have lived a short time in this quiet village, where until the last few days, all has been serene. You know nothing of the strife, of the necessity of fighting, of the cruelty which makes up this border existence. Only two years have hardened me so that I actually pant for the blood of the renegade who has robbed me. A frontiersman must take his choice of succumbing or cutting his way through flesh and bone. Blood will be spilled; if not yours, then your foe's. The pioneers run from the plow to fight; they halt in the cutting of corn to defend themselves, and in winter must battle against cold and hardship, which would be less cruel if there was time in summer to prepare for winter, for the savages leave them hardly an opportunity to plant crops. How many pioneers have given up, and gone back east? Find me any who would not return home tomorrow, if they could. All that brings them out here is the chance for a home, and all that keeps them here is the poor hope of finally attaining their object. Always there is a possibility of future prosperity. But this generation, if it survives, will never see prosperity and happiness. What does this border life engender in a pioneer who holds his own in it? Of all things, not Christianity. He becomes a fighter, keen as the redskin who steals through the coverts."

The serene days of the Village of Peace had passed into history. Soon that depraved vagabond, the French trader, with cheap trinkets and vile whisky, made his appearance. This was all that was needed to inflame the visitors. Where they had been only bold and impudent, they became insulting and abusive. They execrated the Christian Indians for their neutrality; scorned them for worshiping this unknown God, and denounced a religion which made women of strong men.

The slaughtering of cattle commenced; the despoiling of maize fields, and robbing of corn cribs began with the drunkenness.

All this time it was seen that Girty and Elliott consulted often with Pipe and Half King. The latter was the only Huron chief opposed to neutrality toward the Village of Peace, and he was, if possible, more fierce in his hatred than Pipe. The future of the Christian settlement rested with these two chiefs. Girty and Elliott, evidently, were the designing schemers, and they worked diligently on the passions of these simpleminded, but fierce, warlike chiefs.

Greatly to the relief of the distracted missionaries, Heckewelder returned to the village. Jaded and haggard, he presented a travelworn appearance. He made the astonishing assertions that he had been thrice waylaid and assaulted on his way to Goshocking; then detained by a roving band of Chippewas, and soon after his arrival at their camping ground a renegade had run off with a white woman captive, while the Indians west of the village were in an uproar. Zeisberger, however, was safe in the Moravian town of Salem, some miles west of Goshocking. Heckewelder had expected to find the same condition of affairs as existed in the Village of Peace; but he was bewildered by the great array of hostile Indians. Chiefs who had once extended friendly hands to him, now drew back coldly, as they said:

"Washington is dead. The American armies are cut to pieces. The few thousands who had escaped the British are collecting at Fort Pitt to steal the Indian's land."

Heckewelder vigorously denied all these assertions, knowing they had been invented by Girty and Elliott. He exhausted all his skill and patience in the vain endeavor to show Pipe where he was wrong. Half King had been so well coached by the renegades that he refused to listen. The other chiefs maintained a cold reserve that was baffling and exasperating. Wingenund took no active part in the councils; but his presence apparently denoted that he had sided with the others. The outlook was altogether discouraging.

"I'm completely fagged out," declared Heckewelder, that night when he returned to Edwards' cabin. He dropped into a chair as one whose strength is entirely spent, whose indomitable spirit has at last been broken.

"Lie down to rest," said Edwards.

"Oh, I can't. Matters look so black."

"You're tired out and discouraged. You'll feel better tomorrow. The situation is not, perhaps, so hopeless. The presence of these frontiersmen should encourage us."

"What will they do? What can they do?" cried Heckewelder, bitterly. "I tell you never before have I encountered such gloomy, stony Indians. It seems to me that they are in no vacillating state. They act like men whose course is already decided upon, and who are only waiting."

"For what?" asked Jim, after a long silence.

"God only knows! Perhaps for time; possibly for a final decision, and it may be, for a reason, the very thought of which makes me faint."

"Tell us," said Edwards, speaking quietly, for he had ever been the calmest of the missionaries.

"Never mind. Perhaps it's only my nerves. I'm all unstrung, and could suspect anything tonight."

"Heckewelder, tell us?" Jim asked, earnestly.

"My friends, I pray I am wrong. God help us if my fears are correct. I believe the Indians are waiting for Jim Girty."

CHAPTER XXII

Simon Girty lolled on a blanket in Half King's teepee. He was alone, awaiting his allies. Rings of white smoke curled lazily from his lips as he puffed on a long Indian pipe, and gazed out over the clearing that contained the Village of Peace.

Still water has something in its placid surface significant of deep channels, of hidden depths; the dim outlines of the forest is dark with meaning, suggestive of its wild internal character. So Simon Girty's hard, bronzed face betrayed the man. His degenerate brother's features were revolting; but his own were striking, and fell short of being handsome only because of their craggy hardness. Years of revolt, of bitterness, of consciousness of wasted life, had graven their stern lines on that copper, masklike face. Yet despite the cruelty there, the forbidding shade on it, as if a reflection from a dark soul, it was not wholly a bad countenance. Traces still lingered, faintly, of a man in whom kindlier feelings had once predominated.

In a moment of pique Girty had deserted his military post at Fort Pitt, and become an outlaw of his own volition. Previous to that time he had been an able soldier, and a good fellow. When he realized that his step was irrevocable, that even his best friends condemned him, he plunged, with anger and despair in his heart, into a war upon his race. Both of his brothers had long been border ruffians, whose only protection from the outraged pioneers lay in the faraway camps of hostile tribes. George Girty had so sunk his individuality into the savage's that he was no longer a white man. Jim Girty stalked over the borderland with a bloody tomahawk, his long arm outstretched to clutch some unfortunate white woman, and with his hideous smile of death. Both of these men were far lower than the worst savages, and it was almost wholly to their deeds of darkness that Simon Girty owed his infamous name.

Today, White Chief, as Girty was called, awaited his men. A slight tremor of the ground caused him to turn his gaze. The Huron chief, Half King, resplendent in his magnificent array, had entered the teepee. He squatted in a corner, rested the bowl of his great pipe on his knee, and smoked in silence. The habitual frown of his black brow, like a shaded, overhanging cliff; the fire flashing from his eyes, as a shining light is reflected from a dark pool; his closely shut, bulging jaw, all bespoke a nature, lofty in its Indian pride and arrogance, but more cruel than death.

Another chief stalked into the teepee and seated himself. It was Pipe. His countenance denoted none of the intelligence that made Wingenund's face so noble; it was even coarser than Half King's, and his eyes, resembling live coals in the dark; the long, cruel lines of his jaw; the thin, tightly closed lips, which looked as if they could relax only to utter a savage command, expressed fierce cunning and brutality.

"White Chief is idle today," said Half King, speaking in the Indian tongue.

"King, I am waiting. Girty is slow, but sure," answered the renegade.

"The eagle sails slowly round and round, up and up," replied Half King, with majestic gestures, "until his eye sees all, until he knows his time; then he folds his wings and swoops down from the blue sky like the forked fire. So does White Chief. But Half King is impatient."

"Today decides the fate of the Village of Peace," answered Girty, imperturbably.

"Ugh!" grunted Pipe.

Half King vented his approval in the same meaning exclamation.

An hour passed; the renegade smoked in silence; the chiefs did likewise.

A horseman rode up to the door of the teepee, dismounted, and came in. It was Elliott. He had been absent twenty hours. His buckskin suit showed the effect of hard riding through the thickets.

"Hullo, Bill, any sign of Jim?" was Girty's greeting to his lieutenant.

"Nary. He's not been seen near the Delaware camp. He's after that chap who married Winds."

"I thought so. Jim's roundin' up a tenderfoot who will be a bad man to handle if he has half a chance. I saw as much the day he took his horse away from Silver. He finally did fer the Shawnee, an' almost put Jim out. My brother oughtn' to give rein to personal revenge at a time like this." Girty's face did not change, but his tone was one of annoyance.

"Jim said he'd be here today, didn't he?"

"Today is as long as we allowed to wait."

"He'll come. Where's Jake and Mac?"

"They're here somewhere, drinkin' like fish, an' raisin' hell."

Two more renegades appeared at the door, and, entering the teepee, squatted down in Indian fashion. The little wiry man with the weazened face was McKee; the other was the latest acquisition to the renegade force, Jake

Deering, deserter, thief, murderer—everything that is bad. In appearance he was of medium height, but very heavily, compactly built, and evidently as strong as an ox. He had a tangled shock of red hair, a broad, bloated face; big, dull eyes, like the openings of empty furnaces, and an expression of beastliness.

Deering and McKee were intoxicated.

"Bad time fer drinkin'," said Girty, with disapproval in his glance.

"What's that ter you?" growled Deering. "I'm here ter do your work, an' I reckon it'll be done better if I'm drunk."

"Don't git careless," replied Girty, with that cool tone and dark look such as dangerous men use. "I'm only sayin' it's a bad time fer you, because if this bunch of frontiersmen happen to git onto you bein' the renegade that was with the Chippewas an' got thet young feller's girl, there's liable to be trouble."

"They ain't agoin' ter find out."

"Where is she?"

"Back there in the woods."

"Mebbe it's as well. Now, don't git so drunk you'll blab all you know. We've lots of work to do without havin' to clean up Williamson's bunch," replied Girty. "Bill, tie up the tent flaps an' we'll git to council."

Elliott arose to carry out the order, and had pulled in the deerhide flaps, when one of them was jerked outward to disclose the befrilled person of Jim Girty. Except for a discoloration over his eye, he appeared as usual.

"Ugh!" grunted Pipe, who was glad to see his renegade friend.

Half King evinced the same feeling.

"Hullo," was Simon Girty's greeting.

"'Pears I'm on time fer the picnic," said Jim Girty, with his ghastly leer.

Bill Elliott closed the flaps, after giving orders to the guard to prevent any Indians from loitering near the tee-pee.

"Listen," said Simon Girty, speaking low in the Delaware language. "The time is ripe. We have come here to break forever the influence of the white man's religion. Our councils have been held; we shall drive away the missionaries, and burn the Village of Peace."

He paused, leaning forward in his exceeding earnestness, with his bronzed face lined by swelling veins, his whole person made rigid by the murderous thought. Then he hissed between his teeth: *"What shall we do with these Christian Indians?"*

Pipe raised his war club, struck it upon the ground, then handed it to Half King.

Half King took the club and repeated the action.

Both chiefs favored the death penalty.

"Feed 'em to the buzzards," croaked Jim Girty.

Simon Girty knitted his brows in thought. The question of what to do with the converted Indians had long perplexed him.

"No," said he; "let us drive away the missionaries, burn the village, and take the Indians back to camp. We'll keep them there; they'll soon forget."

"Pipe does not want them," declared the Delaware.

"Christian Indians shall never sit round Half King's fire," cried the Huron.

Simon Girty knew the crisis had come; that but few moments were left him to decide as to the disposition of the Christians; and he thought seriously. Certainly he did not want the Christians murdered. However cruel his life, and great his misdeeds, he was still a man. If possible, he desired to burn the village and ruin the religious influence, but without shedding blood. Yet, with all his power, he was handicapped, and that by the very chiefs most nearly under his control. He could not subdue this growing Christian influence without the help of Pipe and Half King. To these savages a thing was either right or wrong. He had sown the seed of unrest and jealousy in the savage breasts, and the fruit was the decree of death. As far as these Indians were concerned, this decision was unalterable.

On the other hand, if he did not spread ruin over the Village of Peace, the missionaries would soon get such a grasp on the tribes that their hold would never be broken. He could not allow that, even if he was forced to sacrifice the missionaries along with their converts, for he saw in the growth of this religion his own downfall. The border must be hostile to the whites, or it could no longer be his home. To be sure, he had aided the British in the Revolution, and could find a refuge among them; but this did not suit him.

He became an outcast because of failure to win the military promotion which he had so much coveted. He had failed among his own people. He had won a great position in an alien race, and he loved his power. To sway men—Indians, if not others—to his will; to avenge himself for the fancied wrong done him; to be great, had been his unrelenting purpose.

He knew he must sacrifice the Christians, or eventually lose his own power. He had no false ideas about the converted Indians. He knew they were innocent; that they were a thousand times better off than the pagan Indians; that they had never harmed him, nor would they ever do so; but if he allowed them to spread their religion there was an end of Simon Girty.

His decision was characteristic of the man. He would sacrifice anyone, or all, to retain his supremacy. He knew the fulfilment of the decree as laid down by Pipe and Half King would be known as his work. His name, infamous now, would have an additional horror, and ever be remembered by posterity in unspeakable loathing, in unsoftening wrath. He knew this, and deep down in his heart awoke a numbered chord of humanity that twinged with strange pain. What awful work he must sanction to keep his vaunted power! More bitter than all was the knowledge that to retain this hold over the Indians he must commit a deed which, so far as the whites were concerned, would take away his great name, and brand him a coward.

He briefly reviewed his stirring life. Singularly fitted for a leader, in a few years he had risen to the most powerful position on the border. He wielded more influence than any chief. He had been opposed to the invasion of the pioneers, and this alone, without his sagacity or his generalship, would have given him control of many tribes. But hatred for his own people, coupled with unerring judgment, a remarkable ability to lead expeditions, and his invariable success, had raised him higher and higher until he stood alone. He was the most powerful man west of the Alleghenies. His fame was such that the British had importuned him to help them, and had actually, in more than one instance, given him command over British subjects.

All of which meant that he had a great, even though an infamous name. No matter what he was blamed for; no matter how many dastardly deeds had been committed by his depraved brothers and laid to his door, he knew he had never done a cowardly act. That which he had committed while he was drunk he considered as having been done by the liquor, and not by the man. He loved his power, and he loved his name.

In all Girty's eventful, ignoble life, neither the alienation from his people, the horror they ascribed to his power, nor the sacrifice of his life to stand high among the savage races, nor any of the cruel deeds committed while at war, hurt him a tithe as much as did this sanctioning the massacre of the Christians.

Although he was a vengeful, unscrupulous, evil man, he had never acted the coward.

Half King waited long for Girty to speak; since he remained silent, the wily Huron suggested they take a vote on the question.

"Let us burn the Village of Peace, drive away the missionaries, and take the Christians back to the Delaware towns—all without spilling blood," said Girty, determined to carry his point, if possible.

"I say the same," added Elliott, refusing the warclub held out to him by Half King.

"Me, too," voted McKee, not so drunk but that he understood the lightninglike glance Girty shot at him.

"Kill 'em all; kill everybody," cried Deering in drunken glee. He took the club and pounded with it on the ground.

Pipe repeated his former performance, as also did Half King, after which he handed the black, knotted symbol of death to Jim Girty.

Three had declared for saving the Christians, and three for the death penalty.

Six pairs of burning eyes were fastened on the Deathshead.

Pipe and Half King were coldly relentless; Deering awoke to brutal earnestness; McKee and Elliott watched with bated breath. These men had formed themselves into a tribunal to decide on the life or death of many, and the situation, if not the greatest in their lives, certainly was one of vital importance.

Simon Girty cursed all the fates. He dared not openly

oppose the voting, and he could not, before those cruel but just chiefs, try to influence his brother's vote.

As Jim Girty took the war club, Simon read in his brother's face the doom of the converted Indians, and he muttered to himself:

"Now tremble an' shrink, all you Christians!"

Jim was not in a hurry. Slowly he poised the war club. He was playing as a cat plays with a mouse; he was glorying in his power. The silence was that of death. *It signified the silence of death.* The war club descended with violence.

"Feed the Christians to ther buzzards!"

CHAPTER XXIII

I have been here before," said Joe to Whispering Winds. "I remember that vine-covered stone. We crawled over it to get at Girty and Silvertip. There's the little knoll; here's the very spot where I was hit by a flying tomahawk. Yes, and there's the spring. Let me see, what did Wetzel call this spot?"

"Beautiful Spring," answered the Indian girl.

"That's it, and it's well named. What a lovely place!"

Nature had been lavish in the beautifying of this inclosed dell. It was about fifty yards wide, and nestled among little, wooded knolls and walls of gray, lichen-covered stone. Though the sun shone brightly into the opening, and the rain had free access to the mossy ground, no stormy winds ever entered this well-protected glade.

Joe reveled in the beauty of the scene, even while he was too weak to stand erect. He suffered no pain from his wound, although he had gradually grown dizzy, and felt as if the ground was rising before him. He was glad to lie upon the mossy ground in the little cavern under the cliff.

Upon examination his wound was found to have opened, and was bleeding. His hunting coat was saturated with blood. Whispering Winds washed the cut, and dressed it with cooling leaves. Then she rebandaged it tightly with Joe's linsey handkerchiefs, and while he rested comfortably she gathered bundles of ferns, carrying them to the little cavern. When she had a large quantity of these she sat down near Joe, and began to weave the long stems into a kind of screen. The fern stalks were four feet long and half a foot wide; these she deftly laced together, making broad screens which would serve to ward off the night dews. This done, she next built a fireplace with flat stones. She found wild apples, plums, and turnips on the knoll above the glade. Then she cooked strips of meat which had been brought with them. Lance grazed on the long grass just within the glade, and Mose caught two rabbits. When darkness settled down Whispering Winds called the dog within the cavern, and hung the screens before the opening.

Several days passed. Joe rested quietly, and began to recover strength. Besides the work of preparing their meals, Whispering Winds had nothing to do save sit near the invalid and amuse or interest him so that he would not fret or grow impatient, while his wound was healing.

They talked about their future prospects. After visiting the Village of Peace, they would go to Fort Henry, where Joe could find employment. They dwelt upon the cabin they would build, and passed many happy moments planning a new home. Joe's love of the wilderness had in no wise diminished; but a blow on his head from a heavy tomahawk, and a vicious stab in the back, had lessened his zeal so far that he understood it was not wise to sacrifice life for the pleasures of the pathless woods. He could have the last without the danger of being shot at from behind every tree. He reasoned that it would be best for him to take his wife to Fort Henry, there find employment, and devote his leisure time to roaming in the forest.

"Will the palefaces be kind to the Indian who has learned to love them?" Whispering Winds asked wistfully of Joe.

"Indeed they will," answered Joe, and he told her the story of Isaac Zane; how he took his Indian bride home; how her beauty and sweetness soon won all the white people's love. "It will be so with you, my wife."

"Whispering Winds knows so little," she murmured.

"Why, you are learning every day, and even if such was not the case, you know enough for me."

"Whispering Winds will be afraid; she fears a little to go."

"I'll be glad when we can be on the move," said Joe, with his old impatient desire for action. "How soon, Winds, can we set off?"

"As many days," answered the Indian girl, holding up five fingers.

"So long? I want to leave this place."

"Leave Beautiful Spring?"

"Yes, even this sweet place. It was a horror for me. I'll never forget the night I first saw that spring shining in the moonlight. It was right above the rock that I looked into the glade. The moon was reflected in the dark pool, and as I gazed into the shadowy depths of the dark water, I suddenly felt an unaccountable terror; but I oughtn't to have the same feeling now. We are safe, are we not?"

"We are safe," murmured Whispering Winds.

"Yet I have the same chill of fear whenever I look at the beautiful spring, and at night as I awake to hear the soft babble of running water, I freeze until my heart feels like cold lead. Winds, I'm not a coward; but I can't help this feeling. Perhaps, it's only the memory of that awful night with Wetzel."

"An Indian feels so when he passes to his unmarked grave," answered Winds, gazing solemnly at him. "Whispering Winds does not like this fancy of yours. Let us leave Beautiful Spring. You are almost well. Ah! if Whispering Winds should lose you! I love you!"

"And I love you, my beautiful wildflower," answered Joe, stroking the dark head so near his own.

A tender smile shone on his face. He heard a slight noise without the cave, and, looking up, saw that which caused the smile to fade quickly.

"Mose!" he called, sharply. The dog was away chasing rabbits.

Whispering Winds glanced over her shoulder with a startled cry, which ended in a scream.

Not two yards behind her stood Jim Girty.

Hideous was his face in its triumphant ferocity. He held a long knife in his hand, and, snarling like a mad wolf, he made a forward lunge.

Joe raised himself quickly; but almost before he could lift his hand in defense, the long blade was sheathed in his breast.

Slowly he sank back, his gray eyes contracting with the old steely flash. The will to do was there, but the power was gone forever.

"Remember, Girty, murderer! I am Wetzel's friend," he cried, gazing at his slayer with unutterable scorn.

Then the gray eyes softened, and sought the blanched face of the stricken maiden.

"Winds," he whispered faintly.

She was as one frozen with horror.

The gray eyes gazed into hers with lingering tenderness; then the film of death came upon them.

The renegade raised his bloody knife, and bent over the prostrate form.

Whispering Winds threw herself upon Girty with the blind fury of a maddened lioness. Cursing fiercely, he stabbed her once, twice, three times. She fell across the body of her lover, and clasped it, convulsively.

Girty gave one glance at his victims; deliberately wiped the gory knife on Winds' leggings, and, with another glance, hurried and fearful, around the glade, he plunged into the thicket.

An hour passed. A dark stream crept from the quiet figures toward the spring. It dyed the moss and the green violet leaves. Slowly it wound its way to the clear water, dripping between the pale blue flowers. The little fall below the spring was no longer snowy white; blood had tinged it red.

A dog came bounding into the glade. He leaped the brook, hesitated on the bank, and lowered his nose to sniff at the water. He bounded up the bank to the cavern.

A long, mournful howl broke the wilderness's quiet.

Another hour passed. The birds were silent; the insects still. The sun sank behind the trees, and the shades of evening gathered.

The ferns on the other side of the glade trembled. A slight rustle of dead leaves disturbed the stillness. The dog whined, then barked. The tall form of a hunter rose out of the thicket, and stepped into the glade with his eyes bent upon moccasin tracks in the soft moss.

The trail he had been following led him to this bloody spring.

"I might hev knowed it," he muttered.

Wetzel, for it was he, leaned upon his long rifle while his keen eyes took in the details of the tragedy. The whining dog, the bloody water, the motionless figures lying in a last embrace, told the sad story.

"Joe an' Winds," he muttered.

Only a moment did he remain lost in sad reflection. A familiar moccasin-print in the sand on the bank pointed westward. He examined it carefully.

"Two hours gone," he muttered. "I might overtake him."

Then his motions became swift. With two blows of his tomahawk he secured a long piece of grapevine. He took a heavy stone from the bed of the brook. He carried Joe to the spring, and, returning for Winds, placed her beside her lover. This done, he tied one end of the grapevine around the stone, and wound the other about the dead bodies.

He pushed them off the bank into the spring. As the lovers sank into the deep pool they turned, exposing first Winds' sad face, and then Joe's. Then they sank out of sight. Little waves splashed on the shore of the pool; the ripple disappeared, and the surface of the spring became tranquil.

Wetzel stood one moment over the watery grave of the maiden who had saved him, and the boy who had loved him. In the gathering gloom his stalwart form assumed gigantic proportions, and when he raised his long arm and shook his clenched fist toward the west, he resembled a magnificent statue of dark menace.

With a single bound he cleared the pool, and then sped out of the glade. He urged the dog on Girty's trail, and followed the eager beast toward the west. As he disappeared, a long, low sound like a sigh of the night wind swelled and moaned through the gloom.

CHAPTER XXIV

When the first ruddy rays of the rising sun crimsoned the eastern sky, Wetzel slowly wound his way down a rugged hill far west of Beautiful Spring. A white dog, weary and footsore, limped at his side. Both man and beast showed evidences of severe exertion.

The hunter stopped in a little cave under a projecting stone, and, laying aside his rifle, began to gather twigs and sticks. He was particular about selecting the wood, and threw aside many pieces which would have burned well; but when he did kindle a flame it blazed hotly, yet made no smoke.

He sharpened a green stick, and, taking some strips of meat from his pocket, roasted them over the hot flame. He fed the dog first. Mose had crouched close on the ground with his head on his paws, and his brown eyes fastened upon the hunter.

"He had too big a start fer us," said Wetzel, speaking as if the dog were human. It seemed that Wetzel's words were a protest against the meaning in those large, sad eyes.

Then the hunter put out the fire, and, searching for a more secluded spot, finally found one on top of the ledge, where he commanded a good view of his surroundings. The weary dog was asleep. Wetzel settled himself to rest, and was soon wrapped in slumber.

About noon he awoke. He arose, stretched his limbs, and then took an easy position on the front of the ledge, where he could look below. Evidently the hunter was waiting for something. The dog slept on. It was the noon-day hour, when the stillness of the forest almost matched that of midnight. The birds were more quiet than at any other time during daylight.

Wetzel reclined there with his head against the stone, and his rifle resting across his knees.

He listened now to the sounds of the forest. The soft breeze fluttering among the leaves, the rain call of the tree frog, the caw of crows from distant hilltops, the sweet songs of the thrush and oriole, were blended together naturally, harmoniously.

But suddenly the hunter raised his head. A note, deeper than the others, a little too strong, came from far down the shaded hollow. To Wetzel's trained ear it was a discord. He manifested no more than this attention, for the birdcall was the signal he had been awaiting. He whistled a note in answer that was as deep and clear as the one which had aroused him.

Moments passed. There was no repetition of the sound. The songs of the other birds had ceased. Besides Wetzel there was another intruder in the woods.

Mose lifted his shaggy head and growled. The hunter patted the dog. In a few minutes the figure of a tall man appeared among the laurels down the slope. He stopped while gazing up at the ledge. Then, with noiseless step, he ascended the ridge, climbed the rocky ledge, and turned the corner of the stone to face Wetzel. The newcomer was Jonathan Zane.

"Jack, I expected you afore this," was Wetzel's greeting.

"I couldn't make it sooner," answered Zane. "After we

left Williamson and separated, I got turned around by a band of several hundred redskins makin' for the Village of Peace. I went back again, but couldn't find any sign of the trail we're huntin'. Then I makes for this meetin' place. I've been goin' for some ten hours, and am hungry."

"I've got some b'ar ready cooked," said Wetzel, handing Zane several strips of meat.

"What luck did you have?"

"I found Girty's trail, an old one, over here some eighteen or twenty miles, an' follored it until I went almost into the Delaware town. It led to a hut in a deep ravine. I ain't often surprised, but I wus then. I found the dead body of that girl, Kate Wells, we fetched over from Fort Henry. That's sad, but it ain't the surprisin' part. I also found Silvertip, the Shawnee I've been lookin' fer. He was all knocked an' cut up, deader'n a stone. There's been somethin' of a scrap in the hut. I calkilate Girty murdered Kate, but I couldn't think then who did fer Silver, though I allowed the renegade might hev done thet, too. I watched round an' seen Girty come back to the hut. He had ten Injuns with him, an' presently they all made fer the west. I trailed them, but didn't calkilate it'd be wise to tackle the bunch singlehanded, so laid back. A mile or so from the hut I came across hoss tracks minglin' with the moccasin prints. About fifteen mile or so from the Delaware town, Girty left his buckskins, an' they went west, while he stuck to the hoss tracks. I was onto his game in a minute. I cut across country fer Beautiful Spring, but I got there too late. I found the warm bodies of Joe and thet Injun girl, Winds. The snake hed murdered them."

"I allow Joe won over Winds, got away from the Delaware town with her, tried to rescue Kate, and killed Silver in the fight. Girty probably was surprised, an' run after he had knifed the girl."

"'Pears so to me. Joe had two knife cuts, an' one was an old wound."

"You say it wez a bad fight?"

"Must hev been. The hut was all knocked in, an' stuff scattered about. Wal, Joe could go some if he onct got started."

"I'll bet he could. He was the likeliest lad I've seen for many a day."

"If he'd lasted, he'd been somethin' of a hunter an' fighter."

"Too bad. But Lord! you couldn't keep him down, no more than you can lots of these wild young chaps that drift out here."

"I'll allow he had the fever bad."

"Did you hev time to bury them?"

"I hedn't time fer much. I sunk them in the spring."

"It's a pretty deep hole," said Zane, reflectively. "Then you and the dog took Girty's trail, but couldn't catch up with him. He's now with the renegade cutthroats and hundreds of riled Indians over there in the Village of Peace."

"I reckon you're right."

A long silence ensued. Jonathan finished his simple repast, drank from the little spring that trickled under the stone, and, sitting down by the dog, smoothed out his long silken hair.

"Lew, we're pretty good friends, ain't we?" he asked, thoughtfully.

"Jack, you an' the colonel are all the friends I ever had, 'ceptin' thet boy lyin' quiet back there in the woods."

"I know you pretty well, and ain't sayin' a word about your runnin' off from me on many a hunt, but I want to speak plain about this fellow Girty."

"Wal?" said Wetzel, as Zane hesitated.

"Twice in the last few years you and I have had it in for

the same men, both white-livered traitors. You remember? First it was Miller, who tried to ruin my sister Betty, and next it was Jim Girty, who murdered our old friend, as good an old man as ever wore moccasins. Wal, after Miller ran off from the fort, we trailed him down to the river, and I points across and says, 'You or me?' and you says, 'Me.' You was Betty's friend, and I knew she'd be avenged. Miller is lyin' quiet in the woods, and violets have blossomed twice over his grave, though you never said a word; but I know it's true because I know you."

Zane looked earnestly into the dark face of his friend, hoping perhaps to get some verbal assurance there that his brief was true. But Wetzel did not speak, and he continued:

"Another day not so long ago we both looked down at an old friend, and saw his white hair matted with blood. He'd been murdered for nothin'. Again you and me trailed a coward and found him to be Jim Girty. I knew you'd been huntin' him for years, and so I says, 'Lew, you or me?' and you says, 'Me.' I give in to you, for I knew you're a better man than me, and because I wanted you to have the satisfaction. Wal, the months have gone by, and Jim Girty's still livin' and carryin' on. Now he's over there after them poor preachers. I ain't sayin', Lew, that you haven't more agin' him than me, but I do say, let me in on it with you. He always has a gang of redskins with him; he's afraid to travel alone, else you'd had him long ago. Two of us'll have more chance to git him. Let me go with you. When it comes to a finish, I'll stand aside while you give it to him. I'd enjoy seein' you cut him from shoulder to hip. After he leaves the Village of Peace we'll hit his trail, camp on it, and stick to it until it ends in his grave."

The earnest voice of the backwoodsman ceased. Both

men rose and stood facing each other. Zane's bronzed face was hard and tense, expressive of an indomitable will; Wetzel's was coldly dark, with fateful resolve, as if his decree of vengeance, once given, was as immutable as destiny. The big, horny hands gripped in a viselike clasp born of fierce passion, but no word was spoken.

Far to the west somewhere, a befrilled and bedizened renegade pursued the wild tenor of his ways; perhaps, even now steeping his soul in more crime, or staining his hands a deeper red, but sleeping or waking, he dreamed not of this deadly compact that meant his doom.

The two hunters turned their stern faces toward the west, and passed silently down the ridge into the depths of the forest. Darkness found them within rifle shot of the Village of Peace. With the dog creeping between them, they crawled to a position which would, in daylight, command a view of the clearing. Then, while one stood guard, the other slept.

When morning dawned they shifted their position to the top of a low, fern-covered cliff, from which they could see every movement in the village. All the morning they watched with that wonderful patience of men who knew how to wait. The visiting savages were quiet, the missionaries moved about in and out of the shops and cabins; the Christian Indians worked industriously in the fields, while the renegades lolled before a prominent teepee.

"This quiet looks bad," whispered Jonathan to Wetzel. No shouts were heared; not a hostile Indian was seen to move.

"They've come to a decision," whispered Jonathan, and Wetzel answered him:

"If they hev, the Christians don't know it."

An hour later the deep pealing of the church bells broke

the silence. The entire band of Christian Indians gathered near the large log structure, and then marched in orderly form toward the maple grove where the service was always held in pleasant weather. This movement brought the Indians within several hundred yards of the cliff where Zane and Wetzel lay concealed.

"There's Heckewelder walking with old man Wells," whispered Jonathan. "There's Young and Edwards, and yes, there's the young missionary, brother of Joe. 'Pears to me they're foolish to hold service in the face of all those riled Injuns."

"Wuss'n foolish," answered Wetzel.

"Look! By gum! As I'm a livin' sinner there comes the whole crowd of hostile redskins. They've got their guns, and—by gum! they're painted. Looks bad, bad! Not much friendliness about that bunch!"

"They ain't intendin' to be peaceable."

"By gum! You're right. There ain't one of them settin' down. 'Pears to me I know some of them redskins. There's Pipe, sure enough, and Kotoxen. By gum! If there ain't Shingiss; he was friendly once."

"None of them's friendly."

"Look! Lew, look! Right behind Pipe. See that long war bonnet. As I'm a born sinner, that's your old friend, Wingenund. 'Pears to me we've rounded up all our acquaintances."

The two bordermen lay close under the tall ferns and watched the proceedings with sharp eyes. They saw the converted Indians seat themselves before the platform. The crowd of hostile Indians surrounded the glade on all sides, except one, which, singularly enough, was next to the woods.

"Look thar!" exclaimed Wetzel, under his breath. He

pointed off to the right of the maple glade. Jonathan gazed in the direction indicated, and saw two savages stealthily slipping through the bushes, and behind trees. Presently these suspicious-acting spies, or scouts, stopped on a little knoll perhaps a hundred yards from the glade.

Wetzel groaned.

"This ain't comfortable," growled Zane, in a low whisper. "Them red devils are up to somethin' bad. They'd better not move round over here."

The hunters, satisfied that the two isolated savages meant mischief, turned their gaze once more toward the maple grove.

"Ah! Simon, you white traitor! See him, Lew, comin' with his precious gang," said Jonathan. "He's got the whole thing fixed, you can plainly see that. Bill Elliott, McKee; and who's that renegade with Jim Girty? I'll allow he must be the fellar we heard was with the Chippewas. Tough lookin' customer; a good mate fer Jim Girty! A fine lot of border hawks!"

"Somethin' comin' off," whispered Wetzel, as Zane's low growl grew unintelligible.

Jonathan felt, rather than saw, Wetzel tremble.

"The missionaries are consultin'. Ah, there comes one! Which? I guess it's Edwards. By gum! who's that Injun stalkin' over from the hostile bunch. Big chief, whoever he is. Blest if it ain't Half King!"

The watchers saw the chief wave his arm and speak with evident arrogance to Edwards, who, however, advanced to the platform and raised his hand to address the Christians.

"Crack!"

A shot rang out from the thicket. Clutching wildly at his breast, the missionary reeled back, staggered, and fell.

"One of those skulkin' redskins has killed Edwards," said Zane. "But, no; he's not dead! He's getting up. Mebbe he ain't hurt bad. By gum! there's Young comin' forward. Of all the fools!"

It was indeed true that Young had faced the Indians. Half King addressed him as he had the other; but Young raised his hand and began speaking.

"Crack!"

Another shot rang out. Young threw up his hands and fell heavily. The missionaries rushed toward him. Mr. Wells ran round the group, wringing his hands as if distracted.

"He's hard hit," hissed Zane, between his teeth. "You can tell that by the way he fell."

Wetzel did not answer. He lay silent and motionless, his long body rigid, and his face like marble.

"There comes the other young fellar—Joe's brother. He'll get plugged, too," continued Zane, whispering rather to himself than to his companion. "Oh, I hoped they'd show some sense! It's noble for them to die for Christianity, but it won't do no good. By gum! Heckewelder has pulled him back. Now, that's good judgment!"

Half King stepped before the Christians and addressed them. He held in his hand a black war club, which he wielded as he spoke.

Jonathan's attention was now directed from the maple grove to the hunter beside him. He had heard a slight metallic click, as Wetzel cocked his rifle. Then he saw the black barrel slowly rise.

"Listen, Lew. Mebbe it ain't good sense. We're after Girty, you remember; and it's a long shot from here—full three hundred yards."

"You're right, Jack, you're right," answered Wetzel, breathing hard.

"Let's wait, and see what comes off."

"Jack, I can't do it. It'll make our job harder; but I can't help it. I can put a bullet just over the Huron's left eye, an' I'm goin' to do it."

"You can't do it, Lew; you can't! It's too far for any gun. Wait! Wait!" whispered Jonathan, laying his hand on Wetzel's shoulder.

"Wait? Man, can't you see what the unnamable villain is doin'?"

"What?" asked Zane, turning his eyes again to the glade.

The converted Indians sat with bowed heads. Half King raised his war club, and threw it on the ground in front of them.

"He's announcin' the death decree!" hissed Wetzel.

"Well! if he ain't!"

Jonathan looked at Wetzel's face. Then he rose to his knees, as had Wetzel, and tightened his belt. He knew that in another instant they would be speeding away through the forest.

"Lew, my rifle's no good fer that distance. But mebbe yours is. You ought to know. It's not sense, because there's Simon Girty, and there's Jim, the men we're after. If you can hit one, you can another. But go ahead, Lew. Plug that cowardly redskin!"

Wetzel knelt on one knee, and thrust the black rifle forward through the fern leaves. Slowly the fatal barrel rose to a level, and became as motionless as the immovable stones.

Jonathan fixed his keen gaze on the haughty countenance of Half King as he stood with folded arms and scornful mien in front of the Christians he had just condemned.

Even as the short, stinging crack of Wetzel's rifle broke

the silence, Jonathan saw the fierce expression of Half King's dark face change to one of vacant wildness. His arms never relaxed from their folded position. He fell, as falls a monarch of the forest trees, a dead weight.

CHAPTER XXV

"Please do not preach today," said Nell, raising her eyes imploringly to Jim's face.

"Nellie, I must conduct the services as usual. I can not shirk my duty, nor let these renegades see I fear to face them."

"I have such a terrible feeling. I am afraid. I don't want to be left alone. Please do not leave me."

Jim strode nervously up and down the length of the room. Nell's worn face, her beseeching eyes and trembling hands touched his heart. Rather than almost anything else, he desired to please her, to strengthen her; yet how could he shirk his duty?

"Nellie, what is it you fear?" he asked, holding her hands tightly.

"Oh, I don't know what—everything. Uncle is growing weaker every day. Look at Mr. Young; he is only a shadow of his former self, and his anxiety is wearing Mr. Heckewelder out. He is more concerned than he dares admit. You needn't shake your head, for I know it. Then those Indians who are waiting, waiting—for God only knows what? Worse than all to me, I saw that renegade, that fearful beast who made away with poor dear Kate!"

Nell burst into tears, and leaned sobbing on Jim's shoulder.

"Nell, I've kept my courage only because of you," replied Jim, his voice trembling slightly.

She looked up quickly. Something in the pale face which was bent over her told her that now, if ever, was the time for a woman to forget herself, and to cheer, to inspire those around her.

"I am a silly baby, and selfish!" she cried, freeing herself from his hold. "Always thinking of myself." She turned away and wiped the tears from her eyes. "Go, Jim, do your duty; I'll stand by and help you all a woman can."

The missionaries were consulting in Heckewelder's cabin. Zeisberger had returned that morning, and his aggressive, dominating spirit was just what they needed in an hour like this. He raised the downcast spirits of the ministers.

"Hold the service? I should say we will," he declared, waving his hands. "What have we to be afraid of?"

"I do not know," answered Heckewelder, shaking his head doubtfully. "I do not know what to fear. Girty himself told me he bore us no ill will; but I hardly believe him. All this silence, this ominous waiting perplexes, bewilders me."

"Gentlemen, our duty at least is plain," said Jim, impressively. "The faith of these Christian Indians in us is so absolute that they have no fear. They believe in God, and in us. These threatening savages have failed signally to impress our Christians. If we do not hold the service they will think we fear Girty, and that might have a bad influence."

"I am in favor of postponing the preaching for a few days. I tell you I am afraid of Girty's Indians, not for myself, for these Christians whom we love so well. I am afraid." Heckewelder's face bore testimony to his anxious dread.

"You are our leader; we have but to obey," said Edwards. "Yet I think we owe it to our converts to stick to our work until we are forced by violence to desist."

"Ah! What form will that violence take?" cried Heckewelder, his face white. "You cannot tell what these savages mean. I fear! I fear!"

"Listen, Heckewelder, you must remember we had this to go through once before," put in Zeisberger earnestly. "In '78 Girty came down on us like a wolf on the fold. He had not so many Indians at his beck and call as now; but he harangued for days, trying to scare us and our handful of Christians. He set his drunken fiends to frighten us, and he failed. We stuck it out and won. He's trying the same game. Let us stand against him, and hold our services as usual. We should trust in God!"

"Never give up!" cried Jim.

"Gentlemen, you are right; you shame me, even though I feel that I understand the situation and its dread possibilities better than any one of you. Whatever befalls we'll stick to our post. I thank you for reviving the spirit in my cowardly heart. We will hold the service today as usual, and to make it more impressive, each shall address the congregation in turn."

"And, if need be, we will give our lives for our Christians," said Young, raising his pale face.

The deep mellow peals of the church bell awoke the slumbering echoes. Scarcely had its melody died away in the forest when a line of Indians issued from the church and marched toward the maple grove. Men, women, youths, maidens, and children.

Glickhican, the old Delaware chief, headed the line. His step was firm, his head erect, his face calm in its noble austerity. His followers likewise expressed in their countenances the steadfastness of their belief. The maiden's heads were bowed, but with shyness, not fear. The children were happy, their bright faces expressive of the joy they felt in the anticipation of listening to their beloved teachers.

This procession passed between rows of painted savages, standing immovable, with folded arms, and somber eyes.

No sooner had the Christians reached the maple grove, when from all over the clearing appeared hostile Indians, who took positions near the knoll where the missionaries stood.

Heckewelder's faithful little band awaited him on the platform. The converted Indians seated themselves as usual at the foot of the knoll. The other savages crowded closely on both sides. They carried their weapons, and maintained the same silence that had so singularly marked their mood of the last twenty-four hours. No human skill could have divined their intention. This coldness might be only habitual reserve, and it might be anything else.

Heckewelder approached at the same time that Simon Girty and his band of renegades appeared. With the renegades were Pipe and Half King. These two came slowly across the clearing, passed through the opening in the crowd, and stopped close to the platform.

Heckewelder went hurriedly up to his missionaries. He seemed beside himself with excitement, and spoke with difficulty.

"Do not preach today. I have been warned again," he said, in a low voice.

"Do you forbid it?" inquired Edwards.

"No, no. I have not that authority, but I implore it. Wait, wait until the Indians are in better mood."

Edwards left the group, and, stepping upon the platform, faced the Christians.

At the same moment Half King stalked majestically from before his party. He carried no weapon save a black, knotted war club. A surging forward of the crowd of savages behind him showed the intense interest which his action had aroused. He walked forward until he stood halfway between the platform and the converts. He ran his evil glance slowly over the Christians, and then rested it upon Edwards.

"Half King's orders are to be obeyed. Let the paleface keep his mouth closed," he cried in the Indian tongue. The imperious command came as a thunderbolt from a clear sky. The missionaries behind Edwards stood bewildered, awaiting the outcome.

But Edwards, without a moment's hesitation, calmly lifted his hand and spoke.

"Beloved Christians, we meet today as we have met before, as we hope to meet in——"

"Spang!"

The whistling of a bullet over the heads of the Christians, accompanied the loud report of a rifle. All present plainly heard the leaden missile strike. Edwards wheeled, clutching his side, breathed hard, and then fell heavily without uttering a cry. He had been shot by an Indian concealed in the thicket.

For a moment no one moved, nor spoke. The missionaries were stricken with horror; the converts seemed turned to stone, and the hostile throng waited silently, as they had for hours.

"He's shot! He's shot! Oh, I feared this!" cried Heckewelder, running forward. The missionaries followed him.

Edwards was lying on his back, with a bloody hand pressed to his side.

"Dave, Dave, how is it with you?" asked Heckewelder, in a voice low with fear.

"Not bad. It's too far out to be bad, but it knocked me over," answered Edwards, weakly. "Give me—water."

They carried him from the platform, and laid him on the grass under a tree.

Young pressed Edwards' hand; he murmured something that sounded like a prayer, and then walked straight upon the platform, as he raised his face, which was sublime with a white light.

"Paleface! Back!" roared Half King, as he waved his war club.

"You Indian dog! Be silent!"

Young's clear voice rolled out on the quiet air so imperiously, so powerful in its wonderful scorn and passion, that the hostile savages were overcome by awe, and the Christians thrilled anew with reverential love.

Young spoke again in a voice which had lost its passion, and was singularly sweet in its richness.

"Beloved Christians, if it is God's will that we must die to prove our faith, then as we have taught you how to live, so we can show you how to die——"

"*Spang!*"

Again a whistling sound came with the bellow of an overcharged rifle; again the sickening thud of a bullet striking flesh.

Young fell backward from the platform.

The missionaries laid him beside Edwards, and then stood in shuddering silence. A smile shone on Young's pale face; a stream of dark blood welled from his breast. His lips moved; he whispered:

"I ask no more—God's will."

Jim looked down once at his brother missionaries; then with blanched face, but resolute and stern, he marched toward the platform.

Heckewelder ran after him, and dragged him back.

"No! no! no! My God! Would you be killed? Oh! I tried to prevent this!" cried Heckewelder, wringing his hands.

One long, fierce, exultant yell pealed throughout the grove. It came from those silent breasts in which was pent up hatred; it greeted this action which proclaimed victory over the missionaries.

All eyes turned on Half King. With measured stride he paced to and fro before the Christian Indians.

Neither cowering nor shrinking marked their manner; to a man, to a child, they rose with proud mien, heads erect and eyes flashing. This mighty chief with his bloodthirsty crew could burn the Village of Peace, could annihilate the Christians, but he could never change their hope and trust in God.

"Blinded fools" cried Half King. "The Huron is wise; he tells no lies. Many moons ago he told the Christians they were sitting halfway between two angry gods, who stood with mouths open wide and looking ferociously at each other. If they did not move back out of the road they would be ground to powder by the teeth of one or the other, or both. Half King urged them to leave the peaceful village, to forget the paleface God; to take their horses, and flocks, and return to their homes. The Christians scorned the Huron King's counsel. The sun has set for the Village of Peace. The time has come. Pipe and the Huron are powerful. They will not listen to the paleface God. They will burn the Village of Peace. Death to the Christians!"

Half King threw the black war club with a passionate energy on the grass before the Indians.

They heard this decree of death with unflinching front. Even the children were quiet. Not a face paled, not an eye was lowered.

Half King cast their doom in their teeth. The Christians eyed him with unspoken scorn.

"My God! My God! It is worse than I thought!" moaned Heckewelder. "Utter ruin! Murder! Murder!"

In the momentary silence which followed his outburst, a tiny cloud of blue-white smoke came from the ferns overhanging a cliff.

"Crack!"

All heard the shot of a rifle; all noticed the difference between its clear, ringing intonation and the loud reports of the other two. All distinctly heard the zip of a bullet as it whistled over their heads.

All? No, not all. One did not hear that speeding bullet. He who was the central figure of this tragic scene, he who had doomed the Christians might have seen that tiny puff of smoke which heralded his own doom, but before the ringing report could reach his ears a small blue hole appeared as if by magic, over his left eye, and pulse, and sense, and life had fled forever.

Half King, great, cruel chieftain, stood still for an instant as if he had been an image of stone; his haughty head lost its erect poise, the fierceness seemed to fade from his dark face, his proud plume waved gracefully as he swayed to and fro, and then fell before the Christians, inert and lifeless.

No one moved; it was as if no one breathed. The superstitious savages awaited fearfully another rifle shot, another lightning stroke, another visitation from the palefaces' God.

But Jim Girty, with a cunning born of his terrible fear, had recognized the ring of that rifle. He had felt the zip of a bullet which could just as readily have found his brain as Half King's. He had stood there as fair a mark as the cruel Huron, yet the Avenger had not chosen him. Was he reserved for a different fate? Was not such a death too merciful for the frontier Deathshead? He yelled in his craven fear:

"Le Vent de la Mort!"

The well-known, dreaded appellation aroused the savages from a fearful stupor into a fierce manifestation of hatred. A tremendous yell rent the air. Instantly the scene changed.

CHAPTER XXVI

In the confusion the missionaries carried Young and Edwards into Mr. Wells' cabin. Nell's calm, white face showed that she had expected some such catastrophe as this, but she of all was the least excited. Heckewelder left them at the cabin and hurried away to consult Captain Williamson. While Zeisberger, who was skilled in surgery, attended to the wounded men, Jim barred the heavy door, shut the rude, swinging windows, and made the cabin temporarily a refuge from prowling savages.

Outside the clamor increased. Shrill yells rent the air, long, rolling war cries sounded above all the din. The measured stamp of moccasined feet, the rush of Indians past the cabin, the dull thud of hatchets struck hard into the trees—all attested to the excitement of the savages, and the imminence of terrible danger.

In the front room of Mr. Wells' cabin Edwards lay on a bed, his face turned to the wall, and his side exposed. There was a bloody hole in his white skin. Zeisberger was probing for the bullet. He had no instruments, save those of his own manufacture, and they were darning needles with bent points, and a long knife blade ground thin.

"There, I have it," said Zeisberger. "Hold still, Dave. There!" As Edwards moaned Zeisberger drew forth the bloody bullet. "Jim, wash and dress this wound. It isn't bad.

Dave will be all right in a couple of days. Now I'll look at George."

Zeisberger hurried into the other room. Young lay with quiet face and closed eyes, breathing faintly. Zeisberger opened the wounded man's shirt and exposed the wound, which was on the right side, rather high up. Nell, who had followed Zeisberger that she might be of some assistance if needed, saw him look at the wound and then turn a pale face away for a second. That hurried shuddering movement of the sober, practical missionary was most significant. Then he bent over Young and inserted one of the probes into the wound. He pushed the steel an inch, two, three, four inches into Young's breast, but the latter neither moved nor moaned. Zeisberger shook his head, and finally removed the instrument. He raised the sufferer's shoulder to find the bed saturated with blood. The bullet wound extended completely through the missionary's body, and was bleeding from the back. Zeisberger folded strips of linsey cloth into small pads and bound them tightly over both apertures of the wound.

"How is he?" asked Jim, when the amateur surgeon returned to the other room, and proceeded to wash the blood from his hands.

Zeisberger shook his head gloomily.

"How is George?" whispered Edwards, who had heard Jim's question.

"Shot through the right lung. Human skill cannot aid him! Only God can save."

"Didn't I hear a third shot?" whispered Dave, gazing round with sad, questioning eyes. "Heckewelder?"

"Is safe. He has gone to see Williamson. You did hear a third shot. Half King fell dead with a bullet over his left eye. He had just folded his arms in a grand pose after his death decree to the Christians."

"A judgment of God!"

"It does seem so, but it came in the form of leaden death from Wetzel's unerring rifle. Do you hear all that yelling? Half King's death has set the Indians wild."

There was a gentle knock at the door, and then the word, "Open," in Heckewelder's voice.

Jim unbarred the door. Heckewelder came in carrying over his shoulder what apparently was a sack of meal. He was accompanied by young Christy. Heckewelder put the bag down, opened it, and lifted out a little Indian boy. The child gazed round with fearful eyes.

"Save Benny! Save Benny!" he cried, running to Nell, and she clasped him closely in her arms.

Heckewelder's face was like marble as he asked concerning Edward's condition.

"I'm not badly off," said the missionary with a smile.

"How's George?" whispered Heckewelder.

No one answered him. Zeisberger raised his hands. All followed Heckewelder into the other room, where Young lay in the same position as when first brought in. Heckewelder stood gazing down into the wan face with its terribly significant smile.

"I brought him out here. I persuaded him to come!" whispered Heckewelder. "Oh, Almighty God!" he cried. His voice broke, and his prayer ended with the mute eloquence of clasped hands and uplifted, appealing face.

"Come out," said Zeisberger, leading him into the larger room. The others followed, and Jim closed the door.

"What's to be done?" said Zeisberger, with his practical common sense. "What did Williamson say? Tell us what you learned?"

"Wait—directly," answered Heckewelder, sitting down and covering his face with his hands. There was a long silence. At length he raised his white face and spoke calmly:

"Gentlemen, the Village of Peace is doomed. I entreated Captain Williamson to help us, but he refused. Said he dared not interfere. I prayed that he would speak at least a word to Girty, but he denied my request."

. "Where are the converts?"

"Imprisoned in the church, every one of them except Benny. Mr. Christy and I hid the child in the meal sack and were thus able to get him here. We must save him."

"Save him?" asked Nell, looking from Heckewelder to the trembling Indian boy.

"Nellie, the savages have driven all our Christians into the church, and shut them up there, until Girty and his men shall give the word to complete their fiendish design. The converts asked but one favor—an hour in which to pray. It was granted. The savages intend to murder them all."

"Oh! Horrible! Monstrous!" cried Nell. "How can they be so inhuman?" She lifted Benny up in her arms. "They'll never get you, my boy. We'll save you—I'll save you!" The child moaned and clung to her neck.

"They are scouring the clearing now for Christians, and will search all the cabins. I'm positive."

"Will they come here?" asked Nell, turning her blazing eyes on Heckewelder.

"Undoubtedly. We must try to hide Benny. Let me think; where would be a good place? We'll try a dark corner of the loft."

"No, no," cried Nell.

"Put Benny in Young's bed," suggested Jim.

"No, no," cried Nell.

"Put him in a bucket and let him down in the well," whispered Edwards, who had listened intently to the conversation.

"That's a capital place," said Heckewelder. "But might he not fall out and drown?"

"Tie him in the bucket," said Jim.

"No, no, no," cried Nell.

"But Nellie, we must decide upon a hiding place, and in a hurry."

"I'll save Benny."

"You? Will you stay here to face those men? Jim Girty and Deering are searching the cabins. Could you bear it to see them? You couldn't."

"Oh! No, I believe it would kill me! That man; that beast! will he come here?" Nell grew ghastly pale, and looked as if about to faint. She shrunk in horror at the thought of again facing Girty. "For God's sake, Heckewelder, don't let him see me! Don't let him come in! Don't!"

Even as the imploring voice ceased a heavy thump sounded on the door.

"Who's there?" demanded Heckewelder.

Thump! Thump!

The heavy blows shook the cabin. The pans rattled on the shelves. No answer came from without.

"Quick! Hide Benny! It's as much as our lives are worth to have him found here," cried Heckewelder in a fierce whisper, as he darted toward the door.

"All right, all right, in a moment," he called out, fumbling over the bar.

He opened the door a moment later and when Jim Girty and Deering entered he turned to his friends with a dread uncertainty in his haggard face.

Edwards lay on the bed with wide-open eyes staring at the intruders. Mr. Wells sat with bowed head. Zeisberger calmly whittled a stick, and Jim stood bolt upright, with a hard light in his eyes.

Nell leaned against the side of a heavy table. Wonderful was the change that had transformed her from a timid, appealing, fear-agonized girl to a woman whose only evidences of unusual excitement were the flame in her eyes and the peculiar whiteness of her face.

Benny was gone!

Heckewelder's glance returned to the visitors. He thought he had never seen such brutal, hideous men.

"Wal, I reckon a preacher ain't agoin' to lie. Hev you seen any Injun Christians round here?" asked Girty, waving a heavy sledgehammer.

"Girty, we have hidden no Indians here," answered Heckewelder, calmly.

"Wal, we'll hev a look, anyway," answered the renegade.

Girty surveyed the room with wolfish eyes. Deering was so drunk that he staggered. Both men, in fact, reeked with the vile fumes of rum. Without another word they proceeded to examine the room, by looking into every box, behind a stone oven, and in the cupboard. They drew the bedclothes from the bed, and with a kick demolished a pile of stove wood. Then the ruffians passed into the other apartments, where they could be heard making thorough search. At length both returned to the large room, when Girty directed Deering to climb the ladder leading to the loft, but because Deering was too much under the influence of liquor to do so, he had to go himself. He rummaged around up there for a few minutes, and then came down.

"Wal, I reckon you wasn't lyin' about it," said Girty, with his ghastly leer.

He and his companion started to go out. Deering had stood with bloodshot eyes fixed on Nell while Girty searched the loft, and as they passed the girl on their way to the open air, the renegade looked at Girty as he motioned with his head toward her. His besotted face expressed some terrible meaning.

Girty had looked at Nell when he first entered, but had not glanced twice at her. As he turned now, before going out of the door, he fixed on her his baleful glance. His aspect was more full of meaning than could have been any words. A horrible power, of which he was boastfully conscious, shone from his little, pointed eyes. His mere presence was deadly. Plainly as if he had spoken was the significance of his long gaze. Anyone could have translated that look.

Once before Nell had faced it, and fainted when its dread meaning grew clear to her. But now she returned his gaze with one in which flashed lightning scorn, and repulsion, in which glowed a wonderful defiance.

The cruel face of this man, the boastful barbarity of his manner, the long, dark, bloody history which his presence recalled, was, indeed, terrifying without the added horror of his intent toward her, but now the self-forgetfulness of a true woman sustained her.

Girty and Deering backed out of the door. Heckewelder closed it, and dropped the bar in place.

Nell fell over the table with a long, low gasp. Then with one hand she lifted her skirt. Benny walked from under it. His big eyes were bright. The young woman clasped him again in her arms. Then she released him, and, laboring under intense excitement, ran to the window.

"There he goes! Oh, the horrible beast! If I only had a gun and could shoot! Oh, if only I were a man! I'd kill him. To think of poor Kate! Ah! he intends the same for me!"

Suddenly she fell upon the floor in a faint. Mr. Wells and Jim lifted her on the bed beside Edwards, where they endeavored to revive her. It was some moments before she opened her eyes.

Jim sat holding Nell's hand. Mr. Wells again bowed his

head. Zeisberger continued to whittle a stick, and Heckewelder paced the floor. Christy stood by with every evidence of sympathy for this distracted group. Outside the clamor increased.

"Just listen!" cried Heckewelder. "Did you ever hear the like? All drunk, crazy, fiendish! They drank every drop of liquor the French traders had. Curses on the vagabond dealers! Rum has made these renegades and savages wild. Oh! my poor, innocent Christians!"

Heckewelder leaned his head against the mantel shelf. He had broken down at last. Racking sobs shook his frame.

"Are you all right again?" asked Jim of Nell.

"Yes."

"I am going out, first to see Williamson, and then the Christians," he said, rising very pale, but calm.

"Don't go!" cried Heckewelder. "I have tried everything. It was all of no use."

"I will go," answered Jim.

"Yes, Jim, go," whispered Nell, looking up into his eyes. It was an earnest gaze in which a faint hope shone.

Jim unbarred the door and went out.

"Wait, I'll go along," cried Zeisberger, suddenly dropping his knife and stick.

As the two men went out a fearful spectacle met their eyes. The clearing was alive with Indians. But such Indians! They were painted demons, maddened by rum. Yesterday they had been silent; if they moved at all it had been with deliberation and dignity. Today they were a yelling, running, blood-seeking mob.

"Awful! Did you ever see human beings like these?" asked Zeisberger.

"No, no!"

"I saw such a frenzy once before, but, of course, only in a small band of savages. Many times have I seen Indians preparing for the warpath, in search of both white men and redskins. They were fierce then, but nothing like this. Everyone of these frenzied fiends is honest. Think of that! Every man feels it his duty to murder these Christians. Girty has led up to this by cunning, and now the time is come to let them loose."

"It means death for all."

"I have given up any thought of escaping," said Zeisberger, with the calmness that had characterized his manner since he returned to the village. "I shall try to get into the church."

"I'll join you there as soon as I see Williamson."

Jim walked rapidly across the clearing to the cabin where Captain Williamson had quarters. The frontiersmen stood in groups, watching the savages with an interest which showed little or no concern.

"I want to see Captain Williamson," said Jim to a frontiersman on guard at the cabin door.

"Wal, he's inside," drawled the man.

Jim thought the voice familiar, and he turned sharply to see the sun-burnt features of Jeff Lynn, the old riverman who had taken Mr. Wells' party to Fort Henry.

"Why, Lynn! I'm glad to see you," exclaimed Jim.

"Purty fair to middlin'," answered Jeff, extending his big hand. "Say, how's the other one, your brother as wus called Joe?"

"I don't know. He ran off with Wetzel, was captured by Indians, and when I last heard of him he had married Wingenund's daughter."

"Wal, I'll be doggoned!" Jeff shook his grizzled head and slapped his leg. "I jest knowed he'd raise somethin'!"

"I'm in a hurry. Do you think Captain Williamson will stand still and let all this go on?"

"I'm afeerd so."

Evidently the captain heard the conversation, for he appeared at the cabin door, smoking a long pipe.

"Captain Williamson, I have come to entreat you to save the Christians from this impending massacre."

"I can't do nuthin'," answered Williamson, removing his pipe to puff forth a great cloud of smoke.

"You have eighty men here!"

"If we interfered Pipe would eat us alive in three minutes. You preacher fellows don't understand this thing. You've got Pipe and Girty to deal with. If you don't know them, you'll be better acquainted by sundown."

"I don't care who they are. Drunken ruffians and savages! That's enough. Will you help us? We are men of your own race, and we come to you for help. Can you withhold it?"

"I won't hev nuthin' to do with this bizness. The chiefs hev condemned the village, an' it'll hev to go. If you fellars hed been careful, no white blood would hev been spilled. I advise you all to lay low till it's over."

"Will you let me speak to your men, to try and get them to follow me?"

"Heckewelder asked the same thing. He was persistent, and I took a vote fer him just to show how my men stood. Eighteen of them said they'd follow him; the rest wouldn't interfere."

"Eighteen! My God!" cried Jim, voicing the passion which consumed him. "You are white men, yet you will stand by and see these innocent people murdered! Man, where's your humanity? Your manhood? These converted Indians are savages no longer, they are Christians. Their children are as good, pure, innocent as your own. Can you remain idle and see these little ones murdered?"

Williamson made no answer, the men who had crowded round were equally silent. Not one lowered his head.

Many looked at the impassioned missionary; others gazed at the savages who were circling around the trees brandishing their weapons. If any pitied the unfortunate Christians, none showed it. They were indifferent, with the indifference of men hardened to cruel scenes.

Jim understood, at last, as he turned from face to face to find everywhere that same imperturbability. These bordermen were like Wetzel and Jonathan Zane. The only good Indian was a dead Indian. Years of war and bloodshed, of merciless cruelty at the hands of redmen, of the hard, border life had rendered these frontiersmen incapable of compassion for any savage.

Jim no longer restrained himself.

"Bordermen you may be, but from my standpoint, from any man's, from God's, you are a lot of coldly indifferent cowards!" exclaimed Jim, with white, quivering lips. "I understand now. Few of you will risk anything for Indians. You will not believe a savage can be a Christian. You don't care if they are all murdered. Any man among you—any man, I say—would step out before those howling fiends and boldly demand that there be no bloodshed. A courageous leader with a band of determined followers could avert this tragedy. You might readily intimidate yonder horde of drunken demons. Captain Williamson, I am only a minister, far removed from a man of war and leader, as you claim to be, but, sir, I curse you as a miserable coward. If I ever get back to civilization I'll brand this inhuman coldness of yours, as the most infamous and dastardly cowardice that ever disgraced a white man. You are worse than Girty!"

Williamson turned a sickly yellow; he fumbled a second with the handle of his tomahawk, but made no answer. The other bordermen maintained the same careless composure. What to them was the raving of a mad preacher?

Jim saw it and turned baffled, fiercely angry, and hopeless. As he walked away Jeff Lynn took his arm, and after they were clear of the crowd of frontiersmen he said:

"Young feller, you give him pepper, an' no mistake. An' mebbe you're right from your side of the fence. But you can't see the Injuns from our side. We hunters hevn't much humanity—I reckon that's what you called it—but we've lost so many friends an' relatives, an' heard of so many murders by the reddys that we look on all of 'em as wild varmints that should be killed on sight. Now, mebbe it'll interest you to know I was the feller who took the vote Williamson told you about, an' I did it 'cause I had an interest in you. I wus watchin' you when Edwards and the other missionary got shot. I like grit in a man, an' I seen you had it clear through. So when Heckewelder comes over I talked to the fellers, an' all I could git interested was eighteen, but they wanted to fight simply fer fightin' sake. Now, old Jeff Lynn is your friend. You just lay low until this is over."

Jim thanked the old riverman and left him. He hardly knew which way to turn. He would make one more effort. He crossed the clearing to where the renegades' teepee stood. McKee and Elliott were sitting on a log. Simon Girty stood beside them, his hard, keen, roving eyes on the scene. The missionary was impressed by the white leader. There was a difference in his aspect, a wilder look than the others wore, as if the man had suddenly awakened to the fury of his Indians. Nevertheless the young man went straight toward him.

"Girty, I come—"

"Git out! You meddlin' preacher!" yelled the renegade, shaking his fist at Jim.

Simon Girty was drunk.

Jim turned from the white fiends. He knew his life to them was not worth a pinch of powder.

"Lost! Lost! All lost!" he exclaimed in despair.

As he went toward the church he saw hundreds of savages bounding over the grass, brandishing weapons, and whooping fiendishly. They were concentrating around Girty's teepee, where already a great throng had congregated. Of all the Indians to be seen not one walked. They leaped by Jim, and ran over the grass nimble as deer.

He saw the eager, venomous fire in their dusky eyes, and the cruelly clenched teeth like those of wolves when they snarl. He felt the hissing breath of many savages as they raced by him. More than one whirled a tomahawk close by Jim's head, and uttered horrible yells in his ear. They were like tigers lusting for blood.

Jim hurried to the church. Not an Indian was visible near the log structure. Even the savage guards had gone. He entered the open door to be instantly struck with reverence and awe.

The Christians were singing.

Miserable and full of sickening dread though Jim was, he could not but realize that the scene before him was one of extraordinary beauty and pathos. The doomed Indians lifted up their voices in song. Never had they sung so feelingly, so harmoniously.

When the song ended Zeisberger, who stood upon a platform, opened his Bible and read:

"In a little wrath I hid my face from thee for a moment, but with everlasting kindness will I have mercy on thee, saith the Lord, thy Redeemer."

In a voice low and tremulous the venerable missionary began his sermon.

The shadow of death hovered over these Christian martyrs; it was reflected in their somber eyes, yet not one was sullen or sad. The children who were too young to understand, but instinctively feeling the tragedy soon to be enacted there, cowered close to their mothers.

Zeisberger preached a touching and impressive, though short, sermon. At its conclusion the whole congregation rose and surrounded the missionary. The men shook his hands, the women kissed them, the children clung to his legs. It was a wonderful manifestation of affection.

Suddenly Glickhican, the old Delaware chief, stepped on the platform, raised his hand, and shouted one Indian word.

A long, low wail went up from the children and youths; the women slowly, meekly bowed their heads. The men, true to the stoicism of their nature and the Christianity they had learned, stood proudly erect awaiting the death that had been decreed.

Glickhican pulled the bell rope.

A deep, mellow tone pealed out.

The sound transfixed all the Christians. No one moved.

Glickhican had given the signal which told the murderers the Christians were ready.

"Come, man, my God! We can't stay here!" cried Jim to Zeisberger.

As they went out both men turned to look their last on the martyrs. The death knell which had rung in the ears of the Christians, was to them the voice of God. Stern, dark visages of men and the sweet, submissive faces of women were uplifted with rapt attention. A light seemed to shine from these faces as if the contemplation of God had illumined them.

As Zeisberger and Jim left the church and hurried toward the cabins, they saw the crowd of savages in a black mass round Girty's teepee. The yelling and leaping had ceased.

Heckewelder opened the door. Evidently he had watched for them.

"Jim! Jim!" cried Nell, when he entered the cabin. "Oh-h! I was afraid. Oh! I am glad you're back safe. See, this noble Indian has come to help us."

Wingenund stood calm and erect by the door.

"Chief, what will you do?"

"Wingenund will show you the way to the big river," answered the chieftain, in his deep bass.

"Run away? No, never! That would be cowardly. Heckewelder, you would not go? Nor you, Zeisberger? We may yet be of use; we may yet save some of the Christians."

"Save the yellow-hair," sternly said Wingenund.

"Oh, Jim, you don't understand. The chief has come to warn me of Girty. He intends to take me as he has others, as he did poor Kate. Did you not see the meaning in his eyes today? How they scorched me! Oh! Jim, take me away! Save me! Do not leave me here to that horrible fate! Oh! Jim, take me away!"

"Nell, I will take you," cried Jim, grasping her hands.

"Hurry! There's a blanket full of things I packed for you," said Heckewelder. "Lose no time. Ah! hear that! My heavens! what a yell!" Heckewelder rushed to the door and looked out. "There they go, a black mob of imps; a pack of hungry wolves! Jim Girty is in the lead. How he leaps! How he waves his sledge! He leads the savages toward the church. Oh, it's the end!"

"Benny, where's Benny?" cried Jim hurriedly, lacing the hunting coat he had flung about him.

"Benny's safe. I've hidden him. I'll get him away from here," answered young Christy. "Go! Now's your time. Godspeed you!"

"I'm ready," declared Mr. Wells. "I—have—finished!"

"There goes Wingenund! He's running. Follow him,

quick! Good-bye! Good-bye! God be with you!" cried Heckewelder.

"Good-bye! Good-bye!"

Jim hurried Nell toward the bushes where Wingenund's tall form could dimly be seen. Mr. Wells followed them. On the edge of the clearing Jim and Nell turned to look back.

They saw a black mass of yelling, struggling, fighting savages crowding around the church.

"Oh Jim, look back! Look back!" cried Nell, holding hard to his hand. "Look back! See if Girty is coming!"

CHAPTER XXVII

At last the fugitives breathed free under the gold and red cover of the woods. Never speaking, never looking back, the guide hurried eastward with long strides. His followers were almost forced to run in order to keep him in sight. He had waited at the edge of the clearing for them, and, relieving Jim of the heavy pack, which he swung lightly over his shoulder, he set a pace that was most difficult to maintain. The young missionary half led, half carried Nell over the stones and rough places. Mr. Wells labored in the rear.

"Oh! Jim! Look back! Look back! See if we are pursued!" cried Nell frequently, with many a fearful glance into the dense thickets.

The Indian took a straight course through the woods. He leaped the brooks, climbed the rough ridges, and swiftly trod the glades that were free of windfalls. His hurry and utter disregard for the plain trail left behind, proved his belief in the necessity of placing many miles between the fugitives and the Village of Peace. Evidently they would be followed, and it would be a waste of valuable time to try to conceal their trail. Gradually the ground began to rise, the way became more difficult, but Wingenund never slackened his pace. Nell was strong, supple, and light of foot. She held her own with Jim, but time and time again they were obliged to wait for her uncle. Once he was far behind. Wingenund halted for them at the height of a ridge where the forest was open.

"Ugh!" exclaimed the chieftain, as they finished the ascent. He stretched a long arm toward the sun; his falcon eye gleamed.

Far in the west a great black and yellow cloud of smoke rolled heavenward. It seemed to rise out of the forest, and to hang low over the trees; then it soared aloft and grew thinner until it lost its distinct line far in the clouds. The setting sun stood yet an hour high over a distant hill, and burned dark red through the great pall of smoke.

"Fire, of course, but——" Jim did not voice his fear; he looked closely at Wingenund.

The chieftain stood silent a moment as was his wont when addressed. The dull glow of the sun was reflected in the dark eyes that gazed far away over the forest and field.

"Fire," said Wingenund, and it seemed that as he spoke a sterner shadow flitted across his bronzed face. "The sun sets tonight over the ashes of the Village of Peace."

He resumed his rapid march eastward. With never a backward glance the saddened party followed. Nell kept close beside Jim, and the old man tramped after them with bowed head. The sun set, but Wingenund never slackened his stride. Twilight deepened, yet he kept on.

"Indian, we can go no further tonight, we must rest," cried Jim, as Nell stumbled against him, and Mr. Wells panted wearily in the rear.

"Rest soon," replied the chief, and kept on.

Darkness had settled down when Wingenund at last halted. The fugitives could see little in the gloom, but they heard the music of running water, and felt soft moss beneath their feet.

They sank wearily down upon a projecting stone. The moss was restful to their tired limbs. Opening the pack they found food with which to satisfy the demands of hunger. Then, close under the stone, the fugitives sank into slumber while the watchful Indian stood silent and motionless.

Jim thought he had just closed his eyes when he felt a gentle pressure on his arm.

"Day is here," said the Indian.

Jim opened his eyes to see the bright red sun crimsoning the eastern hills, and streaming gloriously over the colored forests. He raised himself on his elbow to look around. Nell was still asleep. The blanket was tucked close to her chin. Her chestnut hair was tumbled like a schoolgirl's; she looked as fresh and sweet as the morning.

"Nell, Nell, wake up," said Jim, thinking the while how he would love to kiss those white eyelids.

Nell's eyes opened wide; a smile lay deep in their hazel shadows.

"Where am I? Oh, I remember," she cried, sitting up. "Oh, Jim, I had such a sweet dream. I was at home with Mother and Kate. Oh, to wake to find it all a dream, I am fleeing for life. But, Jim we are safe, are we not?"

"Another day, and we'll be safe."

"Let us fly," she cried, leaping up and shaking out her crumpled skirt. "Uncle, come!"

Mr. Wells lay quietly with his mild blue eyes smiling up at her. He neither moved nor spoke.

"Eat, drink," said the chief, opening the pack.

"What a beautiful place!" exclaimed Nell, taking the bread and meat handed to her. "This is a lovely little glade. Look at those golden flowers, the red and purple leaves, the brown shining moss, and those lichen-covered stones. Why! someone had camped here. See the little cave, the screens of plaited ferns, and the stone fireplace."

"It seems to me this dark spring and those gracefully spreading branches are familiar," said Jim.

"Beautiful Spring," interposed Wingenund.

"Yes, I know this place," cried Nell excitedly. "I remember this glade though it was moonlight when I saw it. Here Wetzel rescued me from Girty."

"Nell, you're right," replied Jim. "How strange we should run across this place again."

Strange fate, indeed, which had brought them again to Beautiful Spring! It was destined that the great scenes of their lives were to be enacted in this mossy glade.

"Come, Uncle, you are lazy," cried Nell, a touch of her old roguishness making playful her voice.

Mr. Wells lay still, and smiled up at them.

"You are not ill?" cried Nell, seeing for the first time how pallid was his face.

"Dear Nellie, I am not ill. I do not suffer, but I am dying," he answered, again with that strange, sweet smile.

"Oh-h-h!" breathed Nell, falling on her knees.

"No, no, Mr. Wells, you are only weak; you will be all right again soon," cried Jim.

"Jim, Nellie, I have known all night. I have lain here wakeful. My heart never was strong. It gave out yesterday, and now it is slowly growing weaker. Put your hand on my breast. Feel. Ah! you see! My life is flickering. God's will be done. I am content. My work is finished. My only regret is that I brought you out to this terrible borderland. But I did not know. If only I could see you safe from the peril of this wilderness, at home, happy, married."

Nell bent over him blinded by her tears, unable to see or speak, crushed by his last overwhelming blow. Jim sat on the other side of the old missionary, holding his hand.

For many moments neither spoke. They glanced at the pale face, watching with eager, wistful eyes for a smile, or listening for a word.

"Come," said the Indian.

Nell silently pointed toward her uncle.

"He is dying," whispered Jim to the Indian.

"Go, leave me," murmured Mr. Wells. "You are still in danger."

"We'll not leave you," cried Jim.

"No, no, no," sobbed Nell, bending over to kiss him.

"Nellie, may I marry you to Jim?" whispered Mr. Wells into her ear. "He has told me how it is with him. He loves you, Nellie. I'd die happier knowing I'd left you with him."

Even at that moment, with her heart almost breaking, Nell's fair face flushed.

"Nell, will you marry me?" asked Jim, softly. Low though it was, he had heard Mr. Wells' whisper.

Nell stretched a little trembling hand over her uncle to Jim, who enclosed it in his own. Her eyes met his. Through her tears shone faintly a light, which, but for the agony that made it dim, would have beamed radiant.

"Find the place," said Mr. Wells, handing Jim a Bible. It was the one he always carried in his pocket.

With trembling hand Jim turned the leaves. At last he found the lines, and handed the book back to the old man.

Simple, sweet, and sad was that marriage service. Nell and Jim knelt with hands clasped over Mr. Wells. The old missionary's voice was faint; Nell's responses were low, and Jim answered with deep and tender feeling. Beside them stood Wingenund, a dark, magnificent figure.

"There! May God bless you!" murmured Mr. Wells, with a happy smile, closing the Bible.

"Nell, my wife!" whispered Jim, kissing her hand.

"Come!" broke in Wingenund's voice, deep, strong, like that of a bell.

Not one of them had observed the chief as he stood erect, motionless, poised like a stag scenting the air. His dark eyes seemed to pierce the purple-golden forest, his keen ear seemed to drink in the singing of the birds and the gentle rustling of leaves. Native to these haunts as were the wild creatures, they were no quicker than the Indian to feel the approach of foes. The breeze had borne faint, suspicious sounds.

"Keep—the Bible," said Mr. Wells, "remember—its—words." His hand closely clasped Nell's, and then suddenly loosened. His pallid face was lighted by a meaning, tender smile which slowly faded—faded, and was gone. The venerable head fell back. The old missionary was dead.

Nell kissed the pale, cold brow, and then rose, half dazed and shuddering. Jim was vainly trying to close the dead man's eyes. She could no longer look. On rising she found herself near the Indian chief. He took her fingers in his great hand, and held them with a strong, warm pressure. Strangely thrilled, she looked up at Wingenund. His somber eyes, fixed piercingly on the forest, and his dark stern face, were, as always, inscrutable. No compassion shone there; no emotion unbefitting a chieftain would ever find expression in that cold face, but Nell felt a certain tenderness in this Indian, a response in his great heart. Felt it so surely, so powerfully that she leaned her head against him. She knew he was her friend.

"Come," said the chief once more. He gently put Nell aside before Jim arose from his sad task.

"We cannot leave him unburied," expostulated Jim.

Wingenund dragged aside a large stone which formed one wall of the cavern. Then he grasped a log which was half covered by dirt, and, exerting his great strength, pulled it from its place. There was a crash, a rumble, the jar of a heavy weight striking the earth, then the rattling of gravel, and, before Nell and Jim realized what had happened, the great rock forming the roof of the cavern slipped down the bank followed by a small avalanche. The cavern was completely covered. Mr. Wells was buried. A mossy stone marked the old missionary's grave.

Nell and Jim were lost in wonder and awe.

"Ugh!" cried the chief, looking toward the opening in the glade.

Fearfully Nell and Jim turned, to be appalled by four naked, painted savages standing with levelled rifles. Behind them stood Deering and Jim Girty.

"Oh, God! We are lost! Lost! Lost!" exclaimed Jim, unable to command himself. Hope died in his heart.

No cry issued from Nell's white lips. She was dazed by this final blow. Having endured so much, this last misfortune, apparently the ruin of her life, brought no added suffering, only a strange, numb feeling.

"Ah-huh! Thought you'd give me the slip, eh?" croaked Girty, striding forward, and as he looked at Wingenund his little, yellow eyes flared like flint. "Does a wolf befriend Girty's captives? Chief you hev led me a hard chase."

Wingenund deigned no reply. He stood as he did so often, still and silent, with folded arms, and a look that was haughty, unresponsive.

The Indians came forward into the glade, and one of them quickly bound Jim's hands behind his back. The savages wore a wild, brutish look. A feverish ferocity, very near akin to insanity, possessed them. They were not quiet a moment, but ran here and there, for no apparent reason, except, possibly, to keep in action with the raging fire in their hearts. The cleanliness which characterized the normal Indian was absent in them; their scant buckskin dress was bedraggled and stained. They were still drunk with rum and the lust for blood. Murder gleamed from the glance of their eyes.

"Jake, come over here," said Girty to his renegade friend. "Ain't she a prize?"

Girty and Deering stood before the poor, stricken girl, and gloated over her fair beauty. She stood as when first transfixed by the horror from which she had been fleeing. Her pale face was lowered, her hands clenched tightly in the folds of her skirt.

Never before had two such coarse, cruel fiends as Deering and Girty encumbered the earth. Even on the border, where the best men were bad, they were the worst. Deering was yet drunk, but Girty had recovered somewhat from the effects of the rum he had absorbed. The former rolled his big eyes and nodded his shaggy head. He was passing judgment, from his point of view, on the fine points of the girl.

"She cer'aintly is," he declared, with a grin. "She's a little beauty. Beats any I ever seen!"

Jim Girty stroked his sharp chin with dirty fingers. His yellow eyes, his burnt saffron skin, his hooked nose, his thin lips—all his evil face seemed to shine with an evil triumph. To look at him was painful. To have him gaze at her was enough to drive any woman mad.

Dark stains spotted the bright frills of his gaudy dress, his buckskin coat and leggings, and dotted his white eagle plumes. Dark stains, horribly suggestive, covered him from head to foot. Bloodstains! The innocent blood of Christians crimsoned his renegade's body, and every dark red blotch cried murder.

"Girl, I burned the Village of Peace to git you," growled Girty. "Come here!"

With a rude grasp that tore open her dress, exposing her beautiful white shoulder and bosom, the ruffian pulled her toward him. His face was transfixed with a fierce joy, a brutal passion.

Deering looked on with a drunken grin, while his renegade friend hugged the almost dying girl. The Indians paced the glade with short strides like leashed tigers. The young missionary lay on the moss with closed eyes. He could not endure the sight of Nell in Girty's arms.

No one noticed Wingenund. He stood back a little, half screened by drooping branches. Once again the chief's dark eyes gleamed, his head turned a trifle aside, and, standing in the statuesque position habitual with him when resting, he listened, as one who hears mysterious sounds. Suddenly his keen glance was riveted on the ferns above the low cliff. He had seen their graceful heads quivering. The two blinding sheets of flame burst from the ferns.

Spang! Spang!

Two rifle reports thundered through the glade. Two Indians staggered and fell in their tracks—dead without a cry.

A huge yellow body, spread out like a panther in his spring, descended with a crash upon Deering and Girty.

The girl fell away from the renegade as he went down with a shrill screech, dragging Deering with him. Instantly began a terrific, whirling, wrestling struggle.

A few feet farther down the cliff another yellow body came crashing down to alight with a thud, to bound erect, to rush forward swift as a leaping deer.

The two remaining Indians had only time to draw their weapons before this lithe, threatening form whirled upon them. Shrill cries, hoarse yells, the clash of steel, and dull blows mingled together. One savage went down, twisted over, writhed, and lay still. The other staggered, warded off lightninglike blows until one passed under his guard, and crashed dully on his head. Then he reeled, rose again, but only to have his skull cloven by a bloody tomahawk.

The victor darted toward the whirling mass.

"Lew, shake him loose! Let him go!" yelled Jonathan Zane, swinging his bloody weapon.

High above Zane's cry, Deering's shouts and curses, Girty's shrieks of fear and fury, above the noise of wrestling bodies and dull blows, rose a deep, booming roar.

It was Wetzel's awful cry of vengeance.

"Shake him loose!" yelled Jonathan.

Baffled, he ran wildly around the wrestlers. Time and time again his gory tomahawk was raised only to be lowered. He found no opportunity to strike. Girty's ghastly countenance gleamed at him from the whirl of legs, and arms and bodies. Then Wetzel's dark face, lighted by merciless eyes, took its place, and that gave way to Deering's broad features. The men being clad alike in buckskin, and their motions so rapid, prevented Zane from lending a helping hand.

Suddenly Deering was propelled from the mass as if by a catapult. His body straightened as it came down with a heavy thud. Zane pounced upon it with catlike quickness. Once more he swung aloft the bloody hatchet; then once more he lowered it, for there was no need to strike. The renegade's side was torn open from shoulder to hip. A deluge of blood poured out upon the moss. Deering choked, a bloody froth formed on his lips. His fingers clutched at nothing. His eyes rolled violently and then were fixed in an awful stare.

The girl lying so quiet in the woods near the old hut was avenged!

Jonathan turned again to Wetzel and Girty, not with any intention to aid the hunter, but simply to witness the end of the struggle.

Without the help of the powerful Deering, how pitifully weak was the Deathshead of the frontier in the hands of the Avenger!

Jim Girty's tomahawk was thrown in one direction and his knife in another. He struggled vainly in the iron grip that held him.

Wetzel rose to his feet clutching the renegade. With his left arm, which had been bared in the fight, he held Girty by the front of his buckskin shirt, and dragged him to that tree which stood alone in the glade. He pushed him against it, and held him there.

The white dog leaped and snarled around the prisoner.

Girty's hands pulled and tore at the powerful arm which forced him hard against the beech. It was a brown arm, and huge with its bulging, knotted, rigid muscles. A mighty arm, strong as the justice which ruled it.

"Girty, thy race is run!" Wetzel's voice cut the silence like a steel whip.

The terrible, ruthless smile, the glittering eyes of doom seemed literally to petrify the renegade.

The hunter's right arm rose slowly. The knife in his hand quivered as if with eagerness. The long blade, dripping with Deering's blood, pointed toward the hilltop.

"Look thar! See 'em! Thar's yer friends!" cried Wetzel.

On the dead branches of trees standing far above the hilltops, were many great, dark birds. They sat motionless as if waiting.

"Buzzards! Buzzards!" hissed Wetzel.

Girty's ghastly face became an awful thing to look upon. No living countenance ever before expressed such fear, such horror, such agony. He foamed at the mouth, he struggled, he writhed. With a terrible fascination he watched that quivering, dripping blade, now poised high.

Wetzel's arm swung with the speed of a shooting star.

He drove the blade into Girty's groin, through flesh and bone, hard and fast into the tree. He nailed the renegade to the beech, there to await his lingering doom.

"*Ah-h! Ah-h! Ah-h!*" shrieked Girty, in cries of agony. He fumbled and pulled at the haft of the knife, but could not loosen it. He beat his breast, he tore his hair. His screams were echoed from the hilltop as if in mockery.

The white dog stood near, his hair bristling, his teeth snapping.

The dark birds sat on the dead branches above the hilltop, as if waiting for their feast.

CHAPTER XXVIII

Zane turned and cut the young missionary's bonds. Jim ran to where Nell was lying on the ground, and tenderly raised her head, calling to her that they were saved. Zane bathed the girl's pale face. Presently she sighed and opened her eyes.

Then Zane looked from the statuelike form of Wingenund to the motionless figure of Wetzel. The chief stood erect with his eyes on the distant hills. Wetzel remained with folded arms, his cold eyes fixed upon the writhing, moaning renegade.

"Lew, look here," said Zane, unhesitatingly, and pointed toward the chief.

Wetzel quivered as if sharply stung; the cold glitter in his eyes changed to lurid fire. With upraised tomahawk he bound across the brook.

"Lew, wait a minute!" yelled Zane.

"Wetzel! wait, wait!" cried Jim, grasping the hunter's arm; but the latter flung him off, as the wind tosses a straw.

"Wetzel, wait, for God's sake, wait!" screamed Nell. She had risen at Zane's call, and now saw the deadly resolve in the hunter's eyes. Fearlessly she flung herself in front of him; bravely she risked her life before his mad rush; frantically she threw her arms around him and clung to his hands desperately.

Wetzel halted; frenzied as he was at the sight of his foe, he could not hurt a woman.

"Girl, let go!" he panted, and his broad breast heaved.

"No, no, no! Listen, Wetzel, you must not kill the chief. He is a friend."

"He is my great foe!"

"Listen, oh! please listen!" pleaded Nell. "He warned me to flee from Girty; he offered to guide us to Fort Henry. He has saved my life. For my sake, Wetzel, do not kill him! Don't let me be the cause of his murder! Wetzel, Wetzel, lower your arm, drop your hatchet. For pity's sake do not spill more blood. Wingenund is a Christian!"

Wetzel stepped back breathing heavily. His white face resembled chiseled marble. With those little hands at his breast he hesitated in front of the chief he had hunted for so many long years.

"Would you kill a Christian?" pleaded Nell, her voice sweet and earnest.

"I reckon not, but this Injun ain't one," replied Wetzel slowly.

"Put away your hatchet. Let me have it. Listen, and I will tell you, after thanking you for this rescue. Do you know of my marriage? Come, please listen! forget for a moment your enmity. Oh! you must be merciful! Brave men are always merciful!"

"Injun, are you a Christian?" hissed Wetzel.

"Oh! I know he is! I know he is!" cried Nell, still standing between Wetzel and the chief.

Wingenund spoke no word. He did not move. His falcon eyes gazed tranquilly at his white foe. Christian or pagan, he would not speak one word to save his life.

"Oh! tell him you are a Christian," cried Nell, running to the chief.

"Yellow-hair, the Delaware is true to his race."

As he spoke gently to Nell a noble dignity shone upon his dark face.

"Injun, my back bears the scars of your braves' whips," hissed Wetzel, once more advancing.

"Deathwind, your scars are deep, but the Delaware's are deeper," came the calm reply. "Wingenund's heart bears two scars. His son lies under the moss and ferns; Deathwind killed him; Deathwind alone knows his grave. Wingenund's daughter, the delight of his waning years, freed the Delaware's great foe, and betrayed her father. Can the Christian God tell Wingenund of his child?"

Wetzel shook like a tree in a storm. Justice cried out in the Indian's deep voice. Wetzel fought for mastery of himself.

"Delaware, your daughter lays there, with her lover," said Wetzel firmly, and pointed into the spring.

"Ugh!" exclaimed the Indian, bending over the dark pool. He looked long into its murky depths. Then he thrust his arm down into the brown water.

"Deathwind tells no lie," said the chief, calmly, and pointed toward Girty. The renegade had ceased struggling, his head was bowed upon his breast. "The white serpent has stung the Delaware."

"What does it mean?" cried Jim.

"Your brother Joe and Whispering Winds lie in the spring," answered Jonathan Zane. "Girty murdered them, and Wetzel buried the two there."

"Oh, is it true?" cried Nell.

"True, lass," whispered Jim, brokenly, holding out his arms to her. Indeed, he needed her strength as much as she needed his. The girl gave one shuddering glance at the spring, and then hid her face on her husband's shoulder.

"Delaware, we are sworn foes," cried Wetzel.

"Wingenund asks no mercy."

"Are you a Christian?"

"Wingenund is true to his race."

"Delaware, begone! Take these weapons an' go. When your shadow falls shortest on the ground, Deathwind starts on your trail."

"Deathwind is the great white chief; he is the great Indian foe; he is as sure as the panther in his leap; as swift as the wild goose in his northern flight. Wingenund never felt fear." The chieftain's sonorous reply rolled through the quiet glade. "If Deathwind thirsts for Wingenund's blood, let him spill it now, for when the Delaware goes into the forest his trail will fade."

"Begone!" roared Wetzel. The fever for blood was once more rising within him.

The chief picked up some weapons of the dead Indians, and with a haughty stride stalked from the glade.

"Oh, Wetzel, thank you, I knew——" Nell's voice broke as she faced the hunter. She recoiled from this changed man.

"Come, we'll go," said Jonathan Zane. "I'll guide you to Fort Henry." He lifted the pack, and led Nell and Jim out of the glade.

They looked back once to picture forever in their minds the lovely spot with its ghastly quiet bodies, the dark, haunting spring, the renegade nailed to the tree, and the tall figure of Wetzel as he watched his shadow on the ground.

When Wetzel also had gone, only two living creatures remained in the glade—the doomed renegade, and the white dog. The gaunt beast watched the man with hungry, mad eyes.

A long moan wailed through the forest. It swelled mournfully on the air, and died away. The doomed man heard it. He raised his ghastly face; his dulled senses seemed to revive. He gazed at the stiffening bodies of the Indians, at the gory corpse of Deering, at the savage eyes of the dog.

Suddenly life seemed to surge strong within him.

"Hells fire! I'm not done fer yet," he gasped. "This damned knife can't kill me; I'll pull it out."

He worked at the heavy knife hilt. Awful curses passed his lips, but the blade did not move. Retribution had spoken his doom.

Suddenly he saw a dark shadow moving along the sunlit ground. It swept past him. He looked up to see a great bird with wide wings sailing far above. He saw another still higher, and then a third. He looked at the hilltop. The quiet, black birds had taken wing. They were floating slowly, majestically upward. He watched their graceful flight. How easily they swooped in wide circles. He remembered that they had fascinated him when a boy, long, long ago, when he had a home. Where was that home? He had one once. Ah, the long, cruel years have rolled back. A youth blotted out by evil returned. He saw a little cottage, he saw the old Virginia homestead, he saw his brothers and his mother.

"Ah-h!" A cruel agony tore his heart. He leaned hard against the knife. With the pain the present returned, but the past remained. All his youth, all his manhood flashed before him. The long, bloody, merciless years faced him, and his crimes crushed upon him with awful might.

Suddenly a rushing sound startled him. He saw a great bird swoop down and graze the treetops. Another followed, and another, and then a flock of them. He saw their gray, spotted breasts and hooked beaks.

"Buzzards," he muttered, darkly eyeing the dead savages. The carrion birds were swooping to their feast.

"By God! He's nailed me fast for buzzards!" he screamed in sudden, awful frenzy. "Nailed fast! Ah-h! Ah-h! Ah-h! Eaten alive by buzzards! Ah-h! Ah-h! Ah-h!"

He shrieked until his voice failed, and then he gasped.

Again the buzzards swooped overhead, this time brushing the leaves. One, a great grizzled bird, settled upon a limb of the giant oak, and stretched its long neck. Another alighted beside him. Others sailed round and round the dead treetop.

The leader arched his wings, and with a dive swooped into the glade. He alighted near Deering's dead body. He was a dark, uncanny bird, with long, scraggy, bare neck, a wreath of white, grizzled feathers, a cruel, hooked beak, and cold eyes.

The carrion bird looked around the glade, and put a great claw on the dead man's breast.

"Ah-h! Ah-h!" shrieked Girty. His agonized yell of terror and horror echoed mockingly from the wooded bluff.

The huge buzzard flapped his wings and flew away, but soon returned to his gruesome feast. His followers, made bold by their leader, floated down into the glade. Their black feathers shone in the sun. They hopped over the moss; they stretched their grizzled necks, and turned their heads sideways.

Girty was sweating blood. It trickled from his ghastly face. All the suffering and horror he had caused in all his long career was as nothing to that which then rended him. He, the renegade, the white Indian, the Deathshead of the frontier, panted and prayed for a merciful breath. He was exquisitely alive. He was human.

Presently the huge buzzard, the leader, raised his hoary head. He saw the man nailed to the tree. The bird bent his head wisely to one side, and then lightly lifted himself into the air. He sailed round the glade, over the fighting buzzards, over the spring, and over the doomed renegade. He flew out of the glade, and in again. He swooped close to Girty. His broad wings scarcely moved as he sailed along.

Girty tried to strike the buzzard as he sailed close by, but his arm fell useless. He tried to scream, but his voice failed.

Slowly the buzzard king sailed by and returned. Every time he swooped a little nearer, and bent his long, scraggy neck.

Suddenly he swooped down, light and swift as a hawk: his wide wings fanned the air; he poised under the tree, and then fastened sharp talons in the doomed man's breast.

CHAPTER XXIX

The fleeting human instinct of Wetzel had given way to the habit of years. His merciless quest for many days had been to kill the frontier fiend. Now that it had been accomplished, he turned his vengeance into its accustomed channel, and once more become the ruthless Indian slayer.

A fierce, tingling joy surged through him as he struck the Delaware's trail. Wingenund had made little or no effort to conceal his tracks; he had gone northwest, straight as a crow flies, toward the Indian encampment. He had a start of sixty minutes, and it would require six hours of rapid traveling to gain the Delaware town.

"Reckon he'll make fer home," muttered Wetzel, following the trail with all possible speed.

The hunter's method of trailing an Indian was singular. Intuition played as great a part as sight. He seemed always to divine his victim's intention. Once on the trail he was as hard to shake off as a bloodhound. Yet he did not, by any means, always stick to the Indian's footsteps. With Wetzel the direction was of the greatest importance.

For half a mile he closely followed the Delaware's plainly marked trail. Then he stopped to take a quick survey of the forest before him. He abruptly left the trail, and, breaking into a run, went through the woods as fleetly and noiselessly as a deer, running for a quarter of a mile, when he stopped to listen. All seemed well, for he lowered his head, and walked slowly along examining the moss and leaves. Presently he came up a little open space where the soil was a sandy loam. He bent over, then rose quickly. He had come upon the Indian's trail. Cautiously he moved forward, stopping every moment to listen. In all the close pursuits of his maturer years he had never been a victim of that most cunning of Indian tricks, an ambush. He relied solely on his ear to learn if foes were close by. The wild creatures of the forest were his informants. As soon as he heard any change in their twittering, humming or playing— whichever way they manifested their joy or fear of life—he became as hard to see, as difficult to hear as a creeping snake.

The Delaware's trail led to a rocky ridge and there disappeared. Wetzel made no effort to find the chief's footprints on the flinty ground, but halted a moment and studied the ridge, the lay of the land around, a ravine on one side, and a dark impenetrable forest on the other. He was calculating his chances of finding the Delaware's trail far on the other side. Indian woodcraft, subtle, wonderful as it may be, is limited to each Indian's ability. Savages, as well as other men, were born unequal. One might leave a faint trail through the forest, while another could be readily traced, and a third, more cunning and skillful than his fellows, have flown under the shady trees, for all the trail he left. But redmen followed the same methods of woodcraft from tradition, as Wetzel had learned after long years of study and experience.

And now, satisfied that he had divined the Delaware's intention, he slipped down the bank of the ravine, and once more broke into a run. He leaped lightly, surefooted as a goat, from stone to stone, over fallen logs, and the brawling brook. At every turn of the ravine, at every open place, he stopped to listen.

Arriving on the other side of the ridge, he left the ravine and passed along the edge of the rising ground. He listened to the birds, and searched the grass and leaves. He found not the slightest indication of a trail where he had expected to find one. He retraced his steps patiently, carefully scrutinized every inch of the ground. But it was all in vain. Wingenund had begun to show his savage cunning. In his warrior days for long years no chief could rival him. His boast had always been that, when Wingenund sought to elude his pursuers, his trail faded among the moss and the ferns.

Wetzel, calm, patient, resourceful, deliberated a moment. The Delaware had not crossed this rock ridge. He had been cunning enough to make his pursuer think such was his intention. The hunter hurried to the eastern end of the ridge for no other reason than apparently that course was the one the savage had the least reason to take. He advanced hurriedly because every moment was precious. Not a crushed blade of grass, a brushed leaf, an overturned pebble nor a snapped twig did he find. He saw that he was getting near to the side of the ridge where the Delaware's trail had abruptly ended. Ah! what was there? A twisted bit of fern, with the drops of dew brushed off. Bending beside the fern, Wetzel examined the grass; it was not crushed. A small plant with triangular leaves of dark green, lay under the fern. Breaking off one of these leaves, he exposed its lower side to the light. The fine, silvery hair or fuzz that grew upon the leaf had been crushed. Wetzel knew that an Indian could tread so softly as not to break the springy grass blades, but the underside of one of these leaves, if a man steps on it, always betrays his passage through the woods. To keen eyes this leaf showed that it had been bruised by a soft moccasin. Wetzel had located the trail, but was still ignorant of its direction. Slowly he traced the shaken ferns and bruised leaves down over the side of the ridge, and at last, near a stone, he found a moccasin print in the moss. It pointed east. The Delaware was traveling in exactly the opposite direction to that which he should be going. He was, moreover, exercising wonderful sagacity in hiding his trail. This, however, did not trouble Wetzel, for if it took him a long time to find the trail, certainly the Delaware had expended as much, or more, in choosing hard ground, logs or rocks on which to tread.

Wetzel soon realized that his own cunning was matched. He trusted no more to his intuitive knowledge, but stuck close to the trail, as a hungry wolf holds to the scent of his quarry.

The Delaware's trail led over logs, stones, and hard-baked ground, up stony ravines, and over cliffs. The wily chief used all of his old skill; he walked backward over moss and sand where his footprints showed plainly; he leaped wide fissures in stony ravines, and then jumped back again; he let himself down over ledges by branches; he crossed creeks and gorges by swinging himself into trees and climbing from one to another; he waded brooks where he found hard bottom, and avoided swampy, soft ground.

With dogged persistence and tenacity of purpose Wetzel stuck to this gradually fading trail. Every additional rod he was force to go more slowly, and take more time in order to find any sign of his enemy's passage through the forests. One thing struck him forcibly. Wingenund was gradually circling to the southwest, a course that took him farther and farther from the Delaware encampment.

Slowly it dawned upon Wetzel that the chief could hardly have any reason for taking this circling course save that of pride and savage joy in misleading, in fooling the foe of the Delawares, in deliberately showing Death-wind that there was one Indian who could laugh at and lose him in the forests. To Wetzel this was bitter as gall. To be led a wild goose chase! His fierce heart boiled with fury. His dark, keen eyes sought the grass and moss with terrible earnestness. Yet in spite of the anger that increased to the white heat of passion, he became aware of some strange sensation creeping upon him. He remembered that the Delaware had offered his life. Slowly, like a shadow, Wetzel passed up and down the ridges, through the brown and yellow aisles of the forest, over the babbling brooks, out upon the golden-flecked fields—always close on the trail.

At last in an open part of the forest, where a fire had once swept away the brush and smaller timber, Wetzel came upon the spot where the Delaware's trail ended.

There in the soft, black ground was a moccasin print. The forest was not dense; there was plenty of light; no logs, stones, or trees were near, and yet over all that glade no further evidence of the Indian's trail was visible.

It faded there as the great chief had boasted it would.

Wetzel searched the burnt ground; he crawled on his hands and knees; again and again he went over the sur-roundings. The fact that one moccasin print pointed west and the other east, showing that the Delaware had turned in his tracks, was the most baffling thing that had ever crossed the hunter in all his wild wanderings.

For the first time in many years he had failed. He took his defeat hard, because he had been successful for so long he thought himself almost infallible, and because the failure lost him the opportunity to kill his great foe.

In his passion he cursed himself for being so weak as to let the prayer of a woman turn him from his life's purpose.

With bowed head and slow, dragging steps he made his way westward. The land was strange to him, but he knew he was going toward familiar ground. For a time he walked quietly, all the time the fierce fever in his veins slowly abating. Calm he always was, except when that unnatural lust for Indians' blood overcame him.

On the summit of a high ridge he looked around to ascertain his bearings. He was surprised to find he had traveled in a circle. A mile or so below him arose the great oak tree which he recognized as the landmark of Beautiful Spring. He found himself standing on the hill, under the very dead tree to which he had directed Girty's attention a few hours previous.

With the idea that he would return to the spring to scalp the dead Indians, he went directly toward the big oak tree. Once out of the forest a wide plain lay between him and the wooded knoll which marked the glade of Beautiful Spring. He crossed this stretch of verdant meadowland, and entered the copse.

Suddenly he halted. His keen sense of the usual harmony of the forest, with its innumerable quiet sounds, had received a severe shock. He sank into the tall weeds and listened. Then he crawled a little further. Doubt became certain. A single note of an oriole warned him, and it needed not the quick notes of a catbird to tell him that near at hand, somewhere, was human life.

Once more Wetzel became a tiger. The hot blood leaped from his heart, firing all his veins and nerves. But calmly noiselessly, certain, cold, deadly as a snake he began the familiar crawling method of stalking his game.

On, on under the briars and thickets, across the hollows

full of yellow leaves, up over stony patches of ground to the fern-covered cliff overhanging the glade he glided—lithe, sinuous, a tiger in movement and in heart.

He parted the long, graceful ferns and gazed with glittering eyes down into the beautiful glade.

He saw not the shining spring nor the purple moss, nor the ghastly white bones—all that buzzards had left of the dead—nor anything, save a solitary Indian standing erect in the glade.

There, within range of his rifle, was his great Indian foe, Wingenund.

Wetzel sank back into the ferns to still the furious exultations which almost consumed him during the moment when he marked his victim. He lay there breathing hard, gripping tightly his rifle, slowly mastering the passion that alone of all things might render his aim futile.

For him it was the third great moment of his life, the last of three moments in which the Indian's life had belonged to him. Once before he had seen that dark, powerful face over the sights of his rifle, and he could not shoot because his one shot must be for another. Again had that lofty, haughty figure stood before him, calm, disdainful, arrogant, and he yielded to a woman's prayer.

The Delaware's life was his to take, and he swore he would have it! He trembled in the ecstasy of his triumphant passion; his great muscles rippled and quivered, for the moment entirely beyond his control. Then his passion calmed. Such power for vengeance had he that he could almost still the very beats of his heart to make sure and deadly his fatal aim. Slowly he raised himself; his eyes of cold fire glittered; slowly he raised the black rifle.

Wingenund stood erect in his old, grand pose, with folded arms, but his eyes, instead of being fixed on the distant hills, were lowered to the ground.

An Indian girl, cold as marble, lay at his feet. Her garments were wet, and clung to her slender form. Her sad face was frozen into an eternal rigidity.

By her side was a newly dug grave.

The bead on the front sight of the rifle had hardly covered the chief's dark face when Wetzel's eye took in these other details. He had been so absorbed in his purpose that he did not dream of the Delaware's reason for returning to the Beautiful Spring.

Slowly Wetzel's forefinger stiffened; slowly he lowered the black rifle.

Wingenund had returned to bury Whispering Winds.

Wetzel's teeth clenched, an awful struggle tore his heart. Slowly the rifle rose, wavered, and fell. It rose again, wavered, and fell. Something terrible was wrong with him; something awful was awakening in his soul.

Wingenund had not made a fool of him. The Delaware had led him a long chase, had given him the slip in the forest, not to boast of it, but to hurry back to give his daughter a Christian burial.

Wingenund was a Christian!

Had he not been, once having cast his daughter from him, he would never have looked upon her face again.

Wingenund was true to his race, but he was a Christian.

Suddenly Wetzel's terrible temptation, his heart-racking struggle ceased. He lowered the long, black rifle. He took one last look at the chieftain's dark, powerful face.

Then the Avenger fled like a shadow through the forest.

CHAPTER XXX

It was late afternoon at Fort Henry. The ruddy sun had already sunk behind the wooded hill, and the long shadows of the trees lengthened on the green square in front of the fort.

Colonel Zane stood in his doorway watching the river with eager eyes. A few minutes before a man had appeared on the bank of the island, and hailed. The colonel had sent his brother Jonathan to learn what was wanted. The latter had already reached the other shore in his flatboat, and presently the little boat put out again with the stranger seated at the stern.

"I thought, perhaps, it might be Wetzel," mused the colonel, "though I never knew of Lew's wanting a boat."

Jonathan brought the man across the river, and up the winding path to where Colonel Zane was waiting.

"Hello! It's young Christy!" exclaimed the colonel, jumping off the steps, and cordially extending his hand. "Glad to see you! Where's Williamson. How did you happen over here?"

"Captain Williamson and his men will make the river eight or ten miles above," answered Christy. "I came across to inquire about the young people who left the Village of Peace. Was glad to learn from Jonathan they got out all right."

"Yes, indeed, we're all glad. Come and sit down. Of

course you'll stay overnight. You look tired and worn. Well, no wonder, when you saw all that Moravian massacre. You must tell me about it. I saw Sam Brady yesterday, and he spoke of seeing you over there. Sam told me a good deal. Ah! here's Jim now."

The young missionary came out of the open door, and the two young men greeted each other warmly.

"How is she?" asked Christy, when the first greetings had been exchanged.

"Nell's just beginning to get over the shock. She'll be glad to see you."

"Jonathan tells me you got married just before Girty came up with you at Beautiful Spring."

"Yes; it is true. In fact, the whole wonderful story is true, yet I cannot believe as yet. You look thin and haggard. When we last met you were well."

"That awful time pulled me down. I was an unwilling spectator of all that horrible massacre, and shall never get over it. I can still see the fiendish savages running about with the reeking scalps of their own people. I actually counted the bodies of forty-nine grown Christians and twenty-seven children. An hour after you left us the church was in ashes, and the next day I saw the burned bodies. Oh! the sickening horror of the scene! It haunts me! That monster Jim Girty killed fourteen Christians with his sledgehammer."

"Did you hear of his death?" asked Colonel Zane.

"Yes, and a fitting end it was to the frontier 'Skull and Crossbones.'"

"It was like Wetzel to think of such a vengeance."

"Has Wetzel came in since?"

"No. Jonathan says he went after Wingenund, and there's no telling when he'll return."

"I hoped he would spare the Delaware."

"Wetzel spare an Indian!"

"But the chief was a friend. He surely saved the girl."

"I am sorry, too, because Wingenund was a fine Indian. But Wetzel is implacable."

"Here's Nell, and Mrs. Clarke too. Come out, both of you," cried Jim.

Nell appeared in the doorway with Colonel Zane's sister. The two girls came down the steps and greeted the young man. The bride's sweet face was white and thin, and there was a shadow in her eyes.

"I am so glad you got safely away from—from there," said Christy, earnestly.

"Tell me of Benny?" asked Nell, speaking softly.

"Oh, yes, I forgot. Why, Benny is safe and well. He was the only Christian Indian to escape the Christian massacre. Heckewelder hid him until it was all over. He is going to have the lad educated."

"Thank Heaven!" murmured Nell.

"And the missionaries?" inquired Jim, earnestly.

"Were all well when I left, except of course, Young. He was dying. The others will remain out there, and try to get another hold, but I fear it's impossible."

"It is impossible, not because the Indian does not want Christianity, but because such white men as the Girtys rule. The beautiful Village of Peace owes its ruin to the renegades," said Colonel Zane impressively.

"Captain Williamson could have prevented the massacre," remarked Jim.

"Possibly. It was a bad place for him, and I think he was wrong not to try," declared the colonel.

"Hullo!" cried Jonathan Zane, getting up from the steps where he sat listening to the conversation.

A familiar soft-moccasined footfall sounded on the path. All turned to see Wetzel come slowly toward them. His buckskin hunting costume was ragged and worn. He looked tired and weary, but the dark eyes were calm.

It was the Wetzel whom they all loved.

They greeted him warmly. Nell gave him her hands, and smiled up at him.

"I'm so glad you've come home safe," she said.

"Safe an' sound, lass, an' glad to find you well," answered the hunter, as he leaned on his long rifle, looking from Nell to Colonel Zane's sister. "Betty, I allus gave you first place among border lasses, but here's one as could run you most any kind of a race," he said, with the rare smile which so warmly lighted his dark, stern face.

"Lew Wetzel making compliments! Well, of all things!" exclaimed the colonel's sister.

Jonathan Zane stood closely scanning Wetzel's features. Colonel Zane, observing his brother's close scrutiny of the hunter, guessed the cause, and said:

"Lew, tell us, did you see Wingenund over the sights of your rifle?"

"Yes," answered the hunter simply.

A chill seemed to strike the hearts of the listeners. That simple answer, coming from Wetzel, meant so much. Nell bowed her head sadly. Jim turned away biting his lip. Christy looked across the valley. Colonel Zane bent over and picked up some pebbles which he threw hard at the cabin wall. Jonathan Zane abruptly left the group, and went into the house.

But the colonel's sister fixed her large, black eyes on Wetzel's face.

"Well?" she asked, and her voice rang.

Wetzel was silent for a moment. He met her eyes with that old, inscrutable smile in his own. A slight shade flitted across his face.

"Betty, I missed him," he said, calmly, and, shouldering his long rifle, he strode away.

Nell and Jim walked along the bluff above the river. Twilight was deepening. The red glow in the west was slowly darkening behind the boldly defined hills.

"So it's all settled, Jim, that we stay here," said Nell.

"Yes, dear. Colonel Zane has offered me work, and a church besides. We are very fortunate, and should be contented. I am happy because you're my wife, and yet I am sad when I think of—him. Poor Joe!"

"Don't you ever think we—we wronged him?" whispered Nell.

"No, he wished it. I think he knew how he would end. No, we did not wrong him; we loved him."

"Yes, I loved him—I loved you both," said Nell softly.

"Then let us always think of him as he would have wished."

"Think of him? Think of Joe? I shall never forget. In winter, spring, and summer I shall remember him, but always most in autumn. For I shall see that beautiful glade with its gorgeous color and the dark, shaded spring where he lies asleep."

The years rolled by with their changing seasons; every autumn the golden flowers bloomed richly, and the colored leaves fell softly upon the amber moss in the glade of Beautiful Spring.

The Indians camped there no more; they shunned the glade and called it the Haunted Spring. They said the spirit of a white dog ran there at night, and the Wind-of-Death mourned over the lonely spot.

At long intervals an Indian chief of lofty frame and

dark, powerful face stalked into the glade to stand for many moments silent and motionless.

And sometimes at twilight when the red glow of the sun had faded to gray, a stalwart hunter slipped like a shadow out of the thicket, and leaned upon a long, black rifle while he gazed sadly into the dark spring, and listened to the sad murmur of the waterfall. The twilight deepened while he stood motionless. The leaves fell into the water with a soft splash, a whippoorwill caroled his melancholy song.

From the gloom of the forest came a low sigh which swelled thrillingly upon the quiet air, and then died away like the wailing of the night wind.

Quiet reigned once more over the dark, murky grave of the boy who gave his love and his life to the wilderness.

THE
LAST TRAIL

CHAPTER I

Twilight of a certain summer day, many years ago, shaded softly down over the wild Ohio valley bringing keen anxiety to a traveler on the lonely river trail. He had expected to reach Fort Henry with his party on this night, thus putting a welcome end to the long, rough, hazardous journey through the wilderness; but the swift, on-coming dusk made it imperative to halt. The narrow, forest-skirted trail, difficult to follow in broad daylight, apparently led into gloomy aisles in the woods. His guide had abandoned him that morning, making the excuse that his services were no longer needed; his teamster was new to the frontier, and, altogether, the situation caused him much uneasiness.

"I wouldn't so much mind another night in camp, if the guide had not left us," he said in a low tone to the teamster.

That worthy shook his shaggy head, and growled while he began unhitching the horses.

"Uncle," said a young man, who had clambered out from the wagon, "we must be within a few miles of Fort Henry."

"How d'ye know we're near the fort?" interrupted the teamster, "or safe, either, fer thet matter? I don't know this country."

"The guide assured me we could easily make Fort Henry by sundown."

"Thet guide! I tell ye, Mr. Sheppard—"

"Not so loud. Do not alarm my daughter," cautioned the man who had been called Sheppard.

"Did ye notice anythin' strange about thet guide?" asked the teamster, lowering his voice. "Did ye see how oneasy he was last night? Did it strike ye he left us in a hurry, kind of excited like, in spite of his offhand manner?"

"Yes, he acted odd, or so it seemed to me," replied Sheppard. "How about you, Will?"

"Now that I think of it, he behaved like a man who expected somebody, or feared something might happen. I fancied, however, that it was simply the manner of a woodsman."

"Wal, I hev my opinion," said the teamster, in a gruff whisper. "Ye was in a hurry to be a-goin', an' wouldn't take no advice. The fur trader at Fort Pitt didn't give this guide Jenks no good send off. Said he wasn't well known round Pitt, 'cept he could handle a knife some."

"What is your opinion?" asked Sheppard, as the teamster paused.

"Wal, the valley below Pitt is full of renegades, outlaws, an' hoss-thieves. The redskins ain't so bad as they used to be, but these white fellers are wusser'n ever. This guide Jenks might be in with them, that's all. Mebbe I'm wrong. I hope so. The way he left us looks bad."

"We won't borrow trouble. If we have come all this way without seeing either Indian or outlaw; in fact, without incident, I feel certain we can perform the remainder of the journey in safety," and then Mr. Sheppard raised his voice. "Here, Helen, you lazy girl, come out of that wagon. We want some supper. Will, you gather some firewood, and we'll soon give this gloomy little glen a more cheerful aspect."

As Mr. Sheppard turned toward the canvas-covered wagon a girl leaped lightly down beside him. She was nearly as tall as he.

"Is this Fort Henry?" she asked, cheerily, beginning to dance around him. "Where's the inn? I'm *so* hungry. How glad I am to get out of that wagon! I'd like to run. Isn't this a lonesome, lovely spot?"

A campfire soon crackled with hiss and sputter, and fragrant wood smoke filled the air. Steaming kettle, and savory steaks of venison cheered the hungry travelers, making them forget for the time the desertion of their guide and the fact that they might be lost. The last glow faded entirely out of the western sky. Night enveloped the forest, and the little glade was a bright spot in the gloom.

The flickering light showed Mr. Sheppard to be a well-preserved old man with gray hair and ruddy, kindly face. The nephew had a boyish, frank expression. The girl was a splendid specimen of womanhood. Her large, laughing eyes were as dark as the shadows beneath the trees.

Suddenly a quick start on Helen's part interrupted the merry flow of conversation. She sat bolt upright with half averted face.

"Cousin, what is the matter?" asked Will, quickly.

Helen remained motionless.

"My dear," said Mr. Sheppard sharply.

"I heard a footstep," she whispered, pointing with trembling finger toward the impenetrable blackness beyond the campfire.

All could hear a soft patter on the leaves. Then distinct footfalls broke the silence.

The tired teamster raised his shaggy head and glanced

fearfully around the glade. Mr. Sheppard and Will gazed doubtfully toward the foliage; but Helen did not change her position. The travelers appeared stricken by the silence and solitude of the place. The faint hum of insects, and the low moan of the night wind, seemed accentuated by the almost painful stillness.

"A panther, most likely," suggested Sheppard, in a voice which he intended should be reassuring. "I saw one to-day slinking along the trail."

"I'd better get my gun from the wagon," said Will.

"How dark and wild it is here!" exclaimed Helen nervously. "I believe I was frightened. Perhaps I fancied it—there! Again—listen. Ah!"

Two tall figures emerged from the darkness into the circle of light, and with swift, supple steps gained the camp-fire before any of the travelers had time to move. They were Indians, and the brandishing of their tomahawks proclaimed that they were hostile.

"Ugh!" grunted the taller savage, as he looked down upon the defenseless, frightened group.

As the menacing figures stood in the glare of the fire gazing at the party with shifty eyes, they presented a frightful appearance. Fierce lineaments, all the more so because of bars of paint, the hideous, shaven heads adorned with tufts of hair holding a single feather, sinewy, copper-colored limbs suggestive of action and endurance, the general aspect of untamed ferocity, appalled the travelers and chilled their blood.

Grunts and chuckles manifested the satisfaction with which the Indians fell upon the half-finished supper. They caused it to vanish with astonishing celerity, and resembled wolves rather than human beings in their greediness.

Helen looked timidly around as if hoping to see those who would aid, and the savages regarded her with ill humor. A movement on the part of any member of the group caused muscular hands to steal toward the tomahawks.

Suddenly the larger savage clutched his companion's knee. Then lifting his hatchet, shook it with a significant gesture in Sheppard's face, at the same time putting a finger on his lips to enjoin silence. Both Indians became statuesque in their immobility. They crouched in an attitude of listening, with heads bent on one side, nostrils dilated, and mouths open.

One, two, three moments passed. The silence of the forest appeared to be unbroken; but ears as keen as those of a deer had detected some sound. The larger savage dropped noiselessly to the ground, where he lay stretched out with his ear to the ground. The other remained immovable; only his beady eyes gave signs of life, and these covered every point.

Finally the big savage rose silently, pointed down the dark trail, and strode out of the circle of light. His companion followed close at his heels. The two disappeared in the black shadows like specters, as silently as they had come.

"Well!" breathed Helen.

"I am immensely relieved!" exclaimed Will.

"What do you make of such strange behavior?" Sheppard asked of the teamster.

"I 'spect they got wind of somebody; most likely thet guide, an'll be back again. If they ain't, it's because they got switched off by some signs or tokens, skeered, perhaps, by the scent of the wind."

Hardly had he ceased speaking when again the circle of light was invaded by stalking forms.

"I thought so! Here comes the skulkin' varmints," whispered the teamster.

But he was wrong. A deep, calm voice spoke the single word: "Friends."

Two men in the brown garb of woodsmen approached. One approached the travelers; the other remained in the background, leaning upon a long, black rifle.

Thus exposed to the glare of the flames, the foremost woodsman presented a singularly picturesque figure. His costume was the fringed buckskins of the border. Fully six feet tall, this lithe-limbed young giant had something of the wild, free grace of the Indian in his posture.

He surveyed the wondering travelers with dark, grave eyes.

"Did the reddys do any mischief?" he asked.

"No, they didn't harm us," replied Sheppard. "They ate our supper, and slipped off into the woods without so much as touching one of us. But, indeed, sir, we are mighty glad to see you."

Will echoed this sentiment, and Helen's big eyes were fastened upon the stranger in welcome and wonder.

"We saw your fire blazin' through the twilight, an' came up just in time to see the Injuns make off."

"Might they not hide in the bushes and shoot us?" asked Will, who had listened to many a border story at Fort Pitt. "It seems as if we'd make good targets in this light."

The gravity of the woodsman's face relaxed.

"You will pursue them?" asked Helen.

"They've melted into the night-shadows long ago," he replied. "Who was your guide?"

"I hired him at Fort Pitt. He left us suddenly this morning. A big man, with black beard and bushy eyebrows. A bit of his ear had been shot or cut out," Sheppard replied.

"Jenks, one of Bing Leggett's border-hawks."

"You have his name right. And who may Bing Leggett be?"

"He's an outlaw. Jenks has been tryin' to lead you into

a trap. Likely he expected those Injuns to show up a day or two ago. Somethin' went wrong with the plan, I reckon. Mebbe he was waitin' for five Shawnees, an' mebbe he'll never see three of 'em again."

Something suggestive, cold, and grim, in the last words did not escape the listeners.

"How far are we from Fort Henry?" asked Sheppard.

"Eighteen miles as a crow flies; longer by trail."

"Treachery!" exclaimed the old man. "We were no more than that this morning. It is indeed fortunate that you found us. I take it you are from Fort Henry, and will guide us there? I am an old friend of Colonel Zane's. He will appreciate any kindness you may show us. Of course you know him?"

"I am Jonathan Zane."

Sheppard suddenly realized that he was facing the most celebrated scout on the border. In Revolutionary times Zane's fame had extended even to the far Atlantic Colonies.

"And your companion?" asked Sheppard with keen interest. He guessed what might be told. Border lore coupled Jonathan Zane with a strange and terrible character, a border Nemesis, a mysterious, shadowy, elusive man, whom few pioneers ever saw, but of whom all knew.

"Wetzel," answered Zane.

With one accord the travelers gazed curiously at Zane's silent companion. In the dim background of the glow cast by the fire, he stood a gigantic figure, dark, quiet, and yet with something intangible in his shadowy outline.

Suddenly he appeared to merge into the gloom as if he really were a phantom. A warning, "Hist!" came from the bushes.

With one swift kick Zane scattered the campfire.

The travelers waited with bated breaths. They could

hear nothing save the beating of their own hearts; they could not even see each other.

"Better go to sleep," came in Zane's calm voice. What a relief it was! "We'll keep watch, an' at daybreak guide you to Fort Henry."

CHAPTER II

Colonel Zane, a rugged, stalwart pioneer, with a strong, dark face, sat listening to his old friend's dramatic story. At its close a genial smile twinkled in his fine dark eyes.

"Well, well, Sheppard, no doubt it was a thrilling adventure to you," he said. "It might have been a little more interesting, and doubtless would, had I not sent Wetzel and Jonathan to look you up."

"You did? How on earth did you know I was on the border? I counted much on the surprise I should give you."

"My Indian runners leave Fort Pitt ahead of any travelers, and acquaint me with particulars."

"I remembered a fleet-looking Indian who seemed to be asking for information about us, when we arrived at Fort Pitt. I am sorry I did not take the fur trader's advice in regard to the guide. But I was in such a hurry to come, and didn't feel able to bear the expense of a raft or boat that we might come by river. My nephew brought considerable gold, and I all my earthly possessions."

"All's well that ends well," replied Colonel Zane cheerily. "But we must thank Providence that Wetzel and Jonathan came up in the nick of time."

"Indeed, yes. I'm not likely to forget those fierce savages. How they slipped off into the darkness! I wonder if Wetzel pursued them? He disappeared last night, and we did not see him again. In fact we hardly had a fair look at him. I question if I should recognize him now, unless by his great stature."

"He was ahead of Jonathan on the trail. That is Wetzel's way. In times of danger he is seldom seen, yet is always near. But come, let us go out and look around. I am running up a log cabin which will come in handy for you."

They passed out into the shade of pine and maples. A winding path led down a gentle slope. On the hillside under a spreading tree a throng of bearded pioneers, clad in faded buckskins and wearing white-ringed coonskin caps, were erecting a log cabin.

"Life here on the border is keen, hard, invigorating," said Colonel Zane. "I tell you, George Sheppard, in spite of your gray hair and your pretty daughter, you have come out West because you want to live among men who do things."

"Colonel, I won't gainsay I've still got hot blood," replied Sheppard, "but I came to Fort Henry for land. My old home in Williamsburg has fallen into ruin together with the fortunes of my family. I brought my daughter and my nephew because I wanted them to take root in new soil."

"Well, George, right glad we are to have you. Where are your sons? I remember them, though 'tis sixteen long years since I left old Williamsburg."

"Gone. The Revolution took my sons. Helen is the last of the family."

"Well, well, indeed that's hard. Independence has cost you colonists as big a price as border-freedom has us pioneers. Come, old friend, forget the past. A new life begins for you here, and it will be one which gives you much. See, up goes a cabin; that will soon be your home."

Sheppard's eye marked the sturdy pioneers and a fast diminishing pile of white-oak logs.

"Ho-heave!" cried a brawny foreman.

A dozen stout shoulders sagged beneath a well-trimmed log.

"Ho-heave!" yelled the foreman.

"See, up she goes," cried the colonel, "and to-morrow night she'll shed rain."

They walked down a sandy lane bounded on the right by a wide, green clearing, and on the left by a line of chestnuts and maples, outposts of the thick forests beyond.

"Yours is a fine site for a house," observed Sheppard, taking in the clean-trimmed field that extended up the hillside, a brook that splashed clear and noisy over the stones to tarry in a little grass-bound lake which forced water through half-hollowed logs into a spring house.

"I think so; this is the fourth time I've put up a cabin on this land," replied the colonel.

"How's that?"

"The redskins are keen to burn things."

Sheppard laughed at the pioneer's reply. "It's not difficult, Colonel Zane, to understand why Fort Henry has stood all these years, with you as its leader. Certainly the location for your cabin is the finest in the settlement. What a view!"

High upon a bluff overhanging the majestic, slow-winding Ohio, the colonel's cabin afforded a commanding position from which to view the picturesque valley. Sheppard's eye first caught the outline of the huge, bold, time-blackened fort which frowned protectingly over surrounding log-cabins; then he saw the wide-sweeping river with its verdant islands, golden, sandy bars, and willow-bordered shores, while beyond, rolling pastures of wavy grass merging into green forests that swept upward with slow swell until lost in the dim purple of distant mountains.

"Sixteen years ago I came out of the thicket upon yonder bluff, and saw this valley. I was deeply impressed by its beauty, but more by its wonderful promise."

"Were you alone?"

"I and my dog. There had been a few white men before me on the river; but I was the first to see this glorious valley from the bluff. Now, George, I'll let you have a hundred acres of well-cleared land. The soil is so rich you can raise two crops in one season. With some stock, and a few good hands, you'll soon be a busy man."

"I didn't expect so much land; I can't well afford to pay for it."

"Talk to me of payment when the farm yields an income. Is this young nephew of yours strong and willing?"

"He is, and has gold enough to buy a big farm."

"Let him keep his money, and make a comfortable home for some good lass. We marry our young people early out here. And your daughter, George, is she fitted for this hard border life?"

"Never fear for Helen."

"The brunt of this pioneer work falls on our women. God bless them, how heroic they've been! The life here is rough for a man, let alone a woman. But it is a man's game. We need girls, girls who will bear strong men. Yet I am always saddened when I see one come out on the border."

"I think I knew what I was bringing Helen to, and she didn't flinch," said Sheppard, somewhat surprised at the tone in which the colonel spoke.

"No one knows until he has lived on the border. Well, well, all this is discouraging to you. Ah! here is Miss Helen with my sister."

The colonel's fine, dark face lost its sternness, and brightened with a smile.

"I hope you rested well after your long ride."

"I am seldom tired, and I have been made most comfortable. I thank you and your sister," replied the girl, giving Colonel Zane her hand, and including both him and his sister in her grateful glance.

The colonel's sister was a slender, handsome young woman, whose dark beauty showed to most effective advantage by the contrast with her companion's fair skin, golden hair, and blue eyes.

Beautiful as was Helen Sheppard, it was her eyes that held Colonel Zane irresistibly. They were unusually large, of a dark purple-blue that changed, shaded, shadowed with her every thought.

"Come, let us walk," Colonel Zane said abruptly, and, with Mr. Sheppard, followed the girls down the path. He escorted them to the fort, showed a long room with little squares cut in the rough-hewn logs, many bullet holes, fire-charred timbers, and dark stains, terribly suggestive of the pain and heroism which the defense of that rude structure had cost.

Under Helen's eager questioning Colonel Zane yielded to his weakness for storytelling, and recited the history of the last siege of Fort Henry; how the renegade Girty swooped down upon the settlement with hundreds of Indians and British soldiers; how for three days of whistling bullets, flaming arrows, screeching demons, fire, smoke, and attack following attack, the brave defenders stood at their posts, there to die before yielding.

"Grand!" breathed Helen, and her eyes glowed. "It was then Betty Zane ran with the powder? Oh! I've heard the story."

"Let my sister tell you of that," said the colonel, smiling.

"You! Was it you?" And Helen's eyes glowed brighter with the light of youth's glory in great deeds.

"My sister has been wedded and widowed since then," said Colonel Zane, reading in Helen's earnest scrutiny of his sister's calm, sad face a wonder if this quiet woman could be the fearless and famed Elizabeth Zane.

Impulsively Helen's hand closed softly over her companion's. Out of the girlish sympathetic action a warm friendship was born.

"I imagine things do happen here," said Mr. Sheppard, hoping to hear more from Colonel Zane.

The colonel smiled grimly.

"Every summer during fifteen years has been a bloody one on the border. The sieges of Fort Henry, and Crawford's defeat, the biggest things we ever knew out here, are matters of history; of course you are familiar with them. But the numberless Indian forays and attacks, the women who have been carried into captivity by renegades, the murdered farmers, in fact, ceaseless war never long directed at any point, but carried on the entire length of the river, are matters known only to the pioneers. Within five miles of Fort Henry I can show you where the laurel bushes grow three feet high over the ashes of two settlements, and many a clearing where some unfortunate pioneer had staked his claim and thrown up a log cabin, only to die fighting for his wife and children. Between here and Fort Pitt there is only one settlement, Yellow Creek, and most of its inhabitants are survivors of abandoned villages farther up the river. Last summer we had the Moravian Massacre, the blackest, most inhuman deed ever committed. Since then Simon Girty and his bloody redskins have lain low."

"You must always have had a big force," said Sheppard.

"We've managed always to be strong enough, though there never were a large number of men here. During the last siege I had only forty in the fort, counting men, women, and boys. But I had pioneers and women who could handle a rifle, and the best bordermen on the frontier."

"Do you make a distinction between pioneers and bordermen?" asked Sheppard.

"Indeed, yes. I am a pioneer; a borderman is an Indian hunter, or scout. For years my cabins housed Andrew Zane, Sam and John McCollock, Bill Metzar, and John and Martin Wetzel, all of whom are dead. Not one saved his scalp. Fort Henry is growing; it has pioneers, rivermen, soldiers, but only two bordermen. Wetzel and Jonathan are the only ones we have left of those great men."

"They must be old?" mused Helen, with a dreamy glow still in her eyes.

"Well, Miss Helen, not in years, as you mean. Life here is old in experience; few pioneers, and no bordermen, live to a great age. Wetzel is about forty, and my brother Jonathan still a young man; but both are old in border lore."

Earnestly, as a man who loves his subject, Colonel Zane told his listeners of these two most prominent characters of the border. Sixteen years previously, when but boys in years, they had cast in their lot with his, and journeyed over the Virginian Mountains, Wetzel to devote his life to the vengeful calling he had chosen, and Jonathan to give rein to an adventurous spirit and love of the wilds. By some wonderful chance, by cunning, woodcraft, or daring, both men had lived through the years of border warfare which had brought to a close the careers of all their contemporaries.

For many years Wetzel preferred solitude to companionship; he roamed the wilderness in pursuit of Indians, his life-long foes, and seldom appeared at the settlement except to bring news of an intended raid of the savages. Jonathan also spent much time alone in the woods, or scouting along the river. But of late years of friendship had ripened between the two bordermen. Mutual interest had brought them together on the trail of a noted renegade, and when, after many long days of patient watching and persistent tracking, the outlaw paid an awful penalty for his bloody deeds, these lone and silent men were friends.

Powerful in build, fleet as deer, fearless and tireless, Wetzel's peculiar bloodhound sagacity, ferocity, and implacability, balanced by Jonathan's keen intelligence and judgment caused these bordermen to become the bane of redmen and renegades. Their fame increased with each succeeding summer, until now the people of the settlement looked upon wonderful deeds of strength and of woodcraft as a matter of course, rejoicing in the power and skill with which these men were endowed.

By common consent the pioneers attributed any mysterious deed, from the finding of a fat turkey on a cabin doorstep, to the discovery of a savage scalped and pulled from his ambush near a settler's spring, to Wetzel and Jonathan. All the more did they feel sure of this conclusion because the bordermen never spoke of their deeds. Sometimes a pioneer living on the outskirts of the settlement would be awakened in the morning by a single rifle shot, and on peering out would see a dead Indian lying almost across his doorstep, while beyond, in the dim, gray mist, a tall figure stealing away. Often in the twilight on a summer evening, while fondling his children and enjoying his smoke after a hard day's labor in the fields, this same settler would see the tall, dark figure of Jonathan Zane step noiselessly out of the thicket, and learn that he must take his family and flee at once to the fort for safety. When a settler was murdered, his children carried into captivity by Indians, and the wife given over to the power of some brutal renegade, tragedies woefully frequent on the border, Wetzel and Jonathan took the trail alone. Many a white woman was returned alive, and, sometimes, unharmed to her relatives; more than one maiden lived to be captured, rescued, and returned to her lover, while almost numberless were the bones of brutal redmen lying in the deep and gloomy woods, or bleaching on the plains, silent, ghastly reminders of the stern justice meted out by these two heroes.

"Such are my two bordermen, Miss Sheppard. The fort there, and all these cabins, would be only black ashes, save for them, and as for us, our wives and children—God only knows."

"Haven't they wives and children, too?" asked Helen.

"No," answered Colonel Zane, with his genial smile. "Such joys are not for bordermen."

"Why not? Fine men like them deserve happiness," declared Helen.

"It is necessary we have such," said the colonel simply, "and they cannot be bordermen unless free as the air blows. Wetzel and Jonathan have never had sweethearts. I believe Wetzel loved a lass once; but he was an Indian-killer whose hands were red with blood. He silenced his heart, and kept to his chosen, lonely life. Jonathan does not seem to realize that women exist to charm, to please, to be loved and married. Once we twitted him about his brothers doing their duty by the border, whereupon he flashed out: 'My life is the border's: my sweetheart is the North Star!'"

Helen dreamily watched the dancing, dimpling waves that broke on the stones of the river shore. All unconscious of the powerful impression the colonel's recital had made upon her, she was feeling the greatness of the lives of these bordermen, and the glory it would now be for her to share with others the pride in their protection.

"Say, Sheppard, look here," said Colonel Zane, on the return to his cabin, "that girl of yours has a pair of eyes. I can't forget the way they flashed! They'll cause more trouble here among my garrison than would a swarm of redskins."

"No? You don't mean it! Out here in this wilderness?" queried Sheppard doubtfully.

"Well, I do."

"O Lord! What a time I've had with that girl! There was one man especially, back home, who made our lives miserable. He was rich and well born; but Helen would have none of him. He got around me, old fool that I am! Practically stole what was left of my estate, and gambled it away when Helen said she'd die before giving herself to him. It was partly on his account that I brought her away. Then there were a lot of moon-eyed beggars after her all the time, and she's young and full of fire. I hoped I'd marry her to some farmer out here, and end my days in peace."

"Peace? With eyes like those? Never on this green earth." And Colonel Zane laughed as he slapped his friend on the shoulder. "Don't worry, old fellow. You can't help her having those changing dark-blue eyes any more than you can help being proud of them. They have won me, already, susceptible old backwoodsman! I'll help you with this spirited young lady. I've had experience, Sheppard, and don't you forget it. First, my sister, a Zane all through, which is saying enough. Then as sweet and fiery a little Indian princess as ever stepped in a beaded moccasin, and since, more than one beautiful, impulsive creature. Being in authority, I suppose it's natural that all the work, from keeping the garrison ready against an attack, to straightening out love affairs, should fall upon me. I'll take the care off your shoulders; I'll keep these young daredevils from killing each other over Miss Helen's favors. I certainly—Hello! There are strangers at the gate. Something's up."

Half a dozen rough-looking men had appeared from round the corner of the cabin, and halted at the gate.

"Bill Elsing, and some of his men from Yellow Creek," said Colonel Zane, as he went toward the group.

"Hullo, kurnel," was the greeting of the foremost, evidently the leader. "We've lost six head of hosses over our way, an' are out lookin' 'em up."

"Say, this horse-stealing business is alarming. What did you come in for?"

"Wal, we meets Jonathan on the ridge about sun up, an' he sent us back lickety-cut. Said he had two of the hosses coralled, an' mebbe Wetzel could git the others."

"That's strange," replied Colonel Zane, thoughtfully.

"'Pears to me Jack and Wetzel hev some redskins treed, an' didn't want us to spile the fun. Mebbe there wasn't scalps enough to go round. Anyway, we come in, an' we'll hang up here to-day."

"Bill, who's doing this horse-stealing?"

"Damn if I know. It's a mighty pert piece of work. I've a mind it's some slick white fellar, with Injuns backin' him."

Helen noted, when she was once more indoors, that Colonel Zane's wife appeared worried. Her usual placid expression was gone. She put off the playful overtures of her two bright boys with unusual indifference, and turned to her husband with anxious questioning as to whether the strangers brought news of Indians. Upon being assured that such was not the case, she looked relieved, and explained to Helen that she had seen armed men come so often to consult the colonel regarding dangerous missions and expeditions, that the sight of a stranger caused her unspeakable dread.

"I am accustomed to danger, yet I can never control my fears for my husband and children," said Mrs. Zane. "The older I grow the more of a coward I am. Oh! this border life is sad for women. Only a little while ago my brother Samuel McColloch was shot and scalped right here on the riverbank. He was going to the spring for a bucket of water. I lost another brother in almost the same way. Every day during the summer a husband and a father falls victim to some murderous Indian. My husband will go in the same way some day. The border claims them all."

"Bessie, you must not show your fears to our new friend. And, Miss Helen, don't believe she's the coward she would make out," said the colonel's sister smilingly.

"Betty is right, Bess, don't frighten her," said Colonel Zane. "I'm afraid I talked too much to-day. But, Miss Helen, you were so interested, and are such a good listener, that I couldn't refrain. Once for all let me say that you will no doubt see stirring life here; but there is little danger of its affecting you. To be sure I think you'll have troubles; but not with Indians or outlaws."

He winked at his wife and sister. At first Helen did not understand his sally, but then she blushed red all over her fair face.

Some time after that, while unpacking her belongings, she heard the clatter of horses' hoffs on the rocky road, accompanied by loud voices. Running to the window, she saw a group of men at the gate.

"Miss Sheppard, will you come out?" called Colonel

Zane's sister from the door. "My brother Jonathan has re-turned."

Helen joined Betty at the door, and looked over her shoulder.

"Wal, Jack, ye got two on 'em, anyways," drawled a voice which she recognized as that of Elsing's.

A man, lithe and supple, slipped from the back of one of the horses, and, giving the halter to Elsing with a single word, turned, and entered the gate. Colonel Zane met him there.

"Well, Jonathan, what's up?"

"There's hell to pay," was the reply, and the speaker's voice rang clear and sharp.

Colonel Zane laid his hand on his brother's shoulder, and thus they stood for a moment, singularly alike, and yet the sturdy pioneer was, somehow, far different from the dark-haired borderman.

"I thought we'd trouble in store from the look on your face," said the colonel calmly. "I hope you haven't very bad news on the first day, for our old friends from Virginia."

"Jonathan," cried Betty when he did not answer the colonel. At her call he half turned, and his dark eyes, steady, strained like those of a watching deer, sought his sister's face.

"Betty, old Jake Lane was murdered by horse thieves yesterday, and Mabel Lane is gone."

"Oh!" gasped Betty; but she said nothing more.

Colonel Zane cursed inaudibly.

"You know, Eb, I tried to keep Lane in the settlement for Mabel's sake. But he wanted to work that farm. I be-lieve horse-stealing wasn't as much of an object as the girl. Pretty women are bad for the border, or any other place, I guess. Wetzel has taken the trail, and I came in because I've serious suspicions—I'll explain to you alone."

The borderman bowed gravely to Helen, with a natural grace, and yet a manner that sat awkwardly upon him. The girl, slightly flushed, and somewhat confused by this meeting with the man around whom her romantic imagination had already woven a story, stood in the doorway after giving him a fleeting glance, the fairest, sweetest picture of girlish beauty ever seen.

The men went into the house; but their voices came distinctly through the door.

"Eb, if Bing Leggett or Girty ever see that big-eyed lass, they'll have her even if Fort Henry has to be burned, an' in case they do get her, Wetzel an' I'll have taken our last trail."

CHAPTER III

Supper over, Colonel Zane led his guests to a side porch, where they were soon joined by Mrs. Zane and Betty. The host's two boys, Noah and Sammy, who had preceded them, were now astride the porch-rail and, to judge by their antics, were riding wild Indian mustangs.

"It's quite cool," said Colonel Zane; "but I want you to see the sunset in the valley. A good many of your future neighbors may come over to-night for a word of welcome. It's the border custom."

He was about to seat himself by the side of Mr. Sheppard, on a rustic bench, when a negro maid appeared in the doorway carrying a smiling, black-eyed baby. Colonel Zane took the child and, holding it aloft, said with fatherly pride:

"This is Rebecca Zane, the first girl baby born to the Zanes, and destined to be the belle of the border."

"May I have her?" asked Helen softly, holding out her arms. She took the child, and placed it upon her knee where its look of solemnity soon changed to one of infantile delight.

"Here come Nell and Jim," said Mrs. Zane, pointing toward the fort.

"Yes, and there comes my brother Silas with his wife, too," added Colonel Zane. "The first couple are James Downs, our young minister, and Nell, his wife. They came out here a year or so ago. James had a brother Joe, the finest young fellow who ever caught the border fever. He was killed by one of the Girtys. His was a wonderful story, and some day you shall hear about the parson and his wife."

"What's the border fever?" asked Mr. Sheppard.

"It's what brought you out here," replied Colonel Zane with a hearty laugh.

Helen gazed with interest at the couple now coming into the yard, and when they gained the porch she saw that the man was big and tall, with a frank, manly bearing, while his wife was a slender little woman with bright, sunny hair, and a sweet, smiling face. They greeted Helen and her father cordially.

Next came Silas Zane, a typical bronzed and bearded pioneer, with his buxom wife. Presently a little group of villagers joined the party. They were rugged men, clad in faded buckskins, and sober-faced women who wore dresses of plain gray linsey. They welcomed the newcomers with simple, homely courtesy. Then six young frontiersmen appeared from around a corner of the cabin, advancing hesitatingly. To Helen they all looked alike, tall, awkward, with brown faces and big hands. When Colonel Zane cheerily cried out to them, they stumbled forward with evident embarrassment, each literally crushing Helen's hand in his horny palm. Afterward they leaned on the rail and stole glances at her.

Soon a large number of villagers were on the porch or in the yard. After paying their respects to Helen and her father they took part in a general conversation. Two or three girls, the latest callers, were surrounded by half a dozen young fellows, and their laughter sounded high above the hum of voices.

Helen gazed upon this company with mingled feelings of relief and pleasure. She had been more concerned regarding the young people with whom her lot might be cast, than the dangers of which others had told. She knew that on the border there was no distinction of rank. Though she came of an old family, and, during her girlhood, had been surrounded by refinement, even luxury, she had accepted cheerfully the reverses of fortune, and was determined to curb the pride which had been hers. It was necessary she should have friends. Warm-hearted, impulsive, and loving, she needed to have around her those in whom she could confide. Therefore it was with sincere pleasure she understood how groundless were her fears and knew that if she did not find good, true friends the fault would be her own. She saw at a glance that the colonel's widowed sister was her equal, perhaps her superior, in education and breeding, while Nellie Downs was as well-bred and gracious a little lady as she had ever met. Then, the other girls, too, were charming, with frank wholesomeness and freedom.

Concerning the young men, of whom there were about a dozen, Helen had hardly arrived at a conclusion. She liked the ruggedness, the signs of honest worth which clung to them. Despite her youth, she had been much sought after because of her personal attractions, and had thus added experience to the natural keen intuition all women possess. The glances of several of the men, particularly the bold regard of one Roger Brandt, whom Colonel Zane introduced, she had seen before, and learned to dislike. On the whole, however, she was delighted with the prospect of new friends and future prosperity, and she felt ever greater pleasure in the certainty that her father shared her gratification.

Suddenly she became aware that the conversation had ceased. She looked up to see the tall, lithe form of Jonathan Zane as he strode across the porch. She could see that a certain constraint had momentarily fallen upon the company. It was an involuntary acknowledgment of the borderman's presence, of a presence that worked on all alike with a subtle, strong magnetism.

"Ah, Jonathan, come out to see the sunset? It's unusually fine to-night," said Colonel Zane.

With hardly more than a perceptible bow to those present, the borderman took a seat near the rail, and, leaning upon it, directed his gaze westward.

Helen sat so near she could have touched him. She was conscious of the same strange feeling, and impelling sense of power, which had come upon her so strongly at first sight of him. More than that, a lively interest had been aroused in her. This borderman was to her a new and novel character. She was amused at learning that here was a young man absolutely indifferent to the charms of the opposite sex, and although hardly admitting such a thing, she believed it would be possible to win him from his indifference. On raising her eyelids, it was with the unconcern which a woman feigns when suspecting she is being regarded with admiring eyes. But Jonathan Zane might not have known of her presence, for all the attention he paid her. Therefore, having a good opportunity to gaze at this borderman of daring deeds, Helen regarded him closely.

He was clad from head to foot in smooth, soft buckskin which fitted well his powerful frame. Beaded moccasins, leggings bound high above the knees, hunting coat laced and fringed, all had the neat, tidy appearance due to good care. He wore no weapons. His hair fell in a raven mass over his shoulders. His profile was regular, with a long, straight nose, strong chin, and eyes black as night. They were now fixed intently on the valley. The whole face gave an impression of serenity, of calmness.

Helen was wondering if the sad, almost stern, tranquillity of that face ever changed, when the baby cooed and held out its chubby little hands. Jonathan's smile, which came quickly, accompanied by a warm light in the eyes, relieved Helen of an unaccountable repugnance she had begun to feel toward the borderman. That smile, brief as a flash, showed his gentle kindness and told that he was not a creature who had set himself apart from human life and love.

As he took little Rebecca, one of his hands touched Helen's. If he had taken heed of the contact, as any ordinary man might well have, she would, perhaps, have thought nothing about it, but because he did not appear to realize that her hand had been almost enclosed in his, she could not help again feeling his singular personality. She saw that this man had absolutely no thought of her. At the moment this did not awaken resentment, for with all her fire and pride she was not vain; but amusement gave place to a respect which came involuntarily.

Little Rebecca presently manifested the faithlessness peculiar to her sex, and had no sooner been taken upon Jonathan's knee than she cried out to go back to Helen.

"Girls are uncommon coy critters," said he, with a grave smile in his eyes. He handed back the child, and once more was absorbed in the setting sun.

Helen looked down the valley to behold the most beautiful spectacle she had ever seen. Between the hills far to the west, the sky flamed with a red and gold light. The sun was poised above the river, and the shimmering waters merged into a ruddy horizon. Long rays of crimson fire crossed the smooth waters. A few purple clouds above caught the refulgence, until aided by the delicate rose and blue space beyond, they became many hued ships sailing on a rainbow sea. Each second saw a gorgeous transformation. Slowly the sun dipped into the golden flood; one

by one the clouds changed from crimson to gold, from gold
to rose, and then to gray; slowly all the tints faded until, as
the sun slipped out of sight, the brilliance gave way to the
soft afterglow of warm lights. These in turn slowly toned
down into gray twilight.

Helen retired to her room soon afterward, and, being
unusually thoughtful, sat down by the window. She reviewed the events of this first day of her new life on the
border. Her impressions had been so many, so varied, that
she wanted to distinguish them. First she felt glad, with
a sweet, warm thankfulness, that her father seemed so
happy, so encouraged by the outlook. Breaking old ties
had been, she knew, no child's play for him. She realized
also that it had been done solely because there had been
nothing left to offer her in the old home, and in a new one
were hope and possibilities. Then she was relieved at getting away from the attentions of a man whose persistence
had been most annoying to her. From thoughts of her
father, and the old life, she came to her new friends of the
present. She was so grateful for their kindness. She certainly would do all in her power to win and keep their
esteem.

Somewhat of a surprise was it to her, that she reserved
for Jonathan Zane the last and most prominent place in her
meditations. She suddenly asked herself how she regarded
this fighting borderman. She recalled her unbounded enthusiasm for the man as Colonel Zane had told of him; then
her first glimpse, and her surprise and admiration at the
lithe-limbed young giant; then incredulity, amusement,
and respect followed in swift order, after which an unaccountable coldness that was almost resentment. Helen was
forced to admit that she did not know how to regard him,
but surely he was a man, throughout every inch of his

superb frame, and one who took life seriously, with neither thought nor time for the opposite sex. And this last brought a blush to her cheek, for she distinctly remembered she had expected, if not admiration, more than passing notice from this hero of the border.

Presently she took a little mirror from a table near where she sat. Holding it to catch the fast-fading light, she studied her face seriously.

"Helen Sheppard, I think on the occasion of your arrival in a new country a little plain talk will be wholesome. Somehow or other, perhaps because of a crowd of idle men back there in the colonies, possibly from your own misguided fancy, you imagined you were fair to look at. It is well to be undeceived."

Scorn spoke in Helen's voice. She was angry because of having been interested in a man, and allowed that interest to betray her into a girlish expectation that he would treat her as all other men had. The mirror, even in the dim light, spoke more truly than she, for it caught the golden tints of her luxuriant hair, the thousand beautiful shadows in her great, dark eyes, the white glory of a face fair as a star, and the swelling outline of neck and shoulders.

With a sudden fiery impetuosity she flung the glass to the floor, where it was broken into several pieces.

"How foolish of me! What a temper I have!" she exclaimed repentantly. "I'm glad I have another glass. Wouldn't Mr. Jonathan Zane, borderman, Indian fighter, hero of a hundred battles, and never a sweetheart, be flattered? No, most decidedly he wouldn't. He never looked at me. I don't think I expected that; I'm sure I didn't want it; but still he might have— Oh! what am I thinking, and he a stranger?"

Before Helen lost herself in slumber on that eventful

evening, she vowed to ignore the borderman; assured herself that she did not want to see him again, and, rather inconsistently, that she would cure him of his indifference.

When Colonel Zane's guests had retired, and the villagers were gone to their homes, he was free to consult with Jonathan.

"Well, Jack," he said, "I'm ready to hear about the horse thieves."

"Wetzel makes it out the man who's runnin' this hoss-stealin' is located right here in Fort Henry," answered the borderman.

The colonel had lived too long on the frontier to show surprise; he hummed a tune while the genial expression faded slowly from his face.

"Last count there were one hundred and ten men at the fort," he replied thoughtfully. "I know over a hundred, and can trust them. There are some new fellows on the boats, and several strangers hanging round Metzar's."

"'Pears to Lew an' me that this fellar is a slick customer, an' one who's been here long enough to know our hosses an' where we keep them."

"I see. Like Miller, who fooled us all, even Betty, when he stole our powder and then sold us to Girty," rejoined Colonel Zane grimly.

"Exactly, only this fellar is slicker an' more desperate than Miller."

"Right you are, Jack, for the man who is trusted and betrays us, must be desperate. Does he realize what he'll get if we ever find out, or is he underrating us?"

"He knows all right, an' is matchin' his cunnin' against our'n."

"Tell me what you and Wetzel learned?"

The borderman proceeded to relate the events that had occurred during a recent tramp in the forest with Wetzel. While returning from a hunt in a swamp several miles over the ridge, back of Fort Henry, they ran across the trail of three Indians. They followed this until darkness set in, when both laid down to rest and wait for the early dawn, that time most propitious for taking the savage by surprise. On resuming the trail they found that other Indians had joined the party they were tracking. To the bordermen this was significant of some unusual activity directed toward the settlement. Unable to learn anything definite from the moccasin traces, they hurried up on the trail to find that the Indians had halted.

Wetzel and Jonathan saw from their covert that the savages had a woman prisoner. A singular feature about it all was that the Indians remained in the same place all day, did not light a campfire, and kept a sharp lookout. The bordermen crept up as close as safe, and remained on watch during the day and night.

Early next morning, when the air was fading from black to gray, the silence was broken by the snapping of twigs and a tremor of the ground. The bordermen believed another company of Indians was approaching; but they soon saw it was a single white man leading a number of horses. He departed before daybreak. Wetzel and Jonathan could not get a clear view of him owing to the dim light; but they heard his voice, and afterwards found the imprint of his moccasins. They did, however, recognize the six horses as belonging to settlers in Yellow Creek.

While Jonathan and Wetzel were consulting as to what it was best to do, the party of Indians divided, four going directly west, and the others north. Wetzel immediately took the trail of the larger party with the prisoner and four of the horses. Jonathan caught two of the animals which the Indians had turned loose, and tied them in the forest. He then started after the three Indians who had gone northward.

"Well?" Colonel Zane said impatiently, when Jonathan hesitated in his story.

"One got away," he said reluctantly. "I barked him as he was runnin' like a streak through the bushes, an' judged that he was hard hit. I got the hosses, an' turned back on the trail of the white man."

"Where did it end?"

"In that hard-packed path near the blacksmith shop. An' the feller steps as light as an Injun."

"He's here, then, sure as you're born. We've lost no horses yet, but last week old Sam heard a noise in the barn, and on going there found Betty's mare out of her stall."

"Some one as knows the lay of the land had been after her," suggested Jonathan.

"You can bet on that. We've got to find him before we lose all the fine horse-flesh we own. Where do these stolen animals go? Indians would steal any kind; but this thief takes only the best."

"I'm to meet Wetzel on the ridge soon, an' then we'll know, for he's goin' to find out where the hosses are taken."

"That'll help some. On the way back you found where the white girl had been taken from. Murdered father, burned cabin, the usual deviltry."

"Exactly."

"Poor Mabel! Do you think this white thief had anything to do with carrying her away?"

"No. Wetzel says that's Bing Leggett's work. The Shawnees were members of his gang."

"Well, Jack, what'll I do?"

"Keep quiet an' wait," was the borderman's answer.

Colonel Zane, old pioneer and frontiersman though he was, shuddered as he went to his room. His brother's dark look, and his deadly calmness, were significant.

CHAPTER IV

To those few who saw Jonathan Zane in the village, it seemed as if he was in his usual quiet and dreamy state. The people were accustomed to his silence, and long since learned that what little time he spent in the settlement was not given to sociability. In the morning he sometimes lay with Colonel Zane's dog, Chief, by the side of a spring under an elm tree, and in the afternoon strolled aimlessly along the river bluff, or on the hillside. At night he sat on his brother's porch smoking a long Indian pipe. Since that day, now a week past, when he had returned with the stolen horses, his movements and habits were precisely what would have been expected of an unsuspicious borderman.

In reality, however, Jonathan was not what he seemed. He knew all that was going on in the settlement. Hardly a bird could have entered the clearing unobserved.

At night, after all the villagers were in bed, he stole cautiously about the stockade, silencing with familiar word the bristling watch-hounds, and went from barn to barn, ending his stealthy tramp at the corral where Colonel Zane kept his thoroughbreds.

But all this scouting by night availed nothing. No unusual event occurred, not even the barking of a dog, a suspicious rustling among the thickets, or whistling of a nighthawk had been heard.

Vainly the borderman strained ears to catch some low night-signal given by waiting Indians to the white traitor within the settlement. By day there was even less to attract the sharp-eyed watcher. The clumsy river boats, half raft, half sawn lumber, drifted down the Ohio on their first and last voyage, discharged their cargoes of grain, liquor, or merchandise, and were broken up. Their crews came back on the long overland journey to Fort Pitt, there to man another craft. The garrison at the fort performed their customary duties; the pioneers tilled the fields; the blacksmith scattered sparks, the wheelwright worked industriously at his bench, and the housewives attended to their many cares. No strangers arrived at Fort Henry. The quiet life of the village was uninterrupted.

Near sunset of a long day Jonathan strolled down the sandy, well-trodden path toward Metzar's inn. He did not drink, and consequently seldom visited the rude, dark, ill-smelling barroom. When occasion demanded his presence there, he was evidently not welcome. The original owner, a sturdy soldier and pioneer, came to Fort Henry when Colonel Zane founded the settlement, and had been killed during Girty's last attack. His successor, another Metzar, was, according to Jonathan's belief, as bad as the whiskey he dispensed. More than one murder had been committed at the inn; countless fatal knife and tomahawk fights had stained red the hard clay floor; and more than one desperate character had been harbored there. Once Colonel Zane sent Wetzel there to invite a thief and outlaw to quit the settlement, with the not unexpected result that it became necessary the robber be carried out.

Jonathan thought of the bad name the place bore all over the frontier, and wondered if Metzar could tell anything about the horse-thieves. When the borderman bent his tall frame to enter the low-studded door he fancied he saw a dark figure disappear into a room just behind the bar. A roughly clad, heavily bearded man turned hastily at the same moment.

"Hullo," he said gruffly.

"H' are you, Metzar. I just dropped in to see if I could make a trade for your sorrel mare," replied Jonathan. Being well aware that the innkeeper would not part with his horse, the borderman had made this announcement as his reason for entering the barroom.

"Nope, I'll allow you can't," replied Metzar.

As he turned to go, Jonathan's eyes roamed around the barroom. Several strangers of shiftless aspect bleared at him.

"They wouldn't steal a pumpkin," muttered Jonathan to himself as he left the inn. Then he added suspiciously, "Metzar was talkin' to someone, an' 'peared uneasy. I never liked Metzar. He'll bear watchin'."

The borderman passed on down the path thinking of what he had heard against Metzar. The colonel had said that the man was prosperous for an innkeeper who took pelts, grain, or meat in exchange for rum. The village gossips disliked him because he was unmarried, taciturn, and did not care for their company. Jonathan reflected also on the fact that Indians were frequently coming to the inn, and this made him distrustful of the proprietor. It was true that Colonel Zane had red-skinned visitors, but there was always good reason for their coming. Jonathan had seen, during the Revolution, more than one trusted man proven to be a traitor, and the conviction settled upon him that some quiet scouting would show up the innkeeper as aiding the horse-thieves if not actually in league with them.

"Good evening, Jonathan Zane."

This greeting in a woman's clear voice brought Jonathan out from his reveries. He glanced up to see Helen Sheppard standing in the doorway of her father's cabin.

"Evenin', miss," he said with a bow, and would have passed on.

"Wait," she cried, and stepped out of the door.

He waited by the gate with a manner which showed that such a summons was novel to him.

Helen, piqued at his curt greeting, had asked him to wait without any idea of what she would say. Coming slowly down the path she felt again a subtle awe of this borderman. Regretting her impulsiveness, she lost confidence.

Gaining the gate she looked up intending to speak; but was unable to do so as she saw how cold and grave was his face, and how piercing were his eyes. She flushed slightly, and then, conscious of an embarrassment new and strange to her, blushed rosy red, making, as it seemed to her, a stupid remark about the sunset. When he took her words literally, and said the sunset was fine, she felt guilty of deceitfulness. Whatever Helen's faults, and they were many, she was honest, and because of not having looked at the sunset, but only wanting him to see her as did other men, the innocent ruse suddenly appeared mean and trifling.

Then, with a woman's quick intuition, she understood that coquetries were lost on this borderman, and, with a smile, got the better of her embarrassment and humiliation by telling the truth.

"I wanted to ask a favor of you, and I'm a little afraid."

She spoke with girlish shyness, which increased as he stared at her.

"Why—why do you look at me so?"

"There's a lake over yonder which the Shawnees say is haunted by a woman they killed," he replied quietly. "You'd do for her spirit, so white an' beautiful in the silver moonlight."

"So my white dress makes me look ghostly," she answered lightly, though deeply conscious of surprise and pleasure at such an unexpected reply from him. This borderman might be full of surprises. "Such a time as I had bringing my dresses out here! I don't know when I can wear them. This is the simplest one."

"An' it's mighty new an' bewilderin' for the border," he replied with a smile in his eyes.

"When these are gone I'll get no more except linsey ones," she said brightly, yet her eyes shone with a wistful uncertainty of the future.

"Will you be happy here?"

"I am happy. I have always wanted to be of some use in the world. I assure you, Master Zane, I am not the butterfly I seem. I have worked hard all day, that is, until your sister Betty came over. All the girls have helped me fix up the cabin until it's more comfortable than I ever dreamed one could be on the frontier. Father is well content here, and that makes me happy. I haven't had time for forebodings. The young men of Fort Henry have been,—well, attentive; in fact, they've been here all the time."

She laughed a little at this last remark, and looked demurely at him.

"It's a frontier custom," he said.

"Oh, indeed? Do all the young men call often and stay late?"

"They do?"

"You didn't," she retorted. "You're the only one who hasn't been to see me."

"I do not wait on the girls," he replied with a grave smile.

"Oh, you don't? Do you expect them to wait on you?" she asked, feeling now she had made this silent man talk, once more at her ease.

"I am a borderman," replied Jonathan. There was a

certain dignity or sadness in his answer which reminded Helen of Colonel Zane's portrayal of a borderman's life. It struck her keenly. Here was this young giant standing erect and handsome before her, as rugged as one of the ash trees of his beloved forest. Who could tell when his strong life might be ended by an Indian hatchet?

"For you, then, is there no such thing as friendship?" she asked.

"On the border men are serious."

This recalled his sister's conversation regarding the attentions of the young men, that they would follow her, fight for her, and give her absolutely no peace until one of them had carried her to his cabin a bride.

She could not carry on the usual conventional conversation with this borderman, but remained silent for a time. She realized more keenly than ever before how different he was from other men, and watched closely as he stood gazing out over the river. Perhaps something she had said caused him to think of the many pleasures and joys he missed. But she could not be certain what was in his mind. She was not accustomed to impassive faces and cold eyes with unlit fires in their dark depths. More likely he was thinking of matters nearer to his wild, free life; of his companion Wetzel somewhere out beyond those frowning hills. Then she remembered that the colonel had told her of his brother's love for nature in all its forms; how he watched the shades of evening fall; lost himself in contemplation of the last copper glow flushing the western sky, or became absorbed in the bright stars. Possibly he had forgotten her presence. Darkness was rapidly stealing down upon them. The evening, tranquil and gray, crept over them with all its mystery. He was a part of it. She could not hope to understand him; but saw clearly that his was no common personality. She wanted to speak, to voice a sympathy strong within her; but she did not know what to say to this borderman.

"If what your sister tells me of the border is true, I may soon need a friend," she said, after weighing well her words. She faced him modestly yet bravely, and looked him straight in the eyes. Because he did not reply she spoke again.

"I mean such a friend as you or Wetzel."

"You may count on both," he replied.

"Thank you," she said softly, giving him her hand. "I shall not forget. One more thing. Will you break a borderman's custom, for my sake?"

"How?"

"Come to see me when you are in the settlement?"

Helen said this in a low voice with just a sob in her breath; but she met his gaze fairly. Her big eyes were all aglow, alight with girlish appeal, and yet proud with a woman's honest demand for fair exchange. Promise was there, too, could he but read it, of wonderful possibilities.

"No," he answered gently.

Helen was not prepared for such a rebuff. She was interested in him, and not ashamed to show it. She feared only that he might misunderstand her; but to refuse her proffered friendship, that was indeed unexpected. Rude she thought it was, while from brow to curving throat her fair skin crimsoned. Then her face grew pale as the moonlight. Hard on her resentment had surged the swell of some new emotion strong and sweet. He refused her friendship because he did not dare accept it; because his life was not his own; because he was a borderman.

While they stood thus, Jonathan looking perplexed and troubled, feeling he had hurt her, but knowing not what to say, and Helen with a warm softness in her eyes, the stalwart figure of a man loomed out of the gathering darkness.

"Ah, Miss Helen! Good evening," he said.

"Is it you, Mr. Brandt?" asked Helen. "Of course you know Mr. Zane."

Brandt acknowledged Jonathan's bow with an awkwardness which had certainly been absent in his greeting to Helen. He started slightly when she spoke the borderman's name.

A brief pause ensued.

"Good night," said Jonathan, and left them.

He had noticed Brandt's gesture of surprise, slight though it was, and was thinking about it as he walked away. Brandt may have been astonished at finding a borderman talking to a girl, and certainly, as far as Jonathan was concerned, the incident was without precedent. But, on the other hand, Brandt may have had another reason, and Jonathan tried to study out what it might be.

He gave but little thought to Helen. That she might like him exceedingly well, did not come into his mind. He remembered his sister Betty's gossip regarding Helen and her admirers, and particularly Roger Brandt; but felt no great concern; he had no curiosity to know more of her. He admired Helen because she was beautiful, yet the feeling was much the same he might have experienced for a gracful deer, a full-foliaged tree, or a dark mossy-stoned bend in a murmuring brook. The girl's face and figure, perfect and alluring as they were, had not awakened him from his indifference.

On arriving at his brother's home, he found the colonel and Betty sitting on the porch.

'Eb, who is this Brandt?" he asked.

"Roger Brandt? He's a French-Canadian; came here from Detroit a year ago. Why do you ask?"

"I want to know more about him."

Colonel Zane reflected a moment, first as to this unusual request from Jonathan, and secondly in regard to what little he really did know of Roger Brandt.

"Well, Jack, I can't tell you much; nothing of him before he showed up here. He says he has been a pioneer, hunter, scout, soldier, trader—everything. When he came to the fort we needed men. It was just after Girty's siege, and all the cabins had been burned. Brandt seemed honest, and was a good fellow. Besides, he had gold. He started the river barges, which came from Fort Pitt. He has surely done the settlement good service, and has prospered. I never talked a dozen times to him, and even then, not for long. He appears to like the young people, which is only natural. That's all I know; Betty might tell you more, for he tried to be attentive to her."

"Did he, Betty?" Jonathan asked.

"He followed me until I showed him I didn't care for company," answered Betty.

"What kind of a man is he?"

"Jack, I know nothing against him, although I never fancied him. He's better educated than the majority of frontiersmen; he's good-natured and agreeable, and the people like him."

"Why don't you?"

Betty looked surprised at his blunt question, and then said with a laugh: "I never tried to reason why; but since you have spoken I believe my dislike was instinctive."

After Betty had retired to her room the brothers remained on the porch smoking.

"Betty's pretty keen, Jack. I never knew her to misjudge a man. Why this sudden interest in Roger Brandt?"

The borderman puffed his pipe in silence.

"Say, Jack," Colonel Zane said suddenly, "do you connect Brandt in any way with this horse-stealing?"

"No more than some, an' less than others," replied Jonathan curtly.

Nothing more was said for a time. To the brothers this hour of early dusk brought the same fullness of peace. From gray twilight to gloomy dusk quiet reigned. The insects of night chirped and chorused with low, incessant hum. From out the darkness came the peeping of frogs.

Suddenly the borderman straightened up, and, removing the pipe from his mouth, turned his ear to the faint breeze, while at the same time one hand closed on the colonel's knee with a warning clutch.

Colonel Zane knew what that clutch signified. Some faint noise, too low for ordinary ears, had roused the borderman. The colonel listened, but heard nothing save the familiar evening sounds.

"Jack, what'd you hear?" he whispered.

"Somethin' back of the barn," replied Jonathan, slipping noiselessly off the steps, lying at full length with his ear close to the ground. "Where's the dog?" he asked.

"Chief must have gone with Sam. Old Sam sometimes goes at this hour to see his daughter."

Jonathan lay on the grass several moments; then suddenly he arose much as a bent sapling springs to place.

"I hear footsteps. Get the rifles," he said in a fierce whisper.

"Damn! There is some one in the barn."

"No; they're outside. Hurry, but softly."

Colonel Zane had but just risen to his feet, when Mrs. Zane came to the door and called him by name.

Instantly from somewhere in the darkness overhanging the road, came a low, warning whistle.

"A signal!" exclaimed Colonel Zane.

"Quick, Eb! Look toward Metzar's light. One, two, three, shadows—Injuns!"

"By the Lord Harry! Now they're gone; but I couldn't mistake those round heads and bristling feathers."

"Shawnees!" said the borderman, and his teeth shut hard like steel on flint.

"Jack, they were after the horses, and some one was on the lookout! By God! right under our noses!"

"Hurry," cried Jonathan, pulling his brother off the porch.

Colonel Zane followed the borderman out of the yard, into the road, and across the grassy square.

"We might find the one who gave the signal," said the colonel. "He was near at hand, and couldn't have passed the house."

Colonel Zane was correct, for whoever had whistled would be forced to take one of two ways of escape; either down the straight road ahead, or over the high stockade fence of the fort.

"There he goes," whispered Jonathan.

"Where? I can't see a blamed thing."

"Go across the square, run around the fort, an' head him off on the road. Don't try to stop him for he'll have weapons, just find out who he is."

"I see him now," replied Colonel Zane, as he hurried off into the darkness.

During a few moments Jonathan kept in view the shadow he had seen first come out of the gloom by the stockade, and thence pass swiftly down the road. He followed swiftly, silently. Presently a light beyond threw a glare across the road. He thought he was approaching a yard where there was a fire, and the flames proved to be from pine cones burning in the yard of Helen Sheppard. He remembered then that she was entertaining some of the young people.

The figure he was pursuing did not pass the glare. Jonathan made certain it disappeared before reaching the light, and he knew his eyesight too well not to trust to it absolutely. Advancing nearer the yard, he heard the murmur of voices and soon saw figures moving about under the trees.

No doubt was in his mind but that the man who gave the signal to warn the Indians, was one of Helen Sheppard's guests.

Jonathan had walked across the street then down the path, before he saw the colonel coming from the opposite direction. Halting under a maple he waited for his brother to approach.

"I didn't meet any one. Did you lose him?" whispered Colonel Zane breathlessly.

"No; he's in there."

"That's Sheppard's place. Do you mean he's hiding there?"

"No!"

Colonel Zane swore, as was his habit when exasperated. Kind and generous man that he was, it went hard with him to believe in the guilt of any of the young men he had trusted. But Jonathan had said there was a traitor among them, and Colonel Zane did not question this assertion. He knew the borderman. During years full of strife, and war, and blood had he lived beside this silent man who said little, but that little was the truth. Therefore Colonel Zane gave way to anger.

"Well, I'm not so damned surprised! What's to be done?"

"Find out what men are there?"

"That's easy. I'll go to see George and soon have the truth."

"Won't do," said the borderman decisively. "Go back to the barn, an' look after the hosses."

When Colonel Zane had obeyed, Jonathan dropped to his hands and knees, and swiftly, with the agile movements of an Indian, gained a corner of the Sheppard yard. He crouched in the shade of a big plum tree. Then, at a favorable opportunity, vaulted the fence and disappeared under a clump of lilac bushes.

The evening wore away no more tediously to the borderman, than to those young frontiersmen who were whispering tender or playful words to their partners. Time and patience were the same to Jonathan Zane. He lay hidden under the fragrant lilacs, his eyes, accustomed to the dark from long practice, losing no movement of the guests. Finally it became evident that the party was at an end. One couple took the initiative, and said good night to their hostess.

"Tom Bennet, I hope it's not you," whispered the borderman to himself, as he recognized the young fellow.

A general movement followed, until the merry party were assembled about Helen near the front gate.

"Jim Morrison, I'll bet it's not you," was Jonathan's comment. "That soldier Williams is doubtful; Hart an' Johnson being strangers, are unknown quantities around here, an' then comes Brandt."

All departed except Brandt, who remained talking to Helen in low, earnest tones. Jonathan lay very quietly, trying to decide what should be his next move in the unraveling of the mystery. He paid little attention to the young couple, but could not help overhearing their conversation.

"Indeed, Mr. Brandt, you frontiersmen are not backward," Helen was saying in her clear voice. "I am surprised to learn that you love me upon such short acquaintance, and am sorry, too, for I hardly know whether I even so much as like you."

"I love you. We men of the border do things rapidly," he replied earnestly.

"So it seems," she said with a soft laugh.

"Won't you care for me?" he pleaded.

"Nothing is surer than that I never know what I am going to do," Helen replied lightly.

"All these fellows are in love with you. They can't help it any more than I. You are the most glorious creature. Please give me hope."

"Mr. Brandt, let go my hand. I'm afraid I don't like such impulsive men."

"Please let me hold your hand."

"Certainly not."

"But I will hold it, and if you look at me like that again I'll do more," he said.

"What, bold sir frontiersman?" she returned, lightly still, but in a voice which rang with a deeper note.

"I'll kiss you," he cried desperately.

"You wouldn't dare."

"Wouldn't I though? You don't know us border fellows yet. You come here with your wonderful beauty, and smile at us with that light in your eyes which makes men mad. Oh, you'll pay for it."

The borderman listened to all this love-making half disgusted, until he began to grow interested. Brandt's back was turned to him, and Helen stood so that the light from the pinecones shone on her face. Her eyes were brilliant, otherwise she seemed a woman perfectly self-possessed. Brandt held her hand despite the repeated efforts she made to free it. But she did not struggle violently, or make an outcry.

Suddenly Brandt grasped her other hand, pulling her toward him.

"These other fellows will kiss you, and I'm going to be the first!" he declared passionately.

Helen drew back, now thoroughly alarmed by the man's fierce energy. She had been warned against this very boldness in frontiersmen; but had felt secure in her own pride and dignity. Her blood boiled at the thought that she must exert strength to escape insult. She struggled violently when Brandt bent his head. Almost sick with fear, she had determined to call for help, when a violent wrench almost toppled her over. At the same instant her wrists were freed; she heard a fierce cry, a resounding blow, and then the sodden thud of a heavy body falling. Recovering her balance, she saw a tall figure beside her, and a man in the act of rising from the ground.

"You?" whispered Helen, recognizing the tall figure as Jonathan's.

The borderman did not answer. He stepped forward, slipping his hand inside his hunting frock. Brandt sprang nimbly to his feet, and with a face which, even in the dim light, could be seen distorted with fury, bent forward to look at the stranger. He, too, had his hand within his coat, as if grasping a weapon; but he did not draw it.

"Zane, a lighter blow would have been easier to forget," he cried, his voice clear and cutting. Then he turned to the girl. "Miss Helen, I got what I deserved. I crave your forgiveness, and ask you to understand a man who was once a gentleman. If I am one no longer, the frontier is to blame. I was mad to treat you as I did."

Thus speaking, he bowed low with the grace of a man sometimes used to the society of ladies, and then went out of the gate.

"Where did you come from?" asked Helen, looking up at Jonathan.

He pointed under the lilac bushes.

"Were you there?" she asked wonderingly. "Did you hear all?"

"I couldn't help hearin'."

"It was fortunate for me; but why—why were you there?"

Helen came a step nearer, and regarded him curiously with her great eyes now black with excitement.

The borderman was silent.

Helen's softened mood changed instantly. There was nothing in his cold face which might have betrayed in him a sentiment similar to that of her admirers.

"Did you spy on me?" she asked quickly, after a moment's thought.

"No," replied Jonathan calmly.

Helen gazed in perplexity at this strange man. She did not know how to explain it; she was irritated, but did her best to conceal it. He had no interest in her, yet had hidden under the lilacs in her yard. She was grateful because he had saved her from annoyance, yet could not fathom his reason for being so near.

"Did you come here to see me?" she asked, forgetting her vexation.

"No."

"What for, then?"

"I reckon I won't say," was the quiet, deliberate refusal.

Helen stamped her foot in exasperation.

"Be careful that I do not put a wrong construction on your strange action," said she coldly. "If you have reasons, you might trust me. If you are only——"

"Sh-s-sh!" he breathed, grasping her wrist, and holding it firmly in his powerful hand. The whole attitude of the man had altered swiftly, subtly. The listlessness was gone. His lithe body became rigid as he leaned forward, his head toward the ground, and turned slightly in a manner that betokened intent listening.

Helen trembled as she felt his powerful frame quiver. Whatever had thus changed him, gave her another glimpse of his complex personality. It seemed to her incredible that with one whispered exclamation this man could change from cold indifference to a fire and force so strong as to dominate her.

Statue-like she remained listening; but hearing no sound, and thrillingly conscious of the hand on her arm.

Far up on the hillside an owl hooted dismally, and an instant later, faint and far away, came an answer so low as to be almost indistinct.

The borderman raised himself erect as he released her.

"It's only an owl," she said in relief.

His eyes gleamed like stars.

"It's Wetzel, an' it means Injuns!"

Then he was gone into the darkness.

CHAPTER V

In the misty morning twilight Colonel Zane, fully armed, paced to and fro before his cabin, on guard. All night he had maintained a watch. He had not considered it necessary to send his family into the fort, to which they had often been compelled to flee. On the previous night Jonathan had come swiftly back to the cabin, and, speaking but two words, seized his weapons, and vanished into the black night. The word were "Injuns! Wetzel!" and there were none others with more power to affect hearers on the border. The colonel believed that Wetzel had signaled to Jonathan.

On the west a deep gully with precipitous sides separated the settlement from a high, wooded bluff. Wetzel often returned from his journeying by this difficult route. He had no doubt seen Indian signs, and had communicated the intelligence to Jonathan by their system of night-bird calls. The nearness of the mighty hunter reassured Colonel Zane.

When the colonel returned from his chase of the previous night, he went directly to the stable, there to find that the Indians had made off with a thoroughbred, and Betty's pony. Colonel Zane was furious, not on account of the value of the horses, but because Bess was his favorite bay, and Betty loved nothing more than her pony Madcap. To have such a march stolen on him after he had heard and seen the thieves was indeed hard. High time it was that these horse thieves be run to earth. No Indian had planned these marauding expeditions. A white man was at the bottom of the thieving, and he should pay for his treachery.

The colonel's temper, however, soon cooled. He realized after thinking over the matter, that he was fortunate it passed off without bloodshed. Very likely the intent had been to get all his horses, perhaps his neighbor's as well, and it had been partly frustrated by Jonathan's keen sagacity. These Shawnees, white leader or not, would never again run such risks.

"It's like a skulking Shawnee," muttered Colonel Zane, "to slip down here under cover of early dusk, when no one but an Indian hunter could detect him. I didn't look for trouble, especially so soon after the lesson we gave Girty and his damned English and redskins. It's lucky Jonathan was here. I'll go back to the old plan of stationing scouts at the outposts until snow flies."

While Colonel Zane talked to himself and paced the path he had selected to patrol, the white mists cleared, and a rosy hue followed the brightening in the east. The birds ceased twittering to break into gay songs, and the cock in the barnyard gave one final clarion-voiced salute to the dawn. The rose in the east deepened into rich red, and then the sun peeped over the eastern hilltops to drench the valley with glad golden light.

A blue smoke curling lazily from the stone chimney of his cabin, showed that Sam had made the kitchen fire, and a little later a rich, savory odor gave pleasing evidence that his wife was cooking breakfast.

"Any sign of Jack?" a voice called from the open door, and Betty appeared.

"Nary sign."

"Of the Indians, then?"

"Well, Betts, they left you a token of their regard," and Colonel Zane smiled as he took a broken halter from the fence.

"Madcap?" cried Betty.

"Yes, they've taken Madcap and Bess."

"Oh, the villains! Poor pony," exclaimed Betty indignantly. "Eb, I'll coax Wetzel to fetch the pony home if he has to kill every Shawnee in the valley."

"Now you're talking, Betts," Colonel Zane replied. "If you could get Lew to do that much, you'd be blessed from one end of the border to the other."

He walked up the road; then back, keeping a sharp lookout on all sides, and bestowing a particularly keen glance at the hillside across the ravine, but could see no sign of the bordermen. As it was now broad daylight he felt convinced that further watch was unnecessary, and went in to breakfast. When he came out again the villagers were astir. The sharp strokes of axes rang out on the clear morning air, and a mellow anvil-clang pealed up from the blacksmith shop. Colonel Zane found his brother Silas and Jim Downs near the gate.

"Morning, boys," he cried cheerily.

"Any glimpse of Jack or Lew?" asked Silas.

"No; but I'm expecting one of 'em any moment."

"How about the Indians?" asked Downs. "Silas roused me out last night; but didn't stay long enough to say more than 'Indians.'"

"I don't know much more than Silas. I saw several of the red devils who stole the horses; but how many, where they've gone, or what we're to expect, I can't say. We've got to wait for Jack or Lew. Silas, keep the garrison in readiness at the fort, and don't allow a man, soldier, or farmer, to leave the clearing until further orders. Perhaps there were only three of those Shawnees, and then again the woods might have been full of them. I take it something's amiss, or Jack and Lew would be in by now."

"Here come Sheppard and his girl," said Silas, pointing down the lane. " 'Pears George is some excited."

Colonel Zane had much the same idea as he saw Sheppard and his daughter. The old man appeared in a hurry, which was sufficient reason to believe him anxious or alarmed, and Helen looked pale.

"Ebenezer, what's this I hear about Indians?" Sheppard asked excitedly. "What with Helen's story about the fort being besieged, and this brother of yours routing honest people from their beds, I haven't had a wink of sleep. What's up? Where are the redskins?"

"Now, George, be easy," said Colonel Zane calmly. "And you, Helen, mustn't be frightened. There's no danger. We did have a visit from Indians last night; but they hurt no one, and got only two horses."

"Oh, I'm so relieved that it's not worse," said Helen.

"It's bad enough, Helen," Betty cried, her black eyes flashing, "my pony Madcap is gone."

"Colonel Zane, come here quick!" cried Downs, who stood near the gate.

With one leap Colonel Zane was at the gate, and, following with his eyes the direction indicated by Downs' trembling finger, he saw two tall, brown figures striding down the lane. One carried two rifles, and the other a long bundle wrapped in a blanket.

"It's Jack and Wetzel," whispered Colonel Zane to Jim. "They've got the girl, and by God! from the way the bundle hangs, I think she's dead. Here," he added, speaking loudly, "you women get into the house."

Mrs. Zane, Betty, and Helen stared.

"Go into the house!" he cried authoritatively.

Without a protest the three women obeyed.

At that moment Nellie Downs came across the lane; Sam shuffled out from the backyard, and Sheppard arose from his seat on the steps. They joined Colonel Zane, Silas, and Jim at the gate.

"I wondered what kept you so late," Colonel Zane said to Jonathan, as he and his companion came up. "You've fetched Mabel, and she's—" The good man could say no more. If he should live an hundred years on the border amid savage murderers, he would still be tender-hearted. Just now he believed the giant borderman by the side of Jonathan held a dead girl, one whom he had danced, when a child, upon his knee.

"Mabel, an' jest alive," replied Jonathan.

"By God! I'm glad!" exclaimed Colonel Zane. "Here, Lew, given her to me."

Wetzel relinquished his burden to the colonel.

"Lew, any bad Indian sign?" asked Colonel Zane as he turned to go into the house.

The borderman shook his head.

"Wait for me," added the colonel.

He carried the girl to that apartment in the cabin which served the purpose of a sitting-room, and laid her on a couch. He gently removed the folds of the blanket, disclosing to view a fragile, white-faced girl.

"Bess, hurry, hurry!" he screamed to his wife, and as she came running in, followed no less hurriedly by Betty, Helen, and Nellie, he continued, "Here's Mabel Lane, alive, poor child; but in sore need of help. First see whether she has any bodily injury. If a bullet must be cut out, or a knife-wound sewed up, it's better she remained unconscious. Betty, run for Bess's instruments, and bring brandy and water. Lively now!" Then he gave vent to an oath and left the room.

Helen, her heart throbbing wildly, went to the side of Mrs. Zane, who was kneeling by the couch. She saw a delicate girl, not over eighteen years old, with a face that would have been beautiful but for the set lips, the closed eyelids, and an expression of intense pain.

"Oh! Oh!" breathed Helen.

"Nell, hand me the scissors," said Mrs. Zane, "and help me take off this dress. Why, it's wet, but, thank goodness! 'tis not with blood. I know that slippery touch too well. There, that's right. Betty, give me a spoonful of brandy. Now heat a blanket, and get one of your linsey gowns for this poor child."

Helen watched Mrs. Zane as if fascinated. The colonel's wife continued to talk while with deft fingers she forced a few drops of brandy between the girl's closed teeth. Then with the adroitness of a skilled surgeon, she made the examination. Helen had heard of this pioneer woman's skill in setting broken bones and treating injuries, and when she looked from the calm face to the steady fingers, she had no doubt as to the truth of what had been told.

"Neither bullet wound, cut, bruise, nor broken bone," said Mrs. Zane. "It's fear, starvation, and the terrible shock."

She rubbed Mabel's hands while gazing at her pale face. Then she forced more brandy between the tightly closed lips. She was rewarded by ever so faint a color tinging the wan cheeks, to be followed by a fluttering of the eyelids. Then the eyes opened wide. They were large, soft, dark, and humid with agony.

Helen could not bear their gaze. She saw the shadow of death, and of worse than death. She looked away, while in her heart rose a storm of passionate fury at the brutes who had made of this tender girl a wreck.

The room was full of women now, sober-faced matrons and grave-eyed girls, yet all wore the same expression, not alone of anger, nor fear, nor pity, but of all combined.

Helen instinctively felt that this was one of the trials of border endurance, and she knew from the sterner faces of the maturer women that such a trial was familiar. Despite all she had been told, the shock and pain were too great, and she went out of the room sobbing.

She almost fell over the broad back of Jonathan Zane who was sitting on the steps. Near him stood Colonel Zane talking with a tall man clad in faded buckskin.

"Lass, you shouldn't have stayed," said Colonel Zane kindly.

"It's—hurt—me—here," said Helen, placing her hand over her heart.

"Yes, I know, I know; of course it has," he replied, taking her hand. "But be brave, Helen, bear up, bear up. Oh! this border is a stern place! Do not think of that poor girl. Come, let me introduce Jonathan's friend, Wetzel!"

Helen looked up and held out her hand. She saw a very tall man with extremely broad shoulders, a mass of raven-black hair, and a tanned face. He stepped forward, and took her hand in his huge, horny palm, pressing it, he stepped back without speaking. Colonel Zane talked to her in a soothing voice; but she failed to hear what he said. This Wetzel, this Indian-hunter whom she had heard called "Deathwind of the Border," this companion, guide, teacher of Jonathan Zane, this borderman of wonderful deeds, stood before her.

Helen saw a cold face, deathly in its pallor, lighted by eyes sloe-black like glinting steel. Striking as were these features, they failed to fascinate as did the strange tracings which apparently showed through the drawn skin. This first repelled, then drew her with wonderful force.

Suffering, of fire, and frost, and iron was written there, and, stronger than all, so potent as to cause fear, could be read the terrible purpose of this man's tragic life.

"You avenged her! Oh! I know you did!" cried Helen, her whole heart leaping with a blaze to her eyes.

She was answered by a smile, but such a smile! Kindly it broke over the stern face, giving a glimpse of a heart still warm beneath that steely cold. Behind it, too, there was something fateful, something deadly.

Helen knew, though the borderman spoke not, that somewhere among the grasses of the broad plains, or on the moss of the wooded hills, lay dead the perpetrators of this outrage, their still faces bearing the ghastly stamp of Deathwind.

CHAPTER VI

Happier days than she had hoped for dawned upon Helen after the first touch of border sorrow. Mabel Lane did not die. Helen and Betty nursed the stricken girl tenderly, weeping for very joy when signs of improvement appeared. She had remained silent for several days, always with that haunting fear in her eyes, and then gradually came a change. Tender care and nursing had due effect in banishing the dark shadow. One morning after a long sleep she awakened with a bright smile, and from that time her improvement was rapid.

Helen wanted Mabel to live with her. The girl's position was pitiable. Homeless, fatherless, with not a relative on the border, yet so brave, so patient that she aroused all the sympathy in Helen's breast. Village gossip was in substance, that Mabel had given her love to a young frontiersman, by name Alex Bennet, who had an affection for her, so it was said, but as yet had made no choice between her and the other lasses of the settlement. What effect Mabel's terrible experience might have on this lukewarm lover, Helen could not even guess; but she was not hopeful as to the future. Colonel Zane and Betty approved of Helen's plan to persuade Mabel to live with her, and the latter's faint protestations they silenced by claiming she could be of great assistance in the management of the house, therefore it was settled.

Finally the day came when Mabel was ready to go with Helen. Betty had given her a generous supply of clothing for all her belongings had been destroyed when the cabin was burned. With Helen's strong young arms around her she voiced her gratitude to Betty and Mrs. Zane and started toward the Sheppard home.

From the green square, where the ground was highest, an unobstructed view could be had of the valley. Mabel gazed down the river to where her home formerly stood. Only a faint, dark spot, like a blur on the green landscape, could be seen. Her soft eyes filled with tears; but she spoke no word.

"She's game and that's why she didn't go under," Colonel Zane said to himself as he mused on the strength and spirit of border women. To their heroism, more than any other thing, he attributed the establishing of homes in this wilderness.

In the days that ensued, as Mabel grew stronger, the girls became very fond of each other. Helen would have been happy at any time with such a sweet companion, but just then, when the poor girl's mind was so sorely disturbed she was doubly glad. For several days, after Mabel was out of danger, Helen's thoughts had dwelt on a subject which caused extreme vexation. She had begun to suspect that she encouraged too many admirers for whom she did not care, and thought too much of a man who did not reciprocate. She was happy and moody in turn. During the moody hours she suspected herself, and in her other ones, scorned the idea that she might ever care for a man who was indifferent. But that thought once admitted, had a trick of returning at odd moments, clouding her cheerful moods.

One sunshiny morning while the May flowers smiled under the hedge, when dew sparkled on the leaves, and the locust-blossoms shone creamy-white amid the soft green of the trees, the girls set about their much-planned flower gardening. Helen was passionately fond of plants, and had brought a jar of seeds of her favorites all the way from her eastern home.

"We'll plant the morning glories so they'll run up the porch, and the dahlias in this long row and the nasturtiums in this round bed," Helen said.

"You have some trailing arbutus," added Mabel, "and must have clematis, wild honeysuckle, and golden glow, for they are all sweet flowers."

"This arbutus is so fresh, so dewy, so fragrant," said Helen, bending aside a lilac bush to see the pale, creeping flowers. "I never saw anything so beautiful. I grow more and more in love with my new home, and friends. I have such a pretty garden to look into, and I never tire of the view beyond."

Helen gazed with pleasure and pride at the garden with its fresh green and lavender-crested lilacs, at the white-blossomed trees, and the vine-covered log cabins with blue smoke curling from their stone chimneys. Beyond, the great bulk of the fort stood guard above the willow-skirted river, and far away over the winding stream the dark hills, defiant, kept their secrets.

"If it weren't for that threatening fort one could imagine this little hamlet, nestling under the great bluff, as quiet and secure as it is beautiful," said Helen. "But that charred stockade fence with its scarred bastions and these lowering portholes, always keep me alive to the reality."

"It wasn't very quiet when Girty was here," Mabel replied thoughtfully.

"Were you in the fort then?" asked Helen breathlessly.

"Oh, yes, I cooled the rifles for the men," replied Mabel calmly.

"Tell me all about it."

Helen listened again to a story she had heard many times; but told by new lips it always gained in vivid interest. She never tired of hearing how the notorious renegade, Girty, rode around the fort on his white horse, giving the defenders an hour in which to surrender; she learned again of the attack, when the British soldiers remained silent on an adjoining hillside, while the Indians yelled exultantly and ran about in fiendish glee, when Wetzel began the battle by shooting an Indian chieftain who had ventured within range of his ever fatal rifle. And when it came to the heroic deeds of that memorable siege Helen could not contain her enthusiasm. She shed tears over little Harry Bennet's death at the south bastion where, though riddled with bullets, he stuck to his post until relieved. Clarke's race across the roof of the fort to extinguish a burning arrow, she applauded with clapping hands. Her great eyes glowed and burned, but she was silent, when hearing how Wetzel ran alone to a break in the stockade, and there, with an ax, the terrible borderman held at bay the whole infuriated Indian mob until the breach was closed. Lastly Betty Zane's never-to-be-forgotten run with the powder to the relief of the garrison and the saving of the fort was something not to cry over or applaud; but to dream of and to glorify.

"Down that slope from Colonel Zane's cabin is where Betty ran with the powder," said Mabel, pointing.

"Did you see her?" asked Helen.

"Yes, I looked out of a porthole. The Indians stopped firing at the fort in their eagerness to shoot Betty. Oh, the banging of guns and yelling of savages was one fearful, dreadful roar! Through all that hail of bullets Betty ran swift as the wind."

"I almost wish Girty would come again," said Helen.

"Don't; he might."

"How long has Betty's husband, Mr. Clarke, been dead?" inquired Helen.

"I don't remember exactly. He didn't live long after the siege. Some say he inhaled the flames while fighting fire inside the stockade."

"How sad!"

"Yes, it was. It nearly killed Betty. But we border girls do not give up easily; we must not," replied Mabel, an unquenchable spirit showing through the sadness of her eyes.

Merry voices interrupted them, and they turned to see Betty and Nell entering the gate. With Nell's bright chatter and Betty's wit, the conversation became indeed vivacious, running from gossip to gowns, and then to that old and ever new theme, love. Shortly afterward the colonel entered the gate, with swinging step and genial smile.

"Well, now, if here aren't four handsome lasses," he said with an admiring glance.

"Eb, I believe if you were single any girl might well suspect you of being a flirt," said Betty.

"No girl ever did. I tell you I was a lady-killer in my day," replied Colonel Zane, straightening his fine form. He was indeed handsome, with his stalwart frame, dark, bronzed face, and rugged, manly bearing.

"Bess said you were; but that it didn't last long after you saw her," cried Betty, mischief gleaming in her dark eye.

"Well, that's so," replied the colonel, looking a trifle crestfallen; "but you know every dog has his day." Then advancing to the porch, he looked at Mabel with a more serious gaze as he asked, "How are you today?"

"Thank you, Colonel Zane, I am getting quite strong."

"Look up the valley. There's a raft coming down the river," said he softly.

Far up the broad Ohio a square patch showed dark against the green water.

Colonel Zane saw Mabel start, and a dark red flush came over her pale face. For an instant she gazed with an expression of appeal, almost fear. He knew the reason. Alex Bennet was on that raft.

"I came over to ask if I can be of any service?"

"Tell him," she answered simply.

"I say, Betts," Colonel Zane cried, "has Helen's cousin cast any more such sheep eyes at you?"

"Oh, Eb, what nonsense!" exclaimed Betty, blushing furiously.

"Well, if he didn't look sweet at you I'm an old fool."

"You're one any way, and you're horrid," said Betty, tears of anger glistening in her eyes.

Colonel Zane whistled softly as he walked down the lane. He went into the wheelwright's shop to see about some repairs he was having made on a wagon, and then strolled on down to the river. Two Indians were sitting on the rude log wharf, together with several frontiersmen and rivermen, all waiting for the raft. He conversed with the Indians, who were friendly Chippewas, until the raft was tied up. The first person to leap on shore was a sturdy young fellow with a shock of yellow hair, and a warm, ruddy skin.

"Hello, Alex, did you have a good trip?" asked Colonel Zane of the youth.

"H'are ye, Colonel Zane. Yes, first-rate trip," replied young Bennet. "Say, I've a word for you. Come aside," and drawing Colonel Zane out of earshot of the others, he continued, "I heard this by accident, not that I didn't spy a bit when I got interested, for I did; but the way it came about was all chance. Briefly, there's a man, evidently an Englishman, at Fort Pitt, whom I overheard say he was out on the border after a Sheppard girl. I happened to hear from one of Brandt's men, who rode into Pitt just before we left, that you had new friends here by that name. This fellow was a handsome chap, no common sort, but lordly, dissipated, and reckless as the devil. He had a servant traveling with him, a sailor, by his gab, who was about the toughest customer I've met in many a day. He cut a fellow in bad shape at Pitt. These two will be on the next boat, due here in a day or so, according to river and weather conditions, an' I thought, considerin' how unusual the thing was, I'd better tell ye."

"Well, well," said Colonel Zane reflectively. He recalled Sheppard's talk about an Englishman. "Alex, you did well to tell me. Was the man drunk when he said he came west after a woman?"

"Sure he was," replied Alex. "But not when he spoke the name. Ye see I got suspicious, an' asked about him. It's this way: Jake Wentz, the trader, told me the fellow asked for the Sheppards when he got off the wagon train. When I first seen him he was drunk, and I heard Jeff Lynn say as how the border was a bad place to come after a woman. That's what made me prick up my ears. Then the Englishman said: 'It is eh? By God! I'd go to hell after a woman I wanted. An' Colonel, he looked it, too."

Colonel Zane remained thoughtful while Alex made up a bundle and forced the haft of an ax under the string; but as the young man started away the colonel suddenly remembered his errand down to the wharf.

"Alex, come back here," he said, and wondered if the lad had good stuff in him. The boatman's face was plain, but not evil, and a close scrutiny of it rather prepossessed the colonel.

"Alex, I've some bad news for you," and then bluntly, with his keen gaze fastened on the young man's face, he told of old Lane's murder, of Mabel's abduction, and of her rescue by Wetzel.

Alex began to curse and swear vengeance.

"Stow all that," said the colonel sharply. "Wetzel followed four Indians who had Mabel and some stolen horses. The redskins quarreled over the girl, and two took the horses, leaving Mabel to the others. Wetzel went after these last, tomahawked them, and brought Mabel home. She was in a bad way, but is now getting over the shock."

"Say, what'd we do here without Wetzel?" Alex said huskily, unmindful of the tears that streamed from his eyes and ran over his brown cheeks. "Poor old Jake! Poor Mabel! Damn me! It's my fault. If I'd 'a done right an' married her as I should, as I wanted to, she wouldn't have had to suffer. But I'll marry her yet, if she'll have me. It was only because I had no farm, no stock, an' only that little cabin as is full now, that I waited."

"Alex, you know me," said Colonel Zane in kindly tones. "Look there, down the clearing half a mile. See that green strip of land along the river, with the big chestnut in the middle and a cabin beyond. There's as fine farming land as can be found on the border, eighty acres, well watered. The day you marry Mabel that farm is yours."

Alex grew red, stammered, and vainly tried to express his gratitude.

"Come along, the sooner you tell Mabel the better," said the colonel with glowing face. He was a good matchmaker. He derived more pleasure from a little charity bestowed upon a deserving person, than from a season's crops.

When they arrived at the Sheppard house the girls were still on the porch. Mabel rose when she saw Alex, standing white and still. He, poor fellow, was embarrassed by the others, who regarded him with steady eyes.

Colonel Zane pushed Alex up on the porch, and said in a low voice: "Mabel, I've just arranged something you're to give Alex. It's a nice little farm, and it'll be a wedding present."

Mabel looked in a bewildered manner from Colonel Zane's happy face to the girls, and then at the red, joyous features of her lover. Only then did she understand, and uttering a strange little cry, put her trembling hands to her bosom as she swayed to and fro.

But she did not fall, for Alex, quick at the last, leaped forward and caught her in his arms.

That evening Helen denied herself to Mr. Brandt and several other callers. She sat on the porch with her father while he smoked his pipe.

"Where's Will?" she asked.

"Gone after snipe, so he said," replied her father.

"Snipe? How funny! Imagine Will hunting! He's surely catching the wild fever Colonel Zane told us about."

"He surely is."

Then came a time of silence. Mr. Sheppard, accustomed to Helen's gladsome spirit and propensity to chatter, noted how quiet she was, and wondered.

"Why are you so still?"

"I'm a little homesick," Helen replied reluctantly.

"No? Well, I declare! This is a glorious country; but not for such as you, dear, who love music and gaiety. I often fear you'll not be happy here, and then I long for the old home, which reminds me of your mother."

"Dearest, forget what I said," cried Helen earnestly. "I'm only a little blue to-day; perhaps not at all homesick."

"Indeed, you always seemed happy."

"Father, I am happy. It's only—only a girl's foolish sentiment."

"I've got something to tell you, Helen, and it has bothered me since Colonel Zane spoke of it to-night. Mordaunt is coming to Fort Henry."

"Mordaunt? Oh, impossible! Who said so? How did you learn?"

"I fear 'tis true, my dear. Colonel Zane told me he had heard of an Englishman at Fort Pitt who asked after us. Moreover, the fellow answers the description of Mordaunt. I am afraid it is he, and come after you."

"Suppose he has—who cares? We owe him nothing. He cannot hurt us."

"But, Helen, he's a desperate man. Aren't you afraid of him?"

"Not I," cried Helen, laughing in scorn. "He'd better have a care. He can't run things with a high hand out here on the border. I told him I would have none of him, and that ended it."

"I'm much relieved. I didn't want to tell you; but it seemed necessary. Well, child, good-night, I'll go to bed."

Long after Mr. Sheppard had retired Helen sat thinking. Memories of the past, and of the unwelcome suitor, Mordaunt, thronged upon her thick and fast. She could see him now with his pale, handsome face, and distinguished bearing. She had liked him, as she had other men, until he involved her father, with himself, in financial ruin, and had made his attentions to her unpleasantly persistent. Then he had followed the fall of fortune with wild dissipation, and became a gambler and a drunkard. But he did not desist in his mad wooing. He became like her shadow, and life grew to be unendurable, until her father planned to emigrate west, when she hailed the news with joy. And now Mordaunt had tracked her to her new home. She was sick with disgust. Then her spirit, always strong, and now freer for this new, wild life of the frontier, rose within her, and she dismissed all thoughts of this man and his passion.

The old life was dead and buried. She was going to be happy here. As for the present, it was enough to think of the little border village, now her home; of her girl friends; of the quiet borderman; and, for the moment, that the twilight was somber and beautiful.

High up on the wooded bluff rising so gloomily over the village, she saw among the trees something silver-bright. She watched it rise slowly from behind the trees, now hidden, now white through rifts in the foliage, until it soared lovely and grand above the black horizon. The ebony shadows of night seemed to lift, as might a sable mantle moved by invisible hands. But dark shadows, safe from the moon-rays, lay under the trees, and a pale, misty vapor hung below the brow of the bluff.

Mysterious as had grown the night before darkness yielded to the moon, this pale, white light flooding the still valley, was even more soft and strange. To one of Helen's temperament no thought was needed; to see was enough. Yet her mind was active. She felt with haunting power the beauty of all before her; in fancy transporting herself far to those silver-tipped clouds, and peopling with dells and shady nooks under the hills with spirits and fairies, maidens and valiant knights. To her the day was as a far-off dream. The great watch stars grew wan before the radiant moon; it reigned alone. The immensity of the world with its glimmering rivers, pensive valleys, and deep, gloomy forests lay revealed under the glory of the clear light.

Absorbed in this contemplation Helen remained a long time gazing with dreamy ecstasy at the moonlit valley until a slight chill disturbed her happy thoughts. She knew she was not alone. Trembling, she stood up to see, easily recognizable in the moonlight, the tall buckskin-garbed figure of Jonathan Zane.

"Well, sir," she called, sharply, yet with a tremor in her voice.

The borderman came forward and stood in front of her. Somehow he appeared changed. The long, black rifle, the dull, glinting weapons made her shudder. Wilder and more untamable he looked than ever. The very silence of the forest clung to him; the fragrance of the grassy plains came faintly from his buckskin garments.

"Evenin', lass," he said in his slow, cool manner.

"How did you get here?" asked Helen presently, because he made no effort to explain his presence at such a late hour.

"I was able to walk."

Helen observed, with a vaulting spirit, one ever ready to rise in arms, that Master Zane was disposed to add humor to his penetrating mysteriousness. She flushed hot and then paled. This borderman certainly possessed the power to vex her, and, reluctantly she admitted, to chill her soul and rouse her fear. She strove to keep back sharp words, because she had learned that this singular individual always gave good reason for his odd actions.

"I think in kindness to me," she said, choosing her words carefully, "you might tell me why you appear so suddenly, as if you had sprung out of the ground."

"Are you alone?"

"Yes. Father is in bed; so is Mabel, and Will has not yet come home. Why?"

"Has no one else been here?"

"Mr. Brandt came, as did some others; but wishing to be alone, I did not see them," replied Helen in perplexity.

"Have you seen Brandt since?"

"Since when?"

"The night I watched by the lilac bush."

"Yes, several times," replied Helen. Something in his tone made her ashamed. "I couldn't very well escape when he called. Are you surprised because after he insulted me I'd see him?"

"Yes."

Helen felt more ashamed.

"You don't love him?" he continued.

Helen was so surprised she could only look into the dark face above her. Then she dropped her gaze, abashed by his searching eyes. But, thinking of his question, she subdued the vague stirrings of pleasure in her breast, and answered coldly:

"No, I do not; but for the service you rendered me I should never have answered such a question."

"I'm glad, an' hope you care as little for the other five men who were here that night."

"I declare, Master Zane, you seem exceedingly interested in affairs of a young woman whom you won't visit, except as you have come to-night."

He looked at her with his piercing eyes.

"You spied upon my guests," she said, in no wise abashed now that her temper was high. "Did you care so very much?"

"Care?" he asked slowly.

"Yes; you were interested to know how many of my admirers were here, what they did, and what they said. You even hint disparagingly of them."

"True, I wanted to know," he replied; "but I don't hint about any man."

"You are so interested you wouldn't call on me when I invited you," said Helen, with poorly veiled sarcasm. It was this that made her bitter; she could never forget that she had asked this man to come to see her, and he had refused.

"I reckon you've mistook me," he said calmly.

"Why did you come? Why do you shadow my friends? This is twice you have done it. Goodness knows how many times you've been here! Tell me."

The borderman remained silent.

"Answer me," commanded Helen, her eyes blazing. She actually stamped her foot. "Borderman or not, you have no right to pry into my affairs. If you are a gentleman, tell me why you came here?"

The eyes Jonathan turned on Helen stilled all the angry throbbing of her blood.

"I come here to learn which of your lovers is the dastard who plotted the abduction of Mabel Lane, an' the thief who stole our hosses. When I find the villain I reckon Wetzel an' I'll swing him to some tree."

The borderman's voice rang sharp and cold, and when he ceased speaking she sank back upon the step, shocked, speechless, to gaze up at him with staring eyes.

"Don't look so, lass; don't be frightened," he said, his voice gentle and kind as it had been hard. He took her hand in his. "You nettled me into replyin'. You have a sharp tongue, lass, and when I spoke I was thinkin' of him. I'm sorry."

"A horse-thief and worse than murderer among my friends!" murmured Helen, shuddering, yet she never thought to doubt his word.

"I followed him here the night of your company."

"Do you know which one?"

"No."

He still held her hand, unconsciously, but Helen knew

it well. A sense of his strength came with the warm pressure, and comforted her. She would need that powerful hand, surely, in the evil days which seemed to darken the horizon.

"What shall I do?" she whispered, shuddering again.

"Keep this secret between you an' me."

"How can I? How can I?"

"You must." His voice was deep and low. "If you tell your father, or any one, I might lose the chance to find this man, for, lass, he's desperate cunnin'. Then he'd go free to rob others, an' mebbe help make off with other poor girls. Lass, keep my secret."

"But he might try to carry me away," said Helen in fearful perplexity.

"Most likely he might," replied the borderman with the smile that came so rarely.

"Oh! Knowing all this, how can I meet any of these men again? I'd betray myself."

"No; you've got too much pluck. It so happens you are the one to help me an' Wetzel rid the border of these hell-hounds, an' you won't fail. I know a woman when it comes to that."

"I—I help you and Wetzel?"

"Exactly."

"Gracious!" cried Helen, half-laughing, half-crying. "And poor me with more trouble coming on the next boat."

"Lass, the colonel told me about the Englishman. It'll be bad for him to annoy you."

Helen thrilled with the depth of meaning in the low voice. Fate surely was weaving a bond between her and this borderman. She felt it in his steady, piercing gaze; in her own tingling blood.

Then as her natural courage dispelled all girlish fears, she faced him, white, resolute, with a look in her eyes that matched his own.

"I will do what I can," she said.

CHAPTER VII

Westward from Fort Henry, far above the eddying river, Jonathan Zane slowly climbed a narrow, hazel-bordered, mountain trail. From time to time he stopped in an open patch among the thickets and breathed deep of the fresh, wood-scented air, while his keen gaze swept over the glades nearby, along the wooded hillsides, and above at the timber-strewn woodland.

This June morning in the wild forest was significant of nature's brightness and joy. Broad-leaved poplars, dense foliage oaks, and vine-covered maples shaded cool, mossy banks, while between the trees the sunshine streamed in bright spots. It shone silver on the glancing silver-leaf, and gold on the colored leaves of the butternut tree. Dewdrops glistened on the ferns; ripples sparkled in the brooks; spiderwebs glowed with wondrous rainbow hues, and the flower of the forest, the sweet, pale-faced daisy, rose above the green like a white star.

Yellow birds flitted among the hazel bushes caroling joyously, and catbirds sang gaily. Robins called; blue jays screeched in the tall, white oaks; woodpeckers hammered in the dead hardwoods, and crows cawed overhead. Squirrels chattered everywhere. Ruffled grouse rose with great bustle and a whirr, flitting like brown flakes through the leaves. From far above came the shrill cry of a hawk, followed by the wilder scream of an eagle.

Wilderness music such as all this fell harmoniously on the borderman's ear. It betokened the gladsome spirit of his wild friends, happy in the warm sunshine above, or in the cool depths beneath the fluttering leaves, and everywhere in those lonely haunts unalarmed and free.

Familiar to Jonathan, almost as the footpath near his home, was this winding trail. On the height above was a safe rendezvous, much frequented by him and Wetzel. Every lichen-covered stone, mossy bank, noisy brook, and giant oak on the way up this mountainside, could have told, had they spoken their secrets, stories of the bordermen. The fragile ferns and slender-bladed grasses peeping from the gray and amber mosses, and the flowers that hung from craggy ledges, had wisdom to impart. A borderman lived under the green treetops, and, therefore, all the nodding branches of sassafras and laurel, the grassy slopes and rocky cliffs, the stately ash trees, kingly oaks, and dark, mystic pines, together with the creatures that dwelt among them, save his deadly red-skinned foes, he loved. Other affection as close and true as this, he had not known. Hearkening thus with single heart to nature's teachings, he learned her secrets. Certain it was, therefore, that the many hours he passed in the woods apart from savage pursuits, were happy and fruitful.

Slowly he pressed on up the ascent, at length coming into open light upon a small plateau marked by huge, rugged, weather-chipped stones. On the eastern side was a rocky promontory, and close to the edge of this cliff, a hundred feet in sheer descent, rose a gnarled, time and tempest-twisted chestnut tree. Here the borderman laid down his rifle and knapsack, and, half-reclining against the tree, settled himself to rest and wait.

This craggy point was the lonely watchtower of eagles. Here on the highest headland for miles around where the bordermen were wont to meet, the outlook was far-reaching and grand.

Below the gray, splintered cliffs sheered down to meet the waving treetops, and then hill after hill, slope after slope, waved and rolled far, far down to the green river. Open grassy patches, bright little islands in that ocean of dark green, shone on the hillsides. The rounded ridges ran straight, curved, or zigzag, but shaped their graceful lines in the descent to make the valley. Long, purple-hued, shadowy depressions in the wide expanse of foliage marked deep clefts between ridges where dark, cool streams bounded on to meet the river. Lower, where the land was level, in open spaces could be seen a broad trail, yellow in the sunlight, winding along with the curves of the watercourse. On a swampy meadow, blue in the distance, a herd of buffalo browsed. Beyond the river, high over the green island, Fort Henry lay peaceful and solitary, the only token of the works of man in all that vast panorama.

Jonathan Zane was as much alone as if one thousand miles, instead of five, intervened between him and the settlement. Loneliness was to him a passion. Other men loved home, the light of woman's eyes, the rattle of dice or the lust of hoarding; but to him this wild, remote promontory, with its limitless view, stretching away to the dim hazy horizon, was more than all the arching joys of civilization.

Hours here, or in the shady valley, recompensed him for the loss of home comforts, the soft touch of woman's hands, the kiss of baby lips, and also for all he suffered in his pitiless pursuits, the hard fare, the steel and blood of a borderman's life.

Soon the sun shone straight overhead, dwarfing the shadow of the chestnut on the rock.

During such a time it was rare that any connected

thought came into the borderman's mind. His dark eyes, now strangely luminous, strayed lingeringly over those purple, undulating slopes. This intense watchfulness had no object, neither had his listening. He watched nothing; he hearkened to the silence. Undoubtedly in this state of rapt absorption his perceptions were acutely alert; but without thought, as were those of the savage in the valley below, or the eagle in the sky above.

Yet so perfectly trained were these perceptions that the least unnatural sound or sight brought him wary and watchful from his dreamy trance.

The slight snapping of a twig in the thicket caused him to sit erect, and reach out toward his rifle. His eyes moved among the dark openings in the thicket. In another moment a tall figure pressed the bushes apart. Jonathan let fall his rifle, and sank back against the tree once more. Wetzel stepped over the rocks toward him.

"Come from Blue Pond?" asked Jonathan as the newcomer took a seat beside him.

Wetzel nodded as he carefully laid aside his long, black rifle.

"Any Injun sign?" continued Jonathan, pushing toward his companion the knapsack of eatables he had brought from the settlement.

"Nary Shawnee track west of this divide," answered Wetzel, helping himself to bread and cheese.

"Lew, we must go eastward, over Bing Legget's way, to find the trail of the stolen horses."

"Likely, an' it'll be a long, hard tramp."

"Who's in Legget's gang now beside Old Horse, the Chippewa, an' his Shawnee pard, Wildfire? I don't know Bing; but I've seen some of his Injuns an' they remember me."

"Never seen Legget but onct," replied Wetzel, "an' that

time I shot half his face off. I've been told by them as have seen him since, that he's got a nasty scar on his temple an' cheek. He's a big man an' knows the woods. I don't know who all's in his gang, nor does anybody. He works in the dark, an' for cunnin' he's got some on Jim Girty, Deerin', an' several more renegades we know of lyin' quiet back here in the woods. We never tackled as bad a gang as his'n; they're all experienced woodsmen, old fighters, an' desperate, outlawed as they be by Injuns an' whites. It would surprise me to find that it's him an' his gang who are runnin' this hoss-thievin'; but bad or no, we're goin' after 'em."

Jonathan told of his movements since he had last seen his companion.

"An' the lass Helen is goin' to help us," said Wetzel, much interested. "It's a good move. Women are keen. Betty put Miller's schemin' in my eye long 'afore I noticed it. But girls have chances were men'd never got."

"Yes, an' she's like Betts, quicker'n lightnin'. She'll find out this hoss-thief in Fort Henry; but Lew, when we do get him we won't be much better off. Where do them hosses go? Who's disposin' of 'em fo this fellar?"

"Where's Brandt from?" asked Wetzel.

"Detroit; he's a French-Canadian."

Wetzel swung sharply around, his eyes glowing like wakening furnaces.

"Bing Legget's a French-Canadian, an' from Detroit. Metzar was once thick with him down Fort Pitt way 'afore he murdered a man an' became an outlaw. We're on the trail, Jack."

"Brandt an' Metzar, with Legget backin' them, an' the horses go overland to Detroit?"

"I calkilate you've hit the mark."

"What'll we do?" asked Jonathan.

"Wait; that's best. We've no call to hurry. We must know the truth before makin' a move, an' as yet we're only suspicious. This lass'll find out more in a week than we could in a year. But Jack, have a care she don't fall into any snare. Brandt ain't any too honest a lookin' chap, an' them renegades is hell for women. The scars you wear prove that well enough. She's a rare, sweet, bloomin' lass, too. I never seen her equal. I remember how her eyes flashed when she said she knew I'd avenged Mabel. Jack, they're wonderful eyes; an' that girl, however sweet an' good as she must be, is chain-lightnin' wrapped up in a beautiful form. Aren't the boys at the fort runnin' arter her!"

"Like mad; it'd make you laugh to see 'em," replied Jonathan calmly.

"There'll be some fights before she's settled for, an' mebbe arter thet. Have a care for her, Jack, an' see that she don't ketch you."

"No more danger than for you."

"I was ketched onct," replied Wetzel.

Jonathan Zane looked up at his companion. Wetzel's head was bowed; but there was no merriment in the serious face exposed to the borderman's scrutiny.

"Lew, you're jokin'."

"Not me. Some day, when you're ketched good, an' I have to go back to the lonely trail, as I did afore you an' me become friends, mebbe then, when I'm the last borderman, I'll tell you."

"Lew, 'cordin' to the way settlers are comin', in a few more years there won't be any need for a borderman. When the Injuns are all gone where'll be our work!"

"'Tain't likely either of us'll ever see them times," said Wetzel, "an' I don't want to. Wal, Jack, I'm off now, an' I'll meet you here every other day."

Wetzel shouldered his long rifle, and soon passed out of sight down the mountainside.

Jonathan arose, shook himself as a big dog might have done, and went down into the valley. Only once did he pause in his descent, and that was when a crackling twig warned him some heavy body was moving near. Silently he sank into the bushes bordering the trail. He listened with his ear close to the ground. Presently he heard a noise as of two hard substances striking together. He resumed his walk, having recognized the grating noise of a deer-hoof striking a rock. Farther down he espied a pair grazing. The buck ran into the thicket; but the doe eyed him curiously.

Less than an hour's rapid walking brought him to the river. Here he plunged into a thicket of willows, and emerged on a sandy strip of shore. He carefully surveyed the riverbank, and then pulled a small birch-bark canoe from among the foliage. He launched the frail craft, paddled across the river, and beached it under a reedy, over-hanging bank.

The distance from this point in a straight line to his destination was only a mile; but a rocky bluff and a ravine necessitated his making a wide detour. While lightly leaping over a brook his keen eye fell on an imprint in the sandy loam. Instantly he was on his knees. The footprint was small, evidently a woman's, and, what was more unusual, instead of the flat, round moccasin-track, it was point, with a sharp, square heel. Such shoes were not worn by border girls. True Betty and Nell had them; but they never went into the woods without moccasins.

Jonathan's experienced eye saw that this imprint was not an hour old. He gazed up at the light. The day was growing short. Already shadows lay in the glens. He would not long have light enough to follow the trail; but he hurried on hoping to find the person who made it before darkness came. He had not traveled many paces before learning that the one who made it was lost. The uncertainty in those hasty steps was as plain to the borderman's eyes, as if it had been written in words on the sand. The course led along the brook, avoiding the rough places, and leading into the open glades and glens; but it drew no nearer to the settlement. A quarter of an hour of rapid trailing enabled Jonathan to discern a dark figure moving among the trees. Abandoning the trail, he cut across a ridge to head off the lost woman. Stepping out of a sassafras thicket, he came face to face with Helen Sheppard.

"Oh!" she cried in alarm, and then the expression of terror gave place to one of extreme relief and gladness. "Oh! Thank goodness! You've found me. I'm lost!"

"I reckon," answered Jonathan grimly. "The settlement's only five hundred yards over that hill."

"I was going the wrong way. Oh! suppose you hadn't come!" exclaimed Helen, sinking on a log and looking up at him with warm, glad eyes.

"How did you lose your way?" Jonathan asked. He saw neither the warmth in her eyes nor the gladness.

"I went up the hillside, only a little way, after flowers, keeping the fort in sight all the time. Then I saw some lovely violets down a little hill, and thought I might venture. I found such loads of them I forgot everything else, and I must have walked on a little way. On turning to go back I couldn't find the little hill. I have hunted in vain for the clearing. It seems as if I have been wandering about for hours. I'm so glad you've found me!"

"Weren't you told to stay in the settlement, inside the clearing?" demanded Jonathan.

"Yes," replied Helen, with her head up.

"Why didn't you?"

"Because I didn't choose."

"You ought to have better sense."

"It seems I hadn't," Helen said quietly, but her eyes belied that calm voice.

"You're a headstrong child," Jonathan added curtly.

"Mr. Zane!" cried Helen with pale face.

"I suppose you've always had your own sweet will; but out here on the border you ought to think a little of others, if not of yourself."

Helen maintained a proud silence.

"You might have run right into prowlin' Shawnees."

"That dreadful disaster would not have caused you any sorrow," she flashed out.

"Of course it would. I might have lost my scalp tryin' to get you back home," said Jonathan, beginning to hesitate. Plainly he did not know what to make of this remarkable young woman.

"Such a pity to have lost all your fine hair," she answered with a touch of scorn.

Jonathan flushed, perhaps for the first time in his life. If there was anything he was proud of, it was his long, glossy hair.

"Miss Helen, I'm a poor hand at words," he said, with a pale, grave face. "I was only speakin' for your own good."

"You are exceedingly kind; but need not trouble yourself."

"Say," Jonathan hesitated, looking half-vexed at the lovely, angry face. Then an idea occurred to him. "Well, I won't trouble. Find your way home yourself."

Abruptly he turned and walked slowly away. He had no idea of allowing her to go home alone; but believed it might be well for her to think so. If she did not call him back he would remain near at hand, and when she showed signs of anxiety or fear he could go to her.

Helen determined she would die in the woods, or be captured by Shawnees, before calling him back. But she watched him. Slowly the tall, strong figure, with its graceful, springy stride, went down the glade. He would be lost to view in a moment, and then she would be alone. How dark it had suddenly become! The gray cloak of twilight was spread over the forest, and in the hollows night already had settled down. A breathless silence pervaded the woods. How lonely! thought Helen, with a shiver. Surely it would be dark before she could find the settlement. What hill hid the settlement from view? She did not know, could not remember which he had pointed out. Suddenly she began to tremble. She had been so frightened before he had found her, and so relieved afterward; and now he was going away.

"Mr. Zane," she cried with a great effort. "Come back."

Jonathan kept slowly on.

"Come back, Jonathan, please."

The borderman retraced his steps.

"Please take me home," she said, lifting a fair face all flushed, tear-stained, and marked with traces of storm. "I was foolish, and silly to come into the woods, and so glad to see you! But you spoke to me—in—in a way no one ever used before. I'm sure I deserved it. Please take me home. Papa will be worried."

Softer eyes and voice than hers never entreated man.

"Come," he said gently, and, taking her by the hand, he led her up the ridge.

Thus they passed through the darkening forest, hand in hand, like a dusky redman and his bride. He helped her over stones and logs, but still held her hand when there was no need of it. She looked up to see him walking, so dark and calm beside her, his eyes ever roving among the trees. Deepest remorse came upon her because of what she had said. There was no sentiment for him in this walk under the dark canopy of the leaves. He realized the responsibility. Any tree might hide a treacherous foe. She would atone for her sarcasm, she promised herself, while walking, ever conscious of her hand in his, her bosom heaving with the sweet, undeniable emotion which came knocking at her heart.

Soon they were out of the thicket, and on the dusty lane. A few moments of rapid walking brought them within sight of the twinkling lights of the village, and a moment later they were at the lane leading to Helen's home. Releasing her hand, she stopped him with a light touch and said:

"Please don't tell papa or Colonel Zane."

"Child, I ought. Some one should make you stay at home."

"I'll stay. Please don't tell. It will worry papa."

Jonathan Zane looked down into her great, dark, wonderful eyes with an unaccountable feeling. He really did not hear what she asked. Something about that upturned face brought to his mind a rare and perfect flower which grew in far-off rocky fastnesses. The feeling he had was intangible, like no more than a breath of fragrant western wind, faint with tidings of some beautiful field.

"Promise me you won't tell."

"Well, lass, have it your own way," replied Jonathan, wondering conscious that it was the first pledge ever asked of him by a woman.

"Thank you. Now we have two secrets, haven't we?" she laughed, with eyes like stars.

"Run home now, lass. Be careful hereafter. I do fear for you with such spirit an' temper. I'd rather be scalped by Shawnees than have Bing Legget so much as set eyes on you."

"You would? Why?" Her voice was like low, soft music.

"Why?" he mused. "It'd seem like a buzzard about to light on a doe."

"Good-night," said Helen abruptly, and, wheeling, she hurried down the lane.

CHAPTER VIII

"Jack," said Colonel Zane to his brother next morning, "to-day is Saturday and all the men will be in. There was high jinks over at Metzar's place yesterday, and I'm looking for more to-day. The two fellows Alex Bennet told me about, came on day-before-yesterday's boat. Sure enough, one's a lordly Englishman, and the other, the cussedest-looking little chap I ever saw. They started trouble immediately. The Englishman, his name is Mordaunt, hunted up the Sheppards and as near as I can make out from George's story, Helen spoke her mind very plainly. Mordaunt and Case, that's his servant, got drunk and raised hell down at Metzar's where they're staying. Brandt and Williams are drinking hard, too, which is something unusual for Brandt. They got chummy at once with the Englishman, who seems to have plenty of gold and is fond of gambling. This Mordaunt is a gentleman, or I never saw one. I feel sorry for him. He appears to be a ruined man. If he lasts a week out here I'll be surprised. Case looks ugly, as if he were spoiling to cut somebody. I want you to keep your eye peeled. The day may pass off as many other days of drinking bouts have, without anything serious, and on the other hand there's liable to be trouble."

Jonathan's preparations were characteristic of the borderman. He laid aside his rifle, and, removing his short coat, buckled on a second belt containing a heavier tomahawk and knife than those he had been wearing. Then he put on his hunting frock, or shirt, and wore it loose with the belts underneath, instead of on the outside. Unfastened, the frock was rather full, and gave him the appearance of a man unarmed and careless.

Jonathan Zane was not so reckless as to court danger, nor, like many frontiersmen, fond of fighting for its own sake. Colonel Zane was commandant of the fort, and, in a land where there was no law, tried to maintain a semblance of it. For years he had kept thieves, renegades, and outlaws away from his little settlement by dealing out stern justice. His word was law, and his bordermen executed it as such. Therefore Jonathan and Wetzel made it their duty to have a keen eye on all that was happening. They kept the colonel posted, and never interfered in any case without orders.

The morning passed quietly. Jonathan strolled here or loitered there; but saw none of the roisterers. He believed they were sleeping off the effects of their orgy on the previous evening. After dinner he smoked his pipe. Betty and Helen passed, and Helen smiled. It struck him suddenly that she had never looked at him in such a way before. There was meaning in that warm, radiant flash. A little sense of vexation, the source of which he did not understand, stirred in him against this girl; but with it came the realization that her white face and big, dark eyes had risen before him often since the night before. He wished, for the first time, that he could understand women better.

"Everything quiet?" asked Colonel Zane, coming out on the steps.

"All quiet," answered Jonathan.

"They'll open up later, I suspect. I'm going over to Sheppard's for a while, and, later, will drop into Metzar's. I'll make him haul in a yard or two. I don't like things I hear about his selling the youngsters rum. I'd like you to be within call."

The borderman strolled down the bluff and along the path which overhung the river. He disliked Metzar more than his brother suspected and with more weighty reason than that of selling rum to minors. Jonathan threw himself at length on the ground and mused over the situation.

"We never had any peace in this settlement, an' never will in our day. Eb is hopeful an' looks at the bright side, always expectin' to-morrow will be different. What have the past sixteen years been! One long bloody fight, an' the next sixteen won't be any better. I make out that we'll have a mix-up soon. Metzar an' Brandt with their allies, whoever they are, will be in it, an' if Bing Legget's in the gang, we've got, as Wetzel said, a long, hard trail, which may be our last. More'n that, there'll be trouble about this chain-lightnin' girl, as Wetzel predicted. Women make trouble anyways; an' when they're winsome an' pretty they cause more; but if they're beautiful an' fiery, bent on havin' their way, as this new lass is, all hell couldn't hold a candle to them. We don't need the Shawnees an' Girtys, an' hoss thieves round this here settlement to stir up excitin' times, now we've got this dark-eyed lass. An' yet any fool could see she's sweet, an' good, an' true as gold."

Toward the middle of the afternoon Jonathan sauntered in the direction of Metzar's inn. It lay on the front of the bluff, with its main doors looking into the road. A long, one-story log structure with two doors, answered as a barroom. The inn proper was a building more pretentious, and joined the smaller one at its western end. Several horses were hitched outside, and two great oxen yoked to a cumbersome mud-crusted wagon stood patiently by.

Jonathan bent his tall head as he entered the noisy

barroom. The dingy place reeked with tobacco smoke and the fumes of vile liquor. It was crowded with men. The lawlessness of the time and place was evident. Gaunt, red-faced frontiersmen reeled to and fro across the saw-dust floor; hunters and fur traders, raftsmen and farmers, swelled the motley crowd; young men, honest-faced, but flushed and wild with drink, hung over the bar; a group of sullen-visaged; serpent-eyed Indians held one corner. The black-bearded proprietor dealt out the rum.

From beyond the barroom, through a door entering upon the back porch, came the rattling of dice. Jonathan crossed the barroom apparently oblivious to the keen glance Metzar shot at him, and went out upon the porch. This also was crowded, but there was more room because of greater space. At one table sat some pioneers drinking and laughing; at another were three men playing with dice. Colonel Zane, Silas, and Sheppard were among the lookers-on at the game. Jonathan joined them, and gazed at the gamesters.

Brandt he knew well enough; he had seen that set, wolfish expression in the riverman's face before. He observed, however, that the man had flushed cheeks and trembling hands, indications of hard drinking. The player sitting next to Brandt was Williams, one of the garrison, and a good-natured fellow, but garrulous and wickedly disposed when drunk. The remaining player Jonathan at once saw was the Englishman, Mordaunt. He was a hand-some man, with fair skin, and long, silken, blond mustache. Heavy lines, and purple shades under his blue eyes, were the unmistakable stamp of dissipation. Reckless, dissolute, bad as he looked, there yet clung something favorable about the man. Perhaps it was his cool, devil-may-care way as he pushed over gold piece after gold piece from the fast diminishing pile before him. His velvet frock and silken doublet had once been elegant; but were now sadly the worse for border roughing.

Behind the Englishman's chair Jonathan saw a short man with a face resembling that of a jackal. The grizzled, stubbly beard, the protruding, vicious mouth, the broad, flat nose, and deep-set, small, glittering eyes made a bad impression on the observer. This man, Jonathan concluded, was the servant, Case, who was so eager with his knife. The borderman made the reflection, that if knife-play was the little man's pastime, he was not likely to go short of sport in that vicinity.

Colonel Zane attracted Jonathan's attention at this moment. The pioneers had vacated the other table, and Silas and Sheppard now sat by it. The colonel wanted his brother to join them.

"Here, Johnny, bring drinks," he said to the serving boy. "Tell Metzar who they're for." Then turning to Sheppard he continued: "He keeps good whiskey, but few of these poor devils ever see it." At the same time Colonel Zane pressed his foot upon that of Jonathan's.

The borderman understood that the signal was intended to call attention to Brandt. The latter had leaned forward, as Jonathan passed by to take a seat with his brother, and said something in a low tone to Mordaunt and Case. Jonathan knew by the way the Englishman and his man quickly glanced up at him, that he had been the subject of the remark.

Suddenly Williams jumped to his feet with an oath.

"I'm cleaned out," he cried.

"Shall we play alone?" asked Brandt of Mordaunt.

"As you like," replied the Englishman, in a tone which showed he cared not a whit whether he played or not.

"I've got work to do. Let's have some more drinks, and play another time," said Brandt.

The liquor was served and drank. Brandt pocketed his pile of Spanish and English gold, and rose to his feet. He was a trifle unsteady; but not drunk.

"Will you gentlemen have a glass with me?" Mordaunt asked of Colonel Zane's party.

"Thank you, some other time, with pleasure. We have our drink now," Colonel Zane said courteously.

Meantime Brandt had been whispering in Case's ear. The little man laughed at something the riverman said. Then he shuffled from behind the table. He was short, his compact build gave promise of unusual strength and agility.

"What are you going to do now?" asked Mordaunt, rising also. He looked hard at Case.

"Shiver my sides, cap'n, if I don't need another drink," replied the sailor.

"You have had enough. Come upstairs with me," said Mordaunt.

"Easy with your hatch, cap'n," grinned Case. "I want to drink with that ther' Injun killer. I've had drinks with buccaneers, and bad men all over the world, and I'm not going to miss this chance."

"Come on; you will get into trouble. You must not annoy these gentlemen," said Mordaunt.

"Trouble is the name of my ship, and she's a trim, fast craft," replied the man.

His loud voice had put an end to the conversation. Men began to crowd in from the barroom. Metzar himself came to see what had caused the excitement.

The little man threw up his cap, whooped, and addressed himself to Jonathan:

"Injun-killer, bad man of the border, will you drink with a jolly old tar from England?"

Suddenly a silence reigned, like that in the depths of the forest. To those who knew the borderman, and few did not know him, the invitation was nothing less than an insult. But it did not appear to them, as to him, like a pre-arranged plot to provoke a fight.

"Will you drink, redskin-hunter?" bawled the sailor.

"No," said Jonathan in his quiet voice.

"Maybe you mean that against old England?" demanded Case fiercely.

The borderman eyed him steadily, inscrutable as to feeling or intent, and was silent.

"Go out there and I'll see the color of your insides quicker than I'd take a drink," hissed the sailor, with his brickred face distorted and hideous to look upon. He pointed with a long-bladed knife that no one had seen him draw, to the green sward beyond the porch.

The borderman neither spoke, nor relaxed a muscle.

"Ho! ho! my brave pirate of the plains!" cried Case, and he leered with braggart sneer into the faces of Jonathan and his companions.

It so happened that Sheppard sat nearest to him, and got the full effect of the sailor's hot, rum-soaked breath. He arose with a pale face.

"Colonel, I can't stand this," he said hastily. "Let's get away from that drunken ruffian."

"Who's a drunken ruffian?" yelled Case, more angry than ever. "I'm not drunk; but I'm going to be, and cut some of you white-livered border mates. Here, you old masthead, drink this to my health, damn you!"

The ruffian had seized a tumbler of liquor from the table, and held it toward Sheppard while he brandished his long knife.

White as snow, Sheppard backed against the wall; but did not take the drink.

The sailor had the floor; no one save him spoke a word. The action had been so rapid that there had hardly been time. Colonel Zane and Silas were as quiet and tense as the borderman.

"Drink!" hoarsely cried the sailor, advancing his knife toward Sheppard's body.

When the sharp point all but pressed against the old man, a bright object twinkled through the air. It struck Case's wrist, knocked the knife from his fingers, and, bounding against the wall, fell upon the floor. It was a tomahawk.

The borderman sprang over the table like a huge catamount, and with movement equally quick, knocked Case with a crash against the wall; closed on him before he could move a hand, and flung him like a sack of meal over the bluff.

The tension relieved, some of the crowd laughed, others looked over the embankment to see how Case had fared, and others remarked that for some reason he had gotten off better than they expected.

The borderman remained silent. He leaned against a post, with broad breast gently heaving, but his eyes sparkled as they watched Brandt, Williams, Mordaunt, and Metzar. The Englishman alone spoke.

"Hardily done," he said, cool and suave. "Sir, yours is an iron hand. I apologize for this unpleasant affair. My man is quarrelsome when under the influence of liquor."

"Metzar, a word with you," cried Colonel Zane curtly.

"Come inside, kunnel," said the innkeeper, plainly ill at ease.

"No; listen here. I'll speak to the point. You've got to stop running this kind of a place. No words, now, you've got to stop. Understand? You know as well as I, perhaps better, the character of your so-called inn. You'll get but one more chance."

"Wal, kunnel, this is a free country," growled Metzar. "I can't help these fellars comin' here lookin' fer blood. I runs an honest place. The men want to drink an' gamble. What's law here? What can you do?"

"You know me, Metzar," Colonel Zane said grimly. "I don't waste words. 'To hell with law!' so you say. I can say that, too. Remember, the next drunken boy I see, or shady deal, or gambling spree, out you go for good."

Metzar lowered his shaggy head and left the porch. Brandt and his friends, with serious faces, withdrew into the barroom.

The borderman walked around the corner of the inn, and up the lane. The colonel, with Silas and Sheppard, followed in more leisurely fashion. At a shout from some one they turned to see a dusty, bloody figure, with ragged clothes, stagger up from the bluff.

"There's that blamed sailor now," said Sheppard. "He's a tough nut. My! What a knock on the head Jonathan gave him. Strikes me, too, that tomahawk came almost at the right time to save me a whole skin."

"I was furious, but not at all alarmed," rejoined Colonel Zane.

"I wondered what made you so quiet."

"I was waiting. Jonathan never acts until the right moment, and then—well, you saw him. The little villain deserved killing. I could have shot him with pleasure. Do you know, Sheppard, Jonathan's aversion to shedding blood is a singular thing. He'd never kill the worst kind of a white man until driven to it."

"That's commendable. How about Wetzel?"

"Well, Lew is different," replied Colonel Zane with a

shudder. "If I told him to take an ax and clean out Metzar's place—God! what a wreck he'd make of it. Maybe I'll have to tell him, and if I do, you'll see something you can never forget."

CHAPTER IX

O n Sunday morning under the bright, warm sun, the little hamlet of Fort Henry lay peacefully quiet, as if no storms had ever rolled and thundered overhead, no roistering ever disturbed its stillness, and no Indian's yell ever horribly broke the quiet.

"'Tis a fine morning," said Colonel Zane, joining his sister on the porch. "Well, how nice you look! All in white for the first time since—well, you do look charming. You're going to church, or course."

"Yes, I invited Helen and her cousin to go. I've persuaded her to teach my Sunday-school class, and I'll take another of older children," replied Betty.

"That's well. The youngsters don't have much chance to learn out here. But we've made one great stride. A church and a preacher means very much to young people. Next shall come the village school."

"Helen and I might teach our classes an hour or two every afternoon."

"It would be a grand thing if you did! Fancy these tots growing up unable to read or write. I hate to think of it; but the Lord knows I've done my best. I've had my troubles in keeping them alive."

"Helen suggested the day school. She takes the greatest interest in everything and everybody. Her energy is remarkable. She simply must move, must do something.

She overflows with kindness and sympathy. Yesterday she cried with happiness when Mabel told her Alex was eager to be married very soon. I tell you, Eb, Helen is a fine character."

"Yes, good as she is pretty, which is saying some," mused the colonel. "I wonder who'll be the lucky fellow to win her."

"It's hard to say. Not that Englishman, surely. She hates him. Jonathan might. You should see her eyes when he is mentioned."

"Say, Betts, you don't mean it?" eagerly asked her brother.

"Yes, I do," returned Betty, nodding her head positively. "I'm not easily deceived about those things. Helen's completely fascinated with Jack. She might be only a sixteen-year-old girl for the way she betrays herself to me."

"Betty, I have a beautiful plan."

"No doubt; you're full of them."

"We can do it, Betty, we can, you and I," he said as he squeezed her arm.

"My dear old matchmaking brother," returned Betty, laughing, "it takes two to make a bargain. Jack must be considered."

"Bosh!" exclaimed the colonel, snapping his fingers. "You needn't tell me any young man—any man, could resist that glorious girl."

"Perhaps not; I couldn't if I were a man. But Jack's not like other people. He'd never realize that she cared for him. Besides, he's a borderman."

"I know, and that's the only serious obstacle. But he could scout around the fort, even if he was married. These long, lonely, terrible journeys taken by him and Wetzel are mostly unnecessary. A sweet wife could soon make him see that. The border will be civilized in a few years, and because of that he'd better give over hunting for Indians. I'd like to see him married and settled down, like all the rest of us, even Isaac. You know Jack's the last of the Zanes, that is, the old Zanes. The difficulty arising from his extreme modesty and bashfulness can easily be overcome."

"How, most wonderful brother?"

"Easy as pie. Tell Jack that Helen is dying of love for him, and tell her that Jack loves—"

"But, dear Eb, that latter part is not true," interposed Betty.

"True, of course it's true, or would be in any man who wasn't as blind as a bat. We'll tell her Jack cares for her; but he is a borderman with stern ideas of duty, and so slow and backward he'd never tell his love even if he had overcome his tricks of ranging. That would settle it with any girl worth her salt, and this one will fetch Jack in ten days, or less."

"Eb, you're a devil," said Betty gayly, and then she added in a more sober vein, "I understand, Eb. Your idea is prompted by love of Jack, and it's all right. I never see him go out of the clearing but I think it may be for the last time, even as on that day so long ago when brother Andrew waved his cap to us, and never came back. Jack is the best man in the world, and I, too, want to see him happy, with a wife, and babies, and a settled occupation in life. I think we might weave a pretty little romance. Shall we try?"

"Try? We'll do it! Now, Betts, you explain it to both. You can do it smoother than I, and telling them is really the finest point of our little plot. I'll help the good work along afterwards. He'll be out presently. Nail him at once."

Jonathan, all unconscious of the deep-laid scheme to

make him happy, soon came out on the porch, and stretched his long arms as he breathed freely of the morning air.

"Hello, Jack, where are you bound?" asked Betty, clasping one of his powerful, buckskin-clad knees with her arm.

"I reckon I'll go over to the spring," he replied, patting her dark, glossy head.

"Do you know I want to tell you something, Jack, and it's quite serious," she said, blushing a little at her guilt; but resolute to carry out her part of the plot.

"Well, dear?" he asked as she hesitated.

"Do you like Helen?"

"That is a question," Jonathan replied after a moment.

"Never mind; tell me," she persisted.

He made no answer.

"Well, Jack, she's—she's wildly in love with you."

The borderman stood very still for several moments. Then, with one step he gained the lawn, and turned to confront her.

"What's that you say?"

Betty trembled a little. He spoke so sharply, his eyes were bent on her so keenly, and he looked so strong, so forceful that she was almost afraid. But remembering that she had said only what, to her mind, was absolutely true, she raised her eyes and repeated the words:

"Helen is wildly in love with you."

"Betty, you wouldn't joke about such a thing; you wouldn't lie to me, I know you wouldn't."

"No, Jack dear."

She saw his powerful frame tremble, even as she had seen more than one man tremble, during the siege, under the impact of a bullet.

Without speaking, he walked rapidly down the path toward the spring.

Colonel Zane came out of his hiding-place behind the porch, and, with a face positively electrifying in its glowing pleasure, beamed upon his sister.

"Gee! Didn't he stalk off like an Indian chief!" he said, chuckling with satisfaction. "By George! Betts, you must have got in a great piece of work. I never in my life saw Jack look like that."

Colonel Zane sat down at Betty's side and laughed softly but heartily.

"We'll fix him all right, the lonely hill-climber! Why, he hasn't a ghost of a chance. Wait until she sees him after hearing your story! I tell you, Betty—why—damme! you're crying!"

He had turned to find her head lowered, while she shaded her face with her hand.

"Now, Betty, just a little innocent deceit like that—what harm?" he said, taking her hand. He was as tender as a woman.

"Oh, Eb, it wasn't that. I didn't mind telling him. Only the flash in his eyes reminded me of—of Alfred."

"Surely it did. Why not? Almost everything brings up a tender memory for some one we've loved and lost. But don't cry, Betty."

She laughed a little, and raised a face with its dark cheeks flushed and tearstained.

"I'm silly, I suppose; but I can't help it. I cry at least once every day."

"Brace up. Here come Helen and Will. Don't let them see you grieved. My! Helen in pure white, too! This is a conspiracy to ruin the peace of the masculine portion of Fort Henry."

Betty went forward to meet her friends while Colonel Zane continued talking, but now to himself. "What a fatal beauty she has!" His eyes swept over Helen with the pleasure of an artist. The fair richness of her skin, the perfect lips, the wavy, shiny hair, the wondrous dark-blue, changing eyes, the tall figure, slender, but strong and swelling with gracious womanhood, made a picture he delighted in and loved to have near him. The girl did not possess for him any of that magnetism, so commonly felt by most of her admirers; but he did feel how subtly full she was of something, which for want of a better term he described in Wetzel's characteristic expression, as "chain-lightning."

He reflected that as he was so much older, that she, although always winsome and earnest, showed nothing of the tormenting, bewildering coquetry of her nature. Colonel Zane prided himself on his discernment, and he had already observed that Helen had different sides of character for different persons. To Betty, Mabel, Nell, and the children, she was frank, girlish, full of fun, and always lovable; to her elders quiet and earnestly solicitous to please; to the young men cold; but with a penetrating, mocking promise haunting that coldness, and sometimes sweetly agreeable, often wilful, and changeable as April winds. At last the colonel concluded that she needed, as did all other spirited young women, the taming influence of a man whom she loved, a home to care for, and children to soften and temper her spirit.

"Well, young friends, I see you count on keeping the Sabbath," he said cheerily. "For my part, Will, I don't see how Jim Downs can preach this morning, before this laurel blossom and that damask rose."

"How poetical! Which is which?" asked Betty.

"Flatterer!" laughed Helen, shaking her finger.

"And a married man, too!" continued Betty.

"Well, being married has not affected my poetical sentiment, nor impaired my eyesight."

"But it has seriously inconvenienced your old propensity of making love to the girls. Not that you wouldn't if you dared," replied Betty with mischief in her eye.

"Now, Will, what do you think of that? Isn't it real sisterly regard? Come, we'll go and look at my thoroughbreds," said Colonel Zane.

"Where is Jonathan?" Helen asked presently. "Something happened at Metzar's yesterday. Papa wouldn't tell me, and I want to ask Jonathan."

"Jack is down by the spring. He spends a great deal of his time there. It's shady and cool, and the water babbles over the stones."

"How much alone he is," said Helen.

Betty took her former position on the steps, but did not raise her eyes while she continued speaking. "Yes, he's more alone than ever lately, and quieter, too. He hardly ever speaks now. There must be something on his mind more serious than horse-thieves."

"What!" Helen asked quickly.

"I'd better not tell—you."

A long moment passed before Helen spoke.

"Please tell me!"

"Well, Helen, we think, Eb and I, that Jack is in love for the first time in his life, and with you, you adorable creature. But Jack's a borderman; he is stern in his principles, thinks he is wedded to his border life, and he knows that he has both red and white blood on his hands. He'd die before he'd speak of his love, because he cannot understand that would do any good, even if you loved him, which is, of course, preposterous."

"Loves me!" breathed Helen softly.

She sat down rather beside Betty, and turned her face away. She still held the young woman's hand which she squeezed so tightly as to make its owner wince. Betty stole a look at her, and saw the rich red blood mantling her cheeks, and her full bosom heave.

Helen turned presently, with no trace of emotion except a singular brilliance of the eyes. She was so slow to speak again that Colonel Zane and Will returned from the corral before she found her voice.

"Colonel Zane, please tell me about last night. When Papa came home to supper he was pale and very nervous. I knew something had happened. But he would not explain, which made me all the more anxious. Won't you please tell me?"

Colonel Zane glanced again at her, and knew what had happened. Despite her self-possession those telltale eyes told her secret. Ever-changing and shadowing with a bounding, rapturous light, they were indeed the windows of her soul. All the emotion of a woman's heart shone there, fear, beauty, wondering appeal, trembling joy, and timid hope.

"Tell you? Indeed I will," replied Colonel Zane, softened and a little remorseful under those wonderful eyes.

No one liked to tell a story better than Colonel Zane. Briefly and graphically he related the circumstances of the affair leading to the attack on Helen's father, and, as the tale progressed, he became quite excited, speaking with animated face and forceful gestures.

"Just as the knife-point touched your father, a swiftly-flying object knocked the weapon to the floor. It was Jonathan's tomahawk. What followed was so sudden I hardly saw it. Like lightning, and flexible as steel, Jonathan jumped over the table, smashed Case against the wall, pulled him up, and threw him over the bank. I tell you, Helen, it was a beautiful piece of action; but not, of course, for a woman's eyes. Now that's all. Your father was not even hurt."

"He saved Papa's life," murmured Helen, standing like a statue.

She wheeled suddenly with that swift bird-like motion habitual to her, and went quickly down the path leading to the spring.

Jonathan Zane, solitary dreamer of dreams as he was, had never been in as strange and beautiful a reverie as that which possessed him on this Sabbath morning.

Deep into his heart had sunk Betty's words. The wonder of it, the sweetness, that alone was all he felt. The glory of this girl had begun, days past, to spread its glamour round him. Swept irresistibly away now, he soared aloft in a dream-castle of fancy with its painted windows and golden walls.

For the first time in his life on the border he had entered the little glade and had no eye for the crystal water flowing over the pebbles and mossy stones, or the plot of grassy ground inclosed by tall, dark trees and shaded by a canopy of fresh green and azure blue. Nor did he hear the music of the soft rushing water, the warbling birds, or the gentle sighing breeze moving the leaves.

Gone, vanished, lost to-day was that sweet companionship of nature. That indefinable and unutterable spirit which flowed so peacefully to him from his beloved woods; that something more than merely affecting his senses, which existed for him in the stony cliffs, and breathed with life through the lonely aisles of the forest, had fled before the fateful power of a woman's love and beauty.

A long time that seemed only a moment passed while he leaned against a stone. A light step sounded on the path.

A vision in pure white entered the glade; two little hands pressed his, and two dark-blue eyes of misty beauty shed their light on him.

"Jonathan, I am come to thank you."

Sweet and tremulous, the voice sounded far away.

"Thank me? For what?"

"You saved Papa's life. Oh! how can I thank you?"

No voice answered for him.

"I had nothing to give but this."

A flower-like face was held up to him; hands light as thistle-down touched his shoulders; dark-blue eyes glowed upon him with all tenderness.

"May I thank you—so?"

Soft lips met his full and lingeringly.

Then came a rush as of wind, a flash of white, and the patter of flying feet. He was alone in the glade.

CHAPTER X

June passed; July opened with unusually warm weather, and Fort Henry had no visits from Indians or horse-thieves, nor any inconvenience except the hot sun. It was the warmest weather for many years, and seriously dwarfed the settlers' growing corn. Nearly all the springs were dry, and a drouth menaced the farmers.

The weather gave Helen an excuse which she was not slow to adopt. Her pale face and languid air perplexed and worried her father and her friends. She explained to them that the heat affected her disagreeably.

Long days had passed since that Sunday morning when she kissed the borderman. What transports of sweet hope and fear were hers then! How shame had scorched her happiness! Yet she still gloried in the act. By that kiss had she awakened to a full consciousness of her love. With insidious stealth and ever-increasing power this flood had increased to full tide, and, bursting its bonds, surged over her with irresistible strength.

During the first days after the dawning of her passion, she lived in its sweetness, hearing only melodious sounds chiming in her soul. The hours following that Sunday were like long dreams. But as all things reach fruition, so this girlish period passed, leaving her a thoughtful woman. She began to gather up the threads of her life where love had broken them, to plan nobly, and to hope and wait.

Weeks passed, however, and her lover did not come. Betty told her that Jonathan made flying trips at break of day to hold council with Colonel Zane; that he and Wetzel were on the trail of Shawnees with stole horses, and both bordermen were in their dark, vengeful, terrible moods. In these later days Helen passed through many stages of feeling. After the exalting mood of hot, young love, came reaction. She fell into the depths of despair. Sorrow paled her face, thinned her cheeks, and lent another shadow, a mournful one, to her great eyes. The constant repression of emotion, the strain of trying to seem cheerful when she was miserable, threatened even her magnificent health. She answered the solicitude of her friends by evasion, and then by that innocent falsehood in which a sensitive soul hides its secrets. Shame was only natural, because since the borderman came not, nor sent her a word, pride whispered that she had wooed him, forgetting modesty.

Pride, anger, shame, despair, however, finally fled before affection. She loved this wild borderman, and knew he loved her in return although he might not understand it himself. His simplicity, his lack of experience with women, his hazardous life and stern duty regarding it, pleaded for him and for her love. For the lack of a little understanding she would never live unhappy and alone while she was loved. Better give a thousand times more than she had sacrificed. He would return to the village some day, when the Indians and the thieves were run down, and would be his own calm, gentle self. Then she would win him, break down his allegiance to this fearful border life, and make him happy in her love.

While Helen was going through one of the fires of life to come out sweeter and purer, if a little pensive and sad, time, which waits not for love, nor life, nor death, was hastening onward, and soon the golden fields of grain were stored. September came with its fruitful promise fulfilled.

Helen entered once more into the quiet, social life of the little settlement, taught her class on Sundays, did all her own work, and even found time to bring a ray of sunshine to more than one sick child's bed. Yet she did not forget her compact with Jonathan, and bent all her intelligence to find some clue that might aid in the capture of the horse-thief. She was still groping in the darkness. She could not, however, banish the belief that the traitor was Brandt. She blamed herself for this, because of having no good reasons for suspicion; but the conviction was there, fixed by intuition. Because a man's eyes were steely gray, sharp like those of a cat's, and capable of the same contraction and enlargement, there was no reason to believe their owner was a criminal. But that, Helen acknowledged with a smile, was the only argument she had. To be sure Brandt had looked capable of anything, the night Jonathan knocked him down; she knew he had incited Case to begin the trouble at Metzar's, and had seemed worried since that time. He had not left the settlement on short journeys, as had been his custom before the affair in the barroom. And not a horse had disappeared from Fort Henry since that time.

Brandt had not discontinued his attentions to her; if they were less ardent it was because she had given him absolutely to understand that she could be his friend only. And she would not have allowed even so much except for Jonathan's plan. She fancied it was possible to see behind Brandt's courtesy, the real subtle, threatening man. Stripped of his kindliness, an assumed virtue, the iron man stood revealed, cold, calculating, cruel.

Mordaunt she never saw but once and then, shocking

and pitiful, he lay dead drunk in the grass by the side of the road, his pale, weary, handsome face exposed to the pitiless rays of the sun. She ran home weeping over his wreck of what had once been so fine a gentleman. Ah! the curse of rum! He had learned his soft speech and courtly bearing in the refinement of a home where a proud mother adored, and gentle sisters loved him. And now, far from the kindred he had disgraced, he lay in the road like a log. How it hurt her! She almost wished she could have loved him, if love might have redeemed. She was more kind to her other admirers, more tolerant of Brandt, and could forgive the Englishman, because the pangs she had suffered through love had softened her spirit.

During this long period the growing friendship of her cousin for Betty had been a source of infinite pleasure to Helen. She hoped and believed a romance would develop between the young widow and Will, and did all in her power, slyly abetted by the matchmaking colonel, to bring the two together.

One afternoon when the sky was clear with that intense blue peculiar to bright days in early autumn, Helen started out toward Betty's, intending to remind that young lady she had promised to hunt for clematis and other fall flowers.

About halfway to Betty's home she met Brandt. He came swinging round a corner with his quick, firm step. She had not seen him for several days, and somehow he seemed different. A brightness, a flash, as of daring expectation, was in his face. The poise, too, of the man had changed.

"Well, I am fortunate. I was just going to your home," he said cheerily. "Won't you come for a walk with me?"

"You may walk with me to Betty's," Helen answered.

"No, not that. Come up the hillside. We'll get some

goldenrod. I'd like to have a chat with you. I may go away—I mean I'm thinking of making a short trip," he added hurriedly. "Please come."

"I promised to go to Betty's."

"You won't come?" His voice trembled with mingled disappointment and resentment.

"No," Helen replied in slight surprise.

"You have gone with the other fellows. Why not with me?" He was white now, and evidently laboring under powerful feelings that must have had their origin in some thought or plan which hinged on the acceptance of his invitation.

"Because I choose not to," Helen replied coldly, meeting his glance fully.

A dark red flush swelled Brandt's face and neck; his gray eyes gleamed balefully with wolfish glare; his teeth were clenched. He breathed hard and trembled with anger. Then, by a powerful effort, he conquered himself; the villainous expression left his face; the storm of rage subsided. Great incentive there must have been for him thus to repress his emotions so quickly. He looked long at her with sinister, intent regard; then, with the laugh of a desperado, a laugh which might have indicated contempt for the failure of his suit, and which was fraught with a world of meaning, of menace, he left her without so much as a salute.

Helen pondered over this sudden change, and felt relieved because she need make no further pretense of friendship. He had shown himself to be what she had instinctively believed. She hurried on toward Betty's, hoping to find Colonel Zane at home, and with Jonathan, for Brandt's hint of leaving Fort Henry, and his evident chagrin at such a slip of speech, had made her suspicious. She was informed by Mrs. Zane that the colonel had gone to a log-raising; Jonathan had not been in for several days, and Betty went away with Will.

"Where did they go?" asked Helen.

"I'm not sure; I think down to the spring."

Helen followed the familiar path through the grove of oaks into the glade. It was quite deserted. Sitting on the stone against which Jonathan had leaned the day she kissed him, she gave way to tender reflection. Suddenly she was disturbed by the sound of rapid footsteps, and looking up, saw the hulking form of Metzar, the innkeeper, coming down the path. He carried a bucket, and meant evidently to get water. Helen did not desire to be seen, and, thinking he would stay only a moment, slipped into a thicket of willows behind the stone. She could see plainly through the foliage. Metzar came into the glade, peered around in the manner of a man expecting to see some one, and then, filling his bucket at the spring, sat down on the stone.

Not a minute elapsed before soft, rapid footsteps sounded in the distance. The bushes parted, disclosing the white, set face and gray eyes of Roger Brandt. With a light spring he cleared the brook and approached Metzar.

Before speaking he glanced around the glade with the fugitive, distrustful glance of a man who suspects even the trees. Then, satisfied by the scrutiny he opened his hunting frock, taking forth a long object which he thrust toward Metzar.

It was an Indian arrow.

Metzar's dull gaze traveled from this to the ominous face of Brandt.

"See there, you! Look at this arrow! Shot by the best Indian on the border into the window of my room. I hadn't been there a minute when it came from the island. God! but it was a great shot!"

"Hell!" gasped Metzar, his dull face quickening with some awful thought.

"I guess it *is* hell," replied Brandt, his face growing whiter and wilder.

"Our game's up?" questioned Metzar with haggard cheek.

"Up? Man! We haven't a day, maybe less, to shake Fort Henry."

"What does it mean?" asked Metzar. He was the calmer of the two.

"It's a signal. The Shawnees, who were in hiding with the horses over by Blueberry swamp, have been flushed by those bordermen. Some of them have escaped; at least one, for no one but Ashbow could shoot that arrow across the river."

"Suppose he hadn't come?" whispered Metzar hoarsely.

Brandt answered him with a dark, shuddering gaze.

A twig snapped in the thicket. Like foxes at the click of a trap, these men whirled with fearsome glances.

"Ugh!" came a low, guttural voice from the bushes, and an Indian of magnificent proportions and somber, swarthy features, entered the glade.

CHAPTER XI

The savage had just emerged from the river, for his graceful, copper-colored body and scanty clothing were dripping with water. He carried a long bow and a quiver of arrows.

Brandt uttered an exclamation of surprise, and Metzar a curse, as the lithe Indian leaped the brook. He was not young. His swarthy face was lined, seamed, and terrible with a dark impassiveness.

"Paleface-brother-get-arrow," he said in halting English, as his eyes flashed upon Brandt. "Chief-want-make-sure."

The white man leaned forward, grasped the Indian's arm, and addressed him in an Indian language. This questioning was evidently in regard to his signal, the whereabouts of others of the party, and why he took such fearful risks almost in the village. The Indian answered with one English word.

"Deathwind!"

Brandt drew back with drawn, white face, while a whistling breath escaped him.

"I knew it, Metz. Wetzel!" he exclaimed in a husky voice.

The blood slowly receded from Metzar's evil, murky face, leaving it haggard.

"Deathwind-on-Chief's-trail-up-Eagle-Rock," continued the Indian. "Deathwind-fooled-not-for-long. Chief-wait-paleface-brothers-at-Two-Islands."

The Indian stepped into the brook, parted the willows, and was gone as he had come, silently.

"We know what to expect," said Brandt in calmer tone as the daring cast of countenance returned to him. "There's an Indian for you! He got away, doubled like an old fox on his trail, and ran in here to give us a chance at escape. Now you know why Bing Legget can't be caught."

"Let's dig at once," replied Metzar, with no show of returning courage such as characterized his companion.

Brandt walked to and fro with bent brows, like one in deep thought. Suddenly he turned upon Metzar eyes which were brightly hard, and reckless with resolve.

"By Heaven! I'll do it! Listen. Wetzel has gone to the top of Eagle Mountain, where he and Zane have a rendezvous. Even he won't suspect the cunning of this Indian; anyway it'll be after daylight to-morrow before he strikes the trail. I've got twenty-four hours, and more, to get this girl, and I'll do it!"

"Bad move to have weight like her on a march," said Metzar.

"Bah! The thing's easy. As for you, go on, push ahead after we're started. All I ask is that you stay by me until the time to cut loose."

"I ain't agoin' to crawfish now," growled Metzar. "Strikes me, too. I'm losin' more'n you."

"You won't be a loser if you can get back to Detroit with your scalp. I'll pay you in horses and gold. Once we reach Legget's place we're safe."

"What's yer plan about gittin' the gal?" asked Metzar.

Brandt leaned forward and spoke eagerly, but in a low tone.

"Git away on hoss-back?" questioned Metzar, visibly

brightening. "Wal, that's some sense. Kin ye trust ther other party?"

"I'm sure I can," rejoined Brandt.

"It'll be a good job, a good job an' all done in daylight, too. Bing Legget couldn't plan better," Metzar said, rubbing his hands.

"We've fooled these Zanes and their fruit-raising farmers for a year, and our time is about up," Brandt muttered. "One more job and we're done. Once with Legget we're safe, and then we'll work slowly back towards Detroit. Let's get out of here now, for some one may come at any moment."

The plotters separated, Brandt going through the grove, and Metzar down the path by which he had come.

Helen, trembling with horror of what she had heard, raised herself cautiously from the willows where she had lain, and watched the innkeeper's retreating figure. When it had disappeared she gave a little gasp of relief. Free now to run home, there to plan what course must be pursued, she conquered her fear and weakness, and hurried from the glade. Luckily, so far as she was able to tell, no one saw her return. She resolved that she would be cool, deliberate, clever, worthy of the borderman's confidence.

First she tried to determine the purport of this interview between Brandt and Metzar. She recalled to mind all that was said, and supplied what she thought had been suggested. Brandt and Metzar were horse-thieves, aids of Bing Legget. They had repaired to the glade to plan. The Indian had been a surprise. Wetzel had routed the Shawnees, and was now on the trail of this chieftain. The Indian warned them to leave Fort Henry and to meet him at a place called Two Islands. Brandt's plan, presumably somewhat changed by the advent of the red-man, was to steal horses, abduct a girl in broad daylight, and before to-morrow's sunset escape to join the ruffian Legget.

"I am the girl," murmured Helen shudderingly, as she relapsed momentarily into girlish fears. But at once she rose above selfish feelings.

Secondly, while it was easy to determine what the outlaws meant, the wisest course was difficult to conceive. She had promised the borderman to help him, and not speak of anything she learned to any but himself. She could not be true to him if she asked advice. The point was clear; either she must remain in the settlement hoping for Jonathan's return in time to frustrate Brandt's villainous scheme, or find the borderman. Suddenly she remembered Metzar's allusion to a second person whom Brandt felt certain he could trust. This meant another traitor in Fort Henry, another horse-thief, another desperado willing to make off with helpless women.

Helen's spirit rose in arms. She had their secret, and could ruin them. She would find the borderman.

Wetzel was on the trail at Eagle Rock. What for? Trailing an Indian who was then five miles east of that rock? Not Wetzel! He was on that track to meet Jonathan. Otherwise, with the redskins near the river, he would have been closer to them. He would meet Jonathan there at sunset to-day, Helen decided.

She paced the room, trying to still her throbbing heart and trembling hands.

"I must be calm," she said sternly. "Time is precious. I have not a moment to lose. I will find him. I've watched that mountain many a time, and can find the trail and the rock. I am in more danger here, than out there in the forest. With Wetzel and Jonathan on the mountain-side, the Indians have fled it. But what about the savage who warned Brandt? Let me think. Yes, he'll avoid the river; he'll go round south of the settlement, and, therefore, can't see me cross. How fortunate that I have paddled a canoe many times across the river. How glad that I made Colonel Zane describe the course up the mountains!"

Her resolution fixed, Helen changed her skirt for one of buckskin, putting on leggins and moccasins of the same serviceable material. She filled the pockets of a short, rain-proof jacket with biscuits, and, thus equipped, sallied forth with a spirit and exultation she could not subdue. Only one thing she feared, which was that Brandt or Metzar might see her cross the river. She launched her canoe and paddled down stream, under cover of the bluff, to a point opposite the end of the island, then straight across, keeping the island between her and the settlement. Gaining the other shore, Helen pulled the canoe into the willows, and mounted the bank. A thicket of willow and alder made progress up the steep incline difficult, but once out of it she faced a long stretch of grassy meadowland. A mile beyond began the green, billowy rise of that mountain which she intended to climb.

Helen's whole soul was thrown into the adventure. She felt her strong young limbs in accord with her heart.

"Now, Mr. Brandt, horse-thief and girl-snatcher, we'll see," she said with scornful lips. "If I can't beat you now I'm not fit to be Betty Zane's friend; and am unworthy of a borderman's trust."

She traversed the whole length of meadowland close under the shadow of the fringed bank, and gained the forest. Here she hesitated. All was so wild and still. No definite course through the woods seemed to invite, and yet all was open. Trees, trees, dark, immovable trees everywhere. The violent trembling of poplar and aspen leaves, when all others were so calm, struck her strangely, and the fearful stillness awed her. Drawing a deep breath she started forward up the gently rising ground.

As she advanced the open forest became darker, and of wilder aspect. The trees were larger and closer together. Still she made fair progress without deviating from the course she had determined upon. Before her rose a ridge, with a ravine on either side, reaching nearly to the summit of the mountain. Here the underbrush was scanty, the fallen trees had slipped down the side, and the rocks were not so numerous, all of which gave her reason to be proud, so far, of her judgment.

Helen, pressing onward and upward, forgot time and danger, while she reveled in the wonder of the forestland. Birds and squirrels fled before her; whistling and wheezing of alarm, or heavy crashings in the bushes, told of frightened wild beasts. A dull, faint roar, like a distant wind, suggested tumbling waters. A single birch tree, gleaming white among the black trees, enlivened the gloomy forest. Patches of sunlight brightened the shade. Giant ferns, just tinging with autumn colors, waved tips of sculptured perfection. Most wonderful of all were the colored leaves, as they floated downward with a sad, gentle rustle.

Helen was brought to a realization of her hazardous undertaking by a sudden roar of water, and the abrupt termination of the ridge in a deep gorge. Grasping a tree she leaned over to look down. It was fully an hundred feet deep, with impassable walls, green-stained and damp, at the bottom of which a brawling, brown brook rushed on its way. Fully twenty feet wide, it presented an insurmountable barrier to farther progress in that direction.

But Helen looked upon it merely as a difficulty to be overcome. She studied the situation, and decided to go to the left because higher ground was to be seen that way.

Abandoning the ridge, she pressed on, keeping as close to the gorge as she dared, and came presently to a fallen tree lying across the dark cleft. Without a second's hesitation, for she knew such would be fatal, she stepped upon the tree and started across, looking at nothing but the log under her feet, while she tried to imagine herself walking across the water gate, at home in Virginia.

She accomplished the venture without a misstep. When safely on the ground once more she felt her knees tremble and a queer, light feeling came into her head. She laughed, however, as she rested a moment. It would take more than a gorge to discourage her, she resolved with set lips, as once again she made her way along the rising ground.

Perilous, if not desperate, work was ahead of her. Broken, rocky ground, matted thicket, and seemingly impenetrable forest, rose darkly in advance. But she was not even tired, and climbed, crawled, twisted, and turned on her way upward. She surmounted a rocky ledge, to face a higher ridge covered with splintered, uneven stones, and the fallen trees of many storms. Once she slipped and fell, spraining her wrist. At length this uphill labor began to wary her. To breathe caused a pain in her side and she was compelled to rest.

Already the gray light of coming night shrouded the forest. She was surprised at seeing the trees become indistinct; because the shadows hovered over the thickets, and noted that the dark, dim outline of the ridges was fading into obscurity.

She struggled on up the uneven slope with a tightening at her heart which was not all exhaustion. For the first time she doubted herself, but it was too late. She could not turn back. Suddenly she felt that she was on a smoother, easier course. Not to strike a stone or break a twig seemed unusual. It might be a path worn by deer going to a spring.

Then into her troubled mind flashed the joyful thought, she had found a trail.

Soft, wiry grass, springing from a wet soil, rose under her feet. A little rill trickled alongside the trail. Mossy, soft-cushioned stones lay imbedded here and there. Young maples and hickories grew breast-high on either side, and the way wound in and out under the lowering shade of forest monarchs.

Swiftly ascending this path she came at length to a point where it was possible to see some distance ahead. The ascent became hardly noticeable. Then, as she turned a bend of the trail, the light grew brighter and brighter, until presently all was open and clear. An oval space, covered with stones, lay before her. A big, blasted chestnut stood nearby. Beyond was the dim, purple haze of distance. Above, the pale, blue sky just faintly rose-tinted by the setting sun. Far to her left the scraggly trees of a low hill were tipped with orange and russet shades. She had reached the summit.

Desolate and lonely was this little plateau. Helen felt immeasurably far away from home. Yet she could see in the blue distance the glancing river, the dark fort, and that cluster of cabins which marked the location of Fort Henry. Sitting upon the roots of the big chestnut tree she gazed around. There were the remains of a small campfire. Beyond, a hollow under a shelving rock. A bed of dry leaves lay packed in this shelter. Some one had been here, and she doubted not that it was the borderman.

She was so tired and her wrist pained so severely that she lay back against the tree trunk, closed her eyes and rested. A weariness, the apathy of utter exhaustion, came over her. She wished the bordermen would hurry and come before she went to sleep.

Drowsily she was sinking into slumber when a long,

low rumble aroused her. How dark it had suddenly become! A sheet of pale light flared across the overcast heavens.

"A storm!" exclaimed Helen. "Alone on this mountaintop with a storm coming. Am I frightened? I don't believe it. At least I'm safe from that ruffian Brandt. Oh! If my borderman would only come!"

Helen changed her position from beside the tree, to the hollow under the stone. It was high enough to permit of her sitting upright, and offered a safe retreat from the storm. The bed of leaves was soft and comfortable. She sat there peering out at the darkening heavens.

All beneath her, southward and westward was gray twilight. The settlement faded from sight; the river grew wan and shadowy. The ruddy light in the west was fast succumbing to the rolling clouds. Darker and darker it became, until only one break in the overspreading vapors admitted the last crimson gleam of sunshine over hills and valley, brightening the river until it resembled a stream of fire. Then the light failed, the glow faded. The intense blackness of night prevailed.

Out of the ebon west came presently another flare of light, a quick, spreading flush, like a flicker from a monster candle; it was followed by a long, low, rumbling roll.

Helen felt in those intervals of unutterably vast silence, that she must shriek aloud. The thunder was a friend. She prayed for the storm to break. She had withstood danger and toilsome effort with fortitude; but could not brave this awful, boding, wilderness stillness.

Flashes of lightning now revealed the rolling, pushing, turbulent clouds, and peals of thunder sounded nearer and louder.

A long swelling moan, sad, low, like the uneasy sigh of the sea, breathed far in the west. It was the wind, the ominous warning of the storm. Sheets of light were now mingled with long, straggling ropes of fire, and the rumblings were often broken by louder, quicker detonations.

Then a period, longer than usual, of inky blackness succeeded the sharp flaring of light. A faint breeze ruffled the leaves of the thicket, and fanned Helen's hot cheek. The moan of the wind became more distinct, then louder, and in another instant like the far-off roar of a rushing river. The storm was upon her. Helen shrank closer against the stone, and pulled her jacket tighter around her trembling form.

A sudden, intense, dazzling, blinding, white light enveloped her. The rocky promontory, the weird, giant chestnut tree, the open plateau, and beyond, the stormy heavens, were all luridly clear in the flash of lightning. She fancied it was possible to see a tall, dark figure emerging from the thicket. As the thunderclap rolled and pealed overhead, she strained her eyes into the blackness waiting for the next lightning flash.

It came with brilliant, dazing splendor. The whole plateau and thicket were as light as in the day. Close by the stone where she lay crept the tall, dark figure of an Indian. With starting eyes she saw the fringed clothing, the long, flying hair, and supple body peculiar to the savage. He was creeping upon her.

Helen's blood ran cold; terror held her voiceless. She felt herself sinking slowly down upon the leaves.

CHAPTER XII

The sun had begun to cast long shadows the afternoon of Helen's hunt for Jonathan, when the borderman, accompanied by Wetzel, led a string of horses along the base of the very mountain she had ascended.

"Last night's job was a good one, I ain't gainsayin'; but the redskin I wanted got away," Wetzel said gloomily.

"He's safe now as a squirrel in a hole. I saw him dartin' among the trees with his white eagle feathers stickin' up like a buck's flag," replied Jonathan. "He can run. If I'd only had my rifle loaded! But I'm not sure he was that arrow-shootin' Shawnee."

"It was him. I saw his bow. We ought'er taken more time an' picked him out," Wetzel replied, shaking his head gravely. "Though mebbe that'd been useless. I think he was hidin'. He's precious shy of his red skin. I've been after him these ten year, an' never ketched him nappin' yet. We'd have done much toward snuffin' out Legget an' his gang if we'd winged the Shawnee."

"He left a plain trail."

"One of his tricks. He's slicker on a trail than any other Injun on the border, unless mebbe it's old Wingenund, the Huron. This Shawnee'd lead us many a mile for nothin', if we'd stick to his trail. I'm long ago used to him. He's doubled like an old fox, run harder'n a skeered fawn, an', if needs be, he'll lay low as a cunnin' buck. I calkilate once over the mountain, he's made a beeline east. We'll go on with the hosses, an' then strike across country to find his trail."

"It 'pears to me, Lew, that we've taken a long time in makin' a show against these hoss-thieves," said Jonathan.

"I ain't sayin' much; but I've felt it," replied Wetzel.

"All summer, an' nothin' done. It was more luck than sense that we run into those Injuns with the hosses. We only got three out of four, an' let the best redskin give us the slip. Here fall is nigh on us, with winter comin' soon, an' still we don't know who's the white traitor in the settlement."

"I said it's to be a long, an' mebbe, our last trail."

"Why?"

"Because these fellars, red or white, are in with a picked gang of the best woodsmen as ever outlawed the border. We'll get the Fort Henry hoss-thief. I'll back the bright-eyed lass for that."

"I haven't seen her lately, an' allow she'd left me word if she learned anythin'."

"Wal, mebbe it's just as well you hain't seen so much of her."

In silence they traveled and, arriving at the edge of the meadow, were about to mount two of the horses, when Wetzel said in a sharp tone:

"Look!"

He pointed to a small, well-defined moccasin track in the black earth on the margin of a rill.

"Lew, it's a woman's, sure's you're born," declared Jonathan.

Wetzel knelt and closely examined the footprint; "Yes, a woman's, an' no Injun."

"What?" Jonathan exclaimed, as he knelt to scrutinize the imprint.

"This ain't half a day old," added Wetzel. "An' not a redskin's moccasin near. What d'you reckon?"

"A white girl, alone," replied Jonathan as he followed the trail a short distance along the brook. "See, she's makin' upland. Wetzel, these tracks could hardly be my sister's, an' there's only one other girl on the border whose feet will match 'em! Helen Sheppard has passed here, on her way up the mountain to find you or me."

"I like your reckonin'."

"She's suddenly discovered somethin', Injuns, horse-thieves, the Fort Henry traitor, or mebbe, an' most likely, some plottin'. Bein' bound to secrecy by me, she's not told my brother. An' it must be call for hurry. She knows we frequent this mountaintop; said Eb told her about the way we get here."

"I'd calkilate about the same."

"What'll you do? Go with me after her?" asked Jonathan.

"I'll take the hosses, an' be at the fort inside of an hour. If Helen's gone, I'll tell her father you're close on her trail. Now listen! It'll be dark soon, an' a storm's comin'. Don't waste time on her trail. Hurry up to the rock. She'll be there, if any lass could climb there. If not, come back in the mornin', hunt her trail out, an' find her. I'm thinkin', Jack, we'll find the Shawnee had somethin' to do with this. Whatever happens after I get back to the fort, I'll expect you hard on my trail."

Jonathan bounded across the brook and with an easy lope began the gradual ascent. Soon he came upon a winding path. He ran along this for perhaps a quarter of an hour, until it became too steep for rapid traveling, when he settled down to a rapid walk. The forest was already dark. A slight rustling of the leaves beneath his feet was the only sound, except at long intervals the distant rumbling of thunder.

The mere possibility of Helen's being alone on that mountain seeking him, made Jonathan's heart beat as it never had before. For weeks he had avoided her, almost forgot her. He had conquered the strange, yearning weakness which assailed him after that memorable Sunday, and once more the silent shaded glens, the mystery of the woods, the breath of his wild, free life had claimed him. But now as this evidence of her spirit, her recklessness, was before him, and he remembered Betty's avowal, a pain, which was almost physical, tore at his heart. How terrible it would be if she came to her death through him! He pictured the big, alluring eyes, the perfect lips, the haunting face, cold in death. And he shuddered.

The dim gloom of the woods soon darkened into blackness. The flashes of lightning, momentarily streaking the foliage, or sweeping overhead in pale yellow sheets, aided Jonathan in keeping the trail.

He gained the plateau just as a great flash illumined it, and distinctly saw the dark hollow where he had taken refuge in many a storm, and where he now hoped to find the girl. Picking his way carefully over the sharp, loose stones, he at last put his hand on the huge rock. Another blue-white, dazzling flash enveloped the scene.

Under the rock he saw a dark form huddled, and a face as white as snow, with wide, horrified eyes.

"Lass," he said, when the thunder had rumbled away. He received no answer, and called again. Kneeling, he groped about until touching Helen's dress. He spoke again; but she did not reply.

Jonathan crawled under the ledge beside the quiet figure. He touched her hands; they were very cold. Bending over, he was relieved to hear her heart beating. He called her name, but still she made no reply. Dipping his hand into a little rill that ran beside the stone, he bathed her face. Soon she stirred uneasily, moaned, and suddenly sat up.

"'Tis Jonathan," he said quickly; "don't be scared."

Another illuminating flare of lightning brightened the plateau.

"Oh! thank Heaven!" cried Helen. "I thought you were an Indian!"

Helen sank trembling against the borderman, who enfolded her in his long arms. Her relief and thankfulness were so great that she could not speak. Her hands clasped and unclasped round his strong fingers. Her tears flowed freely.

The storm broke with terrific fury. A seething torrent of rain and hail came with the rushing wind. Great heaven-broad sheets of lightning played across the black dome overhead. Zigzag ropes, steel-blue in color, shot downward. Crash, and crack, and boom the thunder split and rolled the clouds above. The lightning flashes showed the fall of rain in columns like white waterfalls, borne on the irresistible wind.

The grandeur of the storm awed, and stilled Helen's emotion. She sat there watching the lightning, listening to the peals of thunder, and thrilling with the wonder of the situation.

Gradually the roar abated, the flashes became less frequent, the thunder decreased, as the storm wore out its strength in passing. The wind and rain ceased on the mountaintop almost as quickly as they had begun, and the roar died slowly away in the distance. Far to the eastward flashes of light illumined scowling clouds, and brightened many a dark, wooded hill and valley.

"Lass, how is't I find you here?" asked Jonathan gravely.

With many a pause and broken phrase, Helen told the story of what she had seen and heard at the spring.

"Child, why didn't you go to my brother?" asked Jonathan. "You don't know what you undertook!"

"I thought of everything; but I wanted to find you myself. Besides, I was just as safe alone on this mountain as in the village."

"I don't know but you're right," replied Jonathan thoughtfully. "So Brandt planned to make off with you to-morrow?"

"Yes, and when I heard it I wanted to run away from the village."

"You've done a wondrous clever thing, lass. This Brandt is a bad man, an' hard to match. But if he hasn't shaken Fort Henry by now, his career'll end mighty sudden, an' his bad trails stop short on the hillside among the graves, for Eb will always give outlaws or Injuns descent burial."

"What will the colonel, or anyone, think has become of me?"

"Wetzel knows, lass, for he found your trail below."

"Then he'll tell papa you came after me? Oh! poor papa! I forgot him. Shall we stay here until daylight?"

"We'd gain nothin' by startin' now. The brooks are full, an' in the dark we'd make little distance. You're dry here, an' comfortable. What's more, lass, you're safe."

"I feel perfectly safe, with you," Helen said softly.

"Aren't you tired, lass?"

"Tired? I'm nearly dead. My feet are cut and bruised, my wrist is sprained, and I ache all over. But, Jonathan, I don't care. I am so happy to have my wild venture turn out successfully."

"You can lie here an' sleep while I keep watch."

Jonathan made a move to withdraw his arm, which was still between Helen and the rock but had dropped from her waist.

"I am very comfortable. I'll sit here with you, watching for daybreak. My! how dark it is! I cannot see my hand before my eyes."

Helen settled herself back upon the stone, leaned a very little against his shoulder, and tried to think over her adventure. But her mind refused to entertain any ideas, except those of the present. Mingled with the dreamy lassitude that grew stronger every moment, was a sense of delight in her situation. She was alone on a wild mountain, in the night, with this borderman, the one she loved. By chance and her own foolhardiness this had come about, yet she was fortunate to have it tend to some good beyond her own happiness. All she would suffer from her perilous climb would be aching bones, and, perhaps, a scolding from her father. What she might gain was more than she had dared hope. The breaking up of the horse-thief gang would be a boon to the harassed settlement. How proudly Colonel Zane would smile! Her name would go on that long roll of border honor and heroism. That was not, however, one thousandth part so pleasing, as to be alone with her borderman.

With a sigh of mingled weariness and content, Helen leaned her head on Jonathan's shoulder and fell asleep.

The borderman trembled. The sudden nestling of her head against him, the light caress of her fragrant hair across his cheek, revived a sweet, almost-conquered, almost-forgotten emotion. He felt an inexplicable thrill vibrate through him. No untrodden, ambushed wild, no perilous trail, no dark and bloody encounter had ever made him feel fear as had the kiss of this maiden. He had sternly silenced faint, unfamiliar, yet tender, voices whispering in his heart; and now his rigorous discipline was as if it were not, for at her touch he trembled. Still he did not move away. He knew she had succumbed to weariness, and was fast asleep. He could, gently, without awakening her, have laid her head upon the pillow of leaves; indeed, he thought of doing it, but made no effort. A woman's head softly lying against him was a thing novel, strange, wonderful. For all the power he had then, each tumbling lock of her hair might as well have been a chain linking him fast to the mountain.

With the memory of his former yearning, unsatisfied moods, and the unrest and pain his awakening tenderness had caused him, came a determination to look things fairly in the face, to be just in thought toward this innocent, impulsive girl, and be honest with himself.

Duty commanded that he resist all charm other than that pertaining to his life in the woods. Years ago he had accepted a borderman's destiny, well content to be recompensed by its untamed freedom from restraint; to be always under the trees he loved so well; to lend his cunning and woodcraft in the pioneer's cause; to haunt the savage trails; to live from day to day a menace to the foes of civilization. That was the life he had chosen; it was all he could ever have.

In view of this, justice demanded that he allow no friendship to spring up between himself and this girl. If his sister's belief was really true, if Helen really was interested in him, it must be a romantic infatuation which, not encouraged, would wear itself out. What was he, to win the love of any girl? An unlettered borderman, who knew only the woods, whose life was hard and cruel, whose hands were red with Indian blood, whose vengeance had not spared men even of his own race. He could not believe she really loved him. Wildly impulsive as girls were at times, she had kissed him. She had been grateful, carried away by a generous feeling for him as the protector of her father. When she did not see him for a long time, as he vowed should be the case after he had carried her safely home, she would forget.

Then honesty demanded that he probe his own feelings. Sternly, as if judging a renegade, he searched out in his simple way the truth. This big-eyed lass with her nameless charm would bewitch even a borderman, unless he avoided her. So much he had not admitted until now. Love he had never believed could be possible for him. When she fell asleep her hand had slipped from his arm to his fingers, and now rested there lightly as a leaf. The contact was delight. The gentle night breeze blew a tress of hair across his lips. He trembled. Her rounded shoulder pressed against him until he could feel her slow, deep breathing. He almost held his own breath lest he disturb her rest.

No, he was no longer indifferent. As surely as those pale stars blinked far above, he knew the delight of a woman's presence. It moved him to study the emotion, as he studied all things, which was the habit of his borderman's life. Did it come from knowledge of her beauty, matchless as that of the mountain-laurel? He recalled the dark glance of her challenging eyes, her tall, supple figure, and the bewildering excitement and magnetism of her presence. Beauty was wonderful, but not everything. Beauty belonged to her, but she would have been irresistible without it. Was it not because she was a woman? That was the secret. She was a woman with all a woman's charm to bewitch, to twine round the strength of men as the ivy encircles the oak; with all a woman's weakness to pity and to guard; with all a woman's wilful burning love, and with all a woman's mystery.

At last so much of life was intelligible to him. The renegade committed his worst crimes because even in his outlawed, homeless state, he could not exist without the companionship, if not the love, of a woman. The pioneer's toil and privation were for a woman, and the joy of loving her and living for her. The Indian brave, when not on the war-path, walked hand in hand with a dusky, soft-eyed maiden, and sang to her of moonlit lakes and western winds. Even the birds and beasts mated. The robins returned to their old nest; the eagles paired once and were constant in life and death. The buck followed the doe through the forest. All nature sang that love made life worth living. Love, then, was everything.

The borderman sat out the long vigil of the night watching the stars, and trying to decide that love was not for him. If Wetzel had locked a secret within his breast, and never in all these years spoke of it to his companion, then surely that companion could as well live without love. Stern, dark, deadly work must stain and blot all tenderness from his life, else it would be unutterably barren. The joy of living, of unharrassed freedom he had always known. If a fair face and dark, mournful eyes were to haunt him on every lonely trail, then it were better an Indian should end his existence.

The darkest hour before dawn, as well as the darkest of doubt and longing in Jonathan's life, passed away. A gray gloom obscured the pale, winking stars; the east slowly whitened, then brightened, and at length day broke misty and fresh.

The borderman rose to stretch his cramped limbs. When he turned to the little cavern the girl's eyes were wide open. All the darkness, the shadow, the beauty, and the thought of the past night, lay in their blue depths. He looked away across the valley where the sky was reddening and a pale rim of gold appeared above the hilltops.

"Well, if I haven't been asleep!" exclaimed Helen, with a low, soft laugh.

"You're rested, I hope," said Jonathan, with averted eyes. He dared not look at her.

"Oh, yes, indeed. I am ready to start at once. How gray, how beautiful the morning is! Shall we be long? I hope Papa knows."

In silence the borderman led the way across the rocky plateau, and into the winding, narrow trail. His pale, slightly drawn and stern, face did not invite conversation, therefore Helen followed silently in his footsteps. The way was steep, and at times he was forced to lend her aid. She put her hand in his and jumped lightly as a fawn. Presently a brawling brook, overcrowding its banks, impeded further progress.

"I'll have to carry you across," said Jonathan.

"I'm very heavy," replied Helen, with a smile in her eyes.

She flushed as the borderman put his right arm around her waist. Then a clasp as of steel enclosed her; she felt herself swinging easily into the air, and over the muddy brook.

Farther down the mountain this troublesome brook again crossed the trail, this time much wider and more formidable. Helen looked with some vexation and embarrassment into the borderman's face. It was always the same, stern, almost cold.

"Perhaps I'd better wade," she said hesitatingly.

"Why? The water's deep an' cold. You'd better not get wet."

Helen flushed, but did not answer. With downcast eyes she let herself be carried on his powerful arm.

The wading was difficult this time. The water foamed furiously around his knees. Once he slipped on a stone, and nearly lost his balance. Uttering a little scream Helen grasped at him wildly, and her arm encircled his neck. What was still more trying, when he put her on her feet again, it was found that her hair had become entangled in the porcupine quills on his hunting-coat.

She stood before him while with clumsy fingers he endeavored to untangle the shimmering strands; but in vain. Helen unwound the snarl of wavy hair. Most alluring she was then, with a certain softness on her face, and light and laughter, and something warm in her eyes.

The borderman felt that he breathed a subtle exhilaration which emanated from her glowing, gracious beauty. She radiated with the gladness of life, with an uncontainable sweetness and joy. But, giving no token of his feeling, he turned to march on down through the woods.

From this point the trail broadened, descending at an easier angle. Jonathan's stride lengthened until Helen was forced to walk rapidly, and sometimes run, in order to keep close behind him. A quick journey home was expedient, and in order to accomplish this she would gladly have exerted herself to a greater extent. When they reached the end of the trail where the forest opened clear of brush, finally to merge into the broad, verdant plain, the sun had chased the mist-clouds from the eastern hilltops, and was gloriously brightening the valley.

With the touch of sentiment natural to her, Helen gazed backward for one more view of the mountaintop. The wall of rugged rock she had so often admired from her window at home, which henceforth would ever hold a tender place of remembrance in her heart, rose out of a gray-blue bank of mist. The long swelling slope lay clear to the sunshine. With the rays of the sun gleaming and glistening upon the variegated foliage, and upon the shiny rolling haze above, a beautiful picture of autumn splendor was before her. Tall pines, here and there towered high and lonely over the surrounding trees. Their dark, green, graceful heads stood in bold relief above the gold and yellow crests beneath. Maples, tinged from faintest pink to deepest rose, added warm color to the scene, and chestnuts with their brown-white burrs lent fresher beauty to the undulating slope.

The remaining distance to the settlement was short. Jonathan spoke only once to Helen, then questioning her as to where she had left her canoe. They traversed the meadow, found the boat in the thicket of willows, and were soon under the frowning bluff of Fort Henry. Ascending the steep path, they followed the road leading to Colonel Zane's cabin.

A crowd of boys, men, and women loitering near the bluff arrested Helen's attention. Struck by this unusual occurrence, she wondered what was the cause of such idleness among the busy pioneer people. They were standing in little groups. Some made vehement gestures, others conversed earnestly, and yet more were silent. On seeing Jonathan, a number shouted and pointed toward the inn. The borderman hurried Helen along the path, giving no heed to the throng.

But Helen had seen the cause of all this excitement. At first glance she thought Metzar's inn had been burned; but a second later it could be seen that the smoke came from a smoldering heap of rubbish in the road. The inn, nevertheless, had been wrecked. Windows stared with that vacantness peculiar to deserted houses. The doors were broken from their hinges. A pile of furniture, rude tables, chairs, beds, and other articles, were heaped inside the smoking rubbish. Scattered around lay barrels and kegs all with gaping sides and broken heads. Liquor had stained the road, where it had been soaked up by the thirsty dust.

Upon a shattered cellar door lay a figure covered with a piece of rag carpet. When Helen's quick eyes took in this last, she turned away in horror. That motionless form might be Brandt's. Remorse and womanly sympathy surged over her, for bad as the man had shown himself, he had loved her.

She followed the borderman, trying to compose herself. As they neared Colonel Zane's cabin she saw her father, Will, the colonel, Betty, Nell, Mrs. Zane, Silas Zane, and others whom she did not recognize. They were all looking at her. Helen's throat swelled, and her eyes filled when she got near enough to see her father's haggard, eager face. The others were grave. She wondered guiltily if she had done much wrong.

In another moment she was among them. Tears fell as her father extended his trembling hands to clasp her, and as she hid her burning face on his breast, he cried: "My dear, dear child!" Then Betty gave her a great hug, and Nell flew about them like a happy bird. Colonel Zane's face was pale, and wore a clouded, stern expression. She smiled timidly at him through her tears. "Well! well! well!" he mused, while his gaze softened. That was all he said; but he took her hand and held it while he turned to Jonathan.

The borderman leaned on his long rifle, regarding him with expectant eyes.

"Well, Jack, you missed a little scrimmage this morning. Wetzel got in at daybreak. The storm and horses held him up on the other side of the river until daylight. He told me of your suspicions, with the additional news that he'd found a fresh Indian trail on the island just across from the inn. We went down not expecting to find any one awake; but Metzar was hurriedly packing some of his traps. Half a dozen men were there, having probably stayed all night. That little English cuss was one of them, and another, an ugly fellow, a stranger to us, but evidently a woodsman. Things looked bad. Metzar told a decidedly conflicting story. Wetzel and I went outside to talk over the situation, with the result that I ordered him to clean out the place."

Here Colonel Zane paused to indulge in a grim, meaning laugh.

"Well, he cleaned out the place all right. The ugly stranger got rattlesnake-mad, and yanked out a big knife. Sam is hitching up the team now to haul what's left of him up on the hillside. Metzar resisted arrest, and got badly hurt. He's in the guardhouse. Case, who has been drunk for a week, got in Wetzel's way and was kicked into the middle of next week. He's been spitting blood for the last hour, but I guess he's not much hurt. Brandt flew the coop last night. Wetzel found this hid in his room."

Colonel Zane took a long, feathered arrow from where it lay on a bench, and held it out to Jonathan.

"The Shawnee signal! Wetzel had it right," muttered the borderman.

"Exactly. Lew found where the arrow struck in the wall of Brandt's room. It was shot from the island at the exact spot where Lew came to an end of the Indian's trail in the water."

"That Shawnee got away from us."

"So Lew said. Well, he's gone now. So is Brandt. We're well rid of the gang, if only we never hear of them again."

The borderman shook his head. During the colonel's recital his face changed. The dark eyes had become deadly; the square jaw was shut, the lines of the cheek

had grown tense, and over his usually expressive countenance had settled a chill, lowering shade.

"Lew thinks Brandt's in with Bing Legget. Well, damn
his black traitor heart! He's a good man for the worst and
strongest gang that ever tracked the border."

The borderman was silent; but the furtive, restless
shifting of his eyes over the river and island, hill and valley, spoke more plainly than words.

"You're to take his trail at once," added Colonel Zane.
"I had Bess put you up some bread, meat, and parched
corn. No doubt you'll have a long, hard tramp. Good
luck."

The borderman went into the cabin, presently emerging with a buckskin knapsack strapped to his shoulder.
He set off eastward with a long, swinging stride.

The women had taken Helen within the house where,
no doubt, they could discuss with greater freedom the
events of the previous day.

"Sheppard," said Colonel Zane, turning with a sparkle
in his eyes. "Brandt was after Helen sure as a bad weed
grows fast. And certain as death Jonathan and Wetzel
will see him cold and quiet back in the woods. That's a
border saying, and it means a good deal. I never saw Wetzel so implacable, nor Jonathan so fatally cold but once,
and that was when Miller, another traitor, much like
Brandt, tried to make away with Betty. It would have
chilled your blood to see Wetzel go at that fool this morning. Why did he want to pull a knife on the borderman? It
was a sad sight. Well, these things are justifiable. We
must protect ourselves, and above all, our women. We've
had bad men, and a bad man out here is something you
cannot yet appreciate, come here and slip into the life of
the settlement, because on the border you can never tell
what a man is until he proves himself. There have been

scores of criminals spread over the frontier, and some better men, like Simon Girty, who were driven to outlaw life. Simon must not be confounded with Jim Girty, absolutely the most fiendish desperado who ever lived. Why, even the Indians feared Jim so much that after his death his skeleton remained unmolested in the glade where he was killed. The place is believed to be haunted now, by all Indians and many white hunters, and I believe the bones stand there yet."

"Stand?" asked Sheppard, deeply interested.

"Yes, it stands where Girty stood and died, upright against a tree, pinned, pinned there by a big knife."

"Heavens, man! Who did it?" Sheppard cried in horror.

Again Colonel Zane's laugh, almost metallic, broke grimly from his lips.

"Who? Why, Wetzel, of course. Lew hunted Jim Girty five long years. When he caught him—God! I'll tell you some other time. Jonathan saw Wetzel handle Jim and his pal, Deering, as if they were mere boys. Well, as I said, the border has had, and still has, its bad men. Simon Girty took McKee and Elliott, the Tories, from Fort Pitt, when he deserted, and ten men besides. They're all, except those who are dead, outlaws of the worst type. The other bad men drifted out here from Lord only knows where. They're scattered all over. Simon Girty, since his crowning black deed, the massacre of the Christian Indians, is in hiding. Bing Legget now has the field. He's a hard nut, a cunning woodsman, and capable leader who surrounds himself with only the most desperate Indians and renegades. Brandt is an agent of Legget's and I'll bet we'll hear from him again."

CHAPTER XIII

Jonathan traveled toward the east straight as a crow flies. Wetzel's trail as he pursued Brandt had been left designedly plain. Branches of young maples had been broken by the borderman; they were glaring evidences of his passage. On open ground, or through swampy meadows he had contrived to leave other means to facilitate his comrade's progress. Bits of sumach lay strewn along the way, every red, leafy branch a bright marker of the course; crimson maple leaves served their turn, and even long-bladed ferns were scattered at intervals.

Ten miles east of Fort Henry, at a point where two islands lay opposite each other, Wetzel had crossed the Ohio. Jonathan removed his clothing, and tying these, together with his knapsack, to the rifle, held them above the water while he swam the three narrow channels. He took up the trail again, finding here, as he expected, where Brandt had joined the waiting Shawnee chief. The borderman pressed on harder to the eastward.

About the middle of the afternoon signs betokened that Wetzel and his quarry were not far in advance. Fresh imprints in the grass; crushed asters and moss, broken branches with unwithered leaves, and plots of grassy ground where Jonathan saw that the blades of grass were yet springing back to their original position, proved to the borderman's practiced eye that he was close upon Wetzel.

In time he came to a grove of yellow birch trees. The ground was nearly free from brush, beautifully carpeted with flowers and ferns, and, except where bushy windfalls obstructed the way, was singularly open to the gaze for several hundred yards ahead.

Upon entering this wood Wetzel's plain, intentional markings became manifest, then wavered, and finally disappeared. Jonathan pondered a moment. He concluded that the way was so open and clear, with nothing but grass and moss to mark a trail, that Wetzel had simply considered it waste of time for, perhaps, the short length of this grove.

Jonathan knew he was wrong after taking a dozen steps more. Wetzel's trail, known so well to him, as never to be mistaken, sheered abruptly off to the left, and, after a few yards, the distance between the footsteps widened perceptibly. Then came a point where they were so far apart that they could only have been made by long leaps.

On the instant the borderman knew that some unforeseen peril or urgent cause had put Wetzel to flight, and he now bent piercing eyes around the grove. Retracing his steps to where he had found the break in the trail, he followed up Brandt's tracks for several rods. Not one hundred paces beyond where Wetzel had quit the pursuit, were the remains of a campfire, the embers still smoldering, and moccasin tracks of a small band of Indians. The trail of Brandt and his Shawnee guide met the others at almost right angles.

The Indian, either by accident or design, had guided Brandt to a band of his fellows, and thus led Wetzel almost into an ambush.

Evidence was not clear, however, that the Indians had discovered the keen tracker who had run almost into their midst.

While studying the forest ahead Jonathan's mind was

running over the possibilities. How close was Wetzel? Was he still in flight? Had the savages an inkling of his pursuit? Or was he now working out one of his cunning tricks of woodcraft? The borderman had no other idea than that of following the trail to learn all this. Taking the desperate chances warranted under the circumstances, he walked boldly forward in his comrade's footsteps.

Deep and gloomy was the forest adjoining the birch grove. It was a heavy growth of hardwood trees, interspersed with slender ash and maples, which with their scanty foliage resembled a labyrinth of green and yellow network, like filmy dotted lace, hung on the taller, darker oaks. Jonathan felt safer in this deep wood. He could still see several rods in advance. Following the trail, he was relieved to see that Wetzel's leaps had become shorter and shorter, until they once again were about the length of a long stride. The borderman was, moreover, swinging in a curve to the northeast. This was proof that the borderman had not been pursued, but was making a wide detour to get ahead of the enemy. Five hundred yards farther on the trail turning sharply toward the birch grove in the rear.

The trail was fresh. Wetzel was possibly within signal call; surely within sound of a rifle shot. But even more stirring was the certainty that Brandt and his Indians were inside the circle Wetzel had made.

Once again in sight of the more open woodland, Jonathan crawled on his hands and knees, keeping close to the cluster of ferns, until well within the eastern end of the grove. He lay for some minutes listening. A threatening silence, like the hush before a storm, permeated the wilderness. He peered out from his covert; but, owing to its location in a little hollow, he could not see far. Crawling to the nearest tree he rose to his feet slowly, cautiously.

No unnatural sight or sound arrested his attention. Repeatedly, with the acute, unsatisfied gaze of the borderman who knew that every tree, every patch of ferns, every tangled brush-heap might harbor a foe, he searched the grove with his eyes; but the curly barked birches, the clumps of colored ferns, the bushy windfalls kept their secrets.

For the borderman, however, the whole aspect of the birch-grove had changed. Over the forest was a deep calm. A gentle, barely perceptible wind sighed among the leaves, like rustling silk. The far-off drowsy drum of a grouse intruded on the vast stillness. The silence of the birds betokened a message. That mysterious breathing, that beautiful life of the woods lay hushed, locked in a waiting, brooding silence. Far away among the somber trees, where the shade deepened into impenetrable gloom, lay a menace, invisible and indefinable.

A wind, a breath, a chill, terribly potent, seemed to pass over the borderman. Long experience had given him intuition of danger.

As he moved slightly, with lynx-eyes fixed on the grove before him, a sharp, clear, perfect bird-note broke the ominous quiet. It was like the melancholy cry of an oriole, short, deep, suggestive of lonely forest dells. By a slight variation in the short call, Jonathan recognized it as a signal from Wetzel. The borderman smiled as he realized that with all his stealth, Wetzel had heard or seen him reenter the grove. The signal was a warning to stand still or retreat.

Jonathan's gaze narrowed down to the particular point whence had come the signal. Some two hundred yards ahead in this direction were several large trees standing in a group. With one exception, they all had straight trunks. This deviated from the others in that it possessed an irregular, bulging trunk, or else half-shielded the form of Wetzel. So indistinct and immovable was this irregularity, that the watcher could not be certain. Out of line, somewhat, with this tree which he suspected screened his comrade, lay a huge windfall large enough to conceal in ambush a whole band of savages.

Even as he gazed a sheet of flame flashed from this covert.

Crack!

A loud report followed; then the whistle and zip of a bullet as it whizzed close by his head.

"Shawnee lead!" muttered Jonathan.

Unfortunately the tree he had selected did not hide him sufficiently. His shoulders were so wide that either one or the other was exposed, affording a fine target for a marksman.

A quick glance showed him a change in the knotty tree trunk; the seeming bulge was now the well-known figure of Wetzel.

Jonathan dodged as some object glanced slantingly before his eyes.

Twang. Whizz. Thud. Three familiar and distinct sounds caused him to press hard against the tree.

A tufted arrow quivered in the bark not a foot from his head.

"Close shave! Damn that arrow-shootin' Shawnee!" muttered Jonathan. "An' he ain't in that windfall either." His eyes searched to the left for the source of this new peril.

Another sheet of flame, another report from the windfall. A bullet sang, close overhead, and, glancing on a branch, went harmlessly into the forest.

"Injuns all around; I guess I'd better be makin' tracks," Jonathan said to himself, peering out to learn if Wetzel was still under cover.

He saw the tall figure straighten up; a long, black rifle rise to a level and become rigid; a red fire belch forth, followed by a puff of white smoke.

Spang!

An Indian's horrible, strangely breaking death yell rent the silence.

Then a chorus of plaintive howls, followed by angry shouts, rang through the forest. Naked, painted savages darted out of the windfall toward the tree that had sheltered Wetzel.

Quick as thought Jonathan covered the foremost Indian, and with the crack of his rifle saw the redskin drop his gun, stop in his mad run, stagger sideways, and fall. Then the borderman looked to see what had become of his ally. The cracking of the Indian's rifle told him that Wetzel had been seen by his foes.

With almost incredible fleetness a brown figure with long black hair streaming behind, darted in and out among the trees, flashed through the sunlit glade, and vanished in the dark depths of the forest.

Jonathan turned to flee also, when he heard again the twanging of an Indian's bow. A wind smote his cheek, a shock blinded him, an excruciating pain seized upon his breast. A feathered arrow had pinned his shoulder to the tree. He raised his hand to pull it out; but, slippery with blood, it afforded a poor hold for his fingers. Violently exerting himself, with both hands he wrenched away the weapon. The flint-head lacerating his flesh and scraping his shoulder bones caused sharpest agony. The pain gave away to a sudden sense of giddiness; he tried to run; a dark mist veiled his sight; he stumbled and fell. Then he seemed to sink into a great darkness, and knew no more.

When consciousness returned to Jonathan it was night. He lay on his back, and knew because of his cramped limbs that he had been securely bound. He saw the glimmer of a fire, but could not raise his head. A rustling of leaves in the wind told that he was yet in the woods, and the distant rumble of a waterfall sounded familiar. He felt drowsy; his wound smarted slightly, still he did not suffer any pain. Presently he fell asleep.

Broad daylight had come when again he opened his eyes. The blue sky was directly above, and before him he saw a ledge covered with dwarfed pine trees. He turned his head, and saw that he was in a sort of amphitheater of about two acres in extent enclosed by low cliffs. A cleft in the stony wall let out a brawling brook, and served, no doubt, as entrance to the place. Several rude log cabins stood on that side of the enclosure. Jonathan knew he had been brought to Bing Legget's retreat.

Voices attracted his attention, and, turning his head to the other side, he saw a big Indian pacing near him, and beyond, seven savages and three white men reclining in the shade.

The powerful, dark-visaged savage near him he at once recognized as Ashbow, the Shawnee chief, and noted emissary of Bing Legget. Of the other Indians, three were Delawares, and four Shawnees, all veterans, with swarthy, somber faces and glistening heads on which the scalplocks were trimmed and tufted. Their naked, muscular bodies were painted for the war-path with their strange emblems of death. A trio of white men, nearly as bronzed as their savage comrades, completed the group. One, a desperate-looking outlaw, Jonathan did not know. The blond-bearded giant in the center was Legget. Steel-blue, inhuman eyes, with the expression of a free but hunted animal; a set, mastiff-like jaw, brutal and coarse, individualized him. The last man was the haggard-faced Brandt.

"I tell ye, Brandt, I ain't agoin' against this Injun,"

Legget was saying positively. "He's the best reddy on the border, an' has saved me scores of times. This fellar Zane belongs to him, an' while I'd much rather see the scout knifed right here an' now, I won't do nothin' to interfere with the Shawnee's plans."

"Why does the redskin want to take him away to his village?" Brandt growled. "All Injun vanity and pride."

"It's Injun ways, an' we can't do nothin' to change 'em."

"But you're boss here. You could make him put this borderman out of the way."

"Wal, I ain't agoin' ter interfere. Anyways, Brandt, the Shawnee'll make short work of the scout when he gits him among the tribe. Injuns is Injuns. It's a great honor fer him to get Zane, an' he wants his own people to figger in the finish. Quite nat'r'l, I reckon."

"I understand all that; but it's not safe for us, and it's courting death for Ashbow. Why don't he keep Zane here until you can spare more than three Indians to go with him? These bordermen can't be stopped. You don't know them, because you're new in this part of the country."

"I've been here as long as you, an' agoin' some, too, I reckon," replied Legget complacently.

"But you've not been hunted until lately by these bordermen, and you've had little opportunity to hear of them except from Indians. What can you learn from these silent redskins? I tell you, letting this fellow get out of here alive, even for an hour is a fatal mistake. It's two full days' tramp to the Shawnee village. You don't suppose Wetzel will be afraid of four savages? Why, he sneaked right into eight of us, when we were ambushed, waiting for him. He killed one and then was gone like a streak. It was only a piece of pure luck we got Zane."

"I've reason to know this Wetzel, this Deathwind, as

the Delawares call him. I never seen him though, an' anyways, I reckon I can handle him if ever I get the chance."

"Man, you're crazy!" cried Brandt. "He'd cut you to pieces before you'd have time to draw. He could give you a tomahawk, then take it away and split your head. I tell you I know! You remember Jake Deering? He came from up your way. Wetzel fought Deering and Jim Girty together, and killed them. You know how he left Girty."

"I'll allow he must be a fighter; but I ain't afraid of him."

"That's not the question. I am talking sense. You've got a chance now to put one of these bordermen out of the way. Do it quick! That's my advice."

Brandt spoke so vehemently that Legget seemed impressed. He stroked his yellow beard, and puffed thoughtfully on his pipe. Presently he addressed the Shawnee chief in the native tongue.

"Will Ashbow take five horses for his prisoner?"

The Indian shook his head.

"How many will he take?"

The chief strode with dignity to and fro before his captive. His dark, impassive face gave no clue to his thoughts; but his lofty bearing, his measured, stately walk were indicative of great pride. Then he spoke in his deep bass:

"The Shawnee knows the woods from the Great Lakes where the sun sets, to the Blue Hills where it rises. He has met the great paleface hunters. Only for Deathwind will Ashbow trade his captive."

"See? It ain't no use," said Legget, spreading out his hands. "Let him go. He'll outwit the bordermen if any redskin's able to. The sooner he goes the quicker he'll git back, an' we can go to work. You ought'er be satisfied to git the girl—"

"Shut up!" interrupted Brandt sharply.

" 'Pears to me, Brandt, bein' in love hes kinder worked on your nerves. You used to be game. Now you're afeerd of a bound an' tied man who ain't got long to live."

"I fear no man," answered Brandt, scowling darkly. "But I know what you don't seem to have sense enough to see. If this Zane gets away, which is probable, he and Wetzel will clean up your gang."

"Haw! haw! haw!" roared Legget, slapping his knees. "Then you'd hev little chanst of gittin' the lass, eh?"

"All right. I've no more to say," snapped Brandt, rising and turning on his heel. As he passed Jonathan he paused. "Zane, if I could, I'd get even with you for that punch you once gave me. As it is, I'll stop at the Shawnee village on my way west—"

"With the pretty lass," interposed Legget.

"Where I hope to see your scalp drying in the chief's lodge."

The borderman eyed him steadily; but in silence. Words could not so well have conveyed his thought as did the cold glance of dark scorn and merciless meaning.

Brandt shuffled on with a curse. No coward was he. No man ever saw him flinch. But his intelligence was against him as a desperado. While such as these bordermen lived, an outlaw should never sleep, for he was a marked and doomed man. The deadly, cold-pointed flame which scintillated in the prisoner's eyes was only a gleam of what the border felt towards outlaws.

While Jonathan was considering all he had heard, three more Shawnees entered the retreat, and were at once called aside in consultation by Ashbow. At the conclusion of this brief conference the chief advanced to Jonathan, cut the bonds round his feet, and motioned for him to rise. The prisoner complied to find himself weak and sore, but able to walk. He concluded that his wound, while very painful, was not of a serious nature, and that he would be taken at once on the march toward the Shawnee village.

He was correct, for the chief led him, with the three Shawnees following, toward the outlet of the enclosure. Jonathan's sharp eye took in every detail of Legget's rendezvous. In a corral near the entrance, he saw a number of fine horses, and among them his sister's pony. A more inaccessible, natural refuge than Legget's, could hardly have been found in that country. The entrance was a narrow opening in the wall, and could be held by half a dozen against an army of besiegers. It opened, moreover, on the side of a barren hill, from which could be had a good survey of the surrounding forests and plains.

As Jonathan went with his captors down the hill his hopes, which while ever alive, had been flagging, now rose. The long journey to the Shawnee town led through an untracked wilderness. The Delaware villages lay far to the north; the Wyandot to the west. No likelihood was there of falling in with a band of Indians hunting, because this region, stony, barren, and poorly watered, afforded sparse pasture for deer or bison. From the prisoner's point of view this enterprise of Ashbow's was reckless and vainglorious. Cunning as the chief was, he erred in one point, a great warrior's only weakness, love of show, of pride, of his achievement. In Indian nature this desire for fame was as strong as love of life. The brave risked everything to win his eagle feathers, and the matured warrior found death while keeping bright the glory of the plumes he had won.

Wetzel was in the woods, fleet as a deer, fierce and fearless as a lion. Somewhere among those glades he trod, stealthily, with the ears of a doe and eyes of a hawk strained for sound or sight of his comrade's captors. When he found their trail he would stick to it as the wolf to that of a bleeding buck's. The rescue would not be attempted until the right moment, even though that came within rifle-shot of the Shawnee encampment. Wonderful as his other gifts, was the borderman's patience.

CHAPTER XIV

"G ood morning, Colonel Zane," said Helen cheerily, coming into the yard where the colonel was at work. "Did Will come over this way?"

"I reckon you'll find him if you find Betty," replied Colonel Zane dryly.

"Come to think of it, that's true," Helen said, laughing. "I've a suspicion Will ran off from me this morning."

"He and Betty have gone nutting."

"I declare it's mean of Will," Helen said petulantly. "I have been wanting to go so much, and both he and Betty promised to take me."

"Say, Helen, let me tell you something," said the colonel, resting on his spade and looking at her quizzically. "I told them we hadn't had enough frost yet to ripen hickory nuts and chestnuts. But they went anyhow. Will did remember to say if you came along, to tell you he'd bring the colored leaves you wanted."

"How extremely kind of him. I've a mind to follow them."

"Now see here, Helen, it might be a right good idea for you not to," returned the colonel, with a twinkle and a meaning in his eye.

"Oh, I understand. How singularly dull I've been."

"It's this way. We're mighty glad to have a fine young fellow like Will come along and interest Betty. Lord knows we had a time with her after Alfred died. She's just beginning to brighten up now, and, Helen, the point is that young people on the border must get married. No, my dear, you needn't laugh, you'll have to find a husband same as the other girls. It's not here as it was back east, where a lass might have her fling, so to speak, and take her time choosing. An unmarried girl on the border is a positive menace. I saw, not many years ago, two first-rate youngsters, wild with border fire and spirit, fight and kill each other over a lass who wouldn't choose. Like as not, if she had done so, the three would have been good friends, for out here we're like one big family. Remember this, Helen, and as far as Betty and Will are concerned you will be wise to follow our example: Leave them to themselves. Nothing else will so quickly strike fire between a boy and a girl."

"Betty and Will! I'm sure I'd love to see them care for each other." Then with big, bright eyes bent gravely on him she continued, "May I ask, Colonel Zane, who you have picked out for me?"

"There, now you've said it, and that's the problem. I've looked over every marriageable young man in the settlement, except Jack. Of course you couldn't care for him, a borderman, a fighter, and all that; but I can't find a fellow I think quite up to you."

"Colonel Zane, is not a borderman such as Jonathan worthy a woman's regard?" Helen asked a little wistfully.

"Bless your heart, lass, yes!" replied Colonel Zane heartily. "People out here are not as they are back east. An educated man, polished and all that, but incapable of hard labor, or shrinking from dirt and sweat on his hands, or even blood, would not help us in the winning of the West. Plain as Jonathan is, and with his lack of schooling, he is greatly superior to the majority of young men on the frontier. But, unlettered or not, he is as fine a man as ever stepped in moccasins, or any other kind of foot gear."

"Then why did you say—that—what you did?"

"Well, it's this way," replied Colonel Zane, stealing a glance at her pensive, downcast face. "Girls all like to be wooed. Almost every one I ever knew wanted the young man of her choice to outstrip all her other admirers, and then, for a spell, nearly die of love for her, after which she'd give in. Now, Jack, being a borderman, a man with no occupation except scouting, will never look at a girl, let alone make up to her. I imagine, my dear, it'd take some mighty tall courting to fetch home Helen Sheppard a bride. On the other hand, if some pretty and spirited lass, like, say for instance, Helen Sheppard, would come along and just make Jack forget Indians and fighting, she'd get the finest husband in the world. True, he's wild; but only in the woods. A simpler, kinder, cleaner man cannot be found."

"I believe that, Colonel Zane; but where is the girl who would interest him?" Helen asked with spirit. "These bordermen are unapproachable. Imagine a girl interesting that great, cold, stern Wetzel! All her flatteries, her wiles, the little coquetries that might attract ordinary men, would not be noticed by him, or Jonathan either."

"I grant it'd not be easy, but woman was made to subjugate man, and always, everlastingly, until the end of life here on this beautiful earth, she will do it."

"Do you think Jonathan and Wetzel will catch Brandt?" asked Helen, changing the subject abruptly.

"I'd stake my all that this year's autumn leaves will fall on Brandt's grave."

Colonel Zane's calm, matter-of-fact coldness made Helen shiver.

"Why, the leaves have already begun to fall. Papa told

me Brandt had gone to join the most powerful outlaw band on the border. How can these two men, alone, cope with savages, as I've heard they do, and break up such an outlaw band as Legget's?"

"That's a question I've heard Daniel Boone ask about Wetzel, and Boone, though not a borderman in all the name implies, was a great Indian fighter. I've heard old frontiersmen, grown grizzled on the frontier, use the same words. I've been twenty years with that man, yet I can't answer it. Jonathan, of course, is only a shadow of him; Wetzel is the type of these men who have held the frontier for us. He was the first borderman, and no doubt he'll be the last."

"What have Jonathan and Wetzel that other men do not possess?"

"In them is united a marvelously developed woodcraft, with wonderful physical powers. Imagine a man having a sense, almost an animal instinct, for what is going on in the woods. Take for instance the fleetness of foot. That is one of the greatest factors. It is absolutely necessary to run, to get away when to hold ground would be death. Whether at home or in the woods, the bordermen retreat every day. You wouldn't think they practiced anything of the kind, would you? Well, a man can't be great in anything without keeping at it. Jonathan says he exercises to keep his feet light. Wetzel would just as soon run as walk. Think of the magnificent condition of these men. When a dash of speed is called for, when to be fleet of foot is to elude vengeance-seeking Indians, they must travel as swiftly as the deer. The Zanes were all sprinters. I could do something of the kind; Betty was fast on her feet, as that old fort will testify until the logs rot; Isaac was fleet, too, and Jonathan can get over the ground like a scared buck. But, even so, Wetzel can beat him."

"Goodness me, Helen!" exclaimed the colonel's buxom wife, from the window, "don't you ever get tired hearing Eb talk of Wetzel, and Jack, and Indians? Come in with me. I venture to say my gossip will do you more good than his stories."

Therefore Helen went in to chat with Mrs. Zane, for she was always glad to listen to the colonel's wife, who was so bright and pleasant, so helpful and kindly in her womanly way. In the course of their conversation, which drifted from weaving linsey, Mrs. Zane's occupation at the time, to the costly silks and satins of remembered days, and then to matters of more present interest, Helen spoke of Colonel Zane's hint about Will and Betty.

"Isn't Eb a terror? He's the worst matchmaker you ever saw," declared the colonel's good spouse.

"There's no harm in that."

"No, indeed; it's a good thing, but he makes me laugh, and Betty, he sets her furious."

"The colonel said he had designs on me."

"Of course he has, dear old Eb! How he'd love to see you happily married. His heart is as big as that mountain yonder. He has given this settlement his whole life."

"I believe you. He has such interest, such zeal for everybody. Only the other day he was speaking to me of Mr. Mordaunt, telling how sorry he was for the Englishman, and how much he'd like to help him. It does seem a pity a man of Mordaunt's blood and attainments should sink to utter worthlessness."

"Yes, 'tis a pity for any man, blood or no, and the world's full of such wrecks. I always liked that man's looks. I never had a word with him, of course; but I've seen him often, and something about him appealed to me. I don't believe it was just his handsome face; still I know women are susceptible that way."

"I, too, liked him once as a friend," said Helen feelingly. "Well, I'm glad he's gone."

"Gone?"

"Yes, he left Fort Henry yesterday. He came to say good-bye to me, and, except for his pale face and trembling hands, was much as he used to be in Virginia. Said he was going home to England, and wanted to tell me he was sorry—for—for all he'd done to make papa and me suffer. Drink had broken him, he said, and surely he looked a broken man. I shook hands with him, and then slipped upstairs and cried."

"Poor fellow!" sighed Mrs. Zane.

"Papa said he left Fort Pitt with one of Metzar's men as a guide."

"Then he didn't take the 'little cuss,' as Eb calls his man Case?"

"No, if I remember rightly pap said Case wouldn't go."

"I wish he had. He's no addition to our village."

Voices outside attracted their attention. Mrs. Zane glanced from the window and said: "There come Betty and Will."

Helen went on the porch to see her cousin and Betty entering the yard, and Colonel Zane once again leaning on his spade.

"Gather any hickory nuts from birch or any other kind of trees?" asked the colonel grimly.

"No," replied Will cheerily, "the shells haven't opened yet."

"Too bad the frost is so backward," said Colonel Zane with a laugh. "But I can't see that it makes any difference."

"Where are my leaves?" asked Helen, with a smile and a nod to Betty.

"What leaves?" inquired that young woman, plainly mystified.

"Why, the autumn leaves Will promised to gather with me, then changed his mind, and said he'd bring them."

"I forgot," Will replied a little awkwardly.

Colonel Zane coughed, and then, catching Betty's glance, which had begun to flash, he plied his spade vigorously.

Betty's face had colored warmly at her brother's first question; it toned down slightly when she understood that he was not going to tease her as usual, and suddenly, as she looked over his head, it paled white as snow.

"Eb, look down the lane!" she cried.

Two tall men were approaching with labored tread, one half-supporting his companion.

"Wetzel! Jack! and Jack's hurt!" cried Betty.

"My dear, be calm," said Colonel Zane, in that quiet tone he always used during moments of excitement. He turned toward the bordermen, and helped Wetzel lead Jonathan up the walk into the yard.

From Wetzel's clothing water ran, his long hair was disheveled, his aspect frightful. Jonathan's face was white and drawn. His buckskin hunting-coat was covered with blood, and the hand which he held tightly against his left breast showed dark red stains.

Helen shuddered. Almost fainting, she leaned against the porch, too horrified to cry out, with contracting heart and a chill stealing through her veins.

"Jack! Jack!" cried Betty, in agonized appeal.

"Betty, it's nothin'," said Wetzel.

"Now, Betts, don't be scared of a little blood," Jonathan said with a faint smile flitting across his haggard face.

"Bring water, shears an' some linsey cloth," added Wetzel, as Mrs. Zane came running out.

"Come inside," cried the colonel's wife, as she disappeared again immediately.

"No," replied the borderman, removing his coat, and, with the assistance of his brother, he unlaced his hunting shirt, pulling it down from a wounded shoulder. A great gory hole gaped just beneath his left collarbone.

Although stricken with fear, when Helen saw the bronzed, massive shoulder, the long, powerful arm with its cords of muscles playing under the brown skin, she felt a thrill of admiration.

"Just missed the lung," said Mrs. Zane. "Eb, no bullet ever made that hole."

Wetzel washed the bloody wound, and, placing on it a wad of leaves he took from his pocket, bound up the shoulder tightly.

"What made that hole?" asked Colonel Zane.

Wetzel lifted the quiver of arrows Jonathan had laid on the porch, and, selecting one, handed it to the colonel. The flint-head and a portion of the shaft were stained with blood.

"The Shawnee!" exclaimed Colonel Zane. Then he led Wetzel aside, and began conversing in low tones while Jonathan, with Betty holding his arm, ascended the steps and went within the dwelling.

Helen ran home, and, once in her room, gave vent to her emotions. She cried because of fright, nervousness, relief, and joy. Then she bathed her face, tried to rub some color into her pale cheeks, and set about getting dinner as one in a trance. She could not forget that broad shoulder with its frightful wound. What a man Jonathan must be to receive a blow like that and live! Exhausted, almost spent, had been his strength when he reached home, yet how calm and cool he was! What would she not have given for the faint smile that shone in his eyes for Betty?

The afternoon was long for Helen. When at last supper was over she changed her gown, and, asking Will to accompany her, went down the lane toward Colonel Zane's cabin. At this hour the colonel almost invariably could be found sitting on his doorstep puffing a long Indian pipe, and gazing with dreamy eyes over the valley.

"Well, well, how sweet you look!" he said to Helen; then with a wink of his eyelid, "Hell, Willie, you'll find Elizabeth inside with Jack."

"How is he?" asked Helen eagerly, as Will with a laugh and a retort mounted the steps.

"Jack's doing splendidly. He slept all day. I don't think his injury amounts to much, at least not for such as him or Wetzel. It would have finished ordinary men. Bess says if complications don't set in, blood-poison or something to start a fever, he'll be up shortly. Wetzel believes the two of 'em will be on the trail inside of a week."

"Did they find Brandt?" asked Helen in a low voice.

"Yes, they ran him to his hole, and, as might have been expected, it was Bing Legget's camp. The Indians took Jonathan there."

"Then Jack was captured?"

Colonel Zane related the events, as told briefly by Wetzel, that had taken place during the preceding three days.

"The Indian I saw at the spring carried that bow Jonathan brought back. He must have shot the arrow. He was a magnificent savage."

"He was indeed a great, and a bad Indian, one of the craftiest spies who ever stepped in moccasins; but he lies quiet now on the moss and the leaves. Bing Legget will never find another runner like that Shawnee. Let us go indoors."

He led Helen into the large sitting-room where Jonathan

lay on a couch, with Betty and Will sitting beside him. The colonel's wife and children, Silas Zane, and several neighbors, were present.

"Here, Jack, is a lady inquiring after your health. Betts, this reminds me of the time Isaac came home wounded, after his escape from the Hurons. Strikes me he and his Indian bride should be about due here on a visit."

Helen forgot every one except the wounded man lying so quiet and pale upon the couch. She looked down upon him with eyes strangely dilated, and darkly bright.

"How are you?" she said softly.

"I'm all right, thank you, lass," answered Jonathan.

Colonel Zane contrived, with inimitable skill, to get Betty, Will, Silas, Bessie, and the others interested in some remarkable news he had just heard, or made up, and this left Jonathan and Helen comparatively alone for the moment.

The wise old colonel thought perhaps this might be the right time. He saw Helen's face as she leaned over Jonathan, and that was enough for him. He would have taxed his ingenuity to the utmost to keep the others away from the young couple.

"I was so frightened," murmured Helen.

"Why?" asked Jonathan.

"Oh! You looked so deathly—the blood, and that awful wound!"

"It's nothin', lass."

Helen smiled down upon him. Whether or no the hurt amounted to anything in the borderman's opinion, she knew from his weakness, and his white, drawn face, that the strain of the march home had been fearful. His dark eyes held now nothing of the coldness and glitter so natural to them. They were weary, almost sad. She did not feel afraid of him now. He lay there so helpless, his long, powerful frame as quiet as a sleeping child's! Hitherto an almost indefinable antagonism in him had made itself felt; now there was only gentleness, as of a man too weary to fight longer. Helen's heart swelled with pity, and tenderness, and love. His weakness affected her as had never his strength. With an involuntary gesture of sympathy she placed her hand softly on his.

Jonathan looked up at her with eyes no longer blind. Pain had softened him. For the moment he felt carried out of himself, as it were, and saw things differently. The melting tenderness of her gaze, the glowing softness of her face, the beauty, bewitched him; and beyond that, a sweet, impelling gladness stirred within him and would not be denied. He thrilled as her fingers lightly, timidly touched his, and opened his broad hand to press hers closely and warmly.

"Lass," he whispered, with a huskiness and unsteadiness unnatural to his deep voice.

Helen bent her head closer to him; she saw his lips tremble, and his nostrils dilate; but an unutterable sadness shaded the brightness in his eyes.

"I love you."

The low whisper reached Helen's ears. She seemed to float dreamily away to some beautiful world, with the music of those words ringing in her ears. She looked at him again. Had she been dreaming? No; his dark eyes met hers with a love that he could no longer deny. An exquisite emotion, keen, strangely sweet and strong, yet terrible with sharp pain, pulsated through her being. The revelation had been too abrupt. It was so wonderfully different from what she had ever dared hope. She lowered her head, trembling.

The next moment she felt Colonel Zane's hand on her chair, and heard him say in a cheery voice:

"Well, well, see here, lass, you mustn't make Jack talk too much. See how white and tired he looks."

CHAPTER XV

In forty-eight hours Jonathan Zane was up and about the cabin as though he had never been wounded; the third day he walked to the spring; in a week he was waiting for Wetzel, ready to go on the trail.

On the eighth day of his enforced idleness, as he sat with Betty and the colonel in the yard, Wetzel appeared on a ridge east of the fort. Soon he rounded the stockade fence, and came straight toward them. To Colonel Zane and Betty, Wetzel's expression was terrible. The stern kindliness, the calm, though cold, gravity of his countenance, as they usually saw it, had disappeared. Yet it showed no trace of his unnatural passion to pursue and slay. No doubt that terrible instinct, or lust, was at white heat; but it wore a mask of impenetrable stone-gray gloom.

Wetzel spoke briefly. After telling Jonathan to meet him at sunset on the following day at a point five miles up the river, he reported to the colonel that Legget with his band had left their retreat, moving southward, apparently on a marauding expedition. Then he shook hands with Colonel Zane and turned to Betty.

"Good-bye Betty," he said, in his deep, sonorous voice.

"Good-bye, Lew," answered Betty slowly, as if surprised. "God save you," she added.

He shouldered his rifle, and hurried down the lane, halting before entering the thicket that bounded the clearing, to look back at the settlement. In another moment his dark figure had disappeared among the bushes.

"Betts, I've seen Wetzel go like that hundreds of times, though he never shook hands before; but I feel sort of strange about it now. Wasn't he strange?"

Betty did not answer until Jonathan, who had started to go within, was out of hearing.

"Lew looked and acted the same the morning he struck Miller's trail," Betty replied in a low voice. "I believe, despite his indifference to danger, he realizes that the chances are greatly against him, as they were when he began the trailing of Miller, certain it would lead him into Girty's camp. Then I know Lew has an affection for us, though it is never shown in ordinary ways. I pray he and Jack will come home safe."

"This is a bad trail they're taking up; the worst, perhaps, in border warfare," said Colonel Zane gloomily. "Did you notice how Jack's face darkened when his comrade came? Much of this borderman-life of his is due to Wetzel's influence."

"Eb, I'll tell you one thing," returned Betty, with a flash of her old spirit. "This is Jack's last trail."

"Why do you think so?"

"If he doesn't return he'll be gone the way of all bordermen; but if he comes back once more he'll never get away from Helen."

"Ugh!" exclaimed Zane, venting his pleasure in characteristic Indian way.

"That night after Jack came home wounded," continued Betty, "I saw him, as he lay on the couch, gaze at Helen. Such a look! Eb, she has won."

"I hope so, but I fear, I fear," replied her brother gloomily. "If only he returns that's the thing! Betts, be sure he sees Helen before he goes away."

"I shall try. Here he comes now," said Betty.

"Hello, Jack!" cried the colonel, as his brother came out in somewhat of a hurry. "What have you got? By George! It's that blamed arrow the Shawnee shot into you. Where are you going with it? What the hell—Say—Betts, eh?"

Betty had given him a sharp little kick.

The borderman looked embarrassed. He hesitated and flushed. Evidently he would have liked to avoid his brother's question; but the inquiry came direct. Dissimulation with him was impossible.

"Helen wanted this, an' I reckon that's where I'm goin' with it," he said finally, and walked away.

"Eb, you're a stupid!" exclaimed Betty.

"Hang it! Who'd have thought he was going to give her that blamed, bloody arrow?"

As Helen ushered Jonathan, for the first time, into her cosy little sitting-room, her heart began to thump so hard she could hear it.

She had not seen him since the night he whispered the words which gave such happiness. She had stayed at home, thankful beyond expression to learn every day of his rapid improvement, living in the sweetness of her joy, and waiting for him. And now as he had come, so dark, so grave, so unlike a lover to woo, that she felt a chill steal over her.

"I'm so glad you've brought the arrow," she faltered, "for, of course, coming so far means that you're well once more."

"You asked me for it, an' I've fetched it over. Tomorrow I'm off on a trail I may never return from," he answered simply, and his voice seemed cold.

An immeasurable distance stretched once more between them. Helen's happiness slowly died.

"I thank you," she said with a voice that was tremulous despite all her efforts.

"It's not much of a keepsake."

"I did not ask for it as a keepsake, but because—because I wanted it. I need nothing tangible to keep alive my memory. A few words whispered to me not many days ago will suffice for remembrance—or—or did I dream them?"

Bitter disappointment almost choked Helen. This was not the gentle, soft-voiced man who had said he loved her. It was the indifferent borderman. Again he was the embodiment of his strange, quite woods. Once more he seemed the comrade of the cold, inscrutable Wetzel.

"No, lass, I reckon you didn't dream," he replied.

Helen swayed from sick bitterness and a suffocating sense of pain, back to her old, sweet, joyous, tumultuous heart-throbbing.

"Tell me, if I didn't dream," she said softly, her face flashing warm again. She came close to him and looked up with all her heart in her great dark eyes, and love trembling on her red lips.

Calmness deserted the borderman after one glance at her. He paced the floor; twisted and clasped his hands while his eyes gleamed.

"Lass, I'm only human," he cried hoarsely, facing her again.

But only for a moment did he stand before her; but it was long enough for him to see her shrink a little, the gladness in her eyes giving way to uncertainty and a fugitive hope. Suddenly he began to pace the room again, and to talk incoherently. With the flow of words he gradually grew calmer, and, with something of his natural dignity, spoke more rationally.

"I said I loved you, an' it's true, but I didn't mean to speak. I oughtn't have done it. Somethin' made it so easy, so natural like. I'd have died before letting you know, if any idea had come to me of what I was sayin'. I've fought this feelin' for months. I allowed myself to think of you at first, an' there's the wrong. I went on the trail with your big eyes pictured in my mind, an' before I'd dreamed of it you'd crept into my heart. Life has never been the same since—that kiss. Betty said as how you cared for me, an' that made me worse, only I never really believed. To-day I came over here to say good-bye, expectin' to hold myself well in hand; but the first glance of your eyes unmans me. Nothin' can come of it, lass, nothin' but trouble. Even if you cared, an' I don't dare believe you do, nothin' can come of it! I've my own life to live, an' there's no sweetheart in it. Mebbe, as Lew says, there's one in Heaven. Oh! girl, this has been hard on me. I see you always on my lonely tramps; I see your glorious eyes in the sunny fields an' in the woods, at gray twilight, an' when the stars shine brightest. They haunt me. Ah! you're the sweetest lass as ever tormented a man, an' I love you, I love you!"

He turned to the window only to hear a soft, broken cry, and a flurry of skirts. A rush of wind seemed to envelop him. Then two soft, rounded arms encircled his neck, and a golden head lay on his breast.

"My borderman! My hero! My love!"

Jonathan clasped the beautiful, quivering girl to his heart.

"Lass, for God's sake don't say you love me," he implored, thrilling with contact of her warm arms.

"Ah!" she breathed, and raised her head. Her radiant eyes darkly wonderful with unutterable love, burned into his.

He had almost pressed his lips to the sweet red ones so near his, when he drew back with a start, and his frame straightened.

"Am I a man, or only a coward?" he muttered. "Lass, let me think. Don't believe I'm harsh, nor cold, nor nothin' except that I want to do what's right."

He leaned out of the window while Helen stood near him with a hand on his quivering shoulder. When at last he turned, his face was colorless, white as marble, and sad, and set, and stern.

"Lass, it mustn't be; I'll not ruin your life."

"But you will if you give me up."

"No, no, lass."

"I cannot live without you."

"You must. My life is not mine to give."

"But you love me."

"I am a borderman."

"I will not live without you."

"Hush! lass, hush!"

"I love you."

Jonathan breathed hard; once more the tremor, which seemed pitiful in such a strong man, came upon him. His face was gray.

"I love you," she repeated, her rich voice indescribably deep and full. She opened wide her arms and stood before him with heaving bosom, with great eyes dark with woman's sadness, passionate with woman's promise, perfect in her beauty, glorious in her abandonment.

The borderman bowed and bent like a broken reed.

"Listen," she whispered, coming closer to him, "go if you must leave me; but let this be your last trail. Come back to me, Jack, come back to me! You have had enough of this terrible life; you have won a name that will never be forgotten; you have done your duty to the border. The Indians and outlaws will be gone soon. Take the farm your brother wants you to have, and live for me. We will be happy. I shall learn to keep your home. Oh! my dear, I will recompense you for the loss of all this wild hunting and fighting. Let me persuade you, as much for your sake as for mine, for you are my heart, and soul, and life. Go out upon your last trail, Jack, and come back to me."

"An' let Wetzel go always alone?"

"He is different; he lives only for revenge. What are those poor savages to you? You have a better, nobler life opening."

"Lass, I can't give him up."

"You need not; but give up this useless seeking of adventure. That, you know, is half a borderman's life. Give it up, Jack, if not for your own, then for my sake."

"No—no—never—I can't—I won't be a coward! After all these years I won't desert him. No—no—"

"Do not say more," she pleaded, stealing closer to him until she was against his breast. She slipped her arms around his neck. For love and more than life she was fighting now. "Good-bye, my love." She kissed him, a long, lingering pressure of her soft full lips on his. "Dearest, do not shame me further. Dearest Jack, come back to me, for I love you."

She released him, and ran sobbing from the room.

Unsteady as a blind man, he groped for the door, found it, and went out.

CHAPTER XVI

The longest day in Jonathan Zane's life, the oddest, the most terrible and complex with unintelligible emotions, was that one in which he learned that the wilderness no longer sufficed for him.

He wandered through the forest like a man lost, searching for, he knew not what. Rambling along the shady trails he looked for that contentment which had always been his, but found it not. He plunged into the depths of deep, gloomy ravines; into the fastnesses of heavy-timbered hollows where the trees hid the light of day; he sought the open, grassy hillsides, and roamed far over meadow and plain. Yet something always eluded him. The invisible and beautiful life of all inanimate things sang no more in his heart. The springy moss, the quivering leaf, the telltale bark of the trees, the limpid, misty, eddying pools under green banks, the myriads of natural objects from which he had learned so much, and the manifold joyous life around him, no longer spoke with soul-satisfying faithfulness. The environment of his boyish days, of his youth, and manhood, rendered not a sweetness as of old.

His intelligence, sharpened by the pain of new experience, told him he had been vain to imagine that he, because he was a borderman, could escape the universal destiny of human life. Dimly he could feel the broadening, the awakening into a fuller existence, but he did not welcome this new light. He realized that men had always turned, at some time in their lives, to women even as the cypress leans toward the sun. This weakening of the sterner stuff in him; this softening of his heart, and especially the inquietude, and lack of joy and harmony in his old pursuits of the forest trails bewildered him, and troubled him some. Thousands of times his borderman's trail had been crossed, yet never to his sorrow until now when it had been crossed by a woman.

Sick at heart, hurt in his pride, darkly savage, sad, remorseful, and thrilling with awakened passion, all in turn, he roamed the woodland unconsciously visiting the scenes where he had formerly found contentment.

He paused by many a shady glen, and beautiful quiet glade; by gray cliffs and mossy banks, searching with moody eyes for the spirit which evaded him.

Here in the green and golden woods rose before him a rugged, giant rock, moss-stained, and gleaming with trickling water. Tangled ferns dressed in autumn's russet hue lay at the base of the green-gray cliff, and circled a dark, deep pool dotted with yellow leaves. Half-way up, the perpendicular ascent was broken by a protruding ledge upon which waved broad-leaved plants and rusty ferns. Above, the cliff sheered out with many cracks and seams in its weather-beaten front.

The forest grew to the verge of the precipice. A full-foliaged oak and a luxuriant maple, the former still fresh with its dark green leaves, the latter making a vivid contrast with its pale yellow, purple-red, and orange hues, leaned far out over the bluff. A mighty chestnut grasped with gnarled roots deep into the broken cliff. Dainty plumes of goldenrod swayed on the brink; red berries, amber moss, and green trailing vines peeped over the edge, and every little niche and cranny sported fragile ferns and pale-faced asters. A second cliff, higher than the first, and more heavily wooded, loomed above, and over it sprayed a transparent film of water, thin as smoke, and iridescent in the sunshine. Far above where the glancing rill caressed the mossy cliff and shone like gleaming gold against the dark branches with their green and red and purple leaves, lay the faint blue of the sky.

Jonathan pulled on down the stream with humbler heart. His favorite waterfall had denied him. The gold that had gleamed there was his sweetheart's hair; the red was of her lips; the dark pool with its lights and shades, its unfathomable mystery, was like her eyes.

He came at length to another scene of milder aspect. An open glade where the dancing, dimpling brook raced under dark hemlocks, and where bloodred sumach leaves, and beech leaves like flashes of sunshine, lay against the green. Under a leaning birch he found a patch of purple asters, and a little apart from them, by a mossy stone, a lonely fringed gentian. Its deep color brought to him the dark blue eyes that haunted him, and once again, like one possessed of an evil spirit, he wandered along the merry watercourse.

But finally pain and unrest left him. When he surrendered to his love, peace returned. Though he said in his heart that Helen was not for him, he felt he did not need to torture himself by fighting against resistless power. He could love her without being a coward. He would take up his life where it had been changed, and live it, carrying this bittersweet burden always.

Memory, now that he admitted himself conquered, made a toy of him, bringing the sweetness of fragrant hair, and eloquent eyes, and clinging arms, and dewy lips. A thousand-fold harder to fight than pain was the seductive thought that he had but to go back to Helen to feel again the charm of her presence, to see the grace of her person, to hear the music of her voice, to have again her lips on his.

Jonathan knew then that his trial had but begun; that the pain and suffering of a borderman's broke pride and conquered spirit was nothing; that to steel his heart against the joy, the sweetness, the longing of love was everything.

So a tumult raged within his heart. No bitterness, nor wretchedness stabbed him as before, but a passionate yearning, born of memory, and unquenchable as the fires of the sun, burned there.

Helen's reply to his pale excuses, to his duty, to his life, was that she loved him. The wonder of it made him weak. Was not her answer enough? "I love you!" Three words only; but they changed the world. A beautiful girl loved him, she had kissed him, and his life could never again be the same. She had held out her arms to him—and he, cold, churlish, unfeeling brute, had let her shame herself, fighting for her happiness, for the joy that is a woman's divine right. He had been blind; he had not understood the significance of her gracious action; he had never realized until too late, what it must have cost her, what heart-burning shame and scorn his refusal brought upon her. If she ever looked tenderly at him again with her great eyes; or leaned toward him with her beautiful arms outstretched, he would fall at her feet and throw his duty to the winds, swearing his love was hers always and his life forever.

So love stormed in the borderman's heart.

Slowly the melancholy Indian-summer day waned as Jonathan strode out of the woods into a plain beyond, where he was to meet Wetzel at sunset. A smoky haze like a purple cloud lay upon the gently waving grass. He could not see across the stretch of prairie-land, though at this point he knew it was hardly a mile wide. With the trilling of the grasshoppers alone disturbing the serene quiet of this autumn afternoon, all nature seemed in harmony with the declining season. He stood a while, his thoughts becoming the calmer for the silence and loneliness of this breathing meadow.

When the shadows of the trees began to lengthen, and to steal far out over the yellow grass, he knew the time had come, and glided out upon the plain. He crossed it, and sat down upon a huge stone which lay with one shelving end overhanging the river.

Far in the west the gold-red sun, too fiery for his direct gaze, lost the brilliance of its under circle behind the fringe of the wooded hill. Slowly the red ball sank. When the last bright gleam had vanished in the dark horizon Jonathan turned to search wood and plain. Wetzel was to meet him at sunset. Even as his first glance swept around a light step sounded behind him. He did not move, for that step was familiar. In another moment the tall form of Wetzel stood beside him.

"I'm about as much behind as you was ahead of time," said Wetzel. "We'll stay here fer the night, an' be off early in the mornin'."

Under the shelving side of the rock, and in the shade of the thicket, the bordermen built a little fire and roasted strips of deer-meat. Then, puffing at their long pipes they sat for a long time in silence, while twilight let fall a dark, gray cloak over river and plain.

"Legget's move up the river was a blind, as I suspected," said Wetzel, presently. "He's not far back in the woods from here, an' seems to be waitin' fer somethin' or somebody. Brandt an' seven redskins are with him. We'd hev a good chance at them in the mornin'; now we've got 'em a long ways from their camp, so we'll wait, an' see what deviltry they're up to."

"Mebbe he's waitin' for some Injun band," suggested Jonathan.

"Thar's redskins in the valley an' close to him; but I reckon he's barkin' up another tree."

"Suppose we run into some of these Injuns?"

"We'll hev to take what comes," replied Wetzel, lying down on a bed of leaves.

When darkness enveloped the spot Wetzel lay wrapped in deep slumber, while Jonathan sat against the rock, watching the last flickerings of the campfire.

CHAPTER XVII

Will and Helen hurried back along the river road. Beguiled by the soft beauty of the autumn morning they ventured farther from the fort than ever before, and had been suddenly brought to a realization of the fact by a crackling in the underbrush. Instantly their minds reverted to bears and panthers, such as they had heard invested the thickets round the settlement.

"Oh! Will! I saw a dark form stealing along in the woods from tree to tree!" exclaimed Helen in a startled whisper.

"So did I. It was an Indian, or I never saw one. Walk faster. Once round the bend in the road we'll be within sight of the fort; then we'll run," replied Will. He had turned pale, but maintained his composure.

They increased their speed, and had almost come up to the curve in the road, marked by dense undergrowth on both sides, when the branches in the thicket swayed violently, a sturdy little man armed with a musket appeared from among them.

"Avast! Heave to!" he commanded in a low, fierce voice, leveling his weapon. "One breeze from ye, an' I let sail this broadside."

"What do you want? We have no valuables," said Will, speaking low.

Helen stared at the little man. She was speechless with terror. It flashed into her mind as soon as she recognized the red, evil face of the sailor, that he was the accomplice upon whom Brandt had told Metzar he could rely.

"Shut up! It's not ye I want, nor valuables, but this wench," growled Case. He pushed Will around with the muzzle of the musket, which action caused the young man to turn a sickly white and shrink involuntarily with fear. The hammer of the musket was raised, and might fall at the slightest jar.

"For God's sake! Will, do as he says," cried Helen, who saw murder in Case's eyes. Capture or anything was better than sacrifice of life.

"March!" ordered Case, with the musket against Will's back.

Will hurriedly started forward, jostling Helen, who had preceded him. He was forced to hurry, because every few moments Case pressed the gun to his back or side.

Without another word the sailor marched them swiftly along the road, which now narrowed down to a trail. His intention, no doubt, was to put as much distance between him and the fort as was possible. No more than a mile had been thus traversed when two Indians stepped into view.

"My God! My God!" cried Will as the savages proceeded first to bind Helen's arms behind her, and then his in the same manner. After this the journey was continued in silence, the Indians walking beside the prisoners, and Case in the rear.

Helen was so terrified that for a long time she could not think coherently. It seemed as if she had walked miles, yet did not feel tired. Always in front wound the narrow, leaf-girt trail, and to the left the broad river gleamed at intervals through open spaces in the thickets. Flocks of birds rose in the line of march. They seemed tame, and uttered plaintive notes as if in sympathy.

About noon the trail led to the riverbank. One of the

savages disappeared in a copse of willows, and presently reappeared carrying a birch-bark canoe. Case ordered Helen and Will into the boat, got in himself, and the savages, taking stations at bow and stern, paddled out into the stream. They shot over under the lee of an island, around a rocky point, and across a strait to another island. Beyond this they gained the Ohio shore, and beached the canoe.

"Ahoy! there, cap'n," cried Case, pushing Helen up the bank before him, and she, gazing upward, was more than amazed to see Mordaunt leaning against a tree.

"Mordaunt, had you anything to do with this?" cried Helen breathlessly.

"I had all to do with it," answered the Englishman.

"What do you mean?"

He did not meet her gaze, nor make reply; but turned to address a few words in a low tone to a white man sitting on a log.

Helen knew she had seen this person before, and doubted not he was one of Metzar's men. She saw a rude, bark lean-to, the remains of a campfire, and a pack tied in blankets. Evidently Mordaunt and his men had tarried here awaiting such developments as had come to pass.

"You white-faced hound!" hissed Will, beside himself with rage when he realized the situation. Bound though he was, he leaped up and tried to get at Mordaunt. Case knocked him on the head with the handle of his knife. Will fell with blood streaming from a cut over the temple.

The dastardly act aroused all Helen's fiery courage. She turned to the Englishman with eyes ablaze.

"So you've at last found your level. Border-outlaw! Kill me at once. I'd rather be dead than breathe the same air with such a coward!"

"I swore I'd have you, if not by fair means then by foul," he answered, with dark and haggard face.

"What do you intend to do with me now that I am tied?" she demanded scornfully.

"Keep you a prisoner in the woods till you consent to marry me."

Helen laughed in scorn. Desperate as was the plight, her natural courage had arisen at the cruel blow dealt her cousin, and she faced the Englishman with flashing eyes and undaunted mien. She saw he was again unsteady, and had the cough and catching breath habitual to certain men under the influence of liquor. She turned her attention to Will. He lay as he had fallen, with blood streaming over his pale face and fair hair. While she gazed at him Case whipped out his long knife, and looked up at Mordaunt.

"Cap'n, I'd better loosen a hatch fer him," he said brutally. "He's dead cargo fer us, an' in the way."

He lowered the gleaming point upon Will's chest.

"Oh-h-h!" breathed Helen in horror. She tried to close her eyes but was so fascinated she could not.

"Get up. I'll have no murder," ordered Mordaunt. "Leave him here."

"He's not got a bad cut," said the man sitting on the log. "He'll come to arter a spell, go back to ther fort, an' give an alarm."

"What's that to me?" asked Mordaunt sharply. "We shall be safe. I won't have him with us because some Indian or another will kill him. It's not my purpose to murder any one."

"Ugh!" grunted one of the savages, and pointed eastward with his hand. "Hurry-long-way-go," he said in English. With the Indians in the lead the party turned from the river into the forest.

Helen looked back into the sandy glade and saw Will lying as they had left him, unconscious, with his hands still bound tightly behind him, and blood running over his face. Painful as was the thought of leaving him thus, it afforded her relief. She assured herself he had not been badly hurt, would recover consciousness before long, and, even bound as he was, could make his way back to the settlement.

Her own situation, now that she knew Mordaunt had instigated the abduction, did not seem hopeless. Although dreading Brandt with unspeakable horror, she did not in the least fear the Englishman. He was mad to carry her off like this into the wilderness, but would force her to do nothing. He could not keep her a prisoner long while Jonathan Zane and Wetzel were free to take his trail. What were his intentions? Where was he taking her? Such questions as these, however, troubled Helen more than a little. They brought her thoughts back to the Indians leading the way with lithe and stealthy step. How had Mordaunt associated himself with these savages? Then, suddenly, it dawned upon her that Brandt also might be in this scheme to carry her off. She scouted the idea; but it returned. Perhaps Mordaunt was only a tool; perhaps he himself was being deceived. Helen turned pale at the very thought. She had never forgotten the strange, unreadable, yet threatening, expression which Brandt had worn the day she had refused to walk with him.

Meanwhile the party made rapid progress through the forest. Not a word was spoken, nor did any noise of rustling leaves or crackling twigs follow their footsteps. The savage in the lead chose the open and less difficult ground; he took advantage of glades, mossy places, and rocky ridges. This careful choosing was, evidently, to avoid noise, and make the trail as difficult to follow as possible. Once he stopped suddenly, and listened.

Helen had a good look at the savage while he was in this position. His lean, athletic figure resembled, in its half-clothed condition, a bronzed statue; his powerful visage was set, changeless like iron. His dark eyes seemed to take in all points of the forest before him.

Whatever had caused the halt was an enigma to all save his red-skinned companion.

The silence of the wood was the silence of the desert. No bird chirped; no breath of wind sighed in the treetops; even the aspens remained unagitated. Pale yellow leaves sailed slowly, reluctantly down from above.

But some faint sound, something unusual had jarred upon the exquisitely sensitive ears of the leader, for with a meaning shake of the head to his followers, he resumed the march in a direction at right angles with the original course.

This caution, and evident distrust of the forest ahead, made Helen think again of Jonathan and Wetzel. Those great bordermen might already be on the trail of her captors. The thought thrilled her. Presently she realized, from another long, silent march through forest thickets, glades, aisles, and groves, over rock-strewn ridges, and down mossy-stoned ravines, that her strength was beginning to fail.

"I can go no further with my arms tied in this way," she declared, stopping suddenly.

"Ugh!" uttered the savage before her, turning sharply. He brandished a tomahawk before her eyes.

Mordaunt hurriedly set free her wrists. His pale face flushed a dark, flaming red when she shrank from his touch as if he were a viper.

After they had traveled what seemed to Helen many miles, the vigilance of the leaders relaxed.

On the banks of the willow-skirted stream the Indian guide halted them, and proceeded on alone to disappear in a green thicket. Presently he reappeared, and motioned for them to come on. He led the way over smooth, sandy paths between clumps of willows, into a heavy growth of alder bushes and prickly thorns, at length to emerge upon a beautiful grassy plot enclosed by green and yellow shrubbery. Above the stream, which cut the edge of the glade, rose a sloping, wooded ridge, with huge rocks projecting here and there out of the brown forest.

Several birch-bark huts could be seen; then two rough bearded men lolling upon the grass, and beyond them a group of painted Indians.

A whoop so shrill, so savage, so exultant, that it seemingly froze her blood, rent the silence. A man, unseen before, came crashing through the willows on the side of the ridge. He leaped the stream with the spring of a wild horse. He was big and broad, with disheveled hair, keen, hard face, and wild, gray eyes.

Helen's sight almost failed her; her head whirled dizzily; it was as if her heart had stopped beating and was become a cold, dead weight. She recognized in this man the one whom she feared most of all—Brandt.

He cast one glance full at her, the same threatening, cool, and evil-meaning look she remembered so well, and then engaged the Indian guide in low conversation.

Helen sank at the foot of a tree, leaning against it. Despite her weariness she had retained some spirit until this direful revelation broke her courage. What worse could have happened! Mordaunt had led her, for some reason that she could not divine, into the clutches of Brandt, into the power of Legget and his outlaws.

But Helen was not one to remain long dispirited or hopeless. As this plot thickened, as every added misfortune weighed upon her, when just ready to give up to despair she remembered the bordermen. Then Colonel Zane's tales of their fearless, implacable pursuit when bent on rescue or revenge, recurred to her, and fortitude returned. While she had life she would hope.

The advent of the party with their prisoner enlivened Legget's gang. A great giant of a man, blond-bearded, and handsome in a wild, rugged, uncouth way, a man Helen instinctively knew to be Legget, slapped Brandt on the shoulder.

"Damme, Roge, if she ain't a regular little daisy! Never seed such a purty lass in my life."

Brandt spoke hurriedly, and Legget laughed.

All this time Case had been sitting on the grass, saying nothing, but with his little eyes watchful. Mordaunt stood near him, his head bowed, his face gloomy.

"Say, cap'n, I don't like this mess," whispered Case to his master. "They ain't no crew fer us. I know men, fer I've sailed the seas, an' you're goin' to get what Metz calls the double-cross."

Mordaunt seemed to arouse from his gloomy reverie. He looked at Brandt and Legget who were now in earnest council. Then his eyes wandered toward Helen. She beckoned him to come to her.

"Why did you bring me here?" she asked.

"Brandt understood my case. He planned this thing, and seemed to be a good friend of mine. He said if I once got you out of the settlement, he would give me protection until I crossed the border into Canada. There we could be married," replied Mordaunt unsteadily.

"Then you meant marriage by me, if I could be made to consent?"

"Of course. I'm not utterly vile," he replied, with face lowered in shame.

"Have you any idea what you've done?"

"Done? I don't understand."

"You have ruined yourself, lost your manhood, become

an outlaw, a fugitive, made yourself the worst thing on the border—a girl-thief, and all for nothing."

"No, I have you. You are more to me than all."

"But can't you see? You've brought me out here for Brandt!"

"My God!" exclaimed Mordaunt. He rose slowly to his feet and gazed around like a man suddenly wakened from a dream. "I see it all now! Miserable, drunken wretch that I am!"

Helen saw his face change and lighten as if a cloud of darkness had passed away from it. She understood that love of liquor had made him a party to this plot. Brandt had cunningly worked upon his weakness, proposed a daring scheme; and filled his befogged mind with hopes that, in a moment of clear-sightedness, he would have seen to be vain and impossible. And Helen understood also that the sudden shock of surprise, pain, possible fury, had sobered Mordaunt, probably for the first time in weeks.

The Englishman's face became exceedingly pale. Seating himself on a stone near Case, he bowed his head, remaining silent and motionless.

The conference between Legget and Brandt lasted for some time. When it ended the latter strode toward the motionless figure on the rock.

"Mordaunt, you and Case will do well to follow this Indian at once to the river, where you can strike the Fort Pitt trail," said Brandt.

He spoke arrogantly and authoritatively. His keen, hard face, his steely eyes, bespoke the iron will and purpose of the man.

Mordaunt rose with cold dignity. If he had been a dupe, he was one no longer, as could be plainly read on his calm, pale face. The old listlessness, the unsteadiness had vanished. He wore a manner of extreme quietude; but his eyes were like balls of blazing blue steel.

"Mr. Brandt, I seem to have done you a service, and am no longer required," he said in a courteous tone.

Brandt eyed his man; but judged him wrongly. An English gentleman was new to the border-outlaw.

"I swore the girl should be mine," he hissed.

"Doomed men cannot be choosers!" cried Helen, who had heard him. Her dark eyes burned with scorn and hatred.

All the party heard her passionate outburst. Case arose as if unconcernedly, and stood by the side of his master. Legget and the other two outlaws came up. The Indians turned their swarthy faces.

"Hah! ain't she sassy?" cried Legget.

Brandt looked at Helen, understood the meaning of her words, and laughed. But his face paled, and involuntarily his shifty glance sought the rocks and trees upon the ridge.

"You played me from the first?" asked Mordaunt quietly.

"I did," replied Brandt.

"You meant nothing of your promise to help me across the border?"

"No."

"You intended to let me shift for myself out here in this wilderness?"

"Yes, after this Indian guides you to the river-trail," said Brandt, indicating with his finger the nearest savage.

"I get what you frontier men call 'the double- cross'?"

"That's it," replied Brandt with a hard laugh, in which Legget joined.

A short pause ensued.

"What will you do with the girl?"

"That's my affair."

"Marry her?" Mordaunt's voice was low and quiet.

"No!" cried Brandt. "She flaunted my love in my face, scorned me! She saw that borderman strike me, and by God! I'll get even. I'll keep her here in the woods until I'm tired of her, and when her beauty fades I'll turn her over to Legget."

Scarcely had the words dropped from his vile lips when Mordaunt moved with tigerish agility. He seized a knife from the belt of one of the Indians.

"Die!" he screamed.

Brandt grasped his tomahawk. At the same instant the man who had acted as Mordaunt's guide grasped the Englishman from behind.

Brandt struck ineffectually at the struggling man.

"Fair play!" roared Case, leaping at Mordaunt's second assailant. His long knife sheathed its glittering length in the man's breast. Without even a groan he dropped. "Clear the decks!" Case yelled, sweeping round in a circle. All fell back before that whirling knife.

Several of the Indians started as if to raise their rifles; but Legget's stern command caused them to desist.

The Englishman and the outlaw now engaged in a fearful encounter. The practiced, rugged, frontier desperado apparently had found his match in this pale-faced, slender man. His border skill with the hatchet seemed offset by Mordaunt's terrible rage. Brandt whirled and swung the weapon as he leaped around his antagonist. With his left arm the Englishman sought only to protect his head, while with his right he brandished the knife. Whirling here and there they struggled across the cleared space, plunging out of sight among the willows. During a moment there was a sound as of breaking branches; then a dull blow, horrible to hear, followed by a low moan, and then deep silence.

CHAPTER XVIII

A black weight was seemingly lifted from Helen's weary eyelids. The sun shone; the golden forest surrounded her; the brook babbled merrily; but where were the struggling, panting men? She noticed presently, when her vision had grown more clear, that the scene differed entirely from the willow-glade where she had closed her eyes upon the fight. Then came the knowledge that she had fainted, and, during the time of unconsciousness, been moved.

She lay upon a mossy mound a few feet higher than a swiftly running brook. A magnificent chestnut tree spread its leafy branches above her. Directly opposite, about an hundred feet away, loomed a gray, ragged, moss-stained cliff. She noted this particularly because the dense forest encroaching to its very edge excited her admiration. Such wonderful coloring seemed unreal. Dead gold and bright red foliage flamed everywhere.

Two Indians stood near by silent, immovable. No other of Legget's band was visible. Helen watched the red men.

Sinewy, muscular warriors they were, with bodies partially painted, and long, straight hair, black as burnt wood, interwoven with bits of white bone, and plaited around waving eagle plumes. At first glance their dark faces and dark eyes were expressive of craft, cunning, cruelty, courage, all attributes of the savage.

Yet wild as these savages appeared, Helen did not fear them as she did the outlaws. Brandt's eyes, and Legget's, too, when turned on her, emitted a flame that seemed to scorch and shrivel her soul. When the savages met her gaze, which was but seldom, she imagined she saw intelligence, even pity, in their dusky eyes. Certain it was she did not shrink from them as from Brandt.

Suddenly, with a sensation of relief and joy, she remembered Mordaunt's terrible onslaught upon Brandt. Although she could not recollect the termination of that furious struggle, she did recall Brandt's scream of mortal agony, and the death of the other at Case's hands. This meant, whether Brandt was dead or not, that the fighting strength of her captors had been diminished. Surely as the sun had risen that morning, Helen believed Jonathan and Wetzel lurked on the trail of these renegades. She prayed that her courage, hope, strength, might be continued.

"Ugh!" exclaimed one of the savages, pointing across the open space. A slight swaying of the bushes told that some living thing was moving among them, and an instant later the huge frame of the leader came into view. The other outlaw, and Case, followed closely. Farther down the margin of the thicket the Indians appeared; but without the slightest noise or disturbance of the shrubbery.

It required but a glance to show Helen that Case was in high spirits. His repulsive face glowed with satisfaction. He carried a bundle, which Helen saw, with a sickening sense of horror, was made up of Mordaunt's clothing. Brandt had killed the Englishman. Legget also had a package under his arm, which he threw down when he reached the chestnut tree, to draw from his pocket a long, leather belt, such as travelers use for the carrying of valuables. It was evidently heavy, and the musical clink which accompanied his motion proclaimed the contents to be gold.

Brandt appeared next; he was white and held his hand to his breast. There were dark stains on his hunting coat, which he removed to expose a shirt blotched with red.

"You ain't much hurt, I reckon?" inquired Legget solicitously.

"No; but I'm bleeding bad," replied Brandt coolly. He then called an Indian and went among the willows skirting the stream.

"So I'm to be in this border crew?" asked Case, looking up at Legget.

"Sure," replied the big outlaw. "You're a handy fellar, Case, an' after I break you into border ways you will fit in here tip-top. Now you'd better stick by me. When Eb Zane, his brother Jack, an' Wetzel find out this here day's work, hell will be a cool place compared with their whereabouts. You'll be safe with me, an' this is the only place on the border, I reckon, where you can say your life is your own."

"I'm yer mate, cap'n. I've sailed with soldiers, pirates, sailors, an' I guess I can navigate this borderland. Do we mess here? You didn't come far."

"Wal, I ain't pertikuler, but I don't like eatin' with buzzards," said Legget, with a grin. "Thet's why we moved a bit."

"What's buzzards?"

"Ho! ho! Mebbe you'll hev 'em closer'n you'd like, some day, if you'd only know it. Buzzards are fine birds, most particular birds, as won't eat nothin' but flesh, an' white man or Injun is pie fer 'em."

"Cap'n, I've seed birds as wouldn't wait till a man was dead," said Case.

"Haw! haw! you can't come no sailor yarns on this fellar. Wal, now, we've got ther Englishman's gold. One or t'other of us might jest as well hev it all."

"Right yer are, cap'n. Dice, cards, anyways, so long as I knows the game."

"Here, Jenks, hand over yer clickers, an' bring us a flat stone," said Legget, sitting on the moss and emptying the belt in front of him. Case took a small bag from the dark blue jacket that had so lately covered Mordaunt's shoulders, and poured out its bright contents.

"This coat ain't worth keepin'," he said, holding it up. The garment was rent and slashed, and under the left sleeve was a small, blood-stained hole where one of Brandt's blows had fallen. "Hullo, what's this?" muttered the sailor, feeling in the pocket of the jacket. "Blast my timbers, hooray!"

He held up a small, silver-mounted whiskey flask, unscrewed the lid, and lifted the vessel to his mouth.

"I'm kinder thirsty myself," suggested Legget.

"Cap'n, a nip an' no more," Case replied, holding the flask to Legget's lips.

The outlaw called Jenks now returned with a flat stone which he placed between the two men. The Indians gathered around. With greedy eyes they bent their heads over the gamblers, and watched every movement with breathless interest. At each click of the dice, or clink of gold, they uttered deep exclamations.

"Luck's again' ye, cap'n," said Case, skillfully shaking the ivory cubes.

"Hain't I got eyes?" growled the outlaw.

Steadily his pile of gold diminished, and darker grew his face.

"Cap'n, I'm a bad wind to draw," Case rejoined, drinking again from the flask. His naturally red face had become livid, his skin moist, and his eyes wild with excitement.

"Hullo! If them dice wasn't Jenks's, an' I hadn't played afore with him, I'd swear they's loaded."

"You ain't insinuatin' nothin', cap'n?" inquired Case softly, hesitating with the dice in his hands, his evil eyes glinting at Legget.

"No, you're fair enough," growled the leader. "It's my tough luck."

The game progressed with infrequent runs of fortune for the outlaw, and presently every piece of gold lay in a shining heap before the sailor.

"Clean busted!" exclaimed Legget in disgust.

"Can't you find nothin' more?" asked Case.

The outlaw's bold eyes wandered here and there until they rested upon the prisoner.

"I'll play ther lass against yer pile of gold," he growled. "Best two throws out 'en three. See here, she's as much mine as Brandt's."

"Make it half my pile an' I'll go you."

"Nary time. Bet, or give me back what yer win," replied Legget gruffly.

"She's a trim little craft, no mistake," said Case, critically surveying Helen. "All right, cap'n, I've sportin' blood, an' I'll bet. Yer throw first."

Legget won the first cast, and Case the second. With deliberation the outlaw shook the dice in his huge fist, and rattled them out upon the stone. "Hah!" he cried in delight. He had come within one of the highest score possible. Case nonchalantly flipped the little white blocks. The Indians crowded forward, their dusky eyes shining.

Legget swore in a terrible voice which reechoed from the stony cliff. The sailor was victorious. The outlaw got up, kicked the stone and dice in the brook, and walked away from the group. He strode to and fro under one of the trees. Gruffly he gave an order to the Indians. Several of them began at once to kindle a fire. Presently he called Jenks, who was fishing the dice out of the brook, and began to converse earnestly with him, making fierce gestures and casting lowering glances at the sailor.

Case was too drunk now to see that he had incurred the enmity of the outlaw leader. He drank the last of the rum, and tossed the silver flask to an Indian, who received the present with every show of delight.

Case then, with the slow, uncertain movements of a man whose mind is befogged, began to count his gold; but only to gather up a few pieces when they slipped out of his trembling hands to roll on the moss. Laboriously, seriously, he kept at it with the doggedness of a drunken man. Apparently he had forgotten the others. Failing to learn the value of the coins by taking up each in turn, he arranged them in several piles, and began to estimate his wealth in sections.

In the meanwhile Helen, who had not failed to take in the slightest detail of what was going on, saw that a plot was hatching which boded ill to the sailor. Moreover, she heard Legget and Jenks whispering.

"I kin take him from right here 'atwixt his eyes," said Jenks softly, and tapped his rifle significantly.

"Wal, go ahead, only I rather hev it done quieter," answered Legget. "We're yet a long ways, near thirty miles, from my camp, an' there's no tellin' who's in ther woods. But we've got ter git rid of ther fresh sailor, an' there's no surer way."

Cautiously cocking his rifle, Jenks deliberately raised it to his shoulder. One of the Indian sentinels who stood near at hand, sprang forward and struck up the weapon. He spoke a single word to Legget, pointed to the woods above the cliff, and then resumed his statue-like attitude.

"I told yer, Jenks, that it wouldn't do. The redskin scents somethin' in the woods, an' ther's an Injun I never seed fooled. We mustn't make a noise. Take yer knife an' tomahawk, crawl down below the edge o' the bank an' slip up on him. I'll give half ther gold fer ther job."

Jenks buckled his belt more tightly, gave one threatening glance at the sailor, and slipped over the bank. The bed of the brook lay about six feet below the level of the ground. This afforded an opportunity for the outlaw to get behind Case without being observed. A moment passed. Jenks disappeared round a bend of the stream. Presently his grizzled head appeared above the bank. He was immediately behind the sailor; but still some thirty feet away. This ground must be covered quickly and noiselessly. The outlaw began to crawl. In his right hand he grasped a tomahawk, and between his teeth was a long knife. He looked like a huge, yellow bear.

The savages, with the exception of the sentinel who seemed absorbed in the dense thicket on the cliff, sat with their knees between their hands, watching the impending tragedy.

Nothing but the merest chance, or some extraordinary intervention, could avert Case's doom. He was gloating over his gold. The creeping outlaw made no more noise than a snake. Nearer and nearer he came; his sweaty face shining in the sun; his eyes tigerish; his long body slipping silently over the grass. At length he was within five feet of the sailor. His knotty hands were dug into the sward as he gathered energy for a sudden spring.

At that very moment Case, with his hand on his knife, rose quickly and turned round.

The outlaw, discovered in the act of leaping, had no alternative, and spring he did, like a panther.

The little sailor stepped out of line with remarkable

quickness, and as the yellow body whirled past him, his knife flashed blue-bright in the sunshine.

Jenks fell forward, his knife buried in the grass beneath him, and his outstretched hand still holding the tomahawk.

"Tryin' ter double-cross me fer my gold," muttered the sailor, sheathing his weapon. He never looked to see whether or no his blow had been fatal. "These border fellars might think a man as sails the seas can't handle a knife." He calmly began gathering up his gold, evidently indifferent to further attack.

Helen saw Legget raise his own rifle, but only to have it struck aside as had Jenks's. This time the savage whispered earnestly to Legget, who called the other Indians around him. The sentinel's low throaty tones mingled with the soft babbling of the stream. No sooner had he ceased speaking than the effect of his words showed how serious had been the information, warning or advice. The Indians cast furtive glances toward the woods. Two of them melted like shadows into the red and gold thicket. Another stealthily slipped from tree to tree until he reached the open ground, then dropped into the grass, and was seen no more until his dark body rose under the cliff. He stole along the green-stained wall, climbed a rugged corner, and vanished amid the dense foliage.

Helen felt that she was almost past discernment or thought. The events of the day succeeding one another so swiftly, and fraught with panic, had, despite her hope and fortitude, reduced her to a helpless condition of piteous fear. She understood that the savages scented danger, or had, in their mysterious way, received intelligence such as rendered them wary and watchful.

"Come on, now, an' make no noise," said Legget to Case. "Bring the girl, an' see that she steps light."

"Ay, ay, cap'n," replied the sailor. "Where's Brandt?"

"He'll be comin' soon's his cut stops bleedin'. I reckon he's weak yet."

Case gathered up his goods, and, tucking it under his arm, grasped Helen's arm. She was leaning against the tree, and when he pulled her, she wrenched herself free, rising with difficulty. His disgusting touch and revolting face had revived her sensibilities.

"Yer kin begin duty by carryin' thet," said Case, thrusting the package into Helen's arms. She let it drop without moving a hand.

"I'm runnin' this ship. Yer belong to me," hissed Case, and then he struck her on the head. Helen uttered a low cry of distress, and half-staggered against the tree. The sailor picked up the package. This time she took it, trembling with horror.

"Thet's right. Now, give ther cap'n a kiss," he leered, and jostled against her.

Helen pushed him violently. With agonized eyes she appealed to the Indians. They were engaged tying up their packs. Legget looked on with a lazy grin.

"Oh! oh!" breathed Helen as Case seized her again. She tried to scream, but could not make a sound. The evil eyes, the beastly face, transfixed her with terror.

Case struck her twice, then roughly pulled her toward him.

Half-fainting, unable to move, Helen gazed at the heated, bloated face approaching hers.

When his coarse lips were within a few inches of her lips something hot hissed across her brow. Following so closely as to be an accompaniment, rang out with singular clearness the sharp crack of a rifle.

Case's face changed. The hot, surging flush faded; the expression became shaded, dulled into vacant emptiness;

his eyes rolled wildly, then remained fixed, with a look of dark surprise. He stood upright an instant, swayed with the regular poise of a falling oak, and then plunged backward to the ground. His face, ghastly and livid, took on the awful calm of death.

A very small hole, reddish-blue round the edges, dotted the center of his temple.

Legget stared aghast at the dead sailor; then he possessed himself of the bag of gold.

"Saved me ther trouble," he muttered, giving Case a kick.

The Indians glanced at the little figure, then out into the flaming thickets. Each savage sprang behind a tree with incredible quickness. Legget saw this, and grasping Helen, he quickly led her within cover of the chestnut.

Brandt appeared with his Indian companion, and both leaped to shelter behind a clump of birches near where Legget stood. Brandt's hawk eyes flashed upon the dead Jenks and Case. Without asking a question he seemed to take in the situation. He stepped over and grasped Helen by the arm.

"Who killed Case?" he asked in a whisper, staring at the little blue hole in the sailor's temple.

No one answered.

The two Indians who had gone into the woods to the right of the stream, now returned. Hardly were they under the trees with their party, when the savage who had gone off alone arose out of the grass to the left of the brook, took it with a flying leap, and darted into their midst. He was the sentinel who had knocked up the weapons, thereby saving Case's life twice. He was lithe and supple, but not young. His grave, shadowy-lined, iron visage showed the traces of time and experience. All gazed at him as at one whose wisdom was greater than theirs.

"Old Horse," said Brandt in English. "Haven't I seen bullet holes like this?"

The Chippewa bent over Case, and then slowly straightened his tall form.

"*Deathwind!*" he replied, answering in the white man's language.

His Indian companions uttered low, plaintive murmurs, not signifying fear so much as respect.

Brandt turned as pale as the clean birch-bark on the tree near him. The gray flare of his eyes gave out a terrible light of certainty and terror.

"Legget, you needn't try to hide your trail," he hissed, and it seemed as if there was a bitter, reckless pleasure in these words.

Then the Chippewa glided into the low bushes bordering the creek. Legget followed him, with Brandt leading Helen, and the other Indians brought up the rear, each one sending wild, savage glances into the dark, surrounding forest.

CHAPTER XIX

A dense white fog rose from the river, obscuring all objects, when the bordermen rolled out of their snug bed of leaves. The air was cool and bracing, faintly fragrant with dying foliage and the damp, dewy luxuriance of the ripened season. Wetzel pulled from under the protecting ledge a bundle of bark and sticks he had put there to keep dry, and built a fire, while Jonathan fashioned a cup from a green fruit resembling a gourd, filling it at a spring near by.

"Lew, there's a frosty nip in the water this mornin'," said Jonathan.

"I reckon. It's gettin' along into fall now. Any clear, still night'll fetch all the leaves, an' strip the trees bare as burned timber," answered Wetzel, brushing the ashes off the strip of meat he had roasted. "Get a stick, an' help me cook the rest of this chunk of bison. The sun'll be an hour breakin' up thet mist, an' we can't clear out till then. Mebbe we won't have no chance to light another fire soon."

With these bordermen everything pertaining to their lonely lives, from the lighting of a fire to the trailing of a redskin, was singularly serious. No gladsome song ever came from their lips; there was no jollity around their campfire. Hunters had their moments of rapturous delight; bordermen knew the peace, the content of the wilderness, but their pursuits racked nerve and heart. Wetzel had his moments of frenzied joy, but they passed with the echo of his vengeful yell. Jonathan's happiness, such as it was, had been to roam the forests. That, before a woman's eyes had dispelled it, had been enough, and compensated him for the gloomy, bloody phantoms which haunted him.

The bordermen, having partaken of the frugal breakfast, stowed in their spacious pockets all the meat that was left, and were ready for the day's march. They sat silent for a time waiting for the mist to lift. It broke in places, rolled in huge billows, sailed aloft like great white clouds, and again hung tenaciously to the river and the plain. Away in the west blue patches of sky shone through the rifts, and eastward banks of misty vapor reddened beneath the rising sun. Suddenly from beneath the silver edge of the rising pall the sun burst gleaming gold, disclosing the winding valley with its steaming river.

"We'll make upstream fer Two Islands, an' cross there if so be we've reason," Wetzel had said.

Through the dewy dells, avoiding the wet grass and bushes, along the dark, damp glades with their yellow carpets, under the thinning arches of the trees, down the gentle slops of the ridges, rich with green moss, the bordermen glided like gray shadows. The forest was yet asleep. A squirrel frisked up an oak and barked quarrelsomely at these strange, noiseless visitors. A crow cawed from somewhere overhead. These were the only sounds disturbing the quiet early hour.

As the bordermen advanced the woods lightened and awoke to life and joy. Birds sang, trilled, warbled, or whistled their plaintive songs, peculiar to the dying season, and in harmony with the glory of the earth. Birds that in earlier seasons would have screeched and fought, now sang and fluttered side by side, in fraternal parade on their slow pilgrimage to the far south.

"Bad time fer us, when the birds are so tame, an' chipper. We can't put faith in them these days," said Wetzel. "Seems like they never was wild. I can tell, 'cept at this season, by the way they whistle an' act in the woods, if there's been any Injuns along the trails."

The greater part of the morning passed thus with the bordermen steadily traversing the forest; here, through a spare and gloomy wood, blasted by fire, worn by age, with many a dethroned monarch of bygone times rotting to punk and duff under the ferns, with many a dark, seamed and ragged king still standing, but gray and bald of head and almost ready to take his place in the forest of the past; there, through a maze of young saplings where each ash, maple, hickory, and oak added some new and beautiful hue to the riot of color.

"I just had a glimpse of the lower island, as we passed an opening in the thicket," said Jonathan.

"We ain't far away," replied Wetzel.

The bordermen walked less rapidly in order to proceed with more watchfulness. Every rod or two they stopped to listen.

"You think Legget's across the river?" asked Jonathan.

"He was two days back, an' had his gang with him. He's up to some bad work, but I can't make out what. One thing, I never seen his trail so near Fort Henry."

They emerged at length into a more open forest which skirted the river. At a point still some distance ahead, but plainly in sight, two small islands rose out of the water.

"Hist! What's that?" whispered Wetzel, slipping his hand in Jonathan's arm.

A hundred yards beyond lay a long, dark figure stretched at full length under one of the trees close to the bank.

"Looks like a man," said Jonathan.

"You've hit the mark. Take a good peep roun' now, Jack, fer we're comin' somewhere near the trail we want."

Minutes passed while the patient bordermen searched the forest with their eyes, seeking out every tree within rifle range, or surveyed the level glades, scrutinized the hollows, and bent piercing eyes upon the patches of ferns.

"If there's a redskin around he ain't big enough to hold a gun," said Wetzel, moving forward again, yet still with that same stealthy step and keen caution.

Finally they were gazing down upon the object which had attracted Wetzel's attention.

"Will Sheppard!" cried Jonathan. "Is he dead? What's this mean?"

Wetzel leaned over the prostrate lad, and then quickly turned to his companion.

"Get some water. Take his cap. No, he ain't even hurt bad, unless he's got some wound as don't show."

Jonathan returned with the water, and Wetzel bathed the bloody face. When the gash on Will's forehead was clean, it told the bordermen much.

"Not an hour old, that blow," muttered Wetzel.

"He's comin' to," said Jonathan as Will stirred uneasily and moaned. Presently the lad opened his eyes and sat bolt upright. He looked bewildered for a moment, and felt his head while gazing vaguely at the bordermen. Suddenly he cried:

"I remember! We were captured, brought here, and I was struck down by that villain Case."

"We? Who was with you?" asked Jonathan slowly.

"Helen. We came after flowers and leaves. While in full sight of the fort I saw an Indian. We hurried back," he cried, and proceeded with broken, panting voice to tell his story.

Jonathan Zane leaped to his feet with face deathly white and eyes blue-black, like burning stars.

"Jack, study the trail while I get the lad acrost the river, an' steered fer home," said Wetzel, and then he asked Will if he could swim.

"Yes; but you will find a canoe there in those willows."

"Come, lad, we've no time to spare," added Wetzel, sliding down the bank and entering the willows. He came out almost immediately with the canoe which he launched.

Will turned that he might make a parting appeal to Jonathan to save Helen; but could not speak. The expression on the borderman's face frightened him.

Motionless and erect Jonathan stood, his arms folded and his white, stern face distorted with the agony of remorse, fear, and anguish, which, even as Will gazed, froze into an awful, deadly look of fateful purpose.

Wetzel pushed the canoe off, and paddled with powerful strokes; he left Will on the opposite bank, and returned as swiftly as he could propel the light craft.

The bordermen met each other's glance, and had little need of words. Wetzel's great shoulders began to sag slightly, and his head lowered as his eyes sought the grass; a dark and gloomy shade overcast his features. Thus he passed from borderman to Deathwind. The sough of the wind overhead among the almost naked branches might well have warned Indians and renegades that Deathwind was on the trail!

"Brandt's had a hand in this, an' the Englishman's a fool!" said Wetzel.

"An hour ahead; can we come up with them before they join Brandt an' Legget?"

"We can try, but like as not we'll fail. Legget's gang is thirteen strong by now. I said it! Somethin' told me—a hard trail, a long trail, an' our last trail."

"It's over thirty miles to Legget's camp. We know the woods, an' every stream, an' every cover," hissed Jonathan Zane.

With no further words Wetzel took the trail on the run, and so plain was it to his keen eyes that he did not relax his steady lope except to stop and listen at regular intervals. Jonathan followed with easy swing. Through forest and meadow, over hill and valley, they ran, fleet and tireless. Once, with unerring instinct, they abruptly left the broad trail and cut far across a wide and rugged ridge to come again upon the tracks of the marching band. Then, in open country they reduced their speed to a walk. Ahead, in a narrow valley, rose a thicket of willows, yellow in the sunlight, and impenetrable to human vision. Like huge snakes the bordermen crept into this copse, over the sand, under the low branches, hard on the trail. Finally, in a light, open space, where the sun shone through a network of yellow branches and foliage, Wetzel's hand was laid upon Jonathan's shoulder.

"Listen! Hear that!" he whispered.

Jonathan heard the flapping of wings, and a low, hissing sound, not unlike that made by a goose.

"Buzzards!" he said, with a dark, grim smile. "Mebbe Brandt has begun our work. Come."

Out into the open they crawled to put to flight a flock of huge black birds with grisly, naked necks, hooked beaks, and long, yellow claws. Upon the green grass lay two half-naked men, ghastly, bloody, in terribly limp and lifeless positions.

"Metzar's man Smith, and Mordaunt!"

Jonathan Zane gazed darkly into the steely, sightless eyes of the traitor. Death's awful calm had set the expression; but the man's whole life was there, its better part sadly shining forth among the cruel shadows.

His body was mutilated in a frightful manner. Cuts, stabs, and slashes told the tale of a long encounter, brought to an end by one clean stroke.

"Come here, Lew. You've seen men chopped up; but look at this dead Englishman," called Zane.

Mordaunt lay weltering in a crimson tide. Strangely though, his face was uninjured. A black bruise showed under his fair hair. The ghost of a smile seemed to hover around his set lips, yet almost intangible though it was, it showed that at last he had died a man. His left shoulder, side, and arm showed where the brunt of Brandt's attack had fallen.

"How'd he ever fight so?" mused Jonathan.

"You never can tell," replied Wetzel. "Mebbe he killed this other fellar, too; but I reckon not. Come, we must go slow now, fer Legget is near at hand."

Jonathan brought huge, flat stones from the brook, and laid them over Mordaunt; then, cautiously he left the glade on Wetzel's trail.

Five hundred yards farther on Wetzel had ceased following the outlaw's tracks to cross the creek and climb a ridge. He was beginning his favorite trick of making a wide detour. Jonathan hurried forward, feeling he was safe from observation. Soon he distinguished the tall, brown figure of his comrade gliding ahead from tree to tree, from bush to bush.

"See them maples an' chestnuts down thar," said Wetzel when Jonathan had come up, pointing through an opening in the foliage. "They've stopped fer some reason."

On through the forest the bordermen glided. They kept near the summit of the ridge, under the best cover they could find, and passed swiftly over this half-circle. When beginning once more to draw toward the open grove in the valley, they saw a long, irregular cliff, densely wooded. They swerved a little, and made for this excellent covert.

They crawled the last hundred yards and never took a fern, moved a leaf, or broke a twig. Having reached the brink of the low precipice, they saw the grassy meadow below, the straggling trees, the brook, the group of Indians crowding round the white men.

"See that point of rock thar? It's better cover," whispered Wetzel.

Patiently, with no hurry or excitement, they slowly made their difficult way among the rocks and ferns to the vantage point desired. Taking a position like this was one the bordermen strongly favored. They could see everywhere in front, and had the thick woods at their backs.

"What are they up to?" whispered Jonathan, as he and Wetzel lay close together under a mass of grapevine still tenacious of its broad leaves.

"Dicin'," answered Wetzel. "I can see 'em throw; anyways, nothin' but bettin' ever makes redskins act like that."

"Who's playin'? Where's Brandt?"

"I can make out Legget; see his shaggy head. The other must be Case. Brandt ain't in sight. Nursin' a hurt perhaps. Ah! See thar! Over under the big tree as stands dark-like agin the thicket. Thet's an Injun, an' he looks too quiet an' keen to suit me. We'll have a care of him."

"Must be playin' fer Mordaunt's gold."

"Like as not, for where'd them ruffians get any 'cept they stole it."

"Aha! They're gettin' up! See Legget walk away shakin' his big head. He's mad. Mebbe he'll be madder presently," growled Jonathan.

"Case's left alone. He's countin' his winnin's. Jack, look out fer more work took off our hands."

"By gum! See that Injun knock up a leveled rifle."

"I told you, an' thet redskin hes his suspicions. He's seen us down along ther ridge. There's Helen, sittin' behind the biggest tree. Thet Injun guard, 'afore he moved, kept us from seein' her."

Jonathan made no answer to this; but his breath literally hissed through his clenched teeth.

"Thar goes the other outlaw," whispered Wetzel, as if his comrade could not see. "It's all up with Case. See the sneak bendin' down the bank. Now, thet's a poor way. It'd better be done from the front, walkin' up natural-like, instead of tryin' to cover thet wide stretch. Case'll see him or hear him sure. Thar, he's up now, an' crawlin'. He's too slow, too slow. Aha! I knew it—Case turns. Look at the outlaw spring! Well, did you see thet little cuss whip his knife! One more less fer us to quiet. Thet makes three, Jack, an' mebbe soon, it'll be four."

"They're holdin' a council," said Jonathan.

"I see two Injuns sneakin' off into the woods, an' here comes thet guard. He's a keen redskin, Jack, fer we did come light through the brush. Mebbe it'd be well to stop his scutin'."

"Lew, that villain Case is bullyin' Helen!" cried Jonathan.

"Sh-sh-h," whispered Wetzel.

"See! he's pulled her to her feet. Oh! He struck her! Oh!"

Jonathan leveled his rifle and would have fired, but for the iron grasp on his wrist.

"Hev you lost yer senses? It's full two hundred paces, an' too far fer your piece," said Wetzel in a whisper. "An' it ain't sense to try from here."

"Lend me your gun! Lend me your gun!"

Silently Wetzel handed him the long, black rifle.

Jonathan raised it, but trembled so violently that the barrel wavered like a leaf in the breeze.

"Take it, I can't cover him," groaned Jonathan. "This is new to me. I ain't myself. God! Lew, he struck her again! *Again!* He's tryin' to kiss her! Wetzel, if you're my friend, kill him!"

"Jack, it'd be better to wait, an'—"

"I love her," breathed Jonathan.

The long, black barrel swept up to a level and stopped. White smoke belched from among the green leaves; the report rang throughout the forest.

"Ah! I saw him stop an' pause," hissed Jonathan. "He stands, he sways, he falls! Death for yours, you sailor-beast!"

CHAPTER XX

The bordermen watched Legget and his band disappear into the thicket adjoining the grove. When the last dark, lithe form glided out of sight among the yellowing copse, Jonathan leaped from the low cliff, and had hardly reached the ground before Wetzel dashed down to the grassy turf.

Again they followed the outlaw's trail, darker-faced, fiercer-visaged than ever, with cocked, tightly gripped rifles thrust well before them, and light feet that scarcely brushed the leaves.

Wetzel halted after a long tramp up and down the ridges, and surveyed with keen intent the lay of the land ahead.

"Sooner or later we'll hear from that redskin as discovered us a ways back," whispered he. "I wish we might get a crack at him afore he hinders us bad. I ain't seen many keener Injuns. It's lucky we fixed ther arrow-shootin' Shawnee. We'd never hev beat thet combination. An' fer all of thet I'm worrin' some about the goin' ahead."

"Ambush?" Jonathan asked.

"Like as not. Legget'll send thet Injun back, an' mebbe more'n him. Jack, see them little footprints? They're Helen's. Look how she's draggin' along. Almost tuckered out. Legget can't travel many more miles to-day. He'll make a stand somewheres, an' lose all his redskins afore he gives up the lass."

"I'll never live through to-night with her in that gang. She'll be saved, or dead, before the stars pale in the light of the moon."

"I reckon we're nigh the end for some us. It'll be moonlight an hour after dusk, an' now it's only the middle of the afternoon; we've time enough fer anythin'. Now, Jack, let's not tackle the trail straight. We'll split, an' go round to head 'em off. See thet dead white oak standin' high over thar?"

Jonathan looked out between the spreading branches of a beech, and saw, far over a low meadow, luxuriant with grasses and rushes and bright with sparkling ponds and streams, a dense wood out of which towered a bare, bleached treetop.

"You slip around along the right side of this meader, an' I'll take the left side. Go slow, an' hev yer eyes open. We'll meet under thet big dead tree. I allow we can see it from anywhere around. We'll leave the trail here, an' take it up farther on. Legget's goin' straight for his camp; he ain't losin' an inch. He wants to get in thet rocky hole of his'n."

Wetzel stepped off the trail, glided into the woods, and vanished.

Jonathan turned to the right, traversed the summit of the ridge, softly traveled down its slope, and, after crossing a slow, eddying, quiet stream, gained the edge of the forest on that side of the swamp. A fringe of briars and prickly thorns bordered this wood affording an excellent cover. On the right the land rose rather abruptly. He saw that by walking up a few paces he could command a view of the entire swamp, as well as the ridge beyond, which contained Wetzel, and, probably, the outlaw and his band.

Remembering his comrade's admonition, Jonathan curbed his unusual impatience and moved slowly. The wind swayed the treetops, and rustled the fallen leaves. Birds sang as if thinking the warm, soft weather was summer come again. Squirrels dropped heavy nuts that cracked on the limbs, or fell with a thud to the ground, and they scampered over the dry earth, scratching up the leaves as they barked and scolded. Crows cawed clamorously after a hawk that had darted under the treetops to escape them; deer loped swiftly up the hill, and a lordly elk rose from a wallow in the grassy swamp, crashing into the thicket.

When two-thirds around this oval plain, which was a mile long and perhaps one-fourth as wide, Jonathan ascended the hill to make a survey. The grass waved bright brown and golden in the sunshine, swished in the wind, and swept like a choppy sea to the opposite ridge. The hill was not densely wooded. In many places the red-brown foliage opened upon irregular patches, some black, as if having been burned over, others showing the yellow and purple colors of the low thickets and the gray, barren stones.

Suddenly Jonathan saw something darken one of these sunlit plots. It might have been a deer. He studied the rolling, rounded treetops, the narrow strips between the black trunks, and the open places that were clear in the sunshine. He had nearly come to believe he had seen a small animal or bird flit across the white of the sky far in the background, when he distinctly saw dark figures stealing along past a green-gray rock, only to disappear under colored banks of foliage. Presently, lower down, they reappeared and crossed an open patch of yellow fern. Jonathan counted them. Two were rather yellow in color, the hue of buckskin; another, slight of stature as compared with the first, and light gray by contrast. Then six black, slender, gliding forms crossed the space. Jonathan then lost sight of them, and did not get another glimpse. He knew them to be Legget and his band. The slight figure was Helen.

Jonathan broke into a run, completed the circle around the swamp, and slowed into a walk when approaching the big dead tree where he was to wait for Wetzel.

Several rods beyond the lowland he came to a wood of white oaks, all giants rugged and old, with scarcely a sapling intermingled with them. Although he could not see the objective point, he knew from his accurate sense of distance that he was near it. As he entered the wood he swept its whole length and width with his eyes, he darted forward twenty paces to halt suddenly behind a tree. He knew full well that a sharply moving object was more difficult to see in the woods, than one stationary. Again he ran, fleet and light, a few paces ahead to take up a position as before behind a tree. Thus he traversed the forest. On the other side he found the dead oak of which Wetzel had spoken.

Its trunk was hollow. Jonathan squeezed himself into the blackened space, with his head in a favorable position behind a projecting knot, where he could see what might occur near at hand.

He waited for what seemed to him a long while, during which he neither saw nor heard anything, and then suddenly, the report of a rifle rang out. A single, piercing scream followed. Hardly had the echo ceased when three hollow reports, distinctly different in tone from the first, could be heard from the same direction. In quick succession short, fierce yells attended rather than succeeded, the reports.

Jonathan stepped out of the hiding place, cocked his rifle, and fixed a sharp eye on the ridge before him whence those startling cries had come. The first rifleshot, unlike any other in its short, spiteful, stinging quality, was unmistakably Wetzel's. Zane had heard it, followed many times, as now, by the wild-death-cry of a savage. The other reports were of Indian guns, and the yells were the clamoring, exultant cries of Indians in pursuit.

Far down where the open forest met the gloom of the thickets, a brown figure flashed across the yellow ground. Darting among the trees, across the glades, it moved so swiftly that Jonathan knew it was Wetzel. In another instant a chorus of yelps resounded from the foliage, and three savages burst through the thicket almost at right angles with the fleeing borderman, running to intercept him. The borderman did not swerve from his course; but came on straight toward the dead tree, with the wonderful fleetness that so often had served him well.

Even in that moment Jonathan thought of what desperate chances his comrade had taken. The trick was plain. Wetzel had, most likely, shot the dangerous scout, and, taking to his heels, raced past the others, trusting to his speed and their poor marksmanship to escape with a whole skin.

When within a hundred yards of the oak Wetzel's strength apparently gave out. His speed deserted him; he ran awkwardly, and limped. The savages burst out into full cry like a pack of hungry wolves. They had already emptied their rifles at him, and now, supposing one of the shots had taken effect, redoubled their efforts, making the forest ring with their short, savage yells. One gaunt, dark-bodied Indian with a long, powerful, springy stride easily distanced his companions, and evidently sure of gaining the coveted scalp of the borderman, rapidly closed the gap between them as he swung aloft his tomahawk, yelling the war-cry.

The sight on Jonathan's rifle had several times covered

this savage's dark face; but when he was about to press the trigger Wetzel's fleeting form, also in line with the savage, made it extremely hazardous to take a shot.

Jonathan stepped from his place of concealment, and let out a yell that pealed high over the cries of the savages.

Wetzel suddenly dropped flat on the ground.

With a whipping crack of Jonathan's rifle, the big Indian plunged forward on his face.

The other Indians, not fifty yards away, stopped aghast at the fate of their comrade, and were about to seek the shelter of trees when, with his terrible yell, Wetzel sprang up and charged upon them. He had left his rifle where he fell, but his tomahawk glittered as he ran. The lameness had been a trick, for now he covered ground with a swiftness which caused his former progress to seem slow.

The Indians, matured and seasoned warriors though they were, gave but one glance at this huge, brown figure bearing down upon them like a fiend, and uttering the Indian name of *Deathwind*, wavered, broke, and ran.

One, not so fleet as his companion, Wetzel overtook and cut down with a single stroke. The other gained an hundred-yard start in the slight interval of Wetzel's attack, and, spurred on by a pealing, awful cry in the rear, sped swiftly in and out among the trees until he was lost to view.

Wetzel scalped the two dead savages, and, after returning to regain his rifle, joined Jonathan at the dead oak.

"Jack, you can never tell how things is comin' out. Thet redskin I allowed might worry us a bit, fooled me as slick as you ever saw, an I hed to shoot him. Knowin' it was a case of runnin', I just cut fer this oak, drew the redskins' fire, an' hed 'em arter me quicker 'n you'd say Jack Robinson. I was hopin' you'd be here; but wasn't sure till I'd seen your rifle. Then I kinder got a kink in my leg jest to coax the brutes on."

"Three more quiet," said Jonathan Zane. "What now?"

"We've headed Legget, an' we'll keep nosin' him off his course. Already he's lookin' fer a safe campin' place for the night."

"There is none in these woods, fer him."

"We didn't plan this gettin' between him an' his camp, but couldn't be better fixed. A mile farther along the ridge, is a campin' place, with a spring in a little dell close under a big stone, an' well wooded. Legget's headin' straight fer it. With a couple of Injuns guardin' thet spot, he'll think he's safe. But I know the place, an' can crawl to thet rock the darkest night thet ever was an' never crack a stick."

In the gray of the deepening twilight Jonathan Zane sat alone. An howl hooted dismally in the dark woods beyond the thicket where the borderman crouched waiting for Wetzel. His listening ear detected a soft, rustling sound like the play of a mole under the leaves. A branch trembled and swung back; a soft footstep followed and Wetzel came into the retreat.

"Well?" asked Jonathan impatiently, as Wetzel deliberately sat down and laid his rifle across his knees.

"Easy, Jack, easy. We've an hour to wait."

"The time I've already waited has been long for me."

"They're thar," said Wetzel grimly.

"How far from here?"

"A half-hour's slow crawl."

"Close by?" hissed Jonathan.

"Too near fer you to get excited."

"Let us go; it's as light now as in the gray of mornin'."

"Mornin' would be best. Injuns get sleepy along towards day. I've ever found thet time the best. But we'll be lucky if we ketch these redskins asleep."

"Lew, I can't wait here all night. I won't leave her longer with that renegade. I've got to free or kill her."

"Most likely it'll be the last," said Wetzel simply.

"Well, so be it then," and the borderman hung his head.

"You needn't worry none, 'bout Helen. I jest had a good look at her, not half an hour back. She's tired-out; but full of spunk yet. I seen thet when Brandt went near her. Legget's got his hands full jest now with the redskins. He's hevin' trouble keepin' them on this slow trail. I ain't sayin' they're skeered; but they're mighty restless."

"Will you take the chance now?"

"I reckon you needn't hev asked thet."

"Tell me the lay of the land."

"Wal, if we get to this rock I spoke 'bout, we'll be right over 'em. It's ten feet high, an' we can jump straight amongst 'em. Most likely two or three'll be guardin' the openin' which is a little ways to the right. Ther's a big tree, the only one, low down by the spring. Helen's under it, half-sittin', half-leanin' against the roots. When I first looked, her hands were free; but I saw Brandt bind her feet. An' he had to get an Injun to help him, fer she kicked like a spirited little filly. There's moss under the tree an' there's where the redskins'll lay down to rest."

"I've got that; now out with your plan."

"Wal, I calkilate it's this. The moon'll be up in about an hour. We'll crawl as we've never crawled afore, because Helen's life depends as much on our not makin' a noise, as it does on fightin' when the time comes. If they hear us afore we're ready to shoot, the lass'll be tomahawked quicker 'n lightnin'. If they don't suspicion us, when the right moment comes you shoot Brandt, yell louder'n you ever did afore, leap amongst 'em, an' cut down the first Injun thet's near you on your way to Helen. Swing her over your arm, an' dig int the woods."

"Well?" asked Jonathan when Wetzel finished.

"That's all," the borderman replied grimly.

"An' leave you all alone to fight Legget an' the rest of 'em?"

"I reckon."

"Not to be thought of."

"Ther's no other way."

"There must be! Let me think; I can't, I'm not myself."

"No other way," repeated Wetzel curtly.

Jonathan's broad hand fastened on Wetzel's shoulder and wheeled him around.

"Have I ever left you alone?"

"This's different," and Wetzel turned away again. His voice was cold and hard.

"How is it different? We've had the same thing to do, almost, more than once."

"We've never had as bad a bunch to handle as Legget's. They're lookin' fer us, an' will be hard to beat."

"That's no reason."

"We never had to save a girl one of us loved."

Jonathan was silent.

"I said this'd be my last trail," continued Wetzel. "I felt it, an' I know it'll be yours."

"Why?"

"If you get away with the girl she'll keep you at home, an' it'll be well. If you don't succeed, you'll die tryin', so it's sure your last trail."

Wetzel's deep, cold voice rang with truth.

"Lew, I can't run away an' leave you to fight those devils alone, after all these years we've been together, I can't."

"No other chance to save the lass."

Jonathan quivered with the force of his emotion. His black eyes glittered; his hands grasped at nothing. Once more he was between love and duty. Again he fought over the old battle, but this time it left him weak.

"You love the big-eyed lass, don't you?" asked Wetzel, turning with softened face and voice.

"I have gone mad!" cried Jonathan, tortured by the simple question of his friend. Those big, dear, wonderful eyes he loved so well, looked at him now from the gloom of the thicket. The old, beautiful, soft glow, the tender light, was there, and more, a beseeching prayer to save her.

Jonathan bowed his head, ashamed to let his friend see the tears that dimmed his eyes.

"Jack, we've follered the trail fer years together. Always you've been true an' staunch. This is our last, but whatever bides we'll break up Legget's band to-night; an' the border'll be cleared, mebbe, for always. At least his race is run. Let thet content you. Our time'd have to come, sooner or later, so why not now? I know how it is, that you want to stick by me; but the lass draws you to her. I understand, an' want you to save her. Mebbe you never dreamed it; but I can tell jest how you feel. All the tremblin', an' softness, an' sweetness, an' delight you've got for thet girl, is no mystery to Lew Wetzel."

"You loved a lass?"

Wetzel bowed his head, as perhaps he had never before in all his life.

"Betty—always," he answered softly.

"My sister!" exclaimed Jonathan, and then his hand closed hard on his comrade's, his mind going back to many things, strange in the past, but now explained. Wetzel had revealed his secret.

"An' it's been all my life, since she wasn't higher 'n my knee. There was a time when I might hev been closer to you than I am now. But I was a mad 'an bloody Injun hater, so I never let her know till I seen it was too late. Wal, wal, no more of me. I only told it fer you."

Jonathan was silent.

"An' now to come back where we left off," continued Wetzel. "Let's take a more hopeful look at this comin' fight. Sure I said it was my last trail, but mebbe it's not. You can never tell. Feelin' as we do, I imagine they've no odds on us. Never in my life did I say to you, least of all to any one else, what I was goin' to do; but I'll tell it now. If I land uninjured amongst thet bunch, I'll kill them all."

The giant borderman's low voice hissed, and stung. His eyes glittered with unearthly fire. His face was cold and gray. He spread out his brawny arms and clenched his huge fists, making the muscles of his broad shoulders roll and bulge.

"I hate the thought, Lew, I hate the thought. Ain't there no other way?"

"No other way."

"I'll do it, Lew, because I'd do the same for you; because I have to, because I love her; but God! it hurts."

"Thet's right," answered Wetzel, his deep voice softening until it was singularly low and rich. "I'm glad you've come to it. An' sure it hurts. I want you to feel so at leavin' me to go it alone. If we both get out alive, I'll come many times to see you an' Helen. If you live an' I don't, think of me sometimes; think of the trails we've crossed together. When the fall comes with its soft, cool air, an' smoky mornin's an' starry nights, when the wind's sad among the bare branches, and the leaves drop down, remember they're fallin' on my grave."

Twilight darkened into gloom; the red tinge in the west changed to opal light; through the trees over a dark ridge a rim of silver glinted and moved.

The moon had risen; the hour was come.

The bordermen tightened their belts, replaced their leggins, tied their hunting coats, loosened their hatchets, looked to the priming of their rifles, and were ready.

Wetzel walked twenty paces and turned. His face was white in the moonlight; his dark eyes softened into a look of love as he gripped his comrade's outstretched hand.

Then he dropped flat on the ground, carefully saw to the position of his rifle, and began to creep. Jonathan kept close at his heels.

Slowly but steadily they crawled, minute after minute. The hazel-nut bushes above them had not yet shed their leaves; the ground was clean and hard, and the course fatefully perfect for their deadly purpose.

A slight rustling of their buckskin garments sounded like the rustling of leaves in a faint breeze.

The moon came out above the trees and still Wetzel advanced softly, steadily, surely.

The owl, lonely sentinel of that wood, hooted dismally. Even his night eyes, which made the darkness seem clear as day, missed those gliding figures. Even he, sure guardian of the wilderness, failed the savages.

Jonathan felt soft moss beneath him; he was now in the woods under the trees. The thicket had been passed.

Wetzel's moccasin pressed softly against Jonathan's head. The first signal!

Jonathan crawled forward, and slightly raised himself.

He was on a rock. The trees were thick and gloomy. Below, the little hollow was almost in the wan moonbeams. Dark figures lay close together. Two savages paced noiselessly to and fro. A slight form rolled in a blanket lay against a tree.

Jonathan felt his arm gently squeezed.

The second signal!

Slowly he thrust forward his rifle, and raised it in unison with Wetzel's. Slowly he rose to his feet as if the same muscles guided them both.

Over his head a twig snapped. In the darkness he had not seen a low branch.

The Indian guards stopped suddenly, and became motionless as stone.

They had heard; but too late.

With the blended roar of the rifles both dropped, lifeless.

Almost under the spouting flame and white cloud of smoke, Jonathan leaped behind Wetzel, over the bank. His yells were mingled with Wetzel's vengeful cry. Like leaping shadows the bordermen were upon their foes.

An Indian sprang up, raised a weapon, and fell beneath Jonathan's savage blow, to rise no more. Over his prostrate body the borderman bounded. A dark, nimble form darted upon the captive. He swung high a blade that shone like silver in the moonlight. His shrill war cry of death rang out with Helen's scream of despair. Even as he swung back her head with one hand in her long hair, his arm descended; but it fell upon the borderman's body. Jonathan and the Indian rolled upon the moss. There was a terrific struggle, a whirling blade, a dull blow which silenced the yell, and the borderman rose alone.

He lifted Helen as if she were a child, leaped the brook, and plunged into the thicket.

The noise of the fearful conflict he left behind, swelled high and hideously on the night air. Above the shrill cries of the Indians, and the furious yells of Legget, rose the mad, booming roar of Wetzel. No rifle cracked; but sodden blows, the clash of steel, the threshing of struggling men, told of the dreadful strife.

Jonathan gained the woods, sped through the moonlit glades, and far on under light and shadow.

The shrill cries ceased; only the hoarse yells and the mad roar could be heard. Gradually these also died away, and the forest was still.

CHAPTER XXI

Next morning, when the mist was breaking and rolling away under the warm rays of the Indian-summer sun, Jonathan Zane beached his canoe on the steep bank before Fort Henry. A pioneer, attracted by the borderman's halloo, ran to the bluff and sounded the alarm with shrill whoops. Among the hurrying, brown-clad figures that answered this summons, was Colonel Zane.

"It's Jack, kurnel, an' he's got her!" cried one.

The doughty colonel gained the bluff to see his brother climbing the bank with a white-faced girl in his arms.

"Well?" he asked, looking darkly at Jonathan. Nothing kindly or genial was visible in his manner now; rather grim and forbidding he seemed, thus showing he had the same blood in his veins as the borderman.

"Lend a hand," said Jonathan. "As far as I know she's not hurt."

They carried Helen toward Colonel Zane's cabin. Many women of the settlement saw them as they passed, and looked gravely at one another, but none spoke. This return of an abducted girl was by no means a strange event.

"Somebody run for Sheppard," ordered Colonel Zane, as they entered his cabin.

Betty, who was in the sitting-room, sprang up and cried: "Oh! Eb! Eb! Don't say she's—"

"No, no, Betts, she's all right. Where's my wife? Ah! Bess, here, get to work."

The Colonel left Helen in the tender, skillful hands of his wife and sister, and followed Jonathan into the kitchen.

"I was just ready for breakfast when I heard some one yell," said he. "Come, Jack, eat something."

They ate in silence. From the sitting-room came excited whispers, a joyous cry from Betty, and a faint voice. Then heavy, hurrying footsteps, followed by Sheppard's words of thanksgiving.

"Where's Wetzel?" began Colonel Zane.

The borderman shook his head gloomily.

"Where did you leave him?"

"We jumped Legget's bunch last night, when the moon was about an hour high. I reckon about fifteen miles northeast. I got away with the lass."

"Ah! Left Lew fighting?"

The borderman answered the question with bowed head.

"You got off well. Not a hurt that I can see, and more than lucky to save Helen. Well, Jack, what do you think about Lew?"

"I'm goin' back," replied Jonathan.

"No! no!"

The door opened to admit Mrs. Zane. She looked bright and cheerful. "Hello, Jack; glad you're home. Helen's all right, only faint from hunger and over-exertion. I want something for her to eat—well! you men didn't leave much."

Colonel Zane went into the sitting-room. Sheppard sat beside the couch where Helen lay, white and wan. Betty and Nell were looking on with their hearts in their eyes. Silas Zane was there, and his wife, with several women neighbors.

"Betty, go fetch Jack in here," whispered the colonel in his sister's ear. "Drag him, if you have to," he added fiercely.

The young woman left the room, to reappear directly with her brother. He came in reluctantly.

As the stern-faced borderman crossed the threshold a smile, beautiful to see, dawned in Helen's eyes.

"I'm glad to see you're comin' round," said Jonathan, but he spoke dully as if his mind was on other things.

"She's a little flighty; but a night's sleep will cure that," cried Mrs. Zane from the kitchen.

"What do you think?" interrupted the colonel. "Jack's not satisfied to get back with Helen unharmed, and a whole skin himself; but he's going on the trail again."

"No, Jack, no, no!" cried Betty.

"What's that I hear?" asked Mrs. Zane as she came in. "Jack's going out again? Well, all I want to say is that he's as mad as a March hare."

"Jonathan, look here," said Silas seriously. "Can't you stay home now?"

"Jack, listen," whispered Betty, going close to him. "Not one of us ever expected to see either you or Helen again, and oh! we are so happy. Do not go away again. You are a man; you do not know, you cannot understand all a woman feels. She must sit and wait, and hope, and pray for the safe return of husband or brother or sweetheart. The long days! Oh, the long sleepless nights, with the wail of the wind in the pines, and the rain on the roof! It is maddening. Do not leave us! Do not leave me! Do not leave Helen! Say you will not, Jack."

To these entreaties the borderman remained silent. He stood leaning on his rifle, a tall, dark, strangely sad and stern man.

"Helen, beg him to stay!" implored Betty.

Colonel Zane took Helen's hand, and stroked it, "Yes," he said, "you ask him, lass. I'm sure you can persuade him to stay."

Helen raised her head. "Is Brandt dead?" she whispered faintly.

Still the borderman failed to speak, but his silence was not an affirmative.

"You said you loved me," she cried wildly. "You said you loved me, yet you didn't kill that monster!"

The borderman, moving quickly like a startled Indian, went out of the door.

Once more Jonathan Zane entered the gloomy, quiet aisles of the forest with his soft, tireless tread hardly stirring the leaves.

It was late in the afternoon when he had long left Two Islands behind, and arrived at the scene of Mordaunt's death. Satisfied with the distance he had traversed, he crawled into a thicket to rest.

Daybreak found him again on the trail. He made a short-cut over the ridges and by the time the mist had lifted from the valley he was within stalking distance of the glade. He approached this in the familiar, slow, cautious manner, and halted behind the big rock from which he and Wetzel had leaped. The wood was solemnly quiet. No twittering of birds could be heard. The only sign of life was a gaunt timber wolf slinking away amid the foliage. Under the big tree the savage who had been killed as he would have murdered Helen, lay a crumpled mass where he had fallen. Two dead Indians were in the center of the glade, and on the other side were three more bloody, lifeless forms. Wetzel was not there, nor Legget, nor Brandt.

"I reckoned so," muttered Jonathan as he studied the scene.

The grass had been trampled, the trees barked, the bushes crushed aside.

Jonathan went out of the glade a short distance, and, circling it, began to look for Wetzel's trail. He found it, and near the light footprints of his comrade were the great, broad moccasin tracks of the outlaw. Further searching disclosed the fact that Brandt must have traveled in line with the others.

With the certainty that Wetzel had killed three of the Indians, and, in some wonderful manner characteristic of him, routed the outlaws of whom he was now in pursuit, Jonathan's smoldering emotion burst forth into full flame. Love for his old comrade, deadly hatred of the outlaws, and passionate thirst for their blood, rioted in his heart.

Like a lynx scenting its quarry, the borderman started on the trail, tireless and unswervable. The traces left by the fleeing outlaws and their pursuer were plain to Jonathan. It was not necessary for him to stop. Legget and Brandt, seeking to escape the implacable Nemesis, were traveling with all possible speed, regardless of the broad trail such hurried movements left behind. They knew full well it would be difficult to throw this wolf off the scent; understood that if any attempt was made to ambush the trail, they must cope with woodcraft keener than an Indian's. Flying in desperation, they hoped to reach the rocky retreat, where, like foxes in their burrows, they believed themselves safe.

When the sun sloped low toward the western horizon, lengthening Jonathan's shadow, he slackened pace. He was entering the rocky, rugged country which marked the approach to the distant Alleghenies. From the top of a ridge he took his bearings, deciding that he was within a few miles of Legget's hiding-place.

At the foot of this ridge, where a murmuring brook

sped softly over its bed, he halted. Here a number of horses had forded the brook. They were iron-shod, which indicated almost to a certainty, that they were stolen horses, and in the hands of Indians.

Jonathan saw where the trail of the steeds was merged into that of the outlaws. He suspected that the Indians and Legget had held a short council. As he advanced the borderman found only the faintest impression of Wetzel's trail. Legget and Brandt no longer left any token of their course. They were riding the horses.

All the borderman cared to know was if Wetzel still pursued. He passed on swiftly up a hill, through a wood of birches where the trail showed on a line of broken ferns, then out upon a low ridge where patches of grass grew sparsely. Here he saw in this last ground no indication of his comrade's trail; nothing was to be seen save the imprints of the horses' hoofs. Jonathan halted behind the nearest underbrush. This sudden move on the part of Wetzel was token that, suspecting an ambush, he had made a detour somewhere, probably in the grove of birches.

All the while his eyes searched the long, barren reach ahead. No thicket, fallen tree, or splintered rocks, such as Indians utilized for an ambush, could be seen. Indians always sought the densely matted underbrush, a windfall, or rocky retreat and there awaited a pursuer. It was one of the borderman's tricks of woodcraft that he could recognize such places.

Far beyond the sandy ridge Jonathan came to a sloping, wooded hillside, upon which were scattered big rocks, some mossy and lichen-covered, and one, a giant boulder, with a crown of ferns and laurel gracing its flat surface. It was such a place as the savages would select for ambush. He knew, however, that if an Indian had hidden himself there Wetzel would have discovered him.

When opposite the rock Jonathan saw a broken fern hanging over the edge. The heavy trail of the horses ran close beside it.

Then with that thoroughness of search which made the borderman what he was, Jonathan leaped upon the rock. There, lying in the midst of the ferns, lay an Indian with sullen, somber face set in the repose of death. In his side was a small bullet hole.

Jonathan examined the savage's rifle. It had been discharged. The rock, the broken fern, the dead Indian, the discharged rifle, told the story of that woodland tragedy.

Wetzel had discovered the ambush. Leaving the trail, he had tricked the redskin into firing, then getting a glimpse of the Indian's red body through the sights of his fatal weapon, the deed was done.

With greater caution Jonathan advanced once more. Not far beyond the rock he found Wetzel's trail. The afternoon was drawing to a close. He could not travel much farther, yet he kept on, hoping to overtake his comrade before darkness set in. From time to time he whistled; but got no answering signal.

When the tracks of the horses were nearly hidden by the gathering dusk, Jonathan decided to halt for the night. He whistled one more note, louder and clearer, and awaited the result with strained ears. The deep silence of the wilderness prevailed, suddenly to be broken by a faint, faraway, melancholy call of the hermit-thrush. It was the answering signal the borderman had hoped to hear.

Not many moments elapsed before he heard another call, low, and near at hand, to which he replied. The bushes parted noiselessly on his left, and the tall form of Wetzel appeared silently out of the gloom.

The two gripped hands in silence.

"Hev you any meat?" Wetzel asked, and as Jonathan

handed him his knapsack, he continued, "I was kinder lookin' fer you. Did you get out all right with the lass?"

"Nary a scratch."

The giant borderman grunted his satisfaction.

"How'd Legget an' Brandt get away?" asked Jonathan.

"Cut an' run like scared bucks. Never got a hand on either of 'em."

"How many redskins did they meet back here a spell?"

"They was seven; but now there are only six, an' all snug in Legget's place by this time."

"I reckon we're near his den."

"We're not far off."

Night soon closing down upon the bordermen found them wrapped in slumber, as if no deadly foes were near at hand. The soft night wind sighed dismally among the bare trees. A few bright stars twinkled overhead. In the darkness of the forest the bordermen were at home.

CHAPTER XXII

In Legget's rude log cabin a fire burned low, lightening the forms of the two border outlaws, and showing in the background the dark forms of Indians sitting motionless on the floor. Their dusky eyes emitted a baleful glint, seemingly a reflection of their savage souls caught by the firelight. Legget wore a look of ferocity and sullen fear strangely blended. Brandt's face was hard and haggard, his lips set, his gray eyes smoldering.

"Safe?" he hissed. "Safe you say? You'll see that it's the same now as on the other night, when those border-tigers jumped us and we ran like cowards. I'd have fought it out here, but for you."

"Thet man Wetzel is ravin' mad, I tell you," growled Legget. "I reckon I've stood my ground enough to know I ain't no coward. But this fellar's crazy. He hed the Injuns slashin' each other like a pack of wolves round a buck."

"He's no more mad than you or I," declared Brandt. "I know all about him. His moaning in the woods, and wild yells are only tricks. He knows the Indians' nature, and he makes their very superstition and religion aid him in his fighting. I told you what he'd do. Didn't I beg you to kill Zane when we had a chance? Wetzel would never have taken our trail alone. Now they've beat me out of the girl, and as sure as death will round us up here."

"You don't believe they'll rush us here?" asked Legget.

"They're too keen to take foolish chances, but something will be done we don't expect. Zane was a prisoner here; he had a good look at this place, and you can gamble he'll remember."

"Zane must hev gone back to Fort Henry with the girl."

"Mark what I say, he'll come back!"

"Wal, we kin hold this place against all the men Eb Zane may put out."

"He won't send a man," snapped Brandt passionately. "Remember this, Legget, we're not to fight against soldiers, settlers, or hunters; but bordermen—understand—bordermen! Such as have been developed right here on this bloody frontier, and nowhere else on earth. They haven't fear in them. Both are fleet as deer in the woods. They can't be seen or trailed. They can snuff a candle with a rifle ball in the dark. I've seen Zane do it three times at a hundred yards. And Wetzel! He wouldn't waste powder on practicing. They can't be ambushed, or shaken off a track; they take the scent like buzzards, and have eyes like eagles."

"We kin slip out of here under cover of night," suggested Legget.

"Well, what then? That's all they want. They'd be on us again by sunset. No! we've got to stand our ground and fight. We'll stay as long as we can; but they'll rout us out somehow, be sure of that. And if one of us pokes his nose out to the daylight, it will be shot off."

"You're sore, an' you've lost your nerve," said Legget harshly. "Sore at me 'cause I got sweet on the girl. Ho! ho!"

Brandt shot a glance at Legget which boded no good. His strong hands clenched in an action betraying the reckless rage in his heart. Then he carefully removed his hunting coat, and examined his wound. He retied the bandage, muttering gloomily, "I'm so weak as to be light-headed. If this cut opens again, it's all day for me."

After that the inmates of the hut were quiet. The huge outlaw bowed his shaggy head for a while, and then threw himself on a pile of hemlock boughs. Brandt was not long in seeking rest. Soon both were fast asleep. Two of the savages passed out with cat-like step, leaving the door open. The fire had burned low, leaving a bed of dead coals. Outside in the dark a waterfall splashed softly.

The darkest hour came, and passed, and paled slowly to gray. Birds began to twitter. Through the door of the cabin the light of day streamed in. The two Indian sentinels were building a fire on the stone hearth. One by one the other savages got up, stretched, and yawned, and began the business of the day by cooking their breakfast. It was, apparently, every one for himself.

Legget arose, shook himself like a shaggy dog, and was starting for the door when one of the sentinels stopped him. Brandt, who was now awake, saw the action, and smiled.

In a few moments Indians and outlaws were eating for breakfast roasted strips of venison, with cornmeal baked brown, which served as bread. It was a somber, silent group.

Presently the shrill neigh of a horse startled them. Following it, the whip-like crack of a rifle stung and split the morning air. Hard on this came an Indian's long, wailing death-cry.

"Hah!" exclaimed Brandt.

Legget remained immovable. One of the savages peered out through a little porthole at the rear of the hut. The others continued their meal.

"Whistler'll come in presently to tell us who's doin' the shootin'," said Legget. "He's a keen Injun."

"He's not very keen now," replied Brandt, with bitter

certainty. "He's what the settlers call a good Indian which is to say, dead!"

Legget scowled at his lieutenant.

"I'll go and see," he replied and seized his rifle.

He opened the door, when another rifle-shot rang out. A bullet whistled in the air, grazing the outlaw's shoulder, and imbedded itself in the heavy door-frame.

Legget leaped back with a curse.

"Close shave!" said Brandt coolly. "That bullet came, probably, straight down from the top of the cliff. Jack Zane's there. Wetzel is lower down watching the outlet. We're trapped."

"Trapped," shouted Legget with an angry leer. "We kin live here longer'n the bordermen kin. We've meat on hand, an' a good spring in the back of the hut. How'er we trapped?"

"We won't live twenty-four hours," declared Brandt.

"Why?"

"Because we'll be routed out. They'll find some way to do it, and we'll never have another chance to fight in the open, as we had the other night when they came after the girl. From now on there'll be no sleep, no time to eat, the nameless fear of an unseen foe who can't be shaken off, marching by night, hiding and starving by day, until—! I'd rather be back in Fort Henry at Colonel Zane's mercy."

Legget turned a ghastly face toward Brandt. "Look a here. You're takin' a lot of glee in sayin' these things. I believe you've lost your nerve, or the lettin' out of a little blood hes made you wobbly. We've Injuns here, an' ought to be match fer two men."

Brandt gazed at him with a derisive smile.

"We kin go out an' fight these fellers," continued Legget. "We might try their own game, hidin' an' crawlin' through the woods."

"We two would have to go it alone. If you still had your trusty, trained band of experienced Indians, I'd say that would be just the thing. But Ashbow and the Chippewa are dead; so are the others. This bunch of redskins here may do to steal a few horses; but they don't amount to much against Zane and Wetzel. Besides, they'll cut and run presently, for they're scared and suspicious. Look at the chief; ask him."

The savage Brandt indicated was a big Indian just coming into manhood. His swarthy face still retained some of the frankness and simplicity of youth.

"Chief," said Legget in the Indian tongue. "The great paleface hunter, Deathwind, lies hid in the woods."

"Last night the Shawnee heard the wind of death mourn through the trees," replied the chief gloomily.

"See! What did I say?" cried Brandt. "The superstitious fool! He would begin his death-chant almost without a fight. We can't count on the redskins. What's to be done?"

The outlaw threw himself upon the bed of boughs, and Legget sat down with his rifle across his knees. The Indians maintained the same stoical composure. The moments dragged by into hours.

"Ugh!" suddenly exclaimed the Indian at the end of the hut.

Legget ran to him, and acting upon a motion of the Indian's hand, looked out through the little porthole.

The sun was high. He saw four of the horses grazing by the brook; then gazed scrutinizingly from the steep waterfall, along the green-stained cliff at the dark narrow cleft in the rocks. Here was the only outlet from the inclosure. He failed to discover anything unusual.

The Indian grunted again, and pointed upward.

"Smoke! There's smoke risin' above the trees," cried Legget. "Brandt, come here. What's thet mean?"

Brandt hurried, looked out. His face paled, his lower jaw protruded, quivered, and then was shut hard. He walked away, put his foot on a bench and began to lace his leggings.

"Wal?" demanded Legget.

"The game's up! Get ready to run and be shot at," cried Brandt with a hiss of passion.

Almost as he spoke the roof of the hut shook under a heavy blow.

"What's thet?" No one replied. Legget glanced from Brandt's cold, determined face to the uneasy savages. They were restless, and handling their weapons. The chief strode across the floor with stealthy steps.

"Thud!"

A repetition of the first blow caused the Indians to jump, and drew a fierce imprecation from their outlaw leader.

Brandt eyed him narrowly. "It's coming to you, Legget. They are shooting arrows of fire into the roof from the cliff. Zane is doin' that. He can make a bow and draw one, too. We're to be burned out. Now, damn you! take your medicine! I wanted you to kill him when you had the chance. If you had done so we'd never have come to this. Burned out, do you get that? Burned out!"

"Fire!" exclaimed Legget. He sat down as if the strength had left his legs.

The Indians circled around the room like caged tigers.

"Ugh!" The chief suddenly reached up and touched the birch-bark roof of the hut.

His action brought the attention of all to a faint crackling of burning wood.

"It's caught all right," cried Brandt in a voice which cut the air like a blow from a knife.

"I'll not be smoked like a ham, fer all these tricky bordermen," roared Legget. Drawing his knife he hacked at the heavy buckskin hinges of the rude door. When it dropped free he measured it against the open space. Sheathing the blade, he grasped his rifle in his right hand and swung the door on his left arm. Heavy though it was he carried it easily. The roughly hewn planks afforded a capital shield for all except the lower portion of his legs and feet. He went out of the hut with the screen of wood between himself and the cliff, calling for the Indians to follow. They gathered behind him, breathing hard, clutching their weapons, and seemingly almost crazed by excitement.

Brandt, with no thought of joining this foolhardy attempt to escape from the inclosure, ran to the little porthole that he might see the outcome. Legget and his five redskins were running toward the narrow outlet in the gorge. The awkward and futile efforts of the Indians to remain behind the shield were almost pitiful. They crowded each other for favorable positions, but, struggle as they might, one or two were always exposed to the cliff. Suddenly one, pushed to the rear, stopped simultaneously with the crack of a rifle, threw up his arms, and fell. Another report, differing from the first, rang out. A savage staggered from behind the speeding group with his hand at his side. Then he dropped into the brook.

Evidently Legget grasped this as a golden opportunity, for he threw aside the heavy shield and sprang forward, closely followed by his red-skinned allies. Immediately they came near the cliff, where the trail ran into the gorge, a violent shaking of the dry ferns overhead made manifest the activity of some heavy body. Next instant a huge yellow figure, not unlike a leaping catamount, plunged down with a roar so terrible as to sound inhuman. Legget, Indians, and newcomer rolled along the declivity toward the brook in an indistinguishable mass.

Two of the savages shook themselves free, and bounded to their feet nimbly as cats, but Legget and the other redskin became engaged in a terrific combat. It was a wrestling whirl, so fierce and rapid as to render blows ineffective. The leaves scattered as if in a whirlwind. Legget's fury must have been awful, to judge from his hoarse screams; the Indians' fear maddening, as could be told by their shrieks. The two savages ran wildly about the combatants, one trying to level a rifle, the other to get in a blow with a tomahawk. But the movements of the trio, locked in deadly embrace, were too swift.

Above all the noise of the contest rose that strange, thrilling roar.

"Wetzel!" muttered Brandt, with a chill, creeping shudder as he gazed upon the strife with fascinated eyes.

"Bang!" Again from the cliff came that heavy bellow.

The savage with the rifle shrunk back as if stung, and without a cry fell limply in a heap. His companion, uttering a frightened cry, fled from the glen.

The struggle seemed too deadly, too terrible, to last long. The Indian and the outlaw were at a disadvantage. They could not strike freely. The whirling conflict grew more fearful. During one second the huge, brown, bearish figure of Legget appeared on top; then the dark-bodied, half-naked savage, spotted like a hyena, and finally the lithe, powerful, tiger-shape of the borderman.

Finally Legget wrenched himself free at the same instant that the bloody-stained Indian rolled, writhing in convulsions, away from Wetzel. The outlaw dashed with desperate speed up the trail, and disappeared in the gorge. The borderman sped toward the cliff, leaped on a projecting ledge, grasped an overhanging branch, and pulled himself up. He was out of sight almost as quickly as Legget.

"After his rifle," Brandt muttered, and then realized

that he had watched the encounter without any idea of aiding his comrade. He consoled himself with the knowledge that such an attempt would have been useless. From the moment the borderman sprang upon Legget, until he scaled the cliff, his movements had been incredibly swift. It would have been hardly possible to cover him with a rifle, and the outlaw grimly understood that he needed to be careful of that charge in his weapon.

"By Heavens, Wetzel's a wonder!" cried Brandt in unwilling admiration. "Now he'll go after Legget and the redskin, while Zane stays here to get me. Well, he'll succeed, most likely, but I'll never quit. What's this?"

He felt something slippery and warm on his hand. It was blood running from the inside of his sleeve. A slight pain made itself felt in his side. Upon examination he found, to his dismay, that his wound had reopened. With a desperate curse he pulled a linsey jacket off a peg, tore it into strips, and bound up the injury as tightly as possible.

Then he grasped his rifle, and watched the cliff and the gorge with flaring eyes. Suddenly he found it difficult to breathe; his throat was parched, his eyes smarted. Then the odor of wood smoke brought him to a realization that the cabin was burning. It was only now he understood that the room was full of blue clouds. He sank into the corner, a wolf at bay.

Not many moments passed before the outlaw understood that he could not withstand the increasing heat and stifling vapor of the room. Pieces of burning birch dropped from the roof. The crackling above grew into a steady roar.

"I've got to run for it," he gasped. Death awaited him outside the door, but that was more acceptable than death by fire. Yet to face the final moment when he desired with all his soul to live, required almost superhuman courage. Sweating, panting, he glared around. "God! Is there no other way?" he cried in agony. At this moment he saw an ax on the floor.

Seizing it he attacked the wall of the cabin. Beyond this partition was a hut which had been used for a stable. Half a dozen strokes of the ax opened a hole large enough for him to pass through. With his rifle, and a piece of venison which hung near, he literally fell through the hole, where he lay choking, almost fainting. After a time he crawled across the floor to a door. Outside was a dense laurel thicket, into which he crawled.

The crackling and roaring of the fire grew louder. He could see the column of yellow and black smoke. Once fairly under way, the flames rapidly consumed the pitch-pine logs. In an hour Legget's cabins were a heap of ashes.

The afternoon waned. Brandt lay watchful, slowly recovering his strength. He felt secure under this cover, and only prayed for night to come. As the shadows began to creep down the sides of the cliffs, he indulged in hope. If he could slip out in the dark he had a good chance to elude the borderman. In the passionate desire to escape, he had forgotten his fatalistic words to Legget. He reasoned that he could not be trailed until daylight; that a long night's march would put him far in the lead, and there was just a possibility of Zane's having gone away with Wetzel.

When darkness had set in he slipped out of the covert and began his journey for life. Within a few yards he reached the brook. He had only to follow its course in order to find the outlet to the glen. Moreover, its rush and gurgle over the stones would drown any slight noise he might make.

Slowly, patiently he crawled, stopping every moment to

listen. What a long time he was in coming to the mossy stones over which the brook dashed through the gorge! But he reached them at last. Here if anywhere Zane would wait for him.

With teeth clenched desperately, and an inward tightening of his chest, for at any moment he expected to see the red flame of a rifle, he slipped cautiously over the mossy stones. Finally his hands touched the dewy grass, and a breath of cool wind fanned his hot cheek. He had succeeded in reaching the open. Crawling some rods farther on, he lay still a while and listened. The solemn wilderness calm was unbroken. Rising, he peered about. Behind loomed the black hill with its narrow cleft just discernible. Facing the north star, he went silently out into the darkness.

CHAPTER XXIII

At daylight Jonathan Zane rolled from his snug bed of leaves under the side of a log, and with the flint, steel, and punk he always carried, began building a fire. His actions were far from being hurried. They were deliberate, and seemed strange on the part of a man whose stern face suggested some dark business to be done. When his little fire had been made, he warmed some slices of venison which had already been cooked, and thus satisfied his hunger. Carefully extinguishing the fire and looking to the priming of his rifle, he was ready for the trail.

He stood near the edge of the cliff from which he could command a view of the glen. The black, smoldering ruins of the burned cabins defaced a picturesque scene.

"Brandt must have lit out last night, for I could have seen even a rabbit hidin' in that laurel patch. He's gone, an' it's what I wanted," thought the borderman.

He made his way slowly around the edge of the inclosure and clambered down on the splintered cliff at the end of the gorge. A wide, well-trodden trail extended into the forest below. Jonathan gave scarcely a glance to the beaten path before him; but bent keen eyes to the north, and carefully scrutinized the mossy stones along the brook. Upon a little sandbar running out from the bank he found the light imprint of a hand.

"It was a black night. He'd have to travel by the stars,

an' north's the only safe direction for him," muttered the borderman.

On the bank above he found oblong indentations in the grass, barely perceptible, but owing to the peculiar position of the blades of grass, easy for him to follow.

"He'd better have learned to walk light as an Injun before he took to outlawin'," said the borderman in disdain. Then he returned to the gordge and entered the inclosure. At the foot of the little rise of ground where Wetzel had leaped upon his quarry, was one of the dead Indians. Another lay partly submerged in the brown water.

Jonathan carried the weapons of the savages to a dry place under a projecting ledge in the cliff. Passing on down the glen, he stopped a moment where the cabins had stood. Not a log remained. The horses, with the exception of three, were tethered in the copse of laurel. He recognized two of Colonel Zane's thoroughbreds, and Betty's pony. He cut them loose, positive they would not stray from the glen, and might easily be secured at another time.

He set out upon the trail of Brandt with a long, swinging stride. To him the outcome of that pursuit was but a question of time. The consciousness of superior endurance, speed, and craft spoke in his every movement. The consciousness of being in right, a factor so powerfully potent for victory, spoke in the intrepid front with which he faced the north.

It was a gloomy November day. Gray, steely clouds drifted overhead. The wind wailed through the bare trees, sending dead leaves scurrying and rustling over the brown earth.

The borderman advanced with a step that covered glade and glen, forest and field, with astonishing swiftness. Long since he had seen that Brandt was holding to the lowland. This did not strike him as singular until for the third time he found the trail lead a short distance up the side of a ridge, then descend, seeking a level. With this discovery came the certainty that Brandt's pace was lessening. He had set out with a hunter's stride, but it had begun to shorten. The outlaw had shirked the hills, and shifted from his northern course. Why? The man was weakening; he could not climb; he was favoring a wound.

What seemed more serious for the outlaw, was the fact that he had left a good trail, and entered the low, wild land north of the Ohio. Even the Indians seldom penetrated this tangled belt of laurel and thorn. Owing to the dry season the swamps were shallow, which was another factor against Brandt. No doubt he had hoped to hide his trail by wading, and here it showed up like the track of a bison.

Jonathan kept steadily on, knowing the farther Brandt penetrated into this wilderness the worse off he would be. The outlaw dared not to take to the river until below Fort Henry, which was distant many a weary mile. The trail grew more ragged as the afternoon wore away. When twilight rendered further tracking impossible, the borderman built a fire in a sheltered place, ate his supper, and went to sleep.

In the dim, gray morning light he awoke, fancying he had been startled by a distant rifle shot. He roasted his strips of venison carefully, and ate with a hungry hunter's appreciation, yet sparingly, as befitted a borderman who knew how to keep up his strength upon a long trail.

Hardly had he traveled a mile when Brandt's footprints covered another's. Nothing surprised the borderman; but he had expected this least of all. A hasty examination convinced him that Legget and his Indian ally had fled this way with Wetzel in pursuit.

The morning passed slowly. The borderman kept to the trail like a hound. The afternoon wore on. Over sandy reaches thick with willows, and through long, matted, dried-out cranberry marshes and copses of prickly thorn, the borderman hung to his purpose. His legs seemed never to lose their spring, but his chest began to heave, his head bent, and his face shone with sweat.

At dusk he tired. Crawling into a dry thicket, he ate his scanty meal and fell asleep. When he awoke it was gray daylight. He was wet and chilled. Again he kindled a fire, and sat over it while cooking breakfast.

Suddenly he was brought to his feet by the sound of a rifle shot; then two others followed in rapid succession. Though they were faint, and far away to the west, Jonathan recognized the first, which could have come only from Wetzel's weapon, had he felt reasonably certain of the third, which was Brandt's. There might have been, he reflected grimly, a good reason for Legget's not shooting. However, he knew that Wetzel had rounded up the fugitives, and again he set out.

It was another dismal day, such a one as would be fitting for a dark deed of border justice. A cold, drizzly rain blew from the northwest. Jonathan wrapped a piece of oilskin around his rifle-breech, and faced the downfall. Soon he was wet to the skin. He kept on, but his free stride had shortened. Even upon his iron muscles this soggy, sticky ground had begun to tell.

The morning passed but the storm did not; the air grew colder and darker. The short afternoon would afford him little time, especially as the rain and running rills of water were obliterating the trail.

In the midst of a dense forest of great cottonwoods and sycamores he came upon a little pond, hidden among the bushes, and shrouded in a windy, wet gloom. Jonathan recognized the place. He had been there in winter hunting bears when all the swampland was locked by ice.

The borderman searched along the banks for a time, then went back to the trail, patiently following it. Around the pond it led to the side of a great, shelving rock. He saw an Indian leaning against this, and was about to throw forward his rifle when the strange, fixed, position of the savage told of the tragedy. A wound extended from his shoulder to his waist. Near by on the ground lay Legget. He, too, was dead. His gigantic frame weltered in blood. His big feet were wide apart; his arms spread, and from the middle of his chest protruded the haft of a knife.

The level space surrounding the bodies showed evidence of a desperate struggle. A bush had been rolled upon and crushed by heavy bodies. On the ground was blood as on the stones and leaves. The blade Legget still clutched was red, and the wrist of the hand which held it showed a dark, discolored band, where it had felt the relentless grasp of Wetzel's steel grip. The dead man's buckskin coat was cut into ribbons. On his broad face a demoniacal expression had set in eternal rigidity; the animal terror of death was frozen in his wide staring eyes. The outlaw chief had died as he had lived, desperately.

Jonathan found Wetzel's trail leading directly toward the river, and soon understood that the borderman was on the track of Brandt. The borderman had surprised the worn, starved, sleepy fugitives in the gray, misty dawn. The Indian, doubtless, was the sentinel, and had fallen asleep at his post never to awaken. Legget and Brandt must have discharged their weapons ineffectually. Zane could not understand why his comrade had missed Brandt at a few rods' distance. Perhaps he had wounded the younger outlaw; but certainly he had escaped while Wetzel had closed in on Legget to meet the hardest battle of his career.

While going over his version of the attack, Jonathan

followed Brandt's trail, as had Wetzel, to where it ended in the river. The old borderman had continued on down stream along the sandy shore. The outlaw remained in the water to hide his trail.

At one point Wetzel turned north. This move puzzled Jonathan, and did also the peculiar tracks. It was more perplexing because not far below Zane discovered where the fugitive had left the water to get around a ledge of rock.

The trail was approaching Fort Henry. Jonathan kept on down the river until arriving at the head of the island which lay opposite the settlement. Still no traces of Wetzel! Here Zane lost Brandt's trail completely. He waded the first channel, which was shallow and narrow, and hurried across the island. Walking out upon a sandbar he signaled with his well-known Indian cry. Almost immediately came an answering shout.

While waiting he glanced at the sand, and there, pointing straight toward the fort, he found Brandt's straggling trail!

CHAPTER XXIV

Colonel Zane paced to and fro on the porch. His genial smile had not returned; he was grave and somber. Information had just reached him that Jonathan had hailed from the island, and that one of the settlers had started across the river in a boat.

Betty came out accompanied by Mrs. Zane.

"What's this I hear?" asked Betty, flashing an anxious glance toward the river. "Has Jack really come in?"

"Yes," replied the colonel, pointing to a throng of men on the riverbank.

"Now there'll be trouble," said Mrs. Zane nervously. "I wish with all my heart Brandt had not thrown himself, as he called it, on your mercy."

"So do I," declared Colonel Zane.

"What will be done?" she asked. "There! that's Jack! Silas has hold of his arm."

"He's lame. He has been hurt," replied her husband.

A little procession of men and boys followed the borderman from the river, and from the cabins appeared the settlers and their wives. But there was no excitement except among the children. The crowd filed into the colonel's yard behind Jonathan and Silas.

Colonel Zane silently greeted his brother with an iron grip on the hand which was more expressive than words. No unusual sight was it to see the borderman wet, ragged, bloody, worn with long marches, hollow-eyed and gloomy; yet he had never before presented such an appearance at Fort Henry. Betty ran forward, and, though she clasped his arm, shrank back. There was that in the borderman's presence to cause fear.

"Wetzel?" Jonathan cried sharply.

The colonel raised both hands, palms open, and returned his brother's keen glance. Then he spoke. "Lew hasn't come in. He chased Brandt across the river. That's all I know."

"Brandt's here, then?" hissed the borderman.

The colonel nodded gloomily.

"Where?"

"In the long room over the fort. I locked him in there."

"Why did he come here?"

Colonel Zane shrugged his shoulders. "It's beyond me. He said he'd rather place himself in my hands than be run down by Wetzel or you. He didn't draw, I'll say that for him. He just said, 'I'm your prisoner.' He's in pretty bad shape; barked over the temple, lame in one foot, cut under the arm, starved, and worn out."

"Take me to him," said the borderman, and he threw his rifle on a bench.

"Very well. Come along," replied the colonel. He frowned at those following them. "Here, you women, clear out!" But they did not obey him.

It was a sober-faced group that marched in through the big stockade gate, under the huge, bulging front of the fort, and up the rough stairway. Colonel Zane removed a heavy bar from before a door, and thrust it open with his foot. The long guardroom brilliantly lighted by sunshine coming through the portholes, was empty save for a ragged man lying on a bench.

The noise aroused him; he sat up, and then slowly

labored to his feet. It was the same flaring, wild-eyed Brandt, only fiercer and more haggard. He wore a bloody bandage round his head. When he saw the borderman he backed, with involuntary, instinctive action, against the wall, yet showed no fear.

In the dark glance Jonathan shot at Brandt shone a pitiless implacability; no scorn, nor hate, nor passion, but something which, had it not been so terrible, might have been justice.

"I think Wetzel was hurt in the fight with Legget," said Jonathan deliberately, "an' ask if you know?"

"I believe he was," replied Brandt readily, "I was asleep when he jumped us, and was awakened by the Indian's yell. Wetzel must have taken a snap shot at me as I was getting up, which accounts, probably, for my being alive. I fell, but did not lose consciousness. I heard Wetzel and Legget fighting, and at last struggled to my feet. Although dizzy and bewildered, I could see to shoot; but missed. For a long time, it seemed to me, I watched that terrible fight, and then ran, finally reaching the river, where I recovered somewhat."

"Did you see Wetzel again?"

"Once, about a quarter of a mile behind me. He was staggering along on my trail."

At this juncture there was a commotion among the settlers crowding behind Colonel Zane and Jonathan and Helen Sheppard appeared, white, with her big eyes strangely dilated.

"Oh!" she cried breathlessly, clasping both hands around Jonathan's arm. "I'm not too late? You're not going to—"

"Helen, this is no place for you," said Colonel Zane sternly. "This is business for men. You must not interfere."

Helen gazed at him, at Brandt, and then up at the borderman. She did not loose his arm.

"Outside some one told me you intended to shoot him. Is it true?"

Colonel Zane evaded the searching gaze of those strained, brilliant eyes. Nor did he answer.

As Helen stepped slowly back a hush fell upon the crowd. The whispering, the nervous coughing, and shuffling of feet, ceased.

In those around her Helen saw the spirit of the border. Colonel Zane and Silas wore the same look, cold, hard, almost brutal. The women were strangely grave. Nellie Downs' sweet face seemed changed; there was pity, even suffering on it, but no relenting. Even Betty's face, always so warm, piquant, and wholesome, had taken on a shade of doubt, of gloom, of something almost sullen, which blighted its dark beauty. What hurt Helen most cruelly was the borderman's glittering eyes.

She fought against a shuddering weakness which threatened to overcome her.

"Whose prisoner is Brandt?" she asked of Colonel Zane.

"He gave himself up to me, naturally, as I am in authority here," replied the colonel. "But that signifies little. I can do no less than abide by Jonathan's decree, which, after all, is the decree of the border."

"And that is?"

"Death to outlaws and renegades."

"But cannot you spare him?" implored Helen. "I know he is a bad man; but he might become a better one. It seems like murder to me. To kill him in cold blood, wounded, suffering as he is, when he claimed your mercy. Oh! it is dreadful!"

The usually kind-hearted colonel, soft as wax in the hands of a girl, was now colder and harder than flint.

"It is useless," he replied curtly. "I am sorry for you. We all understand your feelings, that yours are not the principles of the border. If you had lived long here you could appreciate what these outlaws and renegades have done to us. This man is a hardened criminal; he is a thief, a murderer."

"He did not kill Mordaunt," replied Helen quickly. "I saw him draw first and attack Brandt."

"No matter. Come, Helen, cease. No more of this," Colonel Zane cried with impatience.

"But I will not!" exclaimed Helen, with ringing voice and flashing eye. She turned to her girl friends and besought them to intercede for the outlaw. But Nell only looked sorrowfully on, while Betty met her appealing glance with a fire in her eyes that was no dim reflection of her brother's.

"Then I must make my appeal to you," said Helen, facing the borderman. There could be no mistaking how she regarded him. Respect, honor, and love breathed from every line of her beautiful face.

"Why do you want him to go free?" demanded Jonathan. "You told me to kill him."

"Oh, I know. But I was not in my right mind. Listen to me, please. He must have been very different once; perhaps had sisters. For their sake give him another chance. I know he has a better nature. I feared him, hated him, scorned him, as if he were a snake, yet he saved me from that monster Legget!"

"For himself!"

"Well, yes, I can't deny that. But he could have ruined me, wrecked me, yet he did not. At least, he meant marriage by me. He said if I would marry him he would flee over the border and be an honest man."

"Have you no other reason?"

"Yes." Helen's bosom swelled and a glory shone in her splendid eyes. "The other reason is, my own happiness!"

Plain to all, if not through her words, from the light in her eyes, that she could not love a man who was a part to what she considered injustice.

The borderman's white face became flaming red.

It was difficult to refuse this glorious girl any sacrifice she demanded for the sake of the love so openly avowed.

Sweetly and pityingly she turned to Brandt: "Will not you help me?"

"Lass, if it were for me you were asking my life I'd swear it yours for always, and I'd be a man," he replied with bitterness; "but not to save my soul would I ask anything of him."

The giant passions, hate and jealousy, flamed in his gray eyes.

"If I persuade them to release you, will you go away, leave this country, and never come back?"

"I'll promise that, lass, and honestly," he replied.

She wheeled toward Jonathan, and now the rosy color chased the pallor from her cheeks.

"Jack, do you remember when we parted at my home; when you left on this terrible trail, now ended, thank God! Do you remember what an ordeal that was for me? Must I go through it again?"

Bewitchingly sweet she was then, with the girlish charm of coquetry almost lost in the deeper, stranger power of the woman.

The borderman drew his breath sharply; then he wrapped his long arms closely round her. She, understanding that victory was hers, sank weeping upon his breast. For a moment he bowed his face over her, and when he lifted it the dark and terrible gloom had gone.

"Eb, let him go, an' at once," ordered Jonathan. "Give him a rifle, some meat, an' a canoe, for he can't travel, an' turn him loose. Only be quick about it, because if Wetzel comes in, God himself couldn't save the outlaw."

It was an indescribable glance that Brandt cast upon the tearful face of the girl who had saved his life. But without a word he followed Colonel Zane from the room.

The crowd slowly filed down the steps. Betty and Nell lingered behind, their eyes beaming through happy tears. Jonathan, long so cold, showed evidence of becoming as quick and passionate a lover as he had been a borderman. At least, Helen had to release herself from his embrace, and it was a blushing, tearstained face she turned to her friends.

When they reached the stockade gate Colonel Zane was hurrying toward the river with a bag in one hand, and a rifle and a paddle in the other. Brandt limped along after him, the two disappearing over the riverbank.

Betty, Nell, and the lovers went to the edge of the bluff.

They saw Colonel Zane choose a canoe from among a number on the beach. He launched it, deposited the bag in the bottom, handed the rifle and paddle to Brandt, and wheeled about.

The outlaw stepped aboard, and, pushing off slowly, drifted down and out toward mid-stream. When about fifty yards from shore he gave a quick glance around, and ceased paddling. His face gleamed white, and his eyes glinted like bits of steel in the sun.

Suddenly he grasped the rifle, and, leveling it with the swiftness of thought, fired at Jonathan.

The borderman saw the act, even from the beginning, and must have read the outlaw's motive, for as the weapon flashed he dropped flat on the bank. The bullet sang harmlessly over him, imbedding itself in the stockade fence with a distinct thud.

The girls were so numb with horror that they could not even scream.

Colonel Zane swore lustily. "Where's my gun? Get me a gun. Oh! What did I tell you?"

"Look!" cried Jonathan as he rose to his feet.

Upon the sandbar opposite stood a tall, dark, familiar figure.

"By all that's holy, Wetzel!" exclaimed Colonel Zane.

They saw the giant borderman raise a long, black rifle which wavered and fell, and rose again. A little puff of white smoke leaped out, accompanied by a clear, stinging report.

Brandt dropped the paddle he had hurriedly begun plying after his traitor's act. His white face was turned toward the shore as it sank forward to rest at last upon the gunwale of the canoe. Then his body slowly settled, as if seeking repose. His hand trailed outside in the water, drooping inert and lifeless. The little craft drifted downstream.

"You see, Helen, it had to be," said Colonel Zane gently. "What a dastard! A long shot, Jack! Fate itself must have glanced down the sights of Wetzel's rifle."

CHAPTER XXV

A year rolled round; once again Indian summer veiled the golden fields and forests in a soft, smoky haze. Once more from the opal-blue sky of autumn nights, shone the great white stars, and nature seemed wrapped in a melancholy hush.

November the third was the anniversary of a memorable event on the frontier—the marriage of the younger borderman.

Colonel Zane gave it the name of "Independence Day," and arranged a holiday, a feast and dance where all the settlement might meet in joyful thankfulness for the first year of freedom on the border.

With the wiping out of Legget's fierce band, the yoke of the renegades and outlaws was thrown off forever. Simon Girty migrated to Canada and lived with a few Indians who remained true to him. His confederates slowly sank into oblivion. The Shawnee tribe sullenly retreated westward, far into the interior of Ohio; the Delawares buried the war hatchet, and smoked the pipe of peace they had ever before refused. For them the dark, mysterious, fatal wind had ceased to moan along the trails, or sigh through treetops over lonely Indian campfires.

The beautiful Ohio valley had been wrestled from the savages and from those parasites who for years had hung around the necks of the red men.

This day was the happiest of Colonel Zane's life. The task he had set himself, and which he had hardly ever hoped to see completed, was ended. The West had been won. What Boone achieved in Kentucky he had accomplished in Ohio and West Virginia.

The feast was spread on the colonel's lawn. Every man, woman, and child in the settlement was there. Isaac Zane, with his Indian wife and child, had come from the far-off Huron town. Pioneers from Yellow Creek and eastward to Fort Pitt attended. The spirit of the occasion manifested itself in such joyousness as had never before been experienced in Fort Henry. The great feast was equal to the event. Choice cuts of beef and venison, savory viands, wonderful loaves of bread and great plump pies, sweet cider and old wine, delighted the merry party.

"Friends, neighbors, dear ones," said Colonel Zane, "my heart is almost too full for speech. This occasion, commemorating the day of our freedom on the border, is the beginning of the reward for stern labor, hardship, silenced hearths of long, relentless years. I did not think I'd live to see it. The seed we have sown has taken root; in years to come, perhaps, a great people will grow up on these farms we call our homes. And as we hope those coming afterward will remember us, we should stop a moment to think of the heroes who have gone before. Many there are whose names will never be written on the roll of fame, whose graves will be unmarked in history. But we who worked, fought, bled beside them, who saw them die for those they left behind, will render them all justice, honor, and love. To them we give the victory. They were true; then let us, who begin to enjoy the freedom, happiness, and prosperity they won with their lives, likewise be true in memory of them, in deed to ourselves, and in grace to God."

By no means the least of the pleasant features of this pleasant day was the fact that three couples blushingly presented themselves before the colonel, and confided to him their sudden conclusions in regard to the felicitousness of the moment. The happy colonel raced around until he discovered Jim Downs, the minister, and there amid the merry throng he gave the brides away, being the first to kiss them.

It was late in the afternoon when the villagers dispersed to their homes and left the colonel to his own circle. With his strong, dark face beaming, he mounted the old porch step.

"Where are my Zane babies?" he asked. "Ah! here you are! Did anybody ever see anything to beat that? Four wonderful babies! Mother, here's your Daniel—if you'd only named him Eb! Silas, come for Silas junior, bad boy that he is. Isaac, take your Indian princess; ah! little My-eerah with the dusky face. Woe be to him who looks into those eyes when you come to age. Jack, here's little Jonathan, the last of the bordermen, he, too, has beautiful eyes, big like his mother's. Ah! well, I don't believe I have left a wish, unless—"

"Unless?" suggested Betty with her sweet smile.

"It might be—" he said and looked at her.

Betty's warm cheek was close to his as she whispered: "Dear Eb!" The rest only the colonel heard.

"Well! By all that's glorious!" he exclaimed, and attempted to seize her; but with burning face Betty fled.

J ack, dear, how the leaves are falling!" exclaimed Helen. "See them floating and whirling. It reminds me of the day I lay a prisoner in the forest glade praying, waiting for you."

The borderman was silent.

They passed down the sandy lane under the colored maple trees, to a new cottage on the hillside.

"I am perfectly happy to-day," continued Helen. "Everybody seems to be content, except you. For the first time in weeks I see that shade on your face, that look in your eyes. Jack, you do not regret the new life?"

"My love, no, a thousand times no," he answered, smiling down into her eyes. They were changing, shadowing with thought, bright as in other days, and with an added beauty. The wilful spirit had been softened by love.

"Ah, I know, you miss the old friend."

The yellow thicket on the slope opened to let out a tall, dark man who came down with lithe and springy stride.

"Jack, it's Wetzel!" said Helen softly.

No words were spoken as the comrades gripped hands.

"Let me see the boy?" asked Wetzel, turning to Helen.

Little Jonathan blinked up at the grave borderman with great round eyes, and pulled with friendly, chubby fingers at the fringed buckskin coat.

"When you're a man the forest trails will be corn fields," muttered Wetzel.

The bordermen strolled together up the brown hillside, and wandered along the river bluff. The air was cool; in the west the ruddy light darkened behind bold hills; a blue mist streaming in the valley shaded into gray as twilight fell.